PUNITIVE DAMAGE

Chester Oksner

William Morrow and Company, Inc.
New York

Library of Congress Cataloging-in-Publication Data

Oksner, Chester M.
  Punitive damage.

"A Thomas Congdon book"—T.p. verso.
I. Title.
PS3565.K7P8   1987   813'.54   87-7883
ISBN 0-688-07220-8
            A Thomas Congdon Book

Printed in the United States of America

First Edition

1 2 3 4 5 6 7 8 9 10

BOOK DESIGN BY RICHARD ORIOLO

Fic.

To
DOROTHY SARAH
Thank You

PART
ONE

1

"**G**oddammit, Oliver, if you don't want my goddamned case, just say so. There are lots of other goddamned lawyers—"

MacDonald Abraham Oliver rejected a momentary temptation to throw the three-hundred-pound giant out of his Bunker Hill office. He was beginning to like old Charlie Wennerstrom. Not every client could manage one "goddammit" for every half dozen words. Besides, this was the only billion-dollar case he'd been offered all morning.

So all he said was: "Please sit down again, Mr. Wennerstrom."

Drained, dejected by Oliver's apparent lack of enthusiasm, Wennerstrom sat down. The chrome and leather Barcelona chair groaned, but held. The sixty-seven-year-old mountain, disheveled in defeat, glowered at Oliver. Oliver's eyes traced the sequentially matched grain of three walnut-paneled walls as he tried for a decision.

MacDonald Oliver was twenty-seven years younger than Wennerstrom, six inches shorter and 140 pounds lighter. Few people knew that only one of his disconcerting gray eyes was real, the other acrylic plastic. His craggy face was usually described, by people who describe faces, as interesting.

Although MacDonald Oliver wasn't ready to show it, he felt Charlie Wennerstrom's pain. Wennerstrom was tortured and imprisoned by his frustration, straining to escape. Mac Oliver understood torture and imprisonment. He'd been made an expert. He resisted the urge to rub his false eye, instead confining his right hand to its trouser pocket.

Wennerstrom was entitled to an answer. Clearly, he was intelligent and sincere—but that didn't prove he had a real case. Wennerstrom might be another neurotic, just one more lawsuit junkie. Oliver finally spoke. "Your case has obvious liability problems. However, the potential damages are substantial—make that astronomical."

For the first time that morning Wennerstrom's florid baby face smiled a little. "I see. It's a lousy case, but if we can win it at all—"

It was Oliver's turn to smile. "I really don't know what your chances are yet. I need time to assess your case. Study that stack of papers you brought. Give me a few days."

"You realize I haven't enough left to pay a substantial fee?"

Oliver turned serious. "I know. That's partly why I need time. If I'm going to take your case on a contingent fee arrangement, I must be satisfied that it's worth the gamble, and so must my partners." Oliver stood up. "Leave your records with me. I promise you my answer within three days."

After Wennerstrom left, Mac stood, staring at the Los Angeles Harbor Freeway thirty-six stories below, snaking its way to San Pedro.

He spoke the name of the case aloud. "*Wennerstrom* versus *Titan Overland Petroleum Company.*" It did have the ring of a winner. Perhaps really the first billion-dollar verdict in history—if only Charlie wasn't just another crackpot who believed his invention had been stolen.

Jesus, what a case to win.

Black as the crude oil that built them, the twin cylindrical towers of Titan Overland Petroleum Company pointed fifty stories above Bunker

Hill in downtown Los Angeles, only a few blocks from the offices of Sorensen, Oliver, Bradford, and Smith.

While Charlie Wennerstrom was meeting with MacDonald Oliver, another meeting was taking place on one of the upper floors of the North Tower. Satin polished metal letters were mounted on the door:

GRANT RADCLIFFE

VICE-PRESIDENT

REAL ESTATE AND DEVELOPMENT

"Mr. Radcliffe will see you now. Please go right in."

Grant Radcliffe's secretary shuddered as Radcliffe's visitor closed the door behind him. Even though each time he came in he was distantly polite, the man's mere presence terrified her. Perhaps it was his cannonball head, which apparently attached directly to massive shoulders. Or maybe it was that his arms were so long, or his hands so huge. Grant Radcliffe's office conformed to mandatory second-level executive blandness—beige walls, carpet, beige everywhere. Vice-presidential interior decorating was discouraged. Individual creativity was to be wholly channeled into increasing TOPCO's profits and assets.

Radcliffe's angelic face turned away from a wall-mounted chart to face the man. The scene was Beauty and the Beast.

"We've got a problem," the man said.

Radcliffe settled his tall frame into his beige swivel chair and folded his slender arms before speaking. "Yes?"

"Charlie Wennerstrom made an appointment to see MacDonald Oliver." The man consulted a small notebook and grinned a mirthless grin. "Today. Right now, as a matter of fact."

"Who the hell is MacDonald Oliver?"

"Sorensen, Oliver, Bradford, and Smith, attorneys-at-law. You know, the lawyers who took Ford Motor Company for three million last year."

"How do you know?"

"It was in all the papers."

Radcliffe sighed. "Don't be stupid. How do you know Wennerstrom is seeing Oliver today?"

"We've been tapping his phone ever since we cut him off."

"His meeting Oliver doesn't necessarily mean he's after us."
The man raised a massive palm. "Now you're being stupid. Oliver is
a litigation lawyer. That's all he does. And he doesn't take two-bit cases.
Who else but us could Wennerstrom possibly have any reason to sue?"
"Don't be impertinent. You're still working for me. But you're right,
of course. Wennerstrom wants to come after TOPCO."
"And maybe you, too." Another grin, but the cruel eyes were un-
changed.
"Yes, but we'll finesse it. We've merely taken full advantage of the
terms of our joint venture agreement with Wennerstrom. Simply good
business." Radcliffe's remarkably pale blue eyes narrowed. "Tell me
about MacDonald Oliver."
"That's easy. The legal department has checked him out before."
The man's thick fingers reached into his briefcase, retrieving papers.
"This goes deeper than you'll care to hear about this morning. Let me
summarize: MacDonald Abraham Oliver. Vietnam veteran. Special
Forces. Silver Star. Purple Heart. Lost right eye while a prisoner of war.
Escaped." The man shook his head at the feat. "Amazing."
"Discharged as major. Law school, University of California at
Berkeley. Third in class. Editor of *Law Review*. Order of the Coif.
Passed the bar, 1973. Clerked for Justice Crammer, California Su-
preme Court, one summer, then went to work for Nels Sorensen and
Associates, attorneys-at-law. Within two years the old man had reversed
his lifelong tradition as a loner and made Oliver his first partner. Oliver
does nothing but litigation, trial work, mostly civil. Since then the firm
has grown rapidly—nineteen lawyers as of last month. Oliver has a
phenomenal win record, and in heavy cases against top opposition."
"God, a regular war hero. Do we know anything about Oliver himself?"
"Yeah, just a minute." The man rapidly flipped pages. "Here." His
first genuine smile of the morning came as he scanned the pages.
"There are personality sketches by our own lawyers who have been
against him. Oliver seems to be anything you want, depending on
whose opinion you read. Listen to these:
"Tough, aggressive, but courteous gentleman.

"Arrogant, cocky, hot-tempered son of a bitch.

"Extremely intelligent, scholarly lawyer.

"Ordinary intellect, but animallike cunning and deviousness.

"Hard opponent, but keeps word religiously.

"Amoral, unprincipled bastard.

"Want to hear more?"

"No, I'll start liking the son of a bitch. Leave the dossier with me. I'll read the rest later."

"You should have offered Wennerstrom a hundred grand for a full release of his process instead of chopping him off without a nickel. It would have been cheap."

"Don't nag. You're not the motherly type. Anyway, it's too late now. Oliver would instantly smell the fear behind my offer. We'll just wait. Wait and ad-lib."

The man's smile grew. "Wennerstrom's sixty-seven years old and fat. Maybe he can't last too long."

Radcliffe's manicured fingers stroked carefully groomed blond hair. "Restrain yourself. We'll just wait and see."

"MacDonald Oliver, you're fussing with your fake eye again."

Marla Zimmerman, one of the newest associate attorneys in the state, stood, unannounced, at Mac's desk, arms akimbo, legs apart, doing her drill sergeant stance. Marla tried to look intimidating, but the effect was minimal. Even as she stood in high heels before the seated MacDonald Oliver, her eyes were barely higher than his.

Marla continued, "You only do that when you're tense. You always use your right hand."

Mac sighed, put down his notes, and looked up, scowling to mask his affection. "Ah, the office psychiatrist. Good morning, Ms. MZ."

"Mac, you know how I hate that nickname. Anyhow, I haven't time this morning. I only dropped in to discuss that Kiegeloff dissolution you've dumped on me. Mac, those people are animals. But never mind. What's bothering you?"

Marla's large green eyes won. Mac capitulated. "It's the senior partners' meeting in five minutes. You know I need approval to take *Wen-*

nerstrom versus *TOPCO* on a contingent fee. But I have to convince them that we should advance several hundred thousand in costs—"

"The Kiegeloffs have been my whole life lately. You've told me nothing about Wennerstrom yet. Is any case worth advancing hundreds of thousands?"

"This one is. Wennerstrom's developed a method of extracting oil from shale—"

"Shale?"

"Shale is rock, Marla. The U.S.A. has lots of it, and people have been trying to get the oil out of it for thirty years. The impact of Wennerstrom's invention is beyond projection. Within a few years it could literally free this country from dependence on imported oil."

"I thought we had an oil glut."

"Sure, this year we do. But that's mostly because of OPEC's internal disagreement. Those guys supply twenty-five percent of our oil. If OPEC got its act together and elected to turn off the tap, our glut would become a shortage in three weeks. It's precisely because the Wennerstrom Process frees the U.S. from that kind of vulnerability that it is worth billions. But Charlie Wennerstrom doesn't own it anymore. TOPCO has snatched it right out from under him."

The Sorensen, Oliver, Bradford, and Smith conference room walls were lined with several thousand leather-and buckram-bound lawbooks. The books had become more ornamental than functional, since all case and statutory law was accessible through two computer terminals, each housed in its own small room. Nels Sorensen, the seventy-two-year-old founder of the firm, would never give up the library, even though its obsolescence was undeniable. He had nostalgic affection and an anecdote for every volume.

Still spare and straight, even seated, Nels Sorensen looked like a Norwegian sea captain, which was exactly what his father and grandfather had been.

"What are our chances?" asked Sorensen, looking around the group—Timothy George Bradford, Cornell Sepulveda Smith, and Mac Oliver—but obviously meaning the question for Mac.

Sorensen was like a father to Oliver. Sorensen had hired him away from his Supreme Court clerkship only a few months out of law school. Sorensen loved Oliver's vigor and enthusiasm, thrived on it. Sorensen realized he could not hold on to him as a salaried employee and so made MacDonald Oliver his first partner. A remarkable team: enough age difference to be father and son—the white-haired patriarch and the one-eyed war hero out of a war that had so few.

"We really don't know, can't know yet." Mac reined in his ego, straining to be unleashed against one of the world's largest corporations. He remembered to put his right hand into his pocket. He didn't want his anxiety noticed. This audience was tougher than any jury. "We only know what Charlie Wennerstrom knows. Wennerstrom needed financing to prove the process, to obtain the patent. He entered into a joint venture agreement with TOPCO. Suddenly, magically, through some intercorporate mumbo jumbo, Wennerstrom ended up with nothing more than an interest in RL Equities Corp.—a company with paper assets and no income. I've already checked that out. Charlie Wennerstrom has told us the truth—"

"The whole truth?" asked Cornell Sepulveda Smith, affecting a look of good-natured innocence, as if he were the assistant cashier of a suburban branch bank. In fact, Smith's family probably owned the bank. Pudgy, pink, bald Smith was a sixth-generation scion of a powerful California family whose fortune had been founded on citrus ranches in the San Fernando Valley.

"Of course not," Mac replied. "Charlie Wennerstrom doesn't know what went on inside TOPCO's walls—all those devious little minds, scheming to screw him. It's going to take investigation and discovery before we know everything that's knowable. But the rewards can be enormous—"

"The rewards. Tell us about the rewards, Mac," said Timothy Bradford, the remaining senior partner. Timothy George Bradford had been a streetwise Italian boy from East St. Louis who had parlayed good looks, an aggressive boxing style, and a sharp mind into athletic scholarships. He had changed his name before entering Yale Law School: Bradford for Brancussi, George for Giuseppe, and Timothy because he liked the sound of it. His talents as an investor had never matched his success as a lawyer. He was spread too thin financially and was continually short of cash. Still darkly attractive in spite of his excesses, Bradford was charming, devious, and selfish. "Mac," Bradford insisted, "what do you estimate to be the recovery?"

Mac smiled at the transparency of Bradford's greed. He said, "Let me give you the preface first. I don't want to be responsible for causing any of you to go into cardiac arrest. According to Merrill Lynch estimates, TOPCO's annual profit from using the Wennerstrom Process is in excess of a hundred and fifty million dollars. That's at present levels. The life of the patent is seventeen years. Projecting that annual profit over the life of the patent comes to two billion five hundred and fifty million dollars. That's without any adjustment for additional production. Two-point-five billion dollars, gentlemen." Mac paused, hoping that no one would notice that he was sitting on his right hand. God, he wanted this one. The satisfaction of defeating the giant corporation, the status that would follow. He could pick any case he wanted. Not the loftiest of motives, thought Mac, but definitely genuine. He continued: "Sound arguments can be made that if the jury finds fraud, Wennerstrom is entitled to all those profits. If we argue the measure of damages on conservative legal theory, Wennerstrom's forty percent joint venture interest would entitle him to a minimum of forty percent of TOPCO's profit. That's a mere one billion dollars. Our fee then would be forty percent of the recovery or"—Mac pretended to compute—"four hundred million dollars."

"Holy Mary," said Timothy Bradford.

"Impressive number," said Nels Sorensen.

"Perhaps we can have the carpets redone," said Cornell Sepulveda Smith.

Sorensen, Oliver, Bradford, and Smith devised a method of insuring Charlie Wennerstrom's life. That would at least guarantee reimbursement of the firm's advances of court costs in case Charlie died before the trial.

When Mac presented the idea to Wennerstrom, Charlie was amused.

"Is that ethical, lawyer? Seems to me you're creating a conflict of interest. If the case doesn't progress well, I may be worth more to you dead than alive."

The device needed Charlie's daughter's cooperation, too. Laura Wennerstrom was not nearly as amused. As her long legs stalked Mac's office from paneled to window wall and back, her heels dug temporary furrows in the deep maroon carpet. Her black eyes flashed against her fair skin, and the little makeup she wore became redundant as the color rose in her high-boned cheeks. Laura pronounced the scheme, in turn, cold-blooded, mercenary, insensitive, selfish, and, finally, tacky. She also suggested that the reasons for the legal profession's poor public relations were becoming increasingly clear to her.

Charlie sat, quietly observing Laura's passion, secretly delighting in her unconscious imitation of her dead half-Cherokee mother. Charlie doubly adored Laura: once, openly, for herself, especially for her intense feelings, her nearly complete lack of objectivity; and again, secretly, for her unknowing, constant revival of the memory of his beloved Willow.

Mac thought she was obnoxious, naive, spoiled, or any combination thereof. How satisfying it would be to win this big one for old Charlie and somehow put this bitch in her place at the same time.

But the moment, Mac decided, required restraint. "Miss Wennerstrom," he said, "your father is in a joint venture with Sorensen, Oliver, Bradford, and Smith now. As you've already learned from your recent experience, joint ventures often have their seamy aspect."

Laura glared, then softened, "Mr. Oliver, you really know how to hurt a person. All right, sign us up. Just promise that you'll be at least as tough on TOPCO as you are on me."

Mac rarely left the office early, but he wanted to think about the Wennerstrom case without interruption. As he pulled the ice blue BMW 633 CSi onto the southbound Harbor Freeway, he switched the electric sunroof open and let the sunshine in. It was a rare Los Angeles afternoon. Even the smog was clear.

Obviously, he thought, I file suit first and talk later.

As Mac turned onto the westbound Santa Monica Freeway, he decided to check on Abigail. He hadn't paid any attention to her for at least ten days. And, besides, he did some of his best thinking around her. He accelerated past the San Diego Freeway, his usual turnoff, then continued out to Marina del Rey.

Mac parked the car near a row of slips. He sat, savoring the smell, salt air tinged with diesel fuel, and the wind chimes of halyards playfully slapping masts.

We'll start discovery with a search of TOPCO records. That will get us the basic documents needed for further investigation and will also produce a preliminary list of witnesses. I can assign Marla to that.

The laughter of two bikini-clad beauties standing on the deck of a nearby cruiser aroused Mac from his reverie. He walked down the ramp onto the long dock, trying to pick out her form. Mac's spirits always rose when his beauty came into view. There. He stood before thirty-eight feet of gleaming white-hulled sloop, Abigail discreetly painted in dark blue Roman letters on her bow. Mac smiled as he remembered how sullen his wife had become when he named the boat. Mary Kathryn had never quite believed that Abigail was merely a romantic name, reminiscent of whalers and clipper ships.

Mac stepped over the gleaming mahogany toe rail onto the tobacco-colored teak deck. He stood in the cockpit, leaning on the destroyer type of wheel as his good left eye roamed her graceful lines. You sexy bitch, you. Come with me to the South Seas. She could, too, he knew. All she needed was fuel and provisioning.

Mac unlocked the companionway hatch and lowered himelf into the salon: oiled teak panels; blue corduroy settees. A small pseudo-Oriental rug complemented the teak and holly cabin sole. Mac fetched a cold beer from the refrigerator and checked around. Bilge, okay. Shore power on, refrigerator cold, battery voltage up. Mac checked the crankcase oil and coolant level, strained the fuel filter, and started the Westerbeke diesel. The alarm snarled until oil pressure rose to normal. He grabbed a seat cushion and took it, himself and his beer up to the cockpit, where he could stretch in the sun.

Mac felt certain that TOPCO had defrauded Wennerstrom out of his process, although he had no clear idea how it had managed it. And what a chasm between feeling and proving in a courtroom. I'm going to have to spend much more time with Charlie going back over the history of this mess, he thought. A not unpleasant prospect. He really enjoyed Charlie. The old man's mind was an avalanche of ideas. Mac could do without Charlie's daughter, though. A certifiable pain in the— Mac forced himself back to planning trial preparation: records to check; witnesses to interview; law to research. He started making notes. The afternoon flew by.

Mac looked at his watch. Better get home or I'll be stuck in rush-hour traffic, he thought. As he locked *Abigail*, he gave her coaming an affectionate pat.

We need a way to get trial priority. Charlie Wennerstrom's too old to wait three or four years to get to trial. I need a gimmick to speed things up.

Mac left the San Diego Freeway at the Sunset Boulevard turnoff. He downshifted into third as he climbed into the Bel Air section of the south face of the Santa Monica Mountains, which separated the Los Angeles basin from the San Fernando Valley. As mountains go, the Santa Monicas are not impressive. They do serve well as home sites for movie stars, orthodontists, television producers, neurosurgeons, retired call girls, chain store operators, and successful lawyers. The houses that line the narrow, steep, twisting streets of Bel Air range from old Spanish adobe and red-tiled mansions on several acres to contemporary redwood and glass split-levels on city-size lots. Mac turned into the driveway of one of the latter. He pulled into the garage and parked next to the chocolate brown Mercedes 300 TD station wagon. Mary Kathryn must be home.

The house was on a point of jutting rock, fifteen hundred feet above the city, with 270-degree views, from the high rises of downtown Los Angeles across the basin to Catalina Island.

Mac let himself into the kitchen from the garage. "Mary Kathryn, let's celebrate. I've just—"

Mac's wife turned from the range, her face momentarily covered by swirling, softly waved hair, close to the color of burnished copper, more gold than red. Her big eyes filled with tears. "Mac, you must speak to Tracy immediately. Your daughter played hooky—to shoot pool."

Mac could not understand how anyone so tangibly blessed could be so insecure. Any infringement upon Mary Kathryn's cherished view of her world as it should be seemed to tax sorely her ability to cope. Mac knew he should be concerned, for both Mary Kathryn and his daughter, but he couldn't help laughing. "If she played hooky to go shopping, would she then still be yours?"

Mac calmed Mary Kathryn with a kiss and hug. Then he exacted a promise from the seven-year-old delinquent never again to commit hooky while in the third grade. Well, thought Mac, that covers the next three months. He gave Tracy a start with her homework, then sent her off to finish it and to bed.

Mac built a fire in the fireplace, the rock face of which towered twenty feet up to the heavily beamed ceiling. Then he turned up the air-conditioning to compensate. He found the Glen Grant and made two extremely tall scotch and sodas before he brought Mary Kathryn to the thickly carpeted conversation pit. Mac enjoyed just looking at Mary Kathryn. He thought that, even in her baggy velour sweatshirt and jeans, she was still one of the reigning beauties of the Western Hemisphere. Mary Kathryn looked just as she had ten years ago, when she'd stormed Justice Crammer's chambers, doing her impression of Scarlett O'Hara, bearing an invitation to her parents' dinner party. It had been lust at first sight. And mutual.

Mac and Mary Kathryn were married the next year, in the garden of her parents' San Marino mansion, three weeks after her graduation from Marymount College. In addition to their mutual physical attraction, they shared sophomorically romantic ideas about the nature of wedlock. Mac's gorgeous wife naturally would maintain a charming and comfortable home, usually filled with the aroma of freshly baked pie and with precocious, well-behaved children. Twice a week Mary Kathryn's enormously successful husband would undoubtedly bring captains of industry and Saudi princes to dine and to be amused by her anecdotes of the six weeks she'd spent each summer working at her father's newspaper.

Still the same, thought Mac. Lounging in her leather and walnut Eames chair, sipping from French crystal, surrounded by Swedish furniture, Moroccan tapestries, soaring walls, and oversize paintings by Young American Artists. The portrait of a princess.

Should it have been more? Mac wondered. Could it still be? Well, he sighed, it might also be a hell of a lot worse. "A toast to the Belle of Bel Air," he said. "And to the future success of Charles Wennerstrom." He was willing to bet she had nothing on under the sweatshirt.

"Ah, you're going to do it." Mary Kathryn gave Mac a smile that could easily have melted a traffic court judge's heart. "To victory. Tell me all about it."

They brought broiled red snapper, a salad, and a bottle of white Zinfandel to the twenty-five-square-foot rosewood coffee table before the fire.

During dinner Mac told her about the obnoxious display staged by Laura Wennerstrom. Mary Kathryn raised her left eyebrow. "Why," she asked, "doesn't an otherwise intelligent man realize he's been charmed?"

After dinner Mac switched to coffee. Mary Kathryn stayed with the wine. Mac's enthusiasm for the case was obvious, but Mary Kathryn appeared to wonder about the problems. "But TOPCO, one of the giants, a multinational conglomerate. Can you possibly win against the resources of all that?" She emphasized the extent of her real interest in the answer by pulling off her jeans before holding out her wineglass.

Mac poured more wine and kissed her cheek. "I'll seduce them like this." His kisses moved lower. "And attack them like this." Mary Kathryn slid half under him, grabbed his dark, curly hair, and pulled his lean body down to her as she whispered, "And they will surrender—like this." Mac's hands moved under her sweatshirt and confirmed his suspicion.

Later that night, when the stereo automatically switched off and Mary Kathryn's perfumed hair tickled his nose, Mac came half awake. Mary Kathryn was snoring softly into his shoulder. Exotic tropical plants were rustling on the redwood deck. The stars were twinkling through the open sliding glass door.

Mary Kathryn came awake, too. "All right, love?"

Mac sighed and reclosed his eyes. This relationship could be labeled superficial, he supposed. Sometimes he thought they were merely each other's trophies. "Mary Kathryn," he murmured, "this is a definite improvement on your average Hanoi Hilton cell. I just hope the eunuchs remembered to lock up the jewels."

2

*T*wo days after the Wennerstrom Complaint was served on TOPCO, a meeting took place in the offices of O'Malley & Byers, the law firm retained by TOPCO to defend the case.

O'Malley & Byers was so old there had not been an O'Malley or a Byers in the firm for the past two generations. Three years ago the firm had had the opportunity to hire a new Stanford graduate named Joseph O'Malley, who was in no way related to the firm's founder, Samson Augustus O'Malley. Although young O'Malley was valedictorian of his class and editor of the *Law Review* and had impeccable credentials, the O'Malley & Byers partners rejected him on the grounds of his surname. The partners felt that the firm would be held up to public ridicule when it became known that the most lowly associate in the 250-lawyer firm of O'Malley & Byers was the only one named O'Malley.

O'Malley & Byers was controlled by a half dozen gray old men who had risen from their beginnings as gray young men. Although no word was ever spoken concerning it, conformity was prized at O'Malley & Byers. A turtleneck sweater under a tweed jacket would botch the career of even the most promising associate.

The firm's offices occupied the top four floors of a Bunker Hill office building near the Civic Center. Although the suite was served by eight banks of public elevators, it also had two private elevators as well as two private stairways to handle the internal traffic. There were client reception areas and duplicate libraries on each floor. The volume of paper the firm created required three shifts of clerks, stenographers, and secretaries laboring twenty-four hours a day. The three lower floors were decorated in Efficiency Contemporary, but the top level was done in Nineteenth-Century Awesome—deeply carved walnut-paneled walls bearing oil portraits of ancestral partners, Oriental rugs, and heavy velvet drapes. The effect was intimidating. Even corporate vice-presidents tended to whisper as they were led down the corridors.

Jonathan Clark's office was on the top floor. Jonathan Clark wore his steel gray hair long so that he could brush it back from his bushy eyebrows whenever he wanted to appear to be thinking. A modest two-bedroom house in the San Fernando Valley could have been purchased for the price of his gold chain, watch, and cuff links.

Clark's father and grandfather had also been partners in O'Malley & Byers. The Securities and Exchange Commission had affectionately dubbed Clark's father the "greatest criminal corporate mind in America today." Even without nepotism in his favor, Clark should have done well at O'Malley & Byers. He had had good grades at a prestigious law school and spent two dutiful, tedious years in the O'Malley & Byers library, writing memoranda of points and authorities, appellate briefs, and opinion letters, before he was allowed into a courtroom. He always worked hard for the Republican party, and he won more cases than he lost, not a small accomplishment for a defense lawyer. Clark was an accomplished player on emotions of judges and juries, plucking their small passions and prejudices with harpist's sensitivity. He enjoyed the ritual and drama, delighted in courtroom maneuvers.

There was no need to use one of the conference rooms. Clark's office comfortably held the twelve men assembled before the seven-foot carved antique desk.

Clark rose, and notebooks flipped open, ballpoint pens clicked, and twelve motivated faces gave him complete attention. As he pinched his large, hooked nose, he bore a strong resemblance to an overweight Abraham Lincoln. "Gentlemen, we are assembled here to prepare the defense of our client in the case of *Charles Wennerstrom* versus *Titan Overland Petroleum Company*. I have only a few preliminary remarks to make before turning over the meeting to Messrs. Manning and Raedeke, who will give you your assignments. The plaintiff's case seems to be based essentially on his tenuous interpretation of the joint venture agreement and on his uncorroborated testimony of alleged misrepresentations made to him by an officer of our client. I am convinced that this case can be successfully defended. In view of the gravity of the plaintiff's claim of fraud, and the publicity this case will receive, it is imperative that we do so. To that end we must pursue three concurrent strategies: Every opportunity must be taken to delay the trial; plaintiff, and I include his counsel, must be caused maximum expense in the prosecution of his claim; and confusion must be sowed constantly. These are legitimate defense strategies. We would be remiss in our duty to our client if we failed to use them fully. I am confident that if we faithfully adhere to these proven strategies, we will prevail. I need hardly add that a case of this magnitude can directly affect your careers at O'Malley and Byers. Thank you, gentlemen. Carry on, Mr. Manning."

James Manning, a pale, bald skeleton, summarized the case. Attorneys were assigned to investigate the backgrounds of Charles Wennerstrom, Laura Wennerstrom, and Clarence McGovern, the attorney who had represented Charles Wennerstrom in the TOPCO negotiations. The defense hoped to find some discrediting information, which could be used to obscure real issues. Attorneys were directed to make numerous pretrial motions: a motion to quash service of the summons and complaint on the grounds of defective service; a motion to strike the complaint on grounds of bad faith; a motion to change the venue for convenience of witnesses; a motion to inspect plaintiff's records and plaintiff's laboratory; even a motion to examine the plaintiff physically and psychiatrically on the ground that because plaintiff was claiming emotional distress, defendent was entitled to determine his physical and mental condition. Such motions created mountains of paper, consumed lawyers' and the court's time, and caused substantial expense.

Jonathan Clark leaned back in his Connolly leather chair and unwrapped his first cigar of the day. It was a good beginning.

Not long after their first meeting, TOPCO's attorneys filed a motion for a preliminary injunction, enjoining Wennerstrom, pending trial, from selling or transferring any modification of the Wennerstrom Process. The defense did not have strong faith in the success of its motion but believed it to be useful for its confusing and harassing effect. The defense, of course, deduced that Sorensen, Oliver, Bradford, and Smith was on a contingent fee and was probably advancing at least most of Wennerstrom's court costs. Increasing the cost and effort needed to prosecute the plaintiff's claim might discourage plaintiff's forces.

When Mac Oliver read his junior partner's papers opposing the request for preliminary injunction, he realized that Burt Ginter's arguments were persuasive, making TOPCO's chances of obtaining the preliminary injunction dim.

"Burt, I reviewed your points and authorities in opposition to TOPCO's motion. Brilliant stuff. Very effective," said Mac.

Burt was a six-foot-four-inch, gangling spaniel puppy. When he beamed, his ears stuck out six inches. "Thanks, boss. I thought it was good myself."

Mac smiled. "Okay, Burt. Then fix it."

Burt's ears retracted. "Huh?"

Mac said, "It won't do. It's too persuasive. It's liable to win. We want TOPCO's motion to be granted. We want TOPCO to get a preliminary injunction against Charlie Wennerstrom."

"I'm sorry, Mac, I got a little confused. I just assumed that since we represent Charlie Wennerstrom, we want to oppose TOPCO's motion."

"We do, Burt, but not so well. Just good enough so that it doesn't look as if we're taking a dive."

"I understand that you want us to lose this round. But why?"

"The civil calendar in Los Angeles County is so congested it would normally take four years to get this case to trial. Perhaps more, if TOPCO stalls successfully. Charlie Wennerstrom is already sixty-seven. We can't afford—"

"Of course, I get it. Priority for trial. Am I right?"

"Right. If the preliminary injunction is granted, the case is entitled to priority over all other civil cases. We will knock at least two years off the waiting time, and what will a preliminary injunction against Wennerstom cost us? Wennerstrom will only be enjoined from refining a process he's already abandoned."

"Sir, it is an honor to observe your devious mind at work. But why hasn't TOPCO thought of all this?"

"I can only guess they are so delighted at having dreamed up another way to harass us that they've blinded themselves to this consequence. Or perhaps they've thought of it and are so confident of their ability to get continuances and stall off the trial that they think it's a good trade-off. You may have noticed that a lot of differences of opinion occur in lawsuits."

"Yeah. I'll go rewrite my brilliant memo into something really inept. Any other ideas?"

"Send our most pimply-faced junior associate attorney to argue against the motion. Convince him that we're a lead-pipe cinch. He should be sure to tell the judge that it would be an obvious abuse of discretion to grant the motion. And tell him not to forget to spend a lot of time arguing how high TOPCO's bond should be, just in case the judge disagrees with him and decides to grant the injunction anyway."

"Mac, you're an evil person. It's a pleasure to work with you."

Marla Zimmerman had something important to report. Cornell Sepulveda Smith was already in Mac's office, sipping coffee, when she bounced in.

"Ms. MZ," Smith teased, "you are a pleasing sight, indeed. I suppose you've brought us some profound insight, although I would have welcomed you for your freckles alone."

The University of California, Berkeley, honor graduate tried to glower but found it difficult. "It's bad enough being mistaken for a secretary by half the clients around here without being constantly reminded of how damned cute I am. Hi, Mac."

"Good morning, Ms. . . . Zimmerman," said Mac, struggling to appear serious. "What have you got?"

"Something good, I'm sure. I'm not at all sure about how to use it, though." Marla Zimmerman assumed her most professional demeanor, which gave her approximately as much dignity as a high school cheerleader.

"Please proceed, Ms. Zimmerman."

"All right. As you know, TOPCO assigned all right, title and interest in the Wennerstrom Process to Rutherford-Leske Oil, Ltd., in exchange for all of the outstanding shares of Rutherford's wholly owned subsidiary, RL Equities Corp."

"We know, Ms. Zimmerman. Please proceed," Smith suggested.

"Yes, sir. RL Equities Corp. had only one stockholder, of course: Rutherford-Leske Oil, Ltd.—"

Smith was becoming impatient. "I'm sure there is going to be a point. Couldn't you just trust us to understand what you have found without boring us with how you got it?"

Mac intervened. "Patience, Cornell. It may be useful to know. Go on, Ms.—Marla."

Marla Zimmerman smiled her gratitude. It took half an hour to explain how she'd found it before she got to what it was. ". . . And Rutherford-Leske Oil, Ltd., is now forty-eight years old. During that forty-eight years, the Rutherford-Leske stock has always been held by three people. I don't mean the same three people for all those years. Different people have owned the stock over the forty-eight years, but it's always been three stockholders, never more, never less. During the forty-eight-year life of the company its stock has been owned by thirty different individuals. I spent most of yesterday and last night tracking down their backgrounds. I'm not finished, but I've already traced twenty-one of them."

"And?" asked Mac and Smith almost simultaneously.

"And"—Marla Zimmerman paused for another great smile—"I can tell you that at least twenty-one of Rutherford-Leske's stockholders were retired TOPCO officers."

Cornell Sepulveda Smith almost stuttered. "Are you saying that every single Rutherford-Leske Oil, Ltd., stockholder, past and present, whom you've been able to check out is or was a retired TOPCO officer?"

Mac was excited. "You still have nine to check?"

"Yes, nine to go, but my intuition tells me that it's going to come out thirty out of thirty. Here's the list."

Together Mac and Cornell Sepulveda Smith looked at the typewritten list. Thirty names, twenty-one of which had checkmarks beside them. None of the names was known to either man.

"Fascinating coincidence?" asked Smith.

"Infuckingcredible coincidence," said Mac, grinning. "But what precisely is the connection? TOPCO seems to have had some secret connection to Rutherford-Leske Oil, Ltd., but we don't know what."

"That brings me to my problem—our problem," said Marla. "We can't hope to really tie Rutherford-Leske Oil, Ltd., conclusively to TOPCO without subpoenaing TOPCO and Rutherford-Leske Oil, Ltd., records and witnesses for depositions. And of course, we can't do that without tipping our hand to TOPCO—"

"And giving them the opportunity to bury the evidence of any connection," said Mac.

Smith asked, "Marla, are you sure that TOPCO doesn't know what you've got?"

Marla spoke carefully. "Of course, I can't be positive. They've got connections, just as we do, and leaks do sometimes occur. But my information is the result of my own investigation, and you two are the first I've talked to."

"And the last, at least for now," Mac said. "No depositions, no subpoenas, no formal discovery of any kind on this subject. You will continue discreet investigation and report only to Cornell or myself. You know what we need. We want any evidence—"

"That TOPCO exercises any degree of control over Rutherford-Leske Oil, Ltd. Because if we can show that TOPCO controls Rutherford-

Leske, we can argue that TOPCO didn't really sell the Wennerstrom Process at all. They just made it appear that way so they could screw Charlie by keeping the licensing fees for themselves." Marla was exuberant.

Cornell Sepulveda Smith stood. "Coffee all around?"

"And lunch?" added Mac, looking at his watch.

"Could I have a raise, too?" asked Marla.

3

Grant Radcliffe didn't bother to greet his office visitor.

"I'm not delighted at the direction this case has been taking," Radcliffe said. "Harold Rifkin gave away much more than he should have at his deposition. His testimony at the trial may be a problem." Radcliffe wasn't ready to admit, even to himself, that it could be worse than that. Rifkin knew too much.

The man with the cannonball head shrugged his massive shoulders as he sat, uninvited, in a beige chair. "Rifkin? Yeah, your former administrative assistant. Instead of forcing his retirement, you should have let me—"

"Yes, yes. You are much too quick with that suggestion. You cannot solve all of life's problems that way."

The man obviously didn't believe him, but Grant Radcliffe continued. "Anyway, chipping away at the edges does not solve the basic problem. The strength of Wennerstrom's case does not lie in the testimony of peripheral witnesses. The core of Wennerstrom's case is Wennerstrom himself. If Wennerstrom's testimony is believed—"

"So let's attack the basic problem," the man said.

"Interesting choice of words. Do you have anything short of killing in mind?"

"Killing has always been an effective method of solving problems. Don't be hypocritical You don't give a damn about Charles Wennerstrom."

"Of course, I don't. Do not confuse hypocrisy with pragmatism. It is simply that your solution carries enormous risks. Therefore, your way should be considered only as the last alternative, and then only when our potential loss or injury would be too massive to accept, and then only when the risk of such an operation has been reduced to the absolute minimum achievable. Don't you understand that?"

"Of course, I do. It may surprise you that I even agree. But don't you see that Charles Wennerstrom has the potential to destroy you—just possibly even TOPCO itself?"

"A ridiculous exaggeration." Radcliffe tried hard to believe that, but lately his stomach had suggested otherwise.

"No, it's neither ridiculous nor an exaggeration. Listen to me." The man spoke quietly and articulately. He listed the strengths of Wennerstrom's case and flaws in TOPCO's defense, outlining ways in which Wennerstrom's damages against TOPCO could be measured. After he had carefully explained how enormous the damages could be, he leaned back and, with another of his mirthless grins, said, "Now tell me again how it's a ridiculous exaggeration."

Grant Radcliffe was surprised to realize that he was perspiring. He mopped his brow with a fine linen handkerchief. Radcliffe's career plan had been classically simple: superior job performance combined with an advantageous marriage. A substantial verdict against TOPCO could easily be blamed on him. After all, he had engineered the entire transaction. The effect on Radcliffe's future could be chilling. He tried to smile. "God, you're a menace, an assassin with a first-class mind."

The man smiled genuinely at the compliment.

Radcliffe's slim fingers drummed his desktop. "You have not answered my question. Do you have something specific in mind?"

"Several things. Charles Wennerstrom is now sixty-eight and not in the best of health. He just might pass naturally and quietly away, although that is difficult to arrange without detection." The man rubbed his hands. "Charles Wennerstrom works regularly in his old basement lab. A lab which is full of dangerous equipment and materials. He works long, odd hours, often to the point of exhaustion. He has a reputation for absentmindedness, although I'm convinced that he has more than his share of marbles. He just gets distracted when he's concentrating on an experiment. It wouldn't shock anyone if he had an accident some night in that laboratory."

"Do you call that specific?"

"No, I call this specific. Wennerstrom works in that laboratory almost every evening after dinner—occasionally with his daughter's help but usually alone. For the past few months he has been cooking various batches of glob on Bunsen burners, taking samples, labeling and storing them. I don't know what he's trying to accomplish. It just hasn't seemed useful to find out. I have had samples analyzed, however."

Grant Radcliffe stopped drumming.

The man continued. "The materials are all moderately unstable explosives, although it would take another explosion or extreme heat to detonate them. The nights lately have been quite chilly, as is usual this time of year. Wennerstrom keeps the basement windows closed. He usually finishes decanting his samples by one or two A.M., never later than three A.M. Then he turns on a twenty-four-hour music station and falls asleep on his laboratory couch until after sunrise—usually until about seven or seven forty-five, when his daughter wakes him and brings coffee."

"That will kill him?"

The man ignored Radcliffe and continued. "For the past nine nights he has left all four Bunsen burners going full blast, apparently to keep his laboratory warm as he falls asleep. His daughter usually turns them off when she comes in in the morning."

Grant Radcliffe began to look interested.

"The only other heat in that basement laboratory is from an old electric heater which Wennerstrom keeps on the floor at the foot of his couch. Unburned natural gas, being lighter than air, rises to the top of an enclosed air space and fills the space from top to bottom. Each of the four Bunsen burners has an individual valve, but the gas line which serves all four burners has a master manual in-line valve just inside the laboratory door. I have calculated the interior volume of the laboratory and the rate of the flow of gas from the four Bunsen burners. The explosive range is quickly reached in that small volume. The gas will take one to one and one-half hours to achieve a density which will be ignited by the electric heater on the laboratory floor. If the master gas valve is turned off at five A.M., the Bunsen burners will use up the fuel in the line and go out within one minute. If the master gas valve is then reopened, the Bunsen burners, having no pilot lights and having their individual valves still open, will not reignite, but will pour out unburned gas until between six to six-thirty A.M. At that time the electric heater will ignite the gas, causing an explosion, in which, in turn, will detonate the experimental materials stored in the lab, causing a larger explosion, which no one could possibly survive."

Radcliffe was fascinated. "One would have to break in to turn the gas valve off and on. What if Wennerstrom were awakened?"

The man lowered his voice to a whisper. "One would promise to be very quiet. The old man sleeps like, you should excuse the expression, the dead. The daughter would be more likely to awaken, but fortunately her bedroom is at the opposite end of the house. Neither the house itself nor the basement lab has any security. Breaking in would be a little bit tougher than opening a lunch box, but not much."

"What about the sound of escaping gas? What about the smell?"

"As I said, the old guy sleeps like a child. He'll never hear the hissing over the sounds of the radio anyway. The way he sleeps, he would be asphyxiated long before he smelled it. Anyway, the explosion will occur long before asphyxiation is possible."

There was no movement or sound in the room except the faint whir of an air-conditioner.

"And afterward?"

"Afterward the investigators find the remnants of Bunsen burners, an open gas line, pieces of an electric heater, and traces of explosives, which his daughter confirms he has been working with for months. It's obvious that another unfortunate accident has resulted from poor ventilation and failure to use proper safety precautions."

Radcliffe shook his head. "I still do not like murder."

"You don't dislike murder; you only dislike risk. You aren't taking any."

"I cannot condone a killing." Radcliffe didn't quite really believe that.

"How can you condone something you don't even know is going to happen?"

Grant Radcliffe was unmoving, almost hypnotized. "Yes, how could I condone something I didn't even know about?"

The man stood. "Good night then."

Radcliffe stared but said nothing as the man left his office. His desk clock showed that it was time for his appointment with Jonathan Clark. It was only a block to Clark's office. Fresh air would feel good. As Radcliffe walked out of the tower lobby into the street, the wind gusted through the high-rise canyons. The evening rush-hour traffic was starting to build. It would be another cold night.

"Are you all right?" Jonathan Clark asked Radcliffe. "You look pale."

"I'm fine," lied Radcliffe. His visitor had shaken him more than he realized. Radcliffe threw off the memory. "Review the status of the Wennerstrom case for me, please, and give me your updated opinion of our risk of loss. I have to report to our CEO tomorrow and to the full board of directors on Monday."

"Of course," said Clark. He rose from his antique desk and paced his immense Persian carpet. "This is a bit oversimplified, but it's valid enough for our purpose. Wennerstrom is essentially suing for damages on three counts. First, for fraudulent misrepresentation that the Wennerstrom Process was not patentable."

Radcliffe was recovering his presence. "Jonathan, I don't intend to be rude, but I do have a tight schedule. I already know all that. Pearson and the rest of the board will want to know the status of the case, our chances of winning and losing, and the company's maximum exposure to loss."

"Of course," said Clark, annoyed at the interruption. He was just warming up. "It comes down to this. On the basis of current status of discovery, I believe that we have an excellent chance of successfully defending the case."

"Does that mean actually winning or merely keeping the verdict to a low figure?"

"I'm talking about a defense verdict," Clark said. He paused to offer Radcliffe a cigar. Radcliffe waved him off.

"Wennerstrom's breach-of-contract count is premature. We may even be able to get it dismissed without its even getting to the jury. The fraud causes of action are weak. Essentially they are based on the uncorroborated testimony of the plaintiff, Charles Wennerstrom; the plaintiff's daughter, Laura Wennerstrom; and the plaintiff's former attorney, Clarence McGovern. Not exactly an impartial, disinterested group of witnesses. True, TOPCO is a target defendant, as is any large corporation. But jurors are traditionally reluctant to find fraud on flimsy evidence."

"Can you quote odds?" Radcliffe asked. "The board relates to numbers."

"Now that is a difficult game." Clark lit his cigar. "Numbers can be deceptive, but I'll hazard an opinion. Let's say eighty percent on the breach-of-contract cause and seventy percent on the fraud counts. We'll call it seventy percent across the board—a seventy percent chance of a defense verdict."

Color returned to Radcliffe's face. "Excellent. Now what's the worst? What is our maximum exposure to loss if the verdict goes against us?"

"That, too, is difficult to predict. Technically TOPCO's maximum exposure is everything Wennerstrom is asking for in the suit. That could be over a billion dollars, although no jury has ever rendered a verdict even approximating such an astronomical amount. I would set the realistic maximum plaintiff verdict at five million, with a possible additional five million in punitive damages—ten million dollars total. However, I think that the probable amount, if there were a plaintiff's verdict at all, would be closer to five million than ten million."

Radcliffe's pale blue eyes sparkled, and his stomach unclenched. "Excellent, excellent. The board will be relieved." No more than I, he thought. "Is there anything I can do to assist the defense?"

Jonathan Clark hesitated for a moment. "Yes. Harold Rifkin's deposition testimony did not help our defense. Possibly someone could talk persuasively to Rifkin—discreetly, of course. No coercion. But perhaps his memory of events could be jogged so that his recollections are more . . . consistent . . . with the main line of the defense."

"I'll look into that, Jonathan. Thank you. The board will be pleased with your progress. Good night."

When Radcliffe returned to the lobby of Clark's building, he stepped into the nearest telephone booth and dialed an unlisted number. He knew he would hear the familiar taped message. The man never answered the telephone.

A pleasant female voice answered. "This is the John Smith residence. Mr. Smith is not available at this time. At the sound of the tone you may leave a message. . . ."

Radcliffe smiled before he spoke. He didn't know any John Smith. "Aunt Charlotte's operation has been canceled. The doctors feel that it is unnecessary at this time."

Radcliffe felt good as he stepped briskly into the street. The wind had died. It didn't seem nearly as cold.

The man had heard Radcliffe's message over the answering machine's monitor. His first impulse was to call Radcliffe back to find out what had changed his mind. Was Radcliffe merely being squeamish? Too bad. It was going to be an ideally cold night. The operation would have been so simple. It required almost no preparation, really; just a few elementary precautions coming and going. And, the man thought, it was doubly sad because things had been so tedious and routine lately. Not that this operation presented any great challenge. It would serve to stir the blood a little, though. A man needed exercise. It's just too bad I was here to get the message, he thought. Suddenly the man grinned, grinned wider, and laughed out loud. This exercise promised to be too much fun to give up. Yes, it's just too bad I was not here to get the message.

It was 3:00 A.M. when the man got into his dark gray Buick. Nice and cold, he thought. There's a moon, but a person can't have everything. He wore a dark gray suit, a black topcoat, a dark gray hat, black leather gloves, and rubber-soled black oxfords. At a casual glance he looked like a middle-aged businessman coming home from his mistress's apartment. In his topcoat pockets he carried a penlight flash, a small plastic spray bottle of silicone lubricant, and a set of master keys of the brand he knew Wennerstrom's locks to be. He carried no weapons. Maybe I'll get lucky and some fink will try to mug me, he thought. It took thirty minutes, via the Hollywood and Golden State freeways, to drive to Wennerstrom's home in the Los Feliz area. Even in the middle of the night traffic was moderately heavy. The man cruised the neighborhood for a radius of several blocks around Wennerstrom's house, checking for possible stakeouts by city, state, or federal law enforcement agencies, private investigators, process servers, automobile repossessors, suspicious spouses, rapists, or other burglars. The neighborhood was free of competition.

The man parked the Buick and walked the two blocks back to the Wennerstrom's house. He walked around Wennerstrom's block. No television late, late show addicts, no lights on, not a barking dog, not even a mewing cat. As he reapproached Wennerstrom's house, he noticed an open window. That would be Laura's bedroom. He walked soundlessly up the concrete driveway to the side door and opened it with the first key he tried. Good. Haven't lost the touch, he thought. He was in the kitchen. A brief flash of the penlight located the door to the basement, which was ajar. He squeezed through the opening, carefully putting his weight on the top basement step. Silence. Step by step, the well-built old house kept his secret.

Seventeen steps lower, he stood outside the closed laboratory door, listening. He could hear the radio playing. He knew that if Charles Wennerstrom were sleeping or sitting on the couch, Wennerstrom's back would be to the door. He pulled the plastic bottle of lubricant from his pocket and lightly sprayed the hinges and the doorknob. His gloved hand turned the knob. The door was unlocked.

He opened the door enough to stick his head into the room. He smelled something like kerosene. The laboratory was in a flickering blue light, caused by four Bunsen burners on the laboratory counter to his left. Ahead, to his right, he could see the back of the couch and Charlie Wennerstrom's big stocking feet sticking over the arm. On the floor below Charlie's feet the electric heater glowed. Immediately to the right of the door was another counter, with cabinets below.

The man turned and reached for the nearest cabinet door. Stuck. Damn! He got down on one knee facing the cabinet, braced his other knee against the cabinet, and pulled again. The door came silently free. He felt inside the rear of the cabinet where he knew the master gas line valve to be. Something was in the way. A bottle. He slowly, carefully slid it aside. His hand groped for the valve and turned it off. Nothing happened. The blue light continued to flicker. Twenty-nine, thirty, thirty-one. The blue light changed to yellow, flickered again. One by one the four Bunsen burner flames went out. The man turned the valve back on. He strained to hear the hiss of escaping gas but heard nothing over the sounds of the radio. Charlie Wennerstrom didn't make a sound.

The man closed the cabinet door, closed the laboratory door behind him, mounted the steps, and locked the kitchen door behind him as he left the house. As he strolled back to his parked car, he looked at his digital watch: 4:05. Just as choreographed, he gloated as he drove off. Better than the movies.

At four-thirty a white pickup truck, bearing the Southern California Gas Company blue logo on its door, parked in front of the Wennerstrom house. In the predawn light the driver consulted his clipboard to verify the address and the location of the gas meter and main valve. They were mounted on the side of the house. With his wrench he turned off the gas supply to the house, sealing the valve closed with a red cardboard tag. He returned to his truck and drove off. Long before, Southern California Gas had learned the desirability of turning off customers' gas during hours they were unlikely to be awake to argue.

At six-thirty Laura Wennerstrom awoke before her alarm went off. Something was wrong. The house was freezing. She swung her lovely long legs out of bed, put her feet into slippers, and bundled into an old wool robe. She checked the wall thermostat thermometer. Fifty-five degrees. She jiggled the switch, but the forced air furnace did not respond. Laura shivered her way into the kitchen and tried to turn on the gas range burners. Nothing there either. As the sun rose over Southern California, the light also dawned in Laura's mind. She hurried down to the basement lab and gave Charlie Wennerstrom's stocking feet a not entirely friendly slap.

"Father! Charles Wennerstrom!" She asked the rudely half-awakened old man, "What did you do with the check I gave you to mail to the gas company ten days ago?"

At seven the man had a police band scanner, a radio news station, and a television set on. But there was no report of an explosion or fire at the Wennerstrom residence. At nine, unable to contain his curiosity any longer, he drove by the Wennerstrom house, just in time to see happy, smiling Laura Wennerstrom backing out of her driveway, being waved at by Charlie Wennerstrom standing in the kitchen door. The man drove on, unnoticed, shaking his head slowly, side to side.

At ten the man called Grant Radcliffe at his office. "I got your message."

"Obviously in time to cancel," said Radcliffe.

"Obviously."

4

Wennerstrom v. *TOPCO* was assigned to jury trial department 102, Judge Arden Johannsen presiding.

The fourth-floor courtroom, in the block-long Central District Courthouse, was identical with several hundred others with white oak-paneled walls and a waist-high rail separating the audience from the participants. A two-tiered jury box filled with twelve prospective jurors of varying degrees of willingness lined one wall.

Simple, kindly old Judge Johannsen was not known as the brightest judicial light in Los Angeles County, but he was fair. His most serious flaw was the dreaded disease of judges, indecisiveness.

Jonathan Clark was wearing one of his three identical shiny, worn black suits. Clark would appear never to change suits during the trial, regardless of its duration.

MacDonald Oliver chose to project his usual image of understated success, a crisply pressed somber blue suit relieved by a white button-down shirt and Mac's favorite Royal Air Force tie. The tie had no significance. Mac simply liked the red, white, and blue stripes.

Charlie Wennerstrom and Burt Ginter were seated alongside Mac at the counsel table. Mac had insisted on Charlie's presence during jury selection. It was good public relations to have the plaintiff sitting through the dreary process, looking interested and confident. Mac had also learned that clients occasionally displayed remarkable insight in choosing jurors, although he would have had to admit that Charles Wennerstrom had not recently demonstrated remarkable ability to judge character.

Mac had also insisted that Laura stay away. Her strength and looks were unwelcome competition at this stage. Mac wanted to be the focus of the prospective jurors' attention during the selection process. If only he could find a way to keep Jonathan Clark out of the courtroom.

MacDonald Oliver was a happy man that morning. His case was prepared. He had arisen at dawn and run five easy miles along Mulholland Drive. Mary Kathryn had made the supreme sacrifice of also rising early, fixing Mac's favorite breakfast: fresh mango, and scrambled eggs with matzo. At breakfast Tracy had announced her engagement to a boy in her American history class. The wedding was to take place on June 12 in eleven years, since that was a Sunday. Mac was grateful that at least the boy was not in her sex education class. Mac felt good.

It took a day and a half to select a jury agreeable to both sides. Mac had exercised his last challenge on Virgil Smith, an elderly retired Texaco employee. Smith had been a middle executive whose duties had included evaluating contractual claims against the company, and he had seemed overly eager to serve. Mac had also felt that Smith's job experience would make him sympathetic to TOPCO, so he excused Smith. At the next recess Mac found himself standing next to Smith in the men's room. "Why did you excuse me?" Smith wanted to know. "I was all for you. I always thought it was a shame the way they made us screw claimants when I worked at Texaco."

* * *

Mac called Charlie Wennerstrom as his first witness for plaintiff's case. Charlie knew more of the entire Wennerstrom-TOPCO transaction than any other person except, of course, Grant Radcliffe. Mac didn't count on Radcliffe's help.

Charlie was really up for the trial. He looked better than he had in months. Courtesy of Laura, his suit was even pressed. He had slimmed down to a mere 260 pounds. Mac and Laura had conspired to modify Charlie's diet to something closely approaching normality. Charlie had even acceded to a mild dose of exercise, going for daily brisk walks. Sometimes Charlie walked alone, inventing; sometimes with Laura, chatting and joking; sometimes with Mac, going over some aspect of the transaction. Charlie and Mac had achieved instant communication and, although they got along well, did not always agree. Charlie continuously argued that because the facts were on his side, he merely had to testify truthfully. Mac denounced Charlie's view as naive, pointing out that was an example of the attitude that had gotten Charlie into trouble in the first place. Mac tried to convince Charlie that facts do not exist independently in a courtroom. Facts in evidence are inseparable from the manner of their presentation.

"Charlie," Mac said, "the facts are only what the jury decides they are. Suppose three witnesses testify that the light was green, and one testifies the light was red. The jury decides to believe the one witness. In that courtroom the fact is that the light was red. All this leads us to the most significant aspect of life in court. Your demeanor, and mine, will do more to influence what the jury determines to be the 'facts' than anything else that happens in that trial. Behavior and style. It's chemistry, Charlie. You should be able to understand chemistry."

Charlie understood, but he didn't like it. "You're saying that the form will be more important than the substance. That's perverted. How can such a farce achieve justice?"

"It's an imperfect system. You're the inventor. Invent a better one."

On direct examination, Charlie's narrative was easy and flowing. He had gone over the ground with Mac so many times. Only an occasional prompting question was needed. Mac knew that to exert tight control over Charlie by asking too many questions could imply to the jury that

Mac himself did not completely trust his witness. Charlie looked straight at the jury, as instructed by Mac, and told them of his background as a former TOPCO employee. He spoke of his passion for inventing and how it had moved him to form his own research and development company, Wennerstrom Products Associated.

Wennerstrom Products Associated, headed by Charlie Wennerstrom, its president and chief research scientist, also employed a secretary, bookkeeper, laboratory assistant, and computer programmer, all of whom were Charlie's daughter, Laura. He made his traditional joke about working for the WPA and was gratified to see a smile on the face of juror number nine, a gentleman of about Charlie's own age.

"Pick out those whom you sense are responding and talk to them. They will be your advocates inside the jury room," Mac had said.

Charlie testified that his daughter, Laura, deserved a substantial share of the credit for their achievement. He described her as the computer whiz. Charlie inadvertently referred to her as Laurel a couple of times, so Mac had him explain. Laura had been christened Laurel after the genus of tree in the tradition of her mother's tribe. But the Los Angeles School District's computers insisted on relabeling her as Laure L. until the Wennerstrom family accepted the inevitable and renamed her Laura Willow.

Charlie told of his long hours of experimenting, his failures, and successes, which ultimately coalesced into the now-famous Wennerstrom Process. By pumping superheated steam laced with a catalyst into dormant oil wells, Charlie was able to break down shale without extracting or crushing it. The oil thus released could then be treated on the surface or shipped to conventional refineries. Only one barrel of water per barrel of oil was used, borrowed, really, and returned to its source distilled and purified by the process. Air pollution was minimal, no more than that caused by conventional oil drilling, water separation, and pumping.

Charlie broke through while EXXON and other oil giants failed, and on a pittance while they wrote off millions before giving up. The rub was that Charlie needed to construct a pilot plant to prove it worked. The cost was a fraction of what a synfuel plant to produce oil from coal would have cost, a few millions as against billions. Charlie didn't have the first million. He explained how he'd gone to TOPCO, hoping to borrow money to build the pilot plant, and described his first meeting with Radcliffe.

"I told Radcliffe I'd developed the process. Grant Radcliffe already knew all about it. I guess someone—"

"Objection," Jonathan Clark came to his feet. "Conclusion, hearsay, and speculation. The witness has no firsthand knowledge of what Mr. Radcliffe—"

"Sustained," said the judge.

Mac smiled. He had explained the inadmissibility of hearsay testimony to Charlie many times. It was just the way Charlie talked. "Just tell us what Grant Radcliffe said."

Charlie smiled back. He understood. "Oh, yes. He said someone, I don't remember who, had already briefed him on my process and what I was looking for—the financing. He said that he thought that TOPCO would be very interested in the process and would consider the financing. He asked me to prepare some cost estimates and projections. I'd already done them, and I gave him copies. He wanted to study my projections and promised to get back to me promptly. I thanked him, told him I'd look forward to hearing, and I left. It was very brief. Ten minutes, perhaps."

"And did you hear from Radcliffe?"

"Yes, a few days later. He telephoned me from San Francisco. I'm sorry. He said he was calling me from San Francisco. He was rushed for time, but he could spend a few hours with me the next day if I could meet him in Ellwood. He wanted to discuss a proposal."

"Did he say why he wanted to meet in Ellwood?"

"Yes. It's an oil field area. TOPCO was considering leases there."

"Where's Ellwood?"

"Ellwood's just north of Santa Barbara on Highway One-oh-one about one hundred miles from Los Angeles. I agreed to meet him for lunch the next day at The Timbers, which is a restaurant on Highway One-oh-one and Winchester Canyon near Ellwood."

"Relate the conversation to us."

"Well, Radcliffe said that TOPCO was interested in financing the project but that TOPCO would not lend me the money. TOPCO was not in the lending business, he said. He suggested a joint venture. He called it a limited partnership. I would be the limited partner with TOPCO as the general partner, and I would receive forty percent of the business, and—"

Mac had seen one juror's eyebrow lift and thought he had better straighten that one out. "Forty percent of what business?"

"Oh, forty percent of the joint venture, of course." Charlie smiled. "Not forty percent of TOPCO. I would own forty percent of the limited partnership."

"Did Grant Radcliffe tell you that you would own forty percent of the partnership assets?"

"Objection," Clark pounced. "Leading and suggestive. If Mr. Oliver insists on testifying for the witness—"

"Sustained," ruled the judge.

That was a stupid mistake, thought Mac. Leading questions of my own chief witness just make me seem manipulative. Charlie would have gotten around to it. Mac asked, "What did Mr. Radcliffe say?"

"I don't recall his using the word 'assets.' Forty percent of the business would be mine. He definitely used the term 'ownership.' I would own forty percent of the partnership property, he said. TOPCO would be the managing partner. I asked if TOPCO would take care of the patent application. He said he didn't consider the process patentable. That surprised me. He was so adamant."

"Why were you surprised?"

Charlie shrugged. "Simply because I thought the process was clearly patentable."

"Did Radcliffe give you any reasons?"

"Oh, yes. He said the process was an ingenious compilation of existing technologies. I remember those were his exact words because I was so offended by the phrase at the time. Silly of me, of course. But I was rather proud of the invention. I remember asking him why TOPCO was so damned interested in investing several million in it if it wasn't patentable. He said he thought the process was still worth a great deal if we could secretly perfect it for commercial use and get a jump on the competition, although it would not be worth as much as if it were a patentable process."

Mac developed the details of the conversation with additional questions, but he was confident that the two major points had already been made: Radcliffe promised Wennerstrom forty percent ownership of all partnership property. Radcliffe had represented that the Wennerstrom Process was not patentable, an act that the jury could infer he did in order to keep the price down.

"Radcliffe promised to get his lawyers working on a draft of the proposed joint venture agreement as soon as he returned to Los Angeles," Charlie continued. "The next meeting was about three days later at the California Club, on Grand in downtown Los Angeles. Radcliffe was there, and me, and, of course, my daughter, Laura. There was some fuss about that. Apparently the dining room is restricted to males for lunch—pardon me, males at lunchtime. Apparently Radcliffe had not expected Laura. Anyway, he fixed that up right away—got us a private dining room. Laura was amused. Clarence McGovern was there, my attorney, and a gentleman by the name of Harold Rifkin, kind of an assistant to Grant Radcliffe. Five of us."

Charlie testified that at that meeting Radcliffe had presented McGovern and himself with copies of a one-hundred-page draft joint venture agreement, apologizing for the length, and explaining that this was inevitable since it had been written by lawyers.

Mac performed a slow 360-degree turn, appearing to study his notes but actually surveying the courtroom. The bailiff was fidgety, but Charlie was holding the jury's attention. Mac was satisfied. Charlie didn't have to sell the bailiff anything.

Mac led Wennerstrom through testimony as to the rest of the negotiating process and how, with McGovern's approval, Wennerstrom signed the limited partnership agreement and reams of additional documents.

Mac offered the written joint venture agreement in evidence. The written agreement provided for Wennerstrom's ownership of "forty percent interest in the business" with no explicit provision as to whether that interest included ownership of the partnership assets. Mac believed it was desirable to offer the ambiguously inconclusive document as part of the plaintiff's case, thereby minimizing its adverse impact.

Judge Johannsen yawned and glanced at his watch. "Ladies and gentlemen, we will have to adjourn early. I have—a, uh—"

"A meeting, Judge," suggested his clerk.

Charlie Wennerstrom was exuberant as he let his ponderous self down from the witness stand. Charlie waited until the jury was out of earshot before turning to Mac. "How did I do, lawyer?" Obviously he thought he'd done damn well.

"If you'd been this sharp in dealing with TOPCO, we wouldn't have to be here now." Mac smiled.

"I had the wrong lawyer," sighed Charlie.

Mac didn't say anything. He completely agreed.

When Charlie resumed the witness stand the next morning, he was a confident old hand. Laura had re-pressed his suit, and he was eager.

Charlie testified how, with TOPCO's complete cooperation, he had set up the pilot plant and produced shale oil within six months. He testified how immediately after the plant was producing its first shale oil, TOPCO had applied for a patent. Radcliffe had explained that now the partnership had a head start in development of the process, the competition could never catch up, and it would be worth letting out the secret to obtain the patent protection.

Mac asked Charlie if he was surprised at Radcliffe's newfound belief in the process's being patentable. Charlie replied that he was but that he hadn't mentioned it because he felt bound by the joint venture agreement. Charlie said that was also why he hadn't asked Radcliffe whether the process would be worth more when patented.

Clark sat unmoving. At his side Radcliffe doodled on a yellow pad. No one could see that his scribblings all bore strong resemblance to female genital parts.

Then Charlie summarized the complex exchange executed by TOPCO without his knowledge or consent. TOPCO had assigned the Wennerstrom Process patent to Rutherford-Leske Oil, Ltd., in exchange for the stock of Rutherford-Leske Oil Ltd.'s subsidiary, RL Equities

Corp. RL owned abandoned oil field leases and options on dormant oil fields, all potentially rich in shale deposits, but producing no current income.

Charlie's voice started to rise as he testified how he was confused and upset that he hadn't even been consulted and how he had been pacified by Radcliffe's explanation that the eventual profit and tax shelter would be to his ultimate benefit.

Then Charlie summarized how things began to fall apart about a month after the patent was obtained and assigned. His requests for equipment and materials were no longer filled. His salary wasn't paid. He could get no information from Radcliffe or anybody else at TOPCO, until he was finally told that there were no partnership funds for expenses or salary and that there would be none until there were partnership profits. Nobody would predict when that would be.

Charlie was seething red with anger by the time he testified that he owned forty percent of a partnership that owned a company that owned five million dollars' worth of oil rights and real estate, and he didn't have a nickel to pay for his laboratory expenses or salary. "It was outstanding," concluded Charlie, shaking his huge head in renewed disbelief. "I got millions of dollars of income tax shelter and no income."

Mac was delighted. Three jurors were nodding unconscious agreement. Even Judge Johannsen seemed interested. Charlie Wennerstrom had told a complete, lucid story of the transaction from his point of view. Charlie was, after a day and a half on the witness stand, as confident and comfortable as he was likely to become, in preparation for cross-examination. Most important of all, Mac was certain that Wennerstrom had developed considerable sympathy with the jury and possibly even with the judge.

Mac had to resist a feeling of smugness when he finally turned to Jonathan Clark and announced, "No further questions at this time. You may cross-examine."

Jonathan Clark always stood up to cross-examine. He felt the small courtesy pleased the jurors. He knew, too, that his always impressive appearance was even more imposing when he stood. Several inches taller than MacDonald Oliver, almost as tall as Charlie Wennerstrom,

Clark stood, stroking his long gray hair out of his eyes and staring at Wennerstrom.

Clark knew that Charlie Wennerstrom's testimony on direct examination had been effective. He had listened carefully and watched Charlie's impact on several jurors. It was not realistic to hope that the effect of Wennerstrom's testimony could be wholly destroyed, but it must be impaired. Clark knew that he must do substantial damage to plaintiff's case early if he was to have a chance of winning. He must make Wennerstrom hedge, hesitate, show uncertainty; Wennerstrom must be made to qualify his simple, strong statements, compelled to make some admission against his own interest. He would have to be handled carefully. Clark could permit himself no hint of overbearing or browbeating. This jury would resent it. Wennerstrom had established too much rapport. Clark hoped he could turn Wennerstrom's innate candor and intellectual honesty back against him.

Clark's cross-examination began as simply and restrainedly as his black-and-white attire. Clark established Wennerstrom's previous business experience and education, which he made to sound considerable. Wennerstrom was no longer the innocent lamb he had appeared to be. Then Clark went to work on Charlie's employment history, establishing that Charlie had worked for TOPCO for thirty years.

"And your association with Titan had been satisfactory during all those years, had it not, Mr. Wennerstrom?" Clark thought "Titan" sounded more dignified than TOPCO.

"I guess so. I'm not sure what you mean by satisfactory."

"I mean you were not discriminated against. You were treated fairly; you were promoted to a position of responsibility; you were paid a generous wage. Isn't all that so?"

"Well, yes."

"During your thirty years with Titan the company did not breach any contract with you, did it?"

"No."

"During those thirty years you weren't lied to, cheated, or defrauded by the company in any way?"

"No, I wasn't."

"That is what I mean by satisfactory, Mr. Wennerstrom. You had thirty years of an ongoing, continuous, satisfactory business relationship with Titan, isn't that right?"

"Yes, I suppose that's so."

"You came to Titan with this proposition, did you not?"

"Well, no, not exactly."

"Mr. Wennerstrom, you approached Titan, you were not solicited by the company?"

"Yes, that's correct."

"You needed financing, you couldn't do it alone, could you?"

"I had done it. I knew the process would work."

"You needed to build a pilot plant to prove that the process worked, didn't you?"

"Yes, that's so."

"And you didn't have the money to do that, did you?"

"No, I didn't have the money."

"You came to Titan for financing because of your previous long-term satisfactory relationship, isn't that correct?"

"Yes."

"You came to Titan because you had developed a trust for Titan and you hoped that Titan would trust you in return by financing your project, isn't that right?"

"Yes, that's correct."

"And Titan did finance the development of your project. It advanced the millions of dollars necessary to build the pilot plant, didn't it?"

"Yes, of course, it did."

"And Titan built you a first-class, fully equipped laboratory to your own specifications?"

"Yes, they did."

"Throughout the negotiations in this entire transaction you were represented by attorneys of your own choosing, isn't that right?"

"Just one. An attorney: Clarence McGovern."

Jonathan Clark didn't mind keeping Charlie Wennerstrom under tight control with leading questions. Clark wanted the jury to feel that he did not trust Wennerstrom's testimony. He wanted the jury to believe that Wennerstrom needed manipulation in order to wring the whole truth out of him.

Clark accelerated his cross-examination, using only terse, narrow questions designed to compel a yes or no answer.

"When you hired Clarence McGovern as your attorney, you believed he was experienced and competent, didn't you? After negotiations commenced, you continued to have faith in your attorney's experience and competence, isn't that correct? Of course, you would have fired your attorney if he were not experienced or competent, isn't that correct? You kept your attorney throughout all of the negotiations, didn't you? You did not fire your attorney during negotiations, did you? You haven't fired him yet, have you? You consulted with your attorney, he advised you, he reviewed all the documents, you reviewed all the documents, and he was present at all the meetings between yourself and Titan from the time that you retained him, isn't that correct? You accepted all the benefits of this agreement, didn't you? You accepted the laboratory, the equipment, the help, and the salary, isn't that right? You could not have perfected the Wennerstrom Process without the help and the money provided by your agreement with Titan, isn't that true?"

To all of these questions Charlie Wennerstrom could only answer yes.

Clark continued. "Let me show you plaintiff's exhibit one, the joint venture agreement. Have you read it?"

"Yes."

"And your attorney, Clarence McGovern, read it?"

"I assume he did. Yes, he did."

"Point out for me, please, Mr. Wennerstrom, where in the agreement it provides that you shall own forty percent of the assets of the joint venture."

"Well, it doesn't use those words. It provides that I receive forty percent of the profit, and—"

"Nowhere in the joint venture agreement does it provide explicitly that you own forty percent of the joint venture property, does it?"

"Not in those words."

"You understood the terms of the joint venture agreement before you signed it?"

"Not really. I depended on my attorney, of course."

"Yes, you asked your own attorney about those provisions you did not understand?"

"Yes."

"He explained those provisions to you?"

"Yes. He tried to."

Mac shot Charlie a warning glance. No sparring. No laying of blame on McGovern.

"You testified that Mr. Radcliffe initially told you that the process was not patentable. Is that so?"

"Yes."

"But you went forward and signed the joint venture agreement even though you disagreed with Mr. Radcliffe, is that right?"

"Well, yes. It didn't seem— Yes."

"You testified that after the pilot plant was operating, Titan had the process patented. Was that your testimony?"

"Yes, it was."

"Yet you continued to operate within the terms of the joint venture agreement without complaint?"

"Yes."

"Did you believe that the Wennerstrom Process was worth more after the patent was obtained?"

"Yes, I thought it probably was."

"But you nevertheless still continued to work within the terms of the joint venture agreement without any complaint?"

"Yes, I suppose I thought it wouldn't do any good."

"Let me see if I've got this straight, Mr. Wennerstrom. Even though Titan represented to you that your process was not patentable, which was contrary to your own belief, you went forward with the joint venture agreement; after you and your attorney read the proposed joint venture agreement, which nowhere contains the provision regarding your ownership of assets that you say it's supposed to contain, you signed it anyway; and even when Titan had the process patented, after you say it told you it wasn't patentable at all, you still continued under the agreement without complaint. Have I got it right, Mr. Wennerstrom?"

"Yes, but—" Charlie wanted to look to Mac for help but forced himself to face the jury. "Yes, everything you said is correct."

Charlie was simply too honest to perform the intellectual juggling required to counter such cross-examination. Charlie had felt compelled to give the precisely correct answers, even though they resulted in a distorted version of what had actually occurred. In order to establish fraud, Mac had to show that Wennerstrom relied upon TOPCO's fraudulent representation, and not solely on his own judgment or merely upon the advice of his own attorney. Any fraudulent representations not relied upon by Charlie were harmless. Clark's cross-examination had seriously impaired Wennerstrom's showing of reliance on TOPCO's representations. Mac tried not to show it, but he was concerned. A lot of rehabilitation would be required in the days ahead.

5

Mac had to call Clarence McGovern as a witness even though he expected little of him. McGovern had been worthless throughout preparation for trial. His files were incomplete, his notes incoherent; his memory was vague. McGovern obviously was more concerned with saving his own hide than helping Charles Wennerstrom win.

Indeed, a possible malpractice claim against McGovern had been considered. However, Mac had concluded that simultaneous suits against McGovern and TOPCO would be tactically undesirable, amounting to an open concession that TOPCO was not entirely to blame for Wennerstrom's plight. It was doubtful that McGovern's assets were worth pursuing anyway, and McGovern could have avoided any judgment against him by merely filing bankruptcy.

Mac had to call McGovern as a witness because the jury expected it. Of course, the jury would not give McGovern's testimony much credence. He had to agree with his own client, didn't he? But if McGovern failed to testify in corroboration, then Wennerstrom's own testimony became suspect. Clark could capitalize on the omission, arguing that McGovern's failure to testify could only mean that the plaintiff's side was withholding evidence damaging to its own interest.

Mac would be content merely to break even with McGovern's testimony.

On cross-examination, Jonathan Clark repeatedly encouraged McGovern to assert his own proficiency at the expense of Charlie's case.

"In their dealings with you, Titan's attorneys were reasonable and fair, weren't they?" asked Clark.

"Oh, yes," said McGovern, his remarkably full head of brown, curly hair bobbing in agreement.

"Plaintiff Wennerstrom was not cheated or defrauded, was he?"

Mac leaped up. "Objection. Question is argumentative and calls for a conclusion. What is being asked is the ultimate question for the jury to decide."

"Objection sustained," said Judge Johannsen.

Jonathan Clark nodded to Mac before continuing. "It was one of your functions as Charles Wennerstrom's attorney to prevent him from being cheated or defrauded, wasn't it?"

"Yes, it was," agreed McGovern.

"And you did your duty to your client, Charles Wennerstrom, to the very best of your ability, didn't you?" asked Clark.

"Yes, as I would for any client," admitted McGovern.

Clark smiled as he glanced back at Mac before asking, "You would not be doing your job for Wennerstrom if you permitted him to be cheated or defrauded, would you?"

"No, obviously not," said McGovern.

Touché, thought Mac. You got around me nicely with that thrust, Mr. Clark.

It was twelve-oh-five. Judge Johannsen mercifully interrupted McGovern's beating by calling the noon recess. As Mac packed his briefcase, Laura Wennerstrom approached the counsel table. "Mr. Oliver," Laura asked, glancing over at McGovern, who was mopping his chubby brow as he climbed down from the witness stand, "what did you think of that display?"

Mac shrugged. "We knew he was weak."

"A real pillar of Jell-O," said Laura.

Mac laughed. "Can you have lunch with me? I'm planning to put you on next. We should go over your testimony again."

"Of course, Mr. Oliver."

Judge Johannsen had declared an extra hour of noon recess because he had to attend an emergency meeting of the Sons of Vikings. There was time for a leisurely lunch. Mac took Laura to the Los Angeles Athletic Club on Seventh Street. The tables were discreetly placed, permitting private conversation. The food was excellent.

"I've never been here," said Laura as they were guided to a table. "It's such a regal, old-fashioned place. I thought this was one of the last of the men-only oases."

"It was until not long ago. If a man and woman wanted to lunch together, they had to go to the ladies' dining room on the next floor up. Women were always permitted in this room at dinner—provided they were accompanied by men, of course."

"The rationale escapes me," said Laura.

"Lunch was business; dinner was social," explained Mac. "It is now permitted to combine the two. Let's order; then we can talk without interruption."

Laura ordered a glass of dry white wine and avocado stuffed with fresh crab. Mac had a Perrier and Jefferson salad. While in trial, Mac never drank before lunch. It made him drowsy, and that made the afternoon torturous.

"You've seen what Clark is doing to poor Clarence McGovern," said Mac. "You'll have a similar problem."

Laura's dark eyes flashed. "Mr. Oliver, I can barely conceal my contempt for that . . . person. Are you suggesting that I am as spineless as that—that slug?"

"No," said Mac. "I only meant that you, too, will have a hard time with cross-examination. It will be for entirely different reasons. McGovern's weak. Your problem will be caused by your strength."

Laura smiled but looked puzzled.

Mac was wondering why he had never before recognized the beauty of her strong Cherokee features but forced himself to return to the subject.

"You start out with an inherent disadvantage. You're the plaintiff's daughter. The jury anticipates that you will swear to anything to help your father, out of affection and loyalty. Therefore, they'll discount your testimony."

Laura's eyes flashed again. "That makes me angry—"

"I know," said Mac. "Let me finish, please. You have strong opinions. Your emotions are easily aroused. The problem is compounded because Charlie is a sixty-eight-year-old widower. You are his only child and his sole heir. If Charlie wins his case, you would stand to gain—"

"That's despicable," said Laura, using her fork as a weapon to slash her crab. "Those bastards— What's the matter? Mr. Oliver, are you all right?"

MacDonald Oliver was suppressing a wild impulse to lean across the table and kiss Laura Wennerstrom. Mac supposed that the effort of his restraint, although commendable, made him look a little foolish. Mac couldn't believe that had happened to him. Forty minutes ago he still had her categorized as an obnoxious bitch. How the hell had she managed to become so suddenly desirable? He could think of nothing to say but the truth. "You seemed so beautiful I had a sudden urge to kiss you. I'm really sorry."

"Oh, don't be. I think I'm pleased," said Laura. Her high cheekbones blushed. "You are human after all. I thought Mr. Oliver was all steel and technique. But isn't it indiscreet to become involved with your client's daughter? Or is there a technique for that, too?"

"Please," said Mac, "don't make me feel more foolish than I do already. Not only would it be indiscreet—"

Christ, Mac thought, I'm at a loss for words. "Look, I've been married for ten years—to a woman, of course"—oh, God—"and—"

"And," interrupted Laura, "you haven't strayed even once, have you?"

"No, I haven't," confessed Mac, blushing a little himself. "There have been temptations, of course. It's just that I value my life with Mary Kathryn and my daughter so highly that the risk isn't worth—"

"A few hours' roll in the hay." Laura laughed. "You are a surprise, MacDonald Oliver. I didn't like you very much. I'm sure you realized that. I thought you were just a law machine: 'Plug him in and watch him win.' But you may have scruples, possibly even integrity. I'm going to start calling you Mac."

"Thank you for that. I still feel like an ass."

"Even so, shouldn't we be getting back to work?" asked Laura.

"Yes," said Mac. "Where was I before making such a damned fool of myself? Your credibility is naturally suspect because of your relationship with your father and the potential for your monetary gain. Your feelings are always near the surface, easily aroused. Those are facts to live with and must be accepted."

"But if you believe that Jonathan Clark will find it so easy to have his way with me, why do you plan to put me on the witness stand at all?"

"Because the jury expects the plaintiff's daughter to testify. A good daughter is supportive. Besides, even if I don't use you, Clark can still call you as an adverse witness. Or even worse, Clark could point out to the jury that Charlie Wennerstrom's only daughter, Laura, failed to testify on her father's behalf, and that could only mean that—"

"She doesn't agree with her father's version of the facts, or she has something else to hide," said Laura.

"You understand," said Mac. "However, you are not to be your father's advocate. That's my job." Mac looked at his watch. "We'd better get back. Just try hard not to lose your temper. Out of control, you might be made to say anything. I want you to restrain your eagerness to help. You're straining at the leash. . . ."

"But, Mac, I know you don't think I'm a dog."

That evening, as he wheeled the BMW into his driveway and swiftly braked alongside Mary Kathryn's Mercedes, Mac felt a rush of relief. It was as if he had returned from a dangerous patrol knowing he had the next two weeks on the beach.

"Back here, love."

Mac heard Mary Kathryn's voice come from the patio, so he went around to the rear of the house instead of making his usual entrance through the kitchen.

There she stood, burnished hair to her shoulders, golden tan even under the beige nylon string bikini, slender and tall, doing a *Playboy* cover pose while balancing two huge glasses filled with ice cubes and an amber liquid.

"How did—"

"When you wind that Teutonic toy up to four thousand rpm in second gear, your sonic boom precedes you by a mile. Have a drink of your favorite single malt and soda. We're celebrating."

"Thank you. You don't know how much," said Mac as he took a long, grateful pull. "But what occasion?"

"There are three. Tracy's staying overnight at Martha's across the street, the windows have been cleaned, and you've been in trial for one week. Take off your clothes, jump in the pool, and cool down. I fixed a cold salmon vinaigrette and the Pinot Chardonnay is chilled."

Mac obediently stripped. He gathered Mary Kathryn tightly into his arms. "It's been a rough day."

Mary Kathryn pressed close, her nails gently raking down his back. "Hmmm. Hard work doesn't seem to tire you."

Suddenly she leaned forward, toppling Mac backward onto a padded chaise longue. "Enough of this foreplay." She laughed. "Take me now." As Mary Kathryn straddled Mac, she simultaneously cast off her bikini with deft tugs at two cleverly placed strings. Their hands found each other's nipples as they slowly came together. Mac opened his good eye and looked up at her. Mary Kathryn's back was arched, her head thrown back, her eyes closed, her perfect lips parted. The breeze and her motion lifted her copper hair as her small breasts pointed straight to heaven.

My God, thought Mac, she's a Valkyrie.

As they lay together, the sun and the temperature slowly dropped.

"Dinner, darling?" murmured Mary Kathryn.

"Much later," whispered Mac as his hands renewed their exploration. Yes, he thought again, it could be a hell of a lot worse.

* * *

Cold salmon vinaigrette doesn't make a bad breakfast, thought Mac as he downshifted, accelerating onto the fast lane of inbound morning freeway traffic. Mac felt an unfamiliar emotion. What was it? Something last night? He and Mary Kathryn had awakened in the dark and talked by the pool until early morning. She wanted to tell him her ideas for redoing the patio. He thought they were fine. She wanted to plan their vacation. Mac couldn't predict when he would be free. He hadn't mentioned Laura Wennerstrom to Mary Kathryn; the luncheon, his foolish impulse. Was that it? Was the twinge guilt? Mac did not easily recognize guilt, having previously experienced so little of it. Why guilt? he wondered. I haven't done anything. I only wanted to, but I haven't. I wouldn't.

Mac dismissed his uncharacteristic introspection and turned his attention to the morning's business. He would put Laura Wennerstrom on as his next witness. It didn't really matter so much what she testified to. The jury wasn't going to give it much weight anyway. How she said it—that was important. At least they would like her.

Laura Wennerstrom wore a blue and white seersucker suit and an open-necked white shirt. The cover of the spring Brooks Brothers catalog, thought Mac.

After a brief bad marriage Laura had resumed her maiden name and her place in Charlie's home. Apparently insecure in her male relationships, mused Mac. Feels safe with the old man. On direct examination Laura testified to all of the supportive jobs she regularly did for her father. In this way Mac was able to demonstrate her affection and respect for Charlie. Through Laura's testimony Mac was also able to catalog Charlie Wennerstrom's accomplishments and provide insight into his character without the immodesty that would have occurred had Charlie testified to these things himself.

Mac had Laura testify to the physical and mental effect of TOPCO's actions on Charlie. Mac thought the way she had helped Charlie through the ordeal came off well. Then Mac had Laura testify to what the jury had to hear but wouldn't pay any attention to after it had: her corroboration of Charlie's version of every TOPCO meeting she had attended, confirming every TOPCO representation and promise to her father.

Jonathan Clark was not displeased to have Mac bring out Laura's affection for her father on direct examination. This made it easier for him to establish her bias.

Clark's cross-examination quickly established that Laura was Charlie's only heir and the sole ultimate beneficiary of any award in his favor.

Clark then asked Laura about every detail of every conversation at each TOPCO meeting at which she had been present. He asked her again in reverse order, and again in no order at all. Clark asked about what participants wore and what they ate. He asked about the waiters and the china and the decor. Then Clark would ask her again to repeat what each person said. He asked if Laura was certain, positive, or could have been mistaken. Clark wanted to know how she remembered what she did and why she remembered it, and why she remembered some details and not others.

Mac knew what Clark was doing but had no effective way of stopping it. Mac could have postponed it by making a plausible excuse for a recess, but he knew that ultimately Laura would either have to handle Clark's harassment or not. Mac believed that either way, the sooner it was over with, the less impact it would have.

Clark was the ocean's relentless surge, sawing the ship's hawser until finally, from heat and friction, it chafes apart and breaks loose.

After one hour and twenty minutes of Clark's sawing away, Laura's anger and frustration broke loose. She reminded Clark that she had already answered his last question four times. She observed that his memory was obviously no better than that of his client's. In a voice steadily rising in pitch and volume, Laura remarked that a lawyer with a real defense would have other things to do with his time.

Laura became so loud that she awakened Judge Johannsen, who quickly overruled the objection, even though none had been made.

When Laura's temper peaked, Clark easily got her to testify, without realizing what she had said, that her father's prior statements to her regarding his forty percent interest were consistent with the written joint venture agreement provisions regarding forty percent of profits. Clark was able to get Laura not only to admit but to insist that her father knew more about patents than anyone at TOPCO, enabling Clark to argue later that therefore, Wennerstrom could not have justifiably relied on any TOPCO representations regarding nonpatentability of his invention.

When Laura started to shake with frustration, Clark stopped. Gentlemen do not cause ladies distress.

At the recess Laura was tearful. "Oh, Mac, I was so bad. It was just as you warned me. Even though I knew what he was trying to do, I just could not control myself. I really tried. If I've wrecked Charlie's case, I—I'll just die." Laura grabbed her father's hands. Charlie just stood there, not knowing what to say. Charlie found oil much easier to deal with than tears.

"Don't," said Mac. "I think you came through as the dutiful daughter. The rest is not important. The case won't be won or lost on your testimony. It all revolves around Charles Wennerstrom and Grant Radcliffe."

"Grant Radcliffe. That son of a bitch," said Laura.

"No, Laura, you must keep the characters straight. The defense attorney is traditionally the son of a bitch. Grant Radcliffe is the no-good bastard."

6

*M*ac called Harold Rifkin as plaintiff's next witness. Rifkin had been Grant Radcliffe's administrative assistant and a TOPCO assistant vice-president. Shortly after the joint venture agreement had been signed, Rifkin was involuntarily retired at age sixty-four. TOPCO's policy manual prescribed mandatory retirement at age sixty-two for "supervisory management," at age sixty-five for "administrative management," and at the board of directors' discretion for "executive management." It was consoling to Rifkin that his forced retirement proved that he must have reached the executive management level.

As a dedicated employee Harold Rifkin accepted his retirement graciously. He continued to live in his dreary Santa Monica bungalow because it had been his mother's. He had spent thirty years nursing his mother because he was supposed to. He had never married because that would have interfered with nursing his mother. He had never dared a sexual relationship because he was not married. He had frequent asthma attacks because he had never dared a sexual relationship. Harold Rifkin had led a dutiful life.

Harold Rifkin appeared to be a cliché of the mild-mannered gentleman. He was short and slight, and his dark gray suit seemed a size too large. The careful allocation of strands of mousy hair did not effectively dull the glare of pale pink scalp. Harold Rifkin sat in the witness chair and nervously polished rimless glasses.

Mac's background questions established the extent of Rifkin's participation in the Wennerstrom transaction and the fact that he had subsequently retired.

Mac tried to get Rifkin to corroborate the earlier testimony of Radcliffe's misrepresentations regarding nonpatentability and ownership of joint venture property. Mac was certain that Rifkin had knowledge of these things. Rifkin had been present at Radcliffe-Wennerstrom conversations. And he must have had discussions with Grant Radcliffe and TOPCO attorneys. But whenever Mac's questioning came to a significant point, Rifkin's response was, at best, ambivalent. Rifkin's answers were riddled with "I don't remember that," "I'm not sure," "I just don't recall." Rifkin became increasingly apprehensive as the questioning continued, but the quality of his recollection was not improved. The only times that Rifkin appeared to be certain were when he answered, "I don't know." Mac and his assistant trial counsel, Burt Glinter, were disappointed at Harold Rifkin's testimony. Before the trial Burt had taken Rifkin's deposition, in which Rifkin had sworn that Grant Radcliffe had represented to Charlie Wennerstrom that Wennerstrom would own forty percent of the partnership property. Rifkin's testimony clearly contradicted his pretrial deposition.

"This is an obvious case of enforced amnesia," said Burt.

"You're right, but is it curable?" asked Mac.

Neither Mac nor Burt knew how Harold Rifkin had been coerced, although they both were intuitively certain that it had happened.

After Harold Rifkin had given his deposition, Grant Radcliffe had unearthed evidence of some minor Harold Rifkin expense account padding. Grant Radcliffe had privately pointed out to Rifkin that no TOPCO employee was entitled to a pension if his dishonesty during employment

was established. Rifkin could not afford to misunderstand. He immediately commenced saving his pension by losing his memory.

"You'll have to impeach him," whispered Burt.

"Yes, but it's neither satisfying nor effective." Mac raised his voice.
"Mr. Rifkin, a copy of your deposition taken June thirteenth of last year
is on the witness stand before you. Will you please turn to page forty-
eight and read lines two through twenty-three aloud?"

"Lines two through twenty-three, yes," said Rifkin, and began to read.

QUESTION: At that meeting did you hear Mr. Radcliffe say anything to
Mr. Wennerstrom regarding his partnership interest?

ANSWER: Yes. Mr. Radcliffe said that Mr. Wennerstrom would have
a forty percent interest—that the joint venture agreement would
provide that Mr. Wennerstrom owned forty percent of the
partnership.

QUESTION: Of partnership property?

ANSWER: Yes, forty percent of the partnership property.

QUESTION: Did Mr. Wennerstrom or Mr. McGovern say anything in
respect to Mr. Radcliffe's statement?

ANSWER: Mr. Wennerstrom's daughter, Laura Wennerstrom, did.
She wanted to know if Mr. Radcliffe could say more specifically what
that meant.

QUESTION: What forty percent of the partnership property meant?

ANSWER: Yes. Then Mr. Radcliffe said that the company planned to
spend over two million dollars to build the pilot plant and a laboratory and that Mr. Wennerstrom would own forty percent of that after
the return of the company's capital investment. After that, he said,
the sky is the limit.

Mac raised his hand and asked, "Mr. Rifkin, were those the questions
asked and the answers given by you— Mr. Rifkin?"

Rifkin had begun to perspire heavily, although the courtroom was
comfortably air-conditioned. He was gradually turning an unusual
shade. Mac recognized the symptoms immediately.

"Your Honor, declare a recess, please . . . oh, never mind . . .
Bailiff, take him to the jury's men's room . . . NOW."

The bailiff reacted instantly and quickly guided the retching, stumbling Harold Rifkin out of the courtroom.

Judge Johannsen shook off his paralysis. "We will take a fifteen-minute recess," he said. "Mr. Clerk, you will take charge of the jury in the bailiff's absence. Take them—take them into my chambers." Turning to the jury, Judge Johannsen said, "Ladies and gentlemen, feel free to use the, ah, facilities in my chambers." As the last juror filed out, the judge faced the attorneys, but Mac spoke first.

"I apologize, Your Honor. I did not intend to usurp—"

"Nonsense, Mr. Oliver. Thank heaven for your lightning reflexes. You've kept my courtroom clean. We will just wait here until Mr. Rifkin returns. Then we'll see if he's up to continuing."

Jonathan Clark did not like what he had just seen and was casting about for a countermeasure. "Your Honor," Clark said, "I know Mr. Rifkin has not been feeling well. A touch of influenza, I suspect. I believe that it would be appropriate for you to instruct the jury that no inference should be drawn from this . . . unfortunate incident."

"On the contrary, counselor," Judge Johannsen said. "I thought the inference was obvious. However, if you believe that there is some . . . other . . . explanation of the witness's, ah, reaction, you are free to question him regarding it."

"The old codger may have more upstairs than we gave him credit for," Burt whispered.

Ten minutes later a pale, shaken Harold Rifkin returned, followed, but unaided, by the bailiff.

"Mr. Rifkin," the judge asked, "are you feeling all right?"

"Yes, Your Honor, I apologize—"

"No need," said the judge. "Are you able to continue? I don't want to rush you. We can certainly recess for a longer period if you feel unready."

"Thank you, Your Honor. I would prefer to go on. I'll be all right now."

When Harold Rifkin had returned to the witness stand and twelve jurors settled in the jury box, Mac resumed his examination.

"Mr. Rifkin, do you feel well enough to continue?"

"Yes, I'm fine. Thank you."

"Mr. Rifkin, in view of the interruption, I'm going to ask the court reporter to reread the portion of your deposition you just read aloud and my last question."

Mac nodded to the reporter, who read the testimony aloud from his stenotype tape.

"Mr. Rifkin, were those the questions asked and the answers given by you?"

"Yes," answered Rifkin, looking unhappy.

"You realized you were under oath when your deposition was taken?"

"Yes, I knew that."

"And you signed the original transcript of your deposition under penalty of perjury before it was filed with the court?"

"Yes, it's my signature."

"Yet you testified this morning that you did not recall Grant Radcliffe saying anything at that meeting regarding Charlie Wennerstrom's ownership interest in the joint venture property, isn't that right?"

"Yes, I—yes."

"Does the rereading of your deposition refresh your recollection about what Grant Radcliffe actually said?"

"No, not really—"

"Well, Mr. Rifkin, which is correct? Your testimony under oath here this morning or what you testified to under oath at your deposition last June?"

"I . . . was mistaken. Mr. Radcliffe never said those things. I think it was—yes, it must have been Mr. McGovern. Mr. McGovern said that Mr. Wennerstrom should have forty percent of the partnership property."

"And did Mr. McGovern also say, 'The sky is the limit'?" asked Mac.

"Yes, that's it—it must have been."

Mac made sure the jury saw his disbelief before continuing. "Mr. Rifkin, have you had any meetings with TOPCO officers or attorneys since your deposition was taken?"

"Yes, attorneys."

"Anyone else?"

"Yes, Grant Radcliffe."

Grant Radcliffe sat at attention, willing Harold Rifkin to heed the TOPCO line.

"When did you meet with Mr. Radcliffe?"

"Last week."

"Where?"

"The—his office."

"Did you discuss this case?"

"Yes."

"Did you discuss your testimony?"

"He knew I would be testifying."

"Did you discuss your deposition?"

"Mr. Radcliffe refreshed my recollection. I realized my previous testimony—in my deposition—was incorrect. I had been mistaken."

"Didn't you read your deposition before you signed it?"

"Not really."

"Aren't you receiving a pension from TOPCO?"

"Yes." Rifkin was trembling.

"Was your pension discussed?"

Harold Rifkin just shook his head, his handkerchief ready. Mac didn't see any advantage in carrying it further.

After Rifkin was excused, Clark's assistant, Ralph Radecke, jubilantly whispered, "With plaintiff's witnesses like that, who needs a defense?"

"I am not nearly as certain as you seem to be," said Clark, "as to how that episode should be scored."

At the other end of the counsel table Burt was expressing a similar doubt. "I'm confused. Did we gain or lose on that?"

Charlie and Laura Wennerstrom came up. "Mac," said Charlie, "when we started this lawsuit, I had some naive ideas. I thought you just put the true facts in the slot, pulled the lever, and out came justice. Now I realize you also have to line up three cherries. Even though I sometimes worry that you're too damn hard for your own good, I've gained affection for you. I believe we've become friends. I hope we stay that way regardless of the outcome. I'm satisfied that no one could be doing a better job than you are."

Laura was just standing there, her dark eyes big and filling. Mac thought he could drown in them. She took his hand. She didn't say anything. She didn't have to.

Jonathan Clark had saved Grant Radcliffe as his last defense witness. There had been a dull but necessary parade of defense expert witnesses: accountants, who testified to high TOPCO operating expenses caused by its use of the Wennerstrom Process, which were likely to increase in the future; economists, who testified to the future reduced demand for oil, in view of increasing availability of alternate sources of energy; and petroleum engineers, who testified to the awesome technical difficulties already encountered and anticipated in the use of the Wennerstrom Process. Jonathan Clark realized that Grant Radcliffe's testimony was the key to the defense. The jury anticipated Radcliffe's testimony with curiosity.

Mac had seen Grant Radcliffe in the courtroom but had not had the opportunity to observe him closely until Radcliffe's appearance on the witness stand. Mac thought Radcliffe would make a perfect evangelist. His face was saintly. He was taller than Mac and about the same age. He wore expensive clothing with an actor's presence.

On direct examination, Radcliffe denied that he had ever represented to Wennerstrom that the process was not patentable. Radcliffe denied that he ever represented to Wennerstrom that he would have forty percent ownership of the joint venture, as distinguished from forty percent of profits. Radcliffe denied that he had attended a private meeting with Wennerstrom in Ellwood. Radcliffe insisted that he was in the San Francisco Bay Area during all of the week that Wennerstrom said the meeting occurred. Radcliffe showed his appointment diary, which confirmed his recollection. Radcliffe's demeanor was smooth and cool, not that of a man whose word could be easily doubted.

Radcliffe's direct testimony seemed to be nearing a close when the noon recess was called. Mac, Burt, Charlie, and Laura headed for the dreaded courthouse cafeteria. Charlie grumbled, but Mac insisted.

"Not only is it the closest," said Mac, "but you can't eat much, giving us extra time to work."

"My head understands," said Charlie, "but my stomach revolts."

After they were seated, Burt reviewed what they knew about Grant Radcliffe. Charlie Wennerstrom had had the most to do with Radcliffe. Laura had been at a luncheon meeting with him. Burt Ginter had taken Radcliffe's deposition. Harold Rifkin's deposition had added some information. Sorensen, Oliver, Bradford, and Smith personnel had investigated Radcliffe's background.

"Radcliffe comes from an originally well-to-do eastern family," said Burt. "You've heard him talk, he sounds almost British. His father was wiped out financially in the 1929 crash and never did much after that. His mother was a notorious society drunk but seems to have retained her maternal instinct. Somehow she scraped together enough to send her son to exclusive schools and buy him good clothes. Apparently she mooched off rich relatives for this purpose. The man definitely has taste. Did you notice that necktie? Anyway, young Radcliffe seems to have hated his mother and his father impartially. I suspect he was compelled to do a lot of groveling.

"There's a great story about Radcliffe at Princeton. As a sophomore he made one of the Du Pont heiresses pregnant and tried to marry her. He was cut off at the pass by the girl's father, who called him a male gold digger. Radcliffe acted in several college productions. After college our young man came to Hollywood. He tried out for the movies and television but apparently was too pretty. Imagine being constantly told, 'Come back in thirty years; by then you'll look great.'

"Here's an interesting bit. Radcliffe was caught screwing—pardon me, Laura—his agent's girlfriend. As a result, the agent managed to get him blackballed in the entertainment industry. Radcliffe drifted into selling Beverly Hills real estate and did very well. There was a complaint filed against him with the real estate commissioner—something about muscling into another broker's deal—but no action was ever taken. Then Radcliffe went to work for TOPCO as an assistant vice-president in its real estate division. It seems that an aunt, who is a major TOPCO stockholder, helped open that door. Sometime after that Radcliffe met, wooed and married Sarah Channing Chase—anyone remember her? debutante of the year, Junior League, et cetera, et cetera—but most important of all, as Mac already knows, Sarah Channing Chase Radcliffe is the granddaughter of Maynard Chase. Yes, *the* Maynard Chase, chairman of the board of directors of Titan Overland Petroleum Corporation and its largest single stockholder. Whether the marriage or Grant Radcliffe's own merit brought him to the attention of TOPCO's senior executives, we do not know. But since the nuptials Radcliffe has advanced rapidly. He is presently the vice-president in charge of the real estate and development division, which I think means in charge of making deals."

"Young man on his way up," said Mac. "Burt, you spent two days taking his deposition. What was he like?"

"He didn't like answering questions—kept asking me how much longer I was going to take. The man is used to having his own way. I suppose he has a lot of clout at TOPCO. He seemed sort of arrogant but not obnoxious. I caught him in a minor mistake—a date—and I thought he would bite my head off. It's in the transcript—told me to stop putting goddamn words in his mouth and get on with it, he had important things to do."

"He has a temper then?" asked Mac.

"Yes, he has a temper. He doesn't like his mistakes being pointed out. And he doesn't like being crossed."

"I'll work on that," said Mac. "Let's get back."

It was the middle of the afternoon when Clark completed Radcliffe's direct examination. Mac's cross-examination seemed innocuous. Mac was only getting Radcliffe to insist repeatedly that he was not in the Ellwood area on the day testified to by Wennerstrom and that he had never attended any secret meeting with Wennerstrom. Mac was stalling until the end of the day.

When court opened the next morning, Mac asked the judge's permission to interrupt his cross-examination of Radcliffe with a brief foundational witness, who would have evidence pertaining to the cross-examination. Permission was granted.

The foundational witness was a lady from the credit card division of Union Oil. Pursuant to Mac's subpoena, she produced the records of Radcliffe's charge account. The records showed that Grant Radcliffe had signed a credit card receipt for gasoline at a Union Oil service station on the day that Charlie Wennerstrom testified the secret meeting had occurred. The service station was in Ellwood.

Mac then recalled Radcliffe to continue his cross-examination. Jonathan Clark moved for a recess, but because it was only nine thirty-seven, the judge denied the motion. Mac was able to continue his cross-examination without the defense's gaining an opportunity to coach Radcliffe.

Upon being confronted with the evidence of his signed credit card receipt, Radcliffe became angry and flustered.

"It is your signature on the receipt, isn't it, Mr. Radcliffe?" asked Mac.

"No . . . how can I tell . . . it must be . . . I don't see what possible difference the luncheon with Wennerstrom makes anyway. . . ."

"You just forgot about it, didn't you, Mr. Radcliffe?"

"It was a very busy week for me. I had a lot of deals going. Apparently I forgot to enter it in my diary. I think I borrowed a company car in San Jose, drove down to meet Wennerstrom, and drove right back again. I'm not sure. . . ." Radcliffe was floundering now.

"Then you can't be sure what you said to Wennerstrom that day, since you've forgotten the entire event?"

"I'm not sure. I—"

"Then you obviously can't be certain that you didn't tell Charles Wennerstrom that day that the process wasn't patentable?"

"I've already told you. I've forgotten—I don't recall saying that."

"You just don't remember."

"That is what I just said, Mr. Oliver." Radcliffe's pale eyes stabbed. He was beginning to dislike MacDonald Oliver intensely.

"Thank you, Mr. Radcliffe." Mac had more up his sleeve, but he ended his cross-examination there, hoping to sandbag the defense.

"It's fortunate there is no TOPCO service station in Ellwood," whispered Burt.

Radcliffe's testimony had given Jonathan Clark a headache. Clark was grateful that a recess had been called before he had to take Radcliffe on redirect examination. He led Radcliffe into a nearby conference room for private tutoring. He explained that Radcliffe would have no credibility at all if he continued with his wishy-washy failure of memory. Clark insisted that in order to rehabilitate his credibility, Radcliffe should candidly admit that he had made a mistake.

Under Clark's questioning on redirect examination, Radcliffe testified that he had searched his memory. He now recalled that he had represented to Wennerstrom that in his opinion, the process was not patentable. So many events had transpired in the meantime that he had simply forgotten this. He apologized for his lapse of memory. He had said to Wennerstrom that the process was not patentable because that was what he believed at the time. Radcliffe had based his belief on the opinion of TOPCO counsel Raymond Coulter, since deceased. Much later, after the process was perfected, Radcliffe said, he got different advice from different TOPCO counsel. Radcliffe testified that he was later told to apply for the patent because there was nothing to lose. TOPCO had an assured head start on the competition.

Radcliffe supposed that he had really put his earlier statements to Wennerstrom out of his mind because they had become irrelevant. Wennerstrom still got forty percent of the increased profits, even if the patented process had more potential value than if unpatented. Besides, Wennerstrom knew that the process was later patented and had acquiesced in that procedure. Radcliffe grew indignant. He couldn't see what difference it made anyway.

On recross-examination, Mac put in evidence a TOPCO interoffice memo which had been initialed by Radcliffe. The memo stated, "Essential secure patent rights Wennerstrom process. Cost secondary." The memo was dated the week after the secret Ellwood meeting.

Both sides, of course, had known of the memo's existence. It had been produced from TOPCO's records during the discovery process months before the trial. TOPCO had carefully sanitized its records, but the memo had seemed to be so innocuous that it had been disclosed. The memo, in fact, had been innocuous until Radcliffe's unanticipated admission that he had represented that the process was not patentable. Everybody but Mac had overlooked the fact that the formerly harmless memo now became very damaging.

The memo caught Radcliffe in another lie. Radcliffe could not have believed that the Wennerstrom Process was not patentable at the same time he wrote a memo stating it was essential to secure the patent rights.

As this was brought out on Radcliffe's recross-examination, Radcliffe's presence of mind and any last vestige of his credibility were completely destroyed.

On redirect examination, Clark made a final attempt to rehabilitate Radcliffe. But Radcliffe, at this point, was a hopeless cause.

It was completely unnecessary for Mac to examine Radcliffe further. In the eyes of the jury the man had already been demolished. Further cross-examination could not improve plaintiff's position. Mac knew that, but he had an irrational desire to humiliate Radcliffe. Something about Radcliffe demanded it. Mac proceeded to beat an already dead horse.

Mac asked, "You testified that when you represented to Wennerstrom that the process was unpatentable, you believed it was so. Had you forgotten the memo when you gave that testimony?"

Radcliffe seemed dazed. "I suppose so. I don't know."

"Did you think we might not know of that memo so that you could get by without the jury's ever hearing of it?"

Radcliffe didn't even understand the question. "But I wasn't under oath when I wrote it."

"When you're not under oath, you're not particular whether or not you tell the truth?"

"I don't have to be, do I?" Radcliffe wanted to kill Mac by then.

"So your concept of ethics is to tell the truth or not, whichever serves your purpose, so long as you're not under oath?"

Radcliffe clenched his fists, struggling for control. "You can put it that way, if you like, but—"

Mac dismissed him with a disgusted wave. "That's the way you just put it, Mr. Radcliffe."

After the defense rested, it was plaintiff's opportunity for rebuttal. The defense had conceded that Wennerstrom had been promised forty percent of the profits when and if there were any. If Mac could establish that TOPCO never intended to perform that promise, an element of the alleged fraud would be established.

Marla Zimmerman's investigation had uncovered that Rutherford-Leske Oil, Ltd.'s directors and stockholders all had been retired TOPCO senior executives. Rutherford-Leske Oil, Ltd.'s stock had been transferred from one to another with no apparent consideration. It was apparent only that TOPCO exercised some degree of control over Rutherford-Leske Oil, Ltd. in some unknown manner.

Sorensen, Oliver, Bradford, and Smith had chosen to go to trial with the secret of its investigation intact, however incomplete. Even the ingenious Marla had not found a way to unravel the whole mystery without indulging in formal pretrial discovery, such as depositions of Rutherford-Leske Oil, Ltd., and TOPCO officers. But Sorensen, Oliver, Bradford, and Smith had feared that TOPCO, once warned, would find a way to conceal the facts of its relationship with Rutherford-Leske Oil, Ltd.

Mac carefully orchestrated the timing. The subpoena duces tecum that required the production of the Rutherford-Leske Oil, Ltd., records in court at 9:30 on Monday morning had not been served until 4:50 P.M. on the preceding Friday.

The first intimation that Jonathan Clark had was on Monday morning before trial. Clark had gone to his office early to get organized for the day. He received an intercom call from a partner. "Jonathan, I am glad I caught you in," the partner said. "As you know, we represent Rutherford-Leske Oil, Ltd. I received a call from them on Friday. Their minute books and stock transfer records have been subpoenaed by the plaintiff in your trial. I have no idea whether that's significant, but I thought you should know."

Just some routine loose end they want to tie up, supposed Clark as he hung up and went back to work. A few minutes later Clark received a message that the TOPCO corporate secretary had been subpoenaed by the plaintiff. Clark gave the information no significance as he hurriedly changed into his number two black suit for the day's proceedings. Sorensen, Oliver, Bradford, and Smith had been subpoenaing TOPCO officers and employees all during the trial.

As Clark was leaving his office, he was given another message: Grant Radcliffe would not be in court that morning—a medical emergency in his family. Hmmmmph, thought Clark, probably too embarrassed to show up after his fiasco last week.

That morning, when Mac offered the Rutherford-Leske Oil, Ltd., records in evidence as plaintiff's next exhibit, Clark was tempted to object on the grounds of immateriality and irrelevance, but he restrained himself. Better find out what is going on first, he thought. Not good to appear obstructive on routine matters.

After the Rutherford-Leske Oil, Ltd., records were received and marked, Mac called the TOPCO corporate secretary as plaintiff's next witness. A slightly pompous gentleman of ruddy complexion, bearing a silver cavalry mustache, the secretary had held his position for more than twenty years.

"Sir," began Mac, "you have before you plaintiff's exhibits one hundred nineteen and one hundred twenty, the TOPCO records from which can be determined the names of its senior past and present executives. That is, officers with at least the rank of full vice-president."

Jonathan Clark stopped doodling on his legal notepad and sat up straighter.

The witness nodded, and Mac continued. "Also before you are plaintiff's exhibits two hundred twenty-nine and two hundred thirty, the Rutherford-Leske Oil, Ltd., records from which can be identified all past and present directors and shareholders of Rutherford-Leske Oil, Ltd."

"Excuse me for a moment," said the witness. "I am not familiar with the Rutherford-Leske Oil, Ltd., records, you know. . . . Yes, you appear to be correct."

"Thank you," said Mac. "Let's start with the present, please. Is it correct that the current directors and shareholders of Rutherford-Leske Oil, Ltd., are: Patrick Long, Roy Hatch, and Richard Soderberg?"

"Yes," replied the witness, after a moment's search.

"And are Patrick Long, Roy Hatch, and Richard Soderberg also retired senior executives of Titan Overland Petroleum Company?"

"Yes, they are. I know that without consulting the records."

Jonathan Clark began to hear a distant bell faintly clanging.

"And before that, is it correct that Clint Clyman, James LaChance, and Roland Liponi were the directors and shareholders of Rutherford-Leske Oil, Ltd.?"

"Just a moment. Yes, that appears to be so," said the witness.

"And were the same three gentlemen—Clint Clyman, James La-

Chance, and Roland Liponi—also retired senior executives of TOPCO?"

"Yes, they were. They all are deceased, but I knew them all," the witness said.

Jonathan Clark was on his feet. He could hear the alarm bell clearly now. "Objection, Your Honor. This evidence is immaterial and irrelevant. I move to strike this entire line of testimony. It has no bearing on any of the issues of this suit. May we approach the bench, please?"

Judge Johannsen aroused himself and gave permission. Clark, MacDonald Oliver, and the court reporter came to the bench outside the jury's hearing.

"Your Honor," continued Clark, "I have forborne from objecting, waiting patiently for counsel to connect this morning's evidence to the issues. I request that plaintiff's counsel be required to make an offer of proof."

"Mr. Oliver," said Judge Johannsen, "I must concur with Mr. Clark. The relevance of this morning's evidence has escaped me."

"I can assure the court that this evidence is relevant. If I may be allowed to continue, the evidence will become tied into the case."

"I appreciate counsel's assurance," said Clark, "but could he offer something more specific?"

"All right," said Mac, "I will make a formal offer. Plaintiff offers to prove that all of Rutherford-Leske Oil, Ltd.'s directors and shareholders throughout the forty-eight-year existence of that company have been retired senior executives of Titan Overland Petroleum Company."

"So?" said Clark, mustering a disdain that he did not feel. "That may be an interesting statistic, but it is in no way relevant to the issues of this case."

"I tend to agree," said the judge. "Mr. Oliver, what's the point?"

"The point is fundamental to plaintiff's case, Your Honor," said Mac. "Plaintiff claims that although he was promised forty percent of the joint venture profits, TOPCO has never intended to perform that promise. Defendant TOPCO assigned the Wennerstrom Process to Rutherford-Leske Oil, Ltd., in exchange for the stock of its subsidiary corporation, RL Equities Corp. TOPCO contends that even though plaintiff was admittedly promised forty percent of the profits, there are no profits yet since all of the property of RL Equities Corp. is dormant. Its assets consist only of leases and options on oil fields potentially rich in shale deposits, but which are not presently producing any income. Meanwhile, Rutherford-Leske Oil, Ltd., has been making huge profits from licensing the Wennerstrom Process. The offered evidence shows that TOPCO has an interest in and control over Rutherford-Leske Oil, Ltd. The fact that TOPCO assigned the Wennerstrom Process to Rutherford-Leske Oil, Ltd., which it secretly controls, proves that TOPCO never intended to keep its promise to pay Charles Wennerstrom forty percent of the joint venture profits. . . ."

"The offer of proof shows no such thing," said Clark. He now fully realized the significance of the offer, and the importance to the defense of keeping the evidence out. "All the evidence shows is a natural co-incidence, which in no way implies fraud or conspiracy."

"Your Honor," Mac said, "it can be inferred that TOPCO has a financial interest in Rutherford-Leske Oil, Ltd., from the evidence that TOPCO exercises control over Rutherford-Leske. If TOPCO has a financial interest in the company to which it assigned the Wennerstrom Process, it has in effect secretly assigned the process to itself. No clearer evidence of fraud could be hoped for."

"Even if counsel's farfetched deductions were valid," Clark said, "which they are not, there is a basic reason why the offered evidence should not be admitted. This trial is now entering its third month. Plaintiff has put on his case in chief. Titan has completed its defense. Plaintiff is now on rebuttal. Rebuttal evidence must be limited to matters raised by the defense. Even if the offered evidence has relevance, it should have been offered as part of the plaintiff's case in chief. The evidence is being offered now, in the last moments of this trial, in order to take unfair advantage of the defendant. This is an obviously unscrupulous attempt to unfairly surprise defendant so that it will have no chance to counteract the evidence."

"Oh, I think that's a little strong, Mr. Clark," said Judge Johannsen. "After all, the defense did go to some length to prove that there have as yet been no joint venture profits to distribute. No, I think that the offered evidence, if it's relevant at all, is proper rebuttal. Personally, however, I find the inference of fraud from the offered evidence extremely tenuous."

"With respect, Your Honor," said Mac, "the weight of the evidence is for the jury to decide. Mr. Clark is certainly entitled to argue any other inferences he believes the jury should draw."

Judge Johannsen sighed. "I suppose it's better to let it in than to risk reversible error by disallowing it. Defendant's objection is overruled. You may continue with your examination, Mr. Oliver."

MacDonald Oliver returned to the counsel table and resumed questioning. When the corporate secretary's direct examination was completed, it was conclusively established that for every one of the Rutherford-Leske Oil, Ltd., directors and shareholders, a person with an identical name had recently retired as a TOPCO senior executive.

Mac knew that he should stop there. But he was so convinced of a TOPCO/Rutherford-Leske conspiracy that he could not resist. He decided to break one of his own rules by gambling on a question when he was not confident of the answer. "Does TOPCO have any voting control over the management of Rutherford-Leske Oil, Ltd.?" asked Mac.

"Certainly none that I am aware of, counselor," replied the secretary, who was telling the literal truth. Although the secretary's suspicion of a TOPCO/Rutherford-Leske tie had been aroused, he was not voluntarily going to assist the plaintiff against his own company.

Mac decided one stupid question was all he was allowed. "No further questions," he said.

Jonathan Clark was inwardly furious. He was convinced that Radcliffe had concealed essential facts from him. Nevertheless, Clark proceeded calmly with his cross-examination. He was optimistic from the corporate secretary's previous answers that the man personally knew nothing of any TOPCO/Rutherford-Leske conspiracy.

"As I recall, you testified that you personally know the present directors of Rutherford-Leske Oil, Ltd., is that right?" asked Clark.

"Yes, we all worked together at TOPCO before the three gentlemen retired," the secretary answered.

"While they were at TOPCO, did all three have close working relationships?"

"They would have had to. Each of them headed a division that was dependent on the others."

"Before today were you aware that after their retirements all three men had become Rutherford-Leske directors?"

"Yes, I believe I knew that. I never really gave it much thought. It was of no matter to me."

"Then you perceive nothing ulterior about the fact that the three men are shareholders and directors of Rutherford-Leske Oil, Ltd.?"

"It has been quite common for senior TOPCO officers to move into management of other companies after their retirement. Our company policy mandates retirement at a relatively early age. It seems quite natural to me that ex-employees who have known each other and have worked together all of their lives would be attracted to continuing their working relationship."

Thank heaven for good witnesses, thought Clark as he continued. "Does Titan Overland Petroleum Company have any financial interest of any nature in Rutherford-Leske Oil, Ltd.?"

The old gentleman understood the problem perfectly. "I have been TOPCO's secretary for twenty-two years. Before that I was assistant secretary for six years. The corporate secretary has the ultimate responsibility for the management of records of all subsidiary entities. If TOPCO had a financial interest in Rutherford-Leske, I would certainly know about it. I am unaware of any such interest."

MacDonald Oliver knew he was hearing nonsense. There had to be a connection. Years of coincidence were too much to stomach. But would the jury feel the same way? Mac wasn't sure. He wasn't even sure how many of them even understood the testimony. Mac sat there, wanting to examine the witness further but unable to think of any effective way to counter the testimony. Judge Johannsen looked at the wall clock, sighed with relief, and spared Mac further indecision by adjourning until the next morning.

"Doesn't time fly when you're having fun?" asked Burt.

The corporate secretary walked over to Jonathan Clark's side of the courtroom and raised an eyebrow.

"What the hell had been going on?" asked Clark quietly.

"I don't know, but something stinks," the secretary said. "You had better find out what."

Marla Zimmerman had been waiting in the rear of the courtroom. "Mac," she said, "this is important. Harold Rifkin telephoned and wants to talk to you. I told him you would be out to see him right after court. My car is outside."

7

eaving his doctor's office, Harold Rifkin realized he was humming. I am insane, he thought. I have just been told that I'm going to die, and I feel good. Harold returned directly to his Santa Monica bungalow and opened a bottle of Courvoisier VSOP he'd received as a Christmas gift twelve years before but hadn't felt he deserved to drink. As the glow of the cognac spread through him, he dialed the number of Sorensen, Oliver, Bradford, and Smith. He asked for MacDonald Oliver and was connected with Elizabeth Greene, Mac's secretary, who had the good sense to switch him to Marla Zimmerman.

"Marla Zimmerman speaking. May I help you?" Marla instantly suspected the urgency and importance of the call.

"The firm will pay for the ticket," said Mac. He removed the parking violation citation from the windshield as he climbed into Marla Zimmerman's thirteen-year-old Corvette.

"I should think so," said Marla as she peeled the Corvette away from the red-painted curb and expertly accelerated through the narrowing gap between a converging post office van and Cadillac limousine. She threaded the car through Civic Center traffic with such aplomb that they were on the Santa Monica Freeway within minutes, westbound at a highly illegal rate of speed.

"The firm won't pay for this ticket, Marla," said Mac.

"Coward," said Marla, as she slowed the big V8 to sixty-nine miles per hour.

"Marla."

"Nag," said Marla. The speed dropped to sixty-four.

As soon as he returned to his office, Jonathan Clark had a call placed to Grant Radcliffe. Clark unwrapped and lit a large black cigar. His large fingers drummed his polished antique desktop. He was still seething over the day's events.

As the buzzer rang, Clark forced himself to calmness. He picked up the telephone. "Radcliffe? . . . Yes, I'm fine—listen, please, this is important." Jonathan Clark carefully related what had happened at the trial, the damaging evidence suggesting a secret connection between TOPCO and Rutherford-Leske.

"It's too late to waste time lecturing on the desirability of being candid with your own attorney. Today's evidence hurt. Believe that. Although the corporate secretary did his best to bail us out. If you expect me to do anything effective to counter this evidence, I have to know what the hell has been going on. Is there a conspiracy between TOPCO and Rutherford-Leske, or is there possibly some legitimate explanation?"

Radcliffe was silent. First trouble at home and now this. Things were falling apart.

"Radcliffe? Are you there, man?"

"This is disturbing news, Jonathan. I'll have to investigate and call you back," said Radcliffe.

"It had better be promptly. There is damn little time," said Clark, and hung up. On his intercom Clark called the partner who handled the Rutherford-Leske account, and then the partner in charge of

TOPCO matters. Neither gentleman had realized that the Rutherford-Leske directors and shareholders were all retired TOPCO officers. Ironic, thought Clark, disgustedly. My own law firm represents both companies and undoubtedly has copies of their records. Yet no one even suspected the relationship.

Grant Radcliffe had not lied about being disturbed, but he had no need to check anything. Radcliffe knew precisely the relationship between TOPCO and Rutherford-Leske Oil, Ltd. He was one of the few with a need to know. TOPCO had caused Rutherford-Leske Oil, Ltd., to be created forty-eight years ago. Retired senior officers of TOPCO, whose discretion could be trusted, secretly held the Rutherford-Leske Oil, Ltd., stock in trust for TOPCO and managed Rutherford-Leske as TOPCO dictated. Rutherford-Leske Oil, Ltd., had had many uses over the years. Certain insensitive antitrust laws had been evaded. Unpleasant SEC regulations had been frustrated. Undesirable aspects of the Internal Revenue Code had been avoided.

Undisclosed control over Rutherford-Leske had proved to be an extremely convenient device. From the beginning, forty-eight years ago, the director-shareholders of Rutherford-Leske had signed a trust agreement providing that they held the Rutherford-Leske stock as trustees for the benefit of TOPCO. Traditionally the old agreement had been updated every time a shareholder became disabled or died, and a new one substituted. The new nominee signed an addendum. The stock was then transferred to him.

It had always been a function of the TOPCO vice-president for real estate and development to oversee the stock transfers and to act as a liaison between TOPCO and Rutherford-Leske. Since his promotion that job had fallen to Grant Radcliffe.

For the past three years Grant Radcliffe's initials appeared on an addendum to the secret trust agreement every time Rutherford-Leske stock was transferred. TOPCO's chairman of the board and its president were aware of the arrangement. Grant Radcliffe and his predecessors knew. Of course, the forty-eight-year succession of Rutherford-Leske shareholders had to know. There had certainly been no necessity to disclose the arrangement to the TOPCO corporate secretary or to

TOPCO's attorneys. The fewer involved, the more manageable the risk. Up to now the risk had been acceptable, considering the benefits.

Disclosure of the TOPCO-Rutherford connection could cost TOPCO dearly, for which Radcliffe could be blamed, which could wreck Radcliffe's career, destroy Radcliffe's marriage, and devastate Radcliffe's life.

By the time that Marla and Mac reached Harold Rifkin's home, one-third of the brandy had been consumed. Harold was a very cheerful dying man as he explained that he was terminally ill. He offered Marla and Mac drinks as he related that his malignant tumor had been diagnosed as inoperable.

"I will be gone within the year," stated Harold Rifkin.

"Mr. Rifkin," said Marla, "you do seem to be in awfully good spirits for a man who has just received such shocking news."

"Cheers," said Mr. Rifkin as he tossed down another half ounce.

"Why now, Mr. Rifkin? Why are you turning? Is it conscience?" asked Mac.

"Mr. Oliver," said Rifkin, "you might call it that. I think it's even simpler. All my life has been devoted to doing what I've been obligated to do. My duty to my mother, my loyalty to my company. I simply want to start doing what I want to do. I think I'd better get on with it, don't you?"

"We understand the pressures you've been under, and we deeply appreciate your help. What do you have to tell us?" asked Marla.

Harold Rifkin told them everything he remembered. He had been the administrative assistant to Grant Radcliffe and, before that, to Radcliffe's predecessor. He knew about the TOPCO/Rutherford-Leske connection and the trust agreement in Grant Radcliffe's safe. Rifkin's recollection was intermittent. He suspected that the tumor was affecting his memory. Nevertheless, what Rifkin did remember, if accepted by the jury, was more than enough to establish that TOPCO owned Rutherford-Leske Oil, Ltd. TOPCO was indirectly and secretly receiving the profits from the licensing of the Wennerstrom Process to itself as well as to other oil-producing companies.

"I don't hallucinate," said Harold Rifkin. "At least not yet. You can be assured that what I do remember is true."

"I'm convinced of it," said Mac. "What can you tell us about your previous testimony? Do you recall that in court you contradicted your deposition?"

"Yes, I do remember that. It can't be blamed on the tumor. It was then I realized how despicable I'd become."

Harold Rifkin confirmed that Grant Radcliffe had indeed represented that Wennerstrom would receive forty percent ownership of the joint venture assets. He recalled how Grant Radcliffe had coerced him into changing his testimony with the threat of losing his pension.

"I've outwitted that devil, though. Won't need his pension now," said Rifkin. "He is a devil, you know. Drink, anyone?"

"We will need your testimony, of course," said Mac. "If only we could get at that trust agreement. That would be conclusive."

"Subpoena duces tecum?" suggested Marla.

"Useless," said Mac. "TOPCO would simply deny the existence of the document. How can we prove otherwise?"

"Are there any copies?" asked Marla.

"Copy of what?" asked Harold Rifkin. "Excuse me, there goes my mind again. Of course, a copy. When I was forced to retire, I made a copy—don't even know why. I've always liked to keep records of everything. I suppose it made me feel significant."

"You have a copy of the original TOPCO/Rutherford-Leske trust agreement? Out of Radcliffe's safe?" asked Marla.

"Oh, yes, complete with addenda. I even remember the combination. Thirty-three right—oh, you don't care about that," said Rifkin.

"Where?" asked Mac.

"Where? Oh, where? Why, right here. I mean, in my garage or in the one next door. Probably next door. That's newer stuff."

"I don't understand, Mr. Rifkin," said Mac.

"I've been saving TOPCO records for years. Made me comfortable to have a complete set, you know. When my garage filled up, I leased the one next door. Old Mrs. Lansing, number seventy-two-oh-five; I'm seventy-two-oh-three. She doesn't even have a car."

"Mr. Rifkin, could you get the agreement for us now?" asked Marla.

"Might not be so easy," said Harold. "It's in there all right. In one of the garages. All my records are. Kind of a mess, though. I just stacked it all up as I brought it home. I was going to put it all in order when I had time." Harold Rifkin giggled and took another drink.

"Mr. Rifkin, could Marla and I stay and hunt for it?"

"Of course, here's the key. Fits both padlocks. I'll take you over and introduce you to Mrs. Lansing. Then we will all search—"

The telephone rang.

Grant Radcliffe knew that the trust agreement, replete with its addenda, was securely in his office safe. He was confident that the current Rutherford-Leske shareholders would remain strongly silent. Who else knew? There were no copies, were there? No one else had access. Who else could possibly testify? Rifkin! Rifkin knew about the trust. Rifkin had the combination. It had been convenient to trust the meekly obedient Rifkin. Thank God Rifkin's already testified, thought Radcliffe. I suppose it's possible they could recall him, though. It can't hurt if I telephone him and reinforce his loyalty.

When his telephone rang, Rifkin stood rapidly and spilled most of his drink on his lap.

"You take care of yourself," said Marla as Harold Rifkin headed for a change of trousers. "I'll get the telephone."

"Hello? Harold Rifkin's residence." Marla unconsciously fell into her office routine. "Marla Zimmerman speaking. May I help you?"

"This is Grant Radcliffe," he said automatically. "May I speak to Harold Rifkin, please?" Marla Zimmerman? he thought. A vaguely familiar name.

Marla had trouble not gulping. "Mr. Radcliffe, he's in—not able to come to the phone now. May I take a message?"

"No, I'll call back, thank you." Radcliffe hung up, puzzled. Who the devil was Marla Zimmerman? Radcliffe remembered. His deposition had been taken at Sorensen, Oliver, Bradford, and Smith's office. Marla Zimmerman's name was on the entrance door. She came into the deposition room several times, too, handing some records to that Burt Ginter. Radcliffe remembered Burt Ginter's saying, "Thank you, Miss Zimmerman," and recalled noticing how attractive she was. Marla

Zimmerman, an attorney with Sorensen, Oliver, Bradford, and Smith. Grant Radcliffe felt a surge of panic. God. If Marla Zimmerman is with Harold Rifkin, MacDonald Oliver cannot be far behind. Considering what happened in court today, it is obvious what the subject is under discussion.

Drastic action had to be considered. Grant Radcliffe picked up his telephone again and dialed the unlisted number from memory. The familiar female voice answered. "This is the John Smith residence—"

Grant Radcliffe left his message, hung up, and waited. Within thirty seconds Radcliffe's telephone rang. He explained the problem to the man.

"It is apparent," the man said, "there is a Harold Rifkin-Wennerstrom alliance brewing. Considering what Rifkin knows about the trust, and indulging the possibility that he may even have an unauthorized copy of the agreement, I would say that extreme action is appropriate."

"It is imperative there be no testimony regarding that trust agreement," said Radcliffe.

"Yes," said the man as he hung up. He recognized the near hysteria in Radcliffe's voice.

As Harold Rifkin returned from his bedroom wearing dry gray flannels, Marla, a little shaken, announced who the telephone caller had been. Rifkin was visibly upset.

"And I heard you give him your name," said Mac. "Does he know who you are?"

Marla couldn't believe she'd been so stupid. "I brought Burt some exhibits during Radcliffe's deposition. He also may have seen me the few times I've been at the trial. We had better assume the worst."

"The worst may be worse than you think," said a considerably sobered Harold Rifkin. "Grant Radcliffe is ruthless. He cannot afford to have me testify about the trust."

"By now Radcliffe knows what happened today in court. He knows you have knowledge of the secret trust, and he knows that at least one of plaintiff's attorneys is talking to you," said Mac.

"And he knows that the trial resumes at nine-thirty tomorrow morning," said Marla.

"Marla," said Mac, coming to his feet, "call a taxi. Then call the office. Get two bright bodies out here to help you search the garages. Start with the one next door. I'm going to get Mr. Rifkin out of this house. We'll take the cab and check him into the Athletic Club. He'll be safe there until he testifies. After he's testified, they won't dare touch him—no reason to then anyway. They will have nothing left to conceal."

Mac took Rifkin's arm. "Mr. Rifkin, please pack for an overnight stay. I'll help."

Thirty minutes later, when the dark gray Buick passed Harold Rifkin's bungalow at 7203 San Vicente Drive, the house was unlit. The man parked the Buick down the block and walked back. Not much time for subtlety, he thought. At least it's a quiet street. The man could hear the doorbell ringing inside the house, but there was no answer. The man walked around to the rear of the house, then back to the front walk. There were lights on at 7205 and music playing. The man walked next door and rang the front doorbell. When Mrs. Lansing appeared, he explained he was a friend of Mr. Rifkin's who had been invited over but had found the house dark and locked. The man wondered if Mrs. Lansing had any idea what time Mr. Rifkin might be returning. Mrs. Lansing, who didn't miss much that went on in a radius of one city block, didn't know, but mentioned that she had seen Mr. Rifkin leave in a Yellow Cab with another gentleman about twenty minutes ago.

The man thanked her and headed for the nearest telephone booth. Mrs. Lansing wandered back into her garage, carrying a pot of coffee and cookies. Marla and two other well-paid attorneys were on their knees, sorting stacks of paper on the dusty concrete floor.

"The oddest-looking man was just here," Mrs. Lansing announced, "asking for Mr. Rifkin—a friend who Mr. Rifkin had invited over and forgotten, although I can't say that he looked very friendly—"

"Mrs. Lansing, what did you tell him?" asked Marla.

"Nothing, dear. I didn't know when Mr. Rifkin would return. I just mentioned he left in a Yellow Cab—"

"Mrs. Lansing, may I use your telephone, please? It's urgent."

"Of course, dear. Use the one in the kitchen. I'll stay here and finish my coffee so you will have privacy."

Marla thumbed the telephone book rapidly and found the Athletic Club number. Harold Rifkin had been checked in, and Mac, fortunately, was still with him. Marla told Mac what had happened.

"Thank you, Marla," said Mac. "I will take precautions. Call me at home later if you find anything."

Mac hung up and turned to Harold Rifkin. "Mr. Rifkin, can you walk a few blocks?"

Rifkin smiled. "I'm not dead yet. Where are we going?"

"Out to dinner, but throw some overnight things and clothes for tomorrow into my attaché case. There's been a change of plan."

"They're on to me, aren't they?" Harold Rifkin's eyes glittered. "This is great."

As Marla hung up the phone, she glanced at the growing glow outside Mrs. Lansing's kitchen window. "My God! It's Harold Rifkin's garage on fire," she screamed as she dialed for help.

It took the man ten minutes to have his contact trace the taxi's destination. In another twenty minutes the man was at the Los Angeles Athletic Club reception desk, asking for Harold Rifkin.

"Yes, sir," the night clerk said. "Mr. Rifkin has gone out to dinner, but he left a message that he was expecting a caller and asked if you would please wait here. He promised to be back within thirty minutes— by eight o'clock, sir."

MacDonald Oliver and Harold Rifkin leisurely walked four blocks to the Biltmore Hotel, where Harold Rifkin registered as Ben Arnold. Ben's friend paid cash in advance. After dinner Mac took Harold back to his new room.

"You'll be safe here for tonight. I'll pick you up at seven-thirty. We'll have breakfast. Then I'll take you to court myself, Harold."

"Thank you, Mac. I'm having an awfully good time."

At 10:30 P.M. the man left the Athletic Club lobby. He was hungry, disgusted, and convinced he'd been had.

When Mac got home, there was a message from Marla. He called her, and she told him about the fire. Harold Rifkin's house had been virtually destroyed.

"The firemen won't say it was arson, but they've been asking a lot of probing questions. We haven't found anything yet, but we aren't even halfway through. We'll just keep going until we drop. How's that sweet Harold Rifkin?"

"Intact, but I'm going to increase precautions. Call when you strike gold."

When Mac left home the next morning, he made sure that no one was following his BMW. He stopped to pick up Burt at his home. Promptly at seven-thirty they took charge of an ebullient Harold Rifkin and smothered him between them into a corner table in the Biltmore dining room, from which they could easily observe the entrance. Mac told Harold about the destruction of his house and offered to help him find a suitable replacement.

"Don't give it a second thought," said Harold Rifkin. "I've always hated the place. Depressing. I only stayed there because it seemed like I should. It's all insured anyway. Besides, I was thinking of spending a few months in Las Vegas."

After breakfast they guided Harold Rifkin uneventfully into Judge Johannsen's courtroom.

At nine thirty-five, Harold Rifkin was testifying for the plaintiff. Jonathan Clark was stony-faced and icy calm. Grant Radcliffe had not bothered to call him back. Clark had been tempted to alert one of Radcliffe's superior officers to the impending danger but knew it was taboo to override the corporate hierarchy. To hell with him, thought Clark, even though Radcliffe was seated next to Clark, glowering at Rifkin.

On the stand, Harold Rifkin poured it all out. He had testified truthfully at his deposition but had perjured himself at the trial after being threatened with the loss of his pension. Rifkin had heard Radcliffe promise Wennerstrom forty percent ownership of the joint venture property. By the time Rifkin got to the TOPCO/Rutherford-Leske connection the courtroom was charged. The jury was enthralled. The clerk and Judge Johannsen were spellbound. Even the bailiff was attentive.

When Mac asked Harold Rifkin about the provisions of the secret

TOPCO/Rutherford-Leske trust agreement, Jonathan Clark objected. "Counsel is attempting to have the witness testify to the contents of a written instrument which is not in evidence. Evidence Code Section Fifteen Hundred provides that no evidence other than the writing itself is admissible to prove its contents."

But after prodding by Mac, Clark had to concede it was his client's position that the alleged written instrument did not exist. Mac argued, "When a party's rights depend on the contents of a writing that cannot be found after reasonable search, the contents may be proved by secondary evidence. Plaintiff can't subpoena the document from TOPCO. They say it doesn't exist. Harold Rifkin has testified that he had a copy of it and can't find it. Under these circumstances he is entitled to testify to his recollection of the contents of the agreement."

"Fascinating," murmured Judge Johannsen. "Objection overruled. Proceed."

When Harold Rifkin finished his direct testimony, the courtroom was quiet. If Harold Rifkin was telling the truth, then TOPCO effectively owned Rutherford-Leske Oil, Ltd. TOPCO was indirectly receiving the profits from the licensing of the Wennerstrom Process and obviously did not intend to share forty percent with Charles Wennerstrom.

Jonathan Clark's cross-examination was rapierlike. He pointed out that Harold Rifkin was an admitted perjurer. Rifkin had already testified falsely, either at his deposition or at the trial. Why should he expect the jury to believe him now that he was changing his story again?

Clark caught Rifkin in some memory lapses and exacerbated them. Tiring easily, after an hour of cross-examination Harold Rifkin could no longer remember the street address of his home. Could this person be relied upon to recall accurately the terms of a complex legal instrument?

Clark mockingly ridiculed Harold Rifkin's search for the missing document. Rifkin had to admit that he personally had not searched for the document. Only the plaintiff's attorneys had done so. How was that for an impartial effort?

And then the place where the records were supposed to be stored mysteriously burned down last night. How convenient for plaintiff's attorneys to have a witness testify to the existence of an alleged document after they say they can't find it.

Clark made Rifkin admit that he had padded his expense account while employed by TOPCO. Clark reduced him to a disgruntled former employee who has testified vengefully because his pension has been cut off. Rifkin's pension had not, in fact, been terminated, but Radcliffe told Clark it had been. As far as Radcliffe was concerned, it certainly would be the moment he got back to the office.

Clark's cross-examination effectively painted a portrait of a senile, vengeful, thieving perjurer. Pathetic, wrung-out Harold Rifkin. Not much of a witness to place your faith in.

That was when Marla Zimmerman walked in. Marla did not look much better than Harold Rifkin. She had been up all night and had not even changed clothes. But as Marla Zimmerman walked through the courtroom, past the rail, up to the counsel table, and handed MacDonald Oliver a fifty-page document, her face was lit up like the dawn of a new era.

When Mac offered the copy of the TOPCO/Rutherford-Leske trust agreement, with addenda, in evidence, Jonathan Clark made a half-hearted effort to keep it out on the ground that the document had not been properly authenticated. But after Rifkin had testified that he had made the copy from the original in Radcliffe's safe, and identified Grant Radcliffe's initials on the last four addendum sheets, Clark retreated. As the revived Harold Rifkin pointed out the pertinent provisions of the document, Marla Zimmerman slipped back behind the rail and sat between Charlie and Laura Wennerstrom, neither of whom could resist alternately hugging her. No one on the plaintiff's side doubted that the jury would find that TOPCO defrauded Charles Wennerstrom. If Jonathan Clark had been asked, he would have agreed.

Jonathan Clark had thought of the TOPCO preliminary injunction against Wennerstrom as a necessary nuisance, diverting attention from the main issues and with no independent significance. He therefore acceded to his assistant trial attorney's plea to be allowed to examine the witnesses testifying on the injunction issues. The young man, Ralph Radecke, had obtained the preliminary injunction against Wennerstrom, and he still felt satisfaction when he remembered how he had crushed Sorenson, Oliver, Bradford, and Smith's inept opposition at the injunction hearing.

Ralph Radecke felt much larger than his stocky five feet nine. He was an active part of an important trial as he stood and called his next witness. "The defense calls the plaintiff, Charles Wennerstrom, as an adverse witness, pursuant to California Evidence Code Section Seven-seven-six."

With his cross-examination of Wennerstrom, Ralph Radecke reestablished what everyone in the courtroom already knew: that the joint venture agreement contained a covenant not to compete and a provision assigning any Wennerstrom inventions, which were related to the Wennerstrom Process, to the joint venture.

"When did you move out of the laboratory that TOPCO furnished?" Radecke asked.

"When TOPCO ceased paying my salary and expenses."

Radecke established that Wennerstrom had some half-formed ideas about how he could modify the Wennerstrom Process to extract valuable ammonia and phenols as by-products of the shale oil extraction.

"Didn't you move back to the basement laboratory at your home in order to pursue your ideas about the by-product process in secret?"

"No, I'd already had the ideas before I moved back to my basement."

"You admit then that you already had the idea for the by-product process while TOPCO was still paying your salary and expenses?"

"Yes, I just hadn't had time to work on it."

Radecke showed Wennerstrom a letter from TOPCO's chief counsel that had been sent to McGovern and forwarded to Wennerstrom. The letter stated:

It has come to our attention that your client, Charles Wennerstrom, is attempting to develop a modification of the Wennerstrom Process, which will produce certain valuable by-products of the Process. We remind you that the partnership agreement executed by your client contains a Covenant Not to Compete (paragraph 27 E2), as well as a provision assigning any inventions to the partnership, relating to, or arising out of Mr. Wennerstrom's employment by the partnership (paragraph 36 F3). Any fruit of Mr. Wennerstrom's present efforts is partnership property, and Mr. Wennerstrom will be held accountable for same.

"What did you understand when you received the copy of this letter?"

Charlie remembered Mac's opening statement. He decided Mac would not object to a little plagiarism by his own client. "I understood that TOPCO had already dumped on me and now was trying to rub my face in it."

Four jurors grinned.

Radecke colored. "Move to strike the witness's answer as nonresponsive, Your Honor."

"Well, your question was a little broad, Mr. Radecke. Perhaps you could rephrase a narrower question," said the judge, unsuccessfully attempting to repress a smile.

Mr. Radecke, however, felt it would be prudent to go to another question. Jonathan Clark, sitting at the counsel table, was beginning to hear those distant warning bells again. He regretted permitting his young associate to conduct the examination.

Radecke resumed, "Did you keep any diary of your experiments?"

"Yes, I kept notes in a loose-leaf binder."

"And you realized, didn't you, when you got the letter that those notes were the property of your partner, TOPCO?"

"Oh, yes, I realized that."

Radecke pounced for the kill. "And to date you haven't turned those notes over to TOPCO, have you?"

"No, I haven't."

"And what have you done with those notes, Mr. Wennerstrom?"

"First thing I did was I burned them."

Radecke was startled by Wennerstrom's answer. "First thing? What was the next thing you did?"

"Then I got extremely drunk."

It was never clear afterward how it started. Someone in the back of the courtroom started to applaud. Then other spectators began to applaud. Judge Johannsen was violently rapping his gavel. By now even the jury was standing and applauding. The bailiff was desperately trying to restore order by making motions with his hands. Ralph Radecke stood, beet red, paralyzed before the witness stand. Jonathan Clark was on his feet, wildly shouting for the judge's attention. Charlie Wennerstrom sat straight-faced and quiet as if nothing had happened at all. Mac could not resist smiling, but he feared a new problem had been created.

Later, outside the presence of the jury, Jonathan Clark moved for a mistrial.

"The irregularity caused by the scene we have just witnessed is too serious an error to be corrected. Defendant has been precluded from having a fair trial. The jury has been inflamed and has overtly demonstrated its bias by applause. It is unfortunate after so much time and effort have been invested, but this trial must be terminated, and the case retried from the beginning with a different jury," Clark argued.

Although Mac was delighted at the positive emotional impact caused by Charlie's testimony, he anticipated that such irregular reaction would precipitate the mistrial motion. The defense had been battered down during the later rounds. A mistrial would pull the fat out of the fire for TOPCO. It might be months or even years before the case could be retried. Charlie Wennerstrom might not survive. Sorensen, Oliver, Bradford, and Smith would be forced to reincur tremendous expense. With a different judge and jury the result might be quite changed. Plaintiff would lose the element of surprise and the defense would have the opportunity to construct plausible counterevidence. Mac was worried.

"Your Honor," Mac said, "while it must be admitted that the jury's reaction was unusual, no irreparable error has occurred. The jury can be admonished—"

Clark snorted. "Is counsel suggesting that the jurors be instructed to disregard their own applause? That's ludicrous."

"If I may finish, Your Honor," said Mac. "I was going to suggest that the jury be instructed that in spite of their emotional response to the testimony, they are to deliberate quietly on all the evidence before reaching a decision. Any doubt can be resolved by Your Honor's individually questioning each juror to determine if he or she has been rendered incapable of deliberation."

"This carnivallike event was precipitated by the plaintiff's own blatant misconduct," said Clark, "and cannot be cured by an instruction. You cannot unring a bell."

Back and forth the argument raged, Clark desperately trying to abort plaintiff's case, Mac determined to hang on. It was demoralizing to think of starting over. Judge Johannsen sighed and raised his hands.

"Gentlemen—enough. I fear we're just going over the same ground again. I must think this over. Much rests on my decision. We will recess."

"How does an indecisive judge handle this?" asked Burt.

"Mac?" Charlie asked. "I only said what I felt. Did I do something terribly wrong?"

"No, Charlie," said Mac. "The problem seems to be that you may have been too successful."

"Mac, what if we have to start over?" asked Laura.

"Bite your tongue," said Mac, jamming his right hand into his pocket.

Conversation died. No one felt much like talking. Mac waited quietly, Burt doodled, Charlie fidgeted, and Laura paced. Clark, too, sat quietly, staring at the wall clock. Ralph Radecke couldn't bring himself to look at Clark. Grant Radcliffe pretended to read, but inside was all turmoil. He was about to be delivered from the brink of disaster.

In one hour and five minutes Judge Johannsen returned. "I've given this a great deal of thought," Judge Johannsen said. "I cannot place any blame on the plaintiff, Charles Wennerstrom, for this occurrence. Mr. Wennerstrom was asked a question on cross-examination, and he simply answered it directly. I don't know who started the applause. I don't see any practical way of finding out. Whoever it was, I am convinced that it was not a deliberate attempt to influence the jury. As inappropriate as the occurrence was, I believe it was spontaneous and innocent. Whether a breach of procedure occurred is really not relevant. The real question is, What effect will the irregularity have on the jury? If the jury had not participated in the outburst, I could simply admonish it to ignore the demonstration of others. But as Mr. Clark has ably pointed out, the jury cannot be made to disregard its own applause. There was obviously a strong emotional reaction to the testimony, but on reflection, I am not even certain just what testimony triggered the response. Was the reaction to Mr. Wennerstrom's testimony of how he flaunted his disregard of TOPCO's warning letter, or were they simply applauding the elegance of Wennerstrom's final solution—the bottle? One could speculate endlessly. I am satisfied that if the jury's emotional response had been identical, but private, no misconduct would have occurred. In other words, even if we somehow knew that each juror had applauded mentally and silently, that would not be impeaching. This jury has merely done overtly what many juries have done covertly. It has experienced an emotional response. Jurors cannot be barred from having feelings. They can only be instructed that their deliberations are not to be influenced by any sympathy, prejudice, or passion. I do not believe that this jury's ability to reason fairly has been affected. I have concluded that no error has occurred and that it would be pointless to admonish the jury. The motion for mistrial is denied." Judge Johannsen looked over at plaintiff's side of the table. "And no applause, please."

8

The jury had been out for six hours before Mac began to feel the familiar anxiety. Ah, maturity, he thought. Last trial I was getting nervous after only four hours. Of course, he expected the jury to deliberate for a substantial time after hearing a case of this magnitude.

Why start feeling uptight so soon? thought Mac. After all, you've only devoted large chunks of your life and of your professional reputation to this exercise, not to mention two hundred thousand dollars of your firm's money. Relax.

Sweating out the verdict never got easier. Mac's waiting routine was always pretty much the same: back to the office to catch up on urgent work that had been put off, mostly answering postponed telephone calls and letters. It would become increasingly difficult to concentrate. Mac would do some exercises on the office floor. He did two hundred sit-ups. He tried to take a nap. The last few days had been exhausting. He couldn't sleep and drifted into Nels's office, rehashing the trial with the old master: the things that could have been done, different questions on cross-examination, different objections, different arguments. That conversation waned quickly. He glanced at his watch. It was near time for the jury to go to lunch. He taxied back to the courthouse. Mac, he thought, be sitting at the counsel table when they file out of the jury room. There you are, Mac, relaxed, smiling, and confident. Don't dare let any one of them think that you don't care enough to be there. Look at their faces. Happy? Pensive? Frowning? Angry? Do they look back or avoid your eyes? Could anything useful be gleaned from this exercise? Hardly ever, but Mac felt compelled to try anyway.

When the jury went to lunch, Mac started to do the same thing. He thought, I must get away from Charlie Wennerstrom for a while. Even though we're friends, it's the wrong time to be with any client. Lunch would just be a series of what ifs. What if the jury can't decide? What if one of them gets sick? What if the verdict is too low? What if the verdict is too high? It's a good time to be alone. I'm unfit for human company anyway. Mac wasn't hungry, and he hated eating alone. He taxied back the few blocks to his office, picked up his BMW, and drove the short distance to Griffith Park. There Mac roamed the zoo, munching popcorn. He stopped before a pair of relentlessly pacing Bengal tigers. Did they have a jury out, too? Mac tried the monkeys, but they wouldn't perform, just stared at him with sad eyes. Just lost a case, huh? Mac began remembering cases he had lost. The worst memories were of cases that he had been confident about winning, was sure he had won. How could they do that to me? It was a good case. I did everything right. The trial went beautifully, smooth as butter. How could they, it, the system, betray me, MacDonald Abraham Oliver? He caught himself rubbing his blind eye.

Mac glanced at his watch and drove back to the courthouse. He called the office for messages. There was nothing important enough to divert attention from his painful vigil. He went back to the courtroom. The jury had returned from lunch early; that was not surprising, considering the quality of the courthouse food, and was already in the jury room deliberating.

Judge Johannsen was hearing the argument on a motion for a new trial in another case that he had heard before *Wennerstrom v. TOPCO*. Mac listened, halfheartedly trying to figure what the case had been all about. When the arguments concluded, Judge Johannsen thanked both attorneys and told them the matter was under submission. As they filed out of the courtroom, Judge Johannsen stayed on the bench, apparently making notes. In a few minutes he gathered his papers and eased his chunky frame toward his chambers door. He stopped at his clerk's desk and turned.

"Better grant that motion for new trial."

"Grant it, Judge?" The clerk's tone was incredulous.

"I guess you're right. Better deny it." The judge entered his chambers and closed the door.

The clerk shook his head and smiled. Mac shook his head, too, but he couldn't smile. God, what strength of will, he thought. Oh, the crapshootiness of it all. Frightening.

Mac drove the five minutes back to his office. The instant he walked in he was told that Judge Johannsen had heard from the jury and wanted counsel in his chambers immediately.

It can't be a verdict this soon, thought Mac. If it is, it's a defense verdict. There hadn't been time for them to thrash out the damage issues. How did I blow it?

Looking what he hoped was brave and confident, Mac walked out of his office and drove back to the courthouse. Jonathan Clark was already in Judge Johannsen's chambers. He grinned.

"Ah, Mac, come in," said the judge. "The jury has some questions."

Mac hoped he hid his sigh of relief.

"Yes." That was a safe, cool response, wasn't it?

"I'll read you their note, delivered via the bailiff about twenty minutes ago," said the judge. " 'Is there any difference between breach of contract and a promise made without intent to perform? Can we have another hot plate for those who want tea instead of coffee? Aaron Miller, Foreman.' "

The judge continued to look deadpan at Mac and Clark. They looked at the judge. Clark and Mac looked at each other. Clark shrugged.

Mac finally spoke. "It's not so difficult. The plaintiff will stipulate to another hot plate."

The judge and Clark broke up. After things had calmed down, they discussed how to deal with the jury's other question. It was finally agreed that the judge would reinstruct the jury on the elements of breach of contract and of fraudulent promise made without intent to perform.

The bailiff was instructed to return the jury to the courtroom. The judge read the selected instructions.

"Does that answer your first question?" the judge asked.

"Yes, Your Honor," answered the foreman firmly. Some of the jurors didn't look all that certain.

"Good. And you'll have the hot plate by tomorrow morning. Bailiff, please return the jury to the jury room for further deliberation."

The next morning Mac was back at the counsel table in time for the returning jurors to see what he tried to make his cheerfully optimistic countenance. Mac had a terrific hangover and thought how shattered his image would be if he threw up in front of the jury. A sympathetic Charlie Wennerstrom was seated next to Mac. They'd had dinner at Charlie's house and afterward emptied a bottle of Armagnac. Charlie was just as sick as Mac. Jonathan Clark approached from the other end of the table, cold sober and clear-eyed. Disgusting, thought Mac.

"Good morning, gentlemen. Mac, could I speak to you, please?"

"Of course. Excuse me, Charlie," replied Mac. Here it comes, thought Mac. Settlement offer. Be gracious.

"Let's get some coffee, Jonathan."

Jonathan Clark did have an offer. After the standard preliminaries about the jury's still being out, the motions and the appeals still to come, and the expense, delay, and uncertainty of it all, Clark finally got down to it.

"I'm going to offer my full authority on this, Mac. No tedious, petty bargaining."

"Fine, I appreciate that approach. I promise you a prompt, direct response."

"All right. The offer is two million dollars for a dismissal with prejudice and a general release, including any further claims to future joint venture profits or assets."

"Let me be sure I have it straight. Two million settles this suit. TOPCO gets the Wennerstrom Process, and the joint venture is dissolved."

"Yes. Except that"—Clark grinned a rueful grin—"it's Rutherford-Leske Oil, Ltd., that gets the Wennerstrom Process. We figured that based on a five-million-dollar joint venture asset value, Wennerstrom's forty percent share would be two million, the probable maximum compensatory damages if you won—"

"But what about TOPCO's secret profits? Oh, never mind. Let's not reargue the case. I'll talk to Charlie now and try to give you an answer this morning."

"Then you will recommend the settlement?" Clark beamed.

"Good question, Jonathan. Thanks for the coffee—and the offer."

Mac retrieved Charlie from the courtroom and took him back up to the cafeteria.

"After we've taken our costs off the top, there would still be about one-point-eight million dollars left. Your sixty percent of that after deduction of our fee would still be over one million dollars."

"I've never had a million. I could do very well with that much money. What do you think, Mac?"

"Charlie, you're asking me to predict what those twelve people in that jury room are going to do. How the judge will rule on the defense motions if we do get a favorable verdict. How the inevitable appeals will turn out—"

"And how long I'll live. We have to know that, too. You're the lawyer, make a recommendation."

"Okay. The jury's been out for only a day and a half. Nothing remarkable about that, and certainly not suggestive either way, except that we know by now that the jury doesn't see it as an obvious defense verdict case. You could infer from the jury's only question so far that they have determined that TOPCO is liable to some extent, but such inferences are not reliable. I read TOPCO's offer at this stage as signaling that they perceive the risk of a substantial verdict, so they consider two million dollars a reasonable price for elimination of that risk."

Charlie Wennerstrom did his Indian chief impersonation. "White man speak many words. What's your recommendation, lawyer?"

"I'd sure like to hear that verdict."

"So would I. Hold out."

Mac laughed. "Now I know why you don't have any money. You're a closet gambler."

"Sure. I'm an oilman. I suspect the plain truth is that I just want to see those son of a bitches hurt."

When Mac told Clark the offer had been rejected, Clark did not seem surprised. Clark did, however, lift an eyebrow when Mac told him there was no counterproposal.

Mac spent the third morning commuting between his office and the courtroom. In the office he puttered, accomplishing nothing of value. At the courthouse he watched the jury file into the jury room in the morning, out at lunchtime, and back in the afternoon.

Judge Johannsen's clerk offered to bet him five dollars that the verdict would be in plaintiff's favor, but less than ten million dollars. Mac laughed but, out of superstition, refused the bet.

Mac's anxiety mounted. His doubts increased. God, he thought, if I've given that decent old man poor advice and cost him a million—

Mac was in the courthouse cafeteria, drinking bad coffee and trying to read the *Times*, when the bailiff found him.

"Jury just buzzed, Mr. Oliver. They have a verdict."

"Thank you. Be right down." Charlie had gone home early, saying that the strain made him hungry. Just as well he's not here, thought Mac. I can give him good news over the telephone, but the firsthand impact of a defense verdict might kill him.

Clark, the clerk, the reporter, and the bailiff were already in the courtroom. Everybody nodded. Nobody had anything to say. When the clerk saw Mac enter, he buzzed the judge, who came out promptly.

"All present? All right, let's see what we've got. Bring them in, Mr. Bailiff."

Mac turned on his unflinching, intrepid trial attorney look and watched the jurors' faces as they took their places in the jury box. Thank

God, he thought, they aren't avoiding my eye. I got a flicker of a smile from number three, I think. At least I can hope it's not a disaster.

Mac glanced at Clark. Clark sat unmoving, watching the jury just as Mac had been doing, not a hint of emotion on his face. The bailiff, the reporter, and the clerk all wore half-smiles as if somehow, magically, they already knew the verdict.

The judge spoke. "Mrs. Klaus, number four, and Mrs. Conner, number three. You appear to be in the wrong seats. Will you please change places?"

The women blushed, tittered, and switched chairs.

Mac was certain that the exchange had taken at least an hour and a half.

"*Wennerstrom* versus *TOPCO*," the judge said. "The jury is seated, and counsel for both sides are present. Neither the plaintiff nor any officer of the defendant corporation is present. Do counsel stipulate that the verdict may be received without the presence of the parties?"

"Yes, Your Honor," said Mac. For God's sake, yes.

"So stipulated," said Clark.

The judge turned to Mr. Miller, juror number eleven. "Mr. Foreman, have you reached a verdict?"

"Yes, Your Honor, we have." Mr. Miller held up a folded sheet of paper.

The judge continued. "Have you answered all of the special interrogatories submitted to you?"

"Yes, Your Honor." Mr. Miller displayed several more sheets of paper.

Mac was sure that another thirty minutes had passed.

The judge continued. "Mr. Bailiff, please deliver the verdict and the special interrogatory forms to the clerk."

The bailiff crossed the room, took the papers from Mr. Miller, and brought them to the clerk, without looking at them. The clerk unfolded the general verdict and glanced through the several sheets of answer to special interrogatories, all of which he did admirably in slow motion and deadpan. The clerk handed the papers to the judge, who repeated the clerk's performance and handed the papers back to the clerk.

Mac wondered if night was falling.

Judge Johannsen spoke. "Mr. Clerk, please read the verdict."

The clerk rose and cleared his throat.

"Court and cause. We, the jury in the above-entitled cause, find in favor of the plaintiff, Charles Wennerstrom, against the defendant, Titan Overland Petroleum Company, and assess damages in the following sums: general damages, one billion two hundred million dollars; punitive damages, one dollar."

Judge Johannsen spoke again. "Ladies and gentlemen of the jury, is this your verdict?"

There was more. Other things happened and other words were said, but Mac later didn't remember hearing or seeing any of it. He just kept seeing the same green neon sign flashing, and he kept hearing: ONE BILLION DOLLARS—ONE BILLION DOLLARS—ONE BILLION DOLLARS.

By the time Mac returned to his office the party was in full swing. Plastic glasses of champagne everywhere. The entire firm of Sorensen, Oliver, Bradford, and Smith, from Nels Sorensen down to the lowliest mail clerk, was present. Mac was not only their hero but their benefactor. Mac's victory would be translated into substantial cash for every one of them through the firm's bonus plan. Not this year perhaps, but certainly eventually. Mac represented the greatest joy of all—money in the bank.

When Mac entered the reception area, a huge cheer went up. The spontaneous sincerity washed over him in a sweet wave. God, was this what it had been like for Napoleon and Patton? A plastic glass was thrust into his hand, but it was crushed before it reached his lips. Mac was punched, hugged, kissed, stroked, patted, pinched, and squeezed in an orgy of gratitude. Mac was being loved, adored, and damn near deified. Everyone was talking to him at once, shouting to him at once, all the same chorus: beautiful, great, fantastic, awesome, marvelous, outstanding, love you. We all love you, Mac.

Nels was on the opposite side of the room, beaming and rotating like a beacon. Nels waved, spilling champagne in the process. The two men inched toward each other. Nels grabbed Mac by both shoulders and squeezed, a more open display of affection than his Victorian inhibitions had ever before permitted.

"My boy." (First time for that, too.) "Magnificent victory. You must tell me all about the verdict later." Two neighboring celebrants jostled, spilling champagne on Nels's shirtfront. "This is clearly neither the time nor the place. Congratulations."

Timothy Bradford worked his way to Mac. His face was flushed, his speech only a little slurred. "Great, Mac, just great. Hell of a great job. Love you." Timothy Bradford meant it, too. The anticipation of his share of the fee temporarily overshadowed his usual dark thoughts regarding Mac.

Cornell Sepulveda Smith's pink head, the top of which was at the crowd's median shoulder height, bobbed toward him. The man was exuberant as a puppy. "I've been looking into Swiss banks and Bahamian banks. Swiss banks are safer, but Bahamian banks pay more. What do you think, Mac?"

"Why do we want an account at all?"

"We don't want an account, dummy. We want the bank." Smith bobbed away, roaring at his own joke.

Mac's secretary, Elizabeth Greene, waved from the opposite side of the room, and he started toward her.

One of the other secretaries battled her way up to Mac. She was five feet one and ninety-six pounds, five pounds of which had to be her brown eyes. She didn't spill a drop of her champagne. "Telephone, Mac. I know Nels said to hold your calls, but it's Mr. Clark, the TOPCO attorney, calling. He says it can't wait. Okay?"

"Sure. You did right, May. I'll take it in my office."

What could Clark want? thought Mac. Not another settlement offer yet. Much too soon. What could be so urgent? Nothing. Clark is just making a gentlemanly gesture. He wants to congratulate me. Mac smiled, closed the door behind him, and picked up the telephone.

"Hello, Jonathan. Oliver here."

It was not Clark.

"I will get you, Oliver. I will."

Mac knew that voice. Who?

"I will destroy your life as you've done mine."

Of course. Grant Radcliffe.

"I can't speak directly to you about this case, Mr. Radcliffe. It's not ethical for—"

"Just listen then, Oliver. I'm going to make you my life's work. I will fucking demolish you—"

Radcliffe was obviously drunk.

Mac hung up.

He was not frightened. He'd been shot at, kicked, and tortured by professionals. He wasn't afraid, but the vehemence of the man poured into him. Mac suppressed a shudder. Mac's body came out of his office, turned left, and returned to the party, but his spirit stayed behind and sulked.

"Damn you, Radcliffe. You won't ruin my life, but you sure know how to screw up a celebration."

PART
TWO

9

Stacks of file folders covered Mac's desk. He was barely visible. Since The Verdict, association in every major case in the state was being offered to him.

"Mac, if you're back there, here are the three watches you ordered," said Elizabeth Greene, "and Bernie says he's suing. Engraving the inscriptions has given him permanent vision impairment. Mac, even with the discount these were nine thousand dollars. Were the clerk, bailiff, and court reporter really all that helpful?"

"Liz, consider this a modest premium on health and accident insurance. We are trying to keep a one-point-two-billion-dollar verdict healthy. Call department one-oh-two. Find out what's going on. I may be able to catch all three donees at noon."

The presentation of three gold Rolexes was made ten days before TOPCO's Notice of Intention to Move for New Trial was filed. Four hundred pages of affidavits and points and authorities covered every possible ground for a new trial.

O'Malley & Byers had used the full capability of its huge law machine. The sheer weight of the notice was impressive.

Mac, Burt, and Marla met at Mac's office. "It's awesome," said Burt. "Every legal argument ever conceived is in here. No, they forgot to accuse us of bribing the jury. According to this, the verdict is the biggest miscarriage of justice since the Crucifixion."

"Yes"—Mac smiled—"it was a miracle we even got a plaintiff's verdict."

"It's all bullshit, of course," said Marla.

"Ms. MZ!" exclaimed Mac.

"It's true. I read it all. Twice. There isn't one sound, persuasive point in the whole four hundred bullshitty pages."

"It'll take two months to prepare responses to all this garbage," said Burt.

"We don't have two months. We have a statutory ten days, with a possible twenty-day extension," said Mac.

"There goes my weekend," said Marla.

"There goes the whole damned month," said Burt.

"War is hell," said Mac.

The hearing on TOPCO's motion for a new trial took all day. Marla and Burt were on hand to help. Charlie and Laura watched, merely out of curiosity. There was nothing for them to do.

At the end Judge Johannsen thanked the attorneys for their able presentations, announced the matter was under submission, and took to his chambers.

"Mac, I didn't understand ninety-three percent of what was said today by either attorney or the judge," said Charlie Wennerstrom.

"That's because it was all—"

"Bullshit?" said Laura.

"See, she understands," said Marla.

*   *   *

Judge Johannsen was in his chambers, shoes off, stocking feet on his desk, leaning back in his big swivel chair, watching his toes wiggle and his coffee steam.

"Have a cup, Felipe," Judge Johannsen said. "This is a tough one to decide. It's a humungous, huge verdict—"

"World's record," agreed the clerk as he poured a mugful.

"—and I have to confess that I'm uncertain about my ruling on TOPCO's nonsuit motion after the jury applauded plaintiff's testimony. But all in all, I'm inclined to think that it was a fair trial and a fair verdict. I suppose I should deny TOPCO's motion. I just don't know. What do you think, Felipe?"

"I agree, Judge, you're one hundred percent right to deny the motion." The clerk glanced at his new watch. "You'd better get ready for judge's meeting. I'll draw up the order for your signature right now."

The semicircular TOPCO boardroom took up half the top floor of the North TOPCO Tower. The drapes were open, permitting the waiting directors to eavesdrop on the morning sun repainting the San Bernardino Mountains. Maynard Chase, the chairman, always waited until the rest of the board was seated before entering. It gave him a feeling of omnipotence to hear the conversation halt, see heads turn and hear the chorus of "Good morning, Mr. Chairman."

At eighty-three Maynard Chase still had the bearing of a Roman emperor. He'd always had the nose. With seven percent of TOPCO's stock, and majority control of the proxies, he came close to having the empire.

Characteristically, Chase omitted any greeting. "Gentlemen, the critical item on our agenda this morning is our situation in Algeria—not an easy matter to resolve. I hope for some creative proposals. I propose that we clear away the clutter first so that Algeria can be given our full attention. Let's get this *Wennerstrom* versus *TOPCO* thing disposed of. Unless you have been in an isolation ward, you already know that a one-point-two-billion-dollar judgment has been entered against the company—"

"With court costs, it is over one billion two hundred million two hundred thousand, Mr. Chairman."

"Yes, B.J., thank you. The judgment has been stayed, pending our appeal. You should have all received copies of O'Malley and Byers's confidential report on the case. Anyone hasn't read it? Good. There is a lot of legalistic horseshit and conjecture in the report, but it all boils down to one significant fact: Our chances of a reversal stink. The verdict of one-point-two-billion compensatory and only one-dollar punitive damages effectively squashed any chance of reversal based on an excessive award. We have been nailed by this Wennerstrom thing, and short of a miracle, which I haven't seen performed well lately, we are going to pay for it. Anyone differ with the conclusion? Good. B.J., you love figures so much, why don't you tell us all what this appeal is costing?"

"Yes, Mr. Chairman." Everyone but the chairman's granddaughter called him "Mr. Chairman." Nothing about the man encouraged familiarity. B.J. continued to drone out the numbers. ". . . According to the O'Malley and Byers report, the appeal will take at least two years. They put our chances of reversal at less than eleven to one. If we assume two years of appeal without success, accrued interest, bond premiums, and attorneys' fees will add five hundred thirty million dollars to the judgment—"

"B.J.," interrupted Chase, "suppose we assume we could settle the case now for, say, a twenty percent discount?"

"All right, Mr. Chairman. That would save two hundred forty million dollars just in interest. A settlement for eighty percent of the judgment now would save the company seven hundred seventy million dollars, as compared to being compelled to pay off an affirmed judgment after two years of appeal—"

The chairman held up his hand to halt B.J. and turned to another director. "Carlton, at a billion, how long would it take us to amortize the cost of the Wennerstrom Process?"

"Three . . . three and a half years, Mr. Chairman. The way things are booming, perhaps even a little less—"

"Making it rather obvious that it is in the company's interest to bite this particular bullet now," said Maynard Chase.

Another director spoke up. "Mr. Chairman . . . a suggestion. It occurs to me that a settlement offer in installment payments, without interest, over a brief period, say, five years, might be attractive to the plaintiff, as well as to the plaintiff's attorneys. It could substantially reduce their respective income tax liabilities and easily save us several hundred million in interest."

"Good thinking, Harrison. I like that. We will leave the negotiations to O'Malley and Byers, of course, but I move now that we authorize a settlement not to exceed the following terms. . . ."

Everyone at the polished ebony table pulled his pad closer and started taking notes as the chairman stated the details.

Settlement negotiations dragged. O'Malley & Byers was mindful of its loss at the trial and hoped to salvage some face by negotiating the best settlement.

Charlie was ambivalent. He wanted to get his hands on the money and launch new projects. But he didn't want to feel as if he had caved in and let TOPCO walk over him all over again. An easy way out for him was simply to leave the decision to Mac while retaining veto power. Nels prudently divorced himself from the negotiations, relying on Mac's and Cornell Sepulveda Smith's judgment. Only Timothy Bradford pushed for settlement. He had already borrowed a half million dollars in commercial loans against his share of an impending settlement and was forced to renew every ninety days. The interest was eating him up.

O'Malley & Byers opened with $100 million. Mac laughed and refused to counteroffer. O'Malley & Byers upped the offer to $200 million. Mac laughed again, but offered to waive the accrued interest. When the offer got to $300 million, Mac stopped laughing, and agreed to forgive the $202,000 in plaintiff's court costs. When the $500 million offer was made, Mac counteroffered at $1 billion 150 million. At $700 million, Mac countered with $1 billion 50 million.

On June 27 *Wennerstrom v. TOPCO* was finally settled for $999 million, payable one-third down, with the balance payable in two equal annual installments, with no interest due on the unpaid balance.

TOPCO insisted, as a condition of the settlement, that the amount and terms be kept confidential. This enabled TOPCO to publicize afterward that although it had agreed to keep the amount of the settlement confidential, it could say that the amount paid was substantially less than one billion dollars.

On the morning after the settlement was announced, TOPCO's stock dropped only one-half point. By the end of the week TOPCO was selling for one-eighth more than it had been on the date of the settlement.

Charlie Wennerstrom was instantly worth almost $600,000,000 although he only had $199,760,000 in the bank.

Sorensen, Oliver, Bradford, and Smith's share of the first annual settlement installment was $133 million. It posted the largest annual gross of any law firm in history.

The first partners' meeting concerning distribution of the fee was as close as the four dignified senior partners had ever come to a brawl. Each partner's idea of how to deal with the money was regarded by at least two others as harebrained, although no one was impolite enough to say so.

After an hour and a half of bickering it was obvious the discussion was leading nowhere. Nels suggested that Cornell Sepulveda Smith be appointed to study the issues and report back with recommendations. "After all," argued Nels, "Cornell Sepulveda Smith is the only one here with any experience at dealing with such personal wealth. He is also the only one with any objectivity since he's the only one who doesn't need the money."

Timothy Bradford thought that Nels's last remark was debatable. Nels himself was already worth over six million. Nevertheless, everyone agreed that Nels's idea was sound. The burden was thrown on Cornell Sepulveda Smith.

At the next partners' meeting, three days later, Cornell Sepulveda Smith distributed copies of what he called the laundry list.

Although Cornell Sepulveda Smith's recommended distribution was admittedly arbitrary, it had two main virtues: It was simple, and it kept

CAPITAL IMPROVEMENTS (*see appendix*)			$ 1,270,000
CONTRIBUTION TO PENSION FUND			2,000,000
EMPLOYEES' BONUSES:			
14 associate attorneys	@ $50,000	$700,000	
21 secretaries	@ 20,000	420,000	
4 paralegals	@ 20,000	80,000	
2 investigators	@ 20,000	40,000	
1 office manager	@ 20,000	20,000	
1 bookkeeper	@ 20,000	20,000	
2 receptionists	@ 10,000	20,000	
3 clerks	@ 10,000	30,000	

TOTAL EMPLOYEES' BONUSES			$ 1,330,000

PARTNERS' DISTRIBUTION:			
4 senior partners	@ $32,000,000	$128,000,000	
4 junior partners	@ 100,000	400,000	

TOTAL PARTNERS' DISTRIBUTION			128,400,000

TOTAL DISTRIBUTION $133,000,000

the bulk of the fee among the senior partners. The laundry list was approved after remarkably little discussion.

"Thank heaven that's over," said Cornell Sepulveda Smith. "I do have another proposal regarding our beloved colleague MacDonald Abraham Oliver. I propose that we reinstate the six-month sabbatical which he so unselfishly forswore in order to take on the Wennerstrom case and which I submit he has nobly earned."

Mac was tempted to resist the suggestion politely, but it would have been transparently halfhearted. "Hell," he said, "I'll vote for that." So did everyone else.

Cornell Sepulveda Smith resumed. "Since the verdict was handed down six months or so ago, I've been anticipating a substantial settlement and have been working on tentative tax shelters. We still have the opportunity to avoid substantial income taxes this year. My recommendations are also in the appendix."

"Bless you," said Timothy Bradford, who hated paying his income tax only slightly less than paying his alimony.

The day employees' bonuses were distributed, morale at Sorensen, Oliver, Bradford, and Smith zoomed to approximately that of the Marine Corps at the commencement of World War II. For all but a few senior secretaries, the bonuses exceeded annual salaries. There was an epidemic of new clothes, jewelry, and cars. In spite of the anticipated next two years' bonuses, one receptionist declared that she'd never seen so much money in one place in her life and left to spend the year on Maui. One associate attorney also resigned to open his own practice. One secretary quit in protest. She thought a fair bonus would have been at least one million dollars per employee. She reluctantly accepted her twenty thousand dollars, however, and vowed to use it to finance an unfair labor practice suit against the firm. She was never heard of again.

Charlie Wennerstrom insisted on throwing a dinner party on the next Saturday night. The Grand Ballroom of the Century Plaza Hotel was available on short notice for a tall price. The banquet chef recommended a choice of steak or chicken breast, an easily managed and profitable combination. Charlie would have none of such plebeian fare. Finally unfettered by budgetary restraints, Charlie's salivary glands boldly dictated their lavish choices. The planned gastronomic onslaught included such exotica as a Tarama Brandade and Turkey Orloff. While the hotel assistant manager, who had an accountancy background, beamed and rubbed his hands, the chef balked at the enormousness of the enterprise. Charlie insisted on his menu but accepted the compromise of a buffet serving table, thus bringing the exercise within the capability of the hotel staff.

On Saturday evening Charlie, hugely resplendent in a new beige linen suit, flushed and ebullient, warmly greeting everyone whether he knew that person or not, stood at the ballroom entrance. Laura circulated among the guests, introducing the Wennerstrom friends to the Sorensen, Oliver, Bradford, and Smith staffers. Charlie guided each new arrival to one of the two bars set up just inside the entrance, managing to get his own glass continuously filled in the process.

Dinner was a great success. Although half the food was unfamiliar to three-quarters of the guests, no one's appetite seemed to be impaired. Charlie lumbered among the tables, explaining the origin and preparation of the dishes and demonstrating how each should be eaten. As host Charlie also bore the responsibility of ensuring that no bad wine passed any guest's lips. Charlie fulfilled this task nobly by continuously sampling the bottles as he weaved about the room.

Charlie offered toasts to MacDonald Abraham Oliver, to Sorensen, Oliver, Bradford, and Smith, and to the American jury system. Laura had somehow located a small orchestra that could play anything. Charlie tried to dance with every girl in the place. Perhaps he did. No one counted.

Mac tried one dance with Laura but made a feeble excuse to cut it short. She made him uncomfortable as hell.

Charlie smothered Mac and Mary Kathryn in his arms while he explained his plans for deriving synthetic fuel from horse manure. Mac suggested that if they had enough horses to furnish the manure, they wouldn't need the fuel. Unabashed, Charlie bored them close to sobriety with a brilliant elucidation of his concept for freeing hydrogen fuel from seawater, through electrolysis powered by tidal action.

It was a happy, exhausted semibillionaire whom Laura and the doorman finally coerced into a taxi at one-thirty on Sunday morning. "Do you realize what that cost?" asked Laura as the cab headed for the Los Feliz district.

"Less than half your new Mercedes," replied Charlie.

"What new Mercedes? Charlie Wennerstrom, you are drunk."

"Irrelevant and immaterial, Your Honor. Thousands of people are drunk. Do I do that well?"

With the cabdriver's help, Laura coaxed Charlie into bed. Charlie was instantly out cold. He began snoring magnificently as Laura closed his bedroom door.

At 3:40 A.M. the noise awakened Laura. She had been dreaming something about white horses. Laura could not immediately identify the noise. Then she realized it was Charlie and dashed into his bedroom. Charlie was sitting upright, sweating profusely, eyes bulging, inhaling deeply. He seemed to be pointing to his chest as he gasped. Laura could make out "can't . . . my . . . air."

Indigestion or heart attack. Better treat it as a heart attack. Charlie, don't you die, don't you die on me now. We are just coming to the good part.

By 4:15 A.M. Laura was in the Los Angeles County General corridor waiting for the doctor to come out. Her efforts at CPR had failed, as had the heroic measures of the paramedics.

"Miss Wennerstrom, I'm sorry. We tried everything. He's gone." Laura nodded her head. She already knew that.

By 7:30 A.M. Laura had been back in the house, sitting on the edge of Charlie's old bed for the past two hours. Not moving, just sitting.

Before Mac answered his telephone he knew it would be bad. No one called with good news at seven forty-five on Sunday morning.

When Mac hung up, Mary Kathryn spoke. "What is it?" Mac told her. Mary Kathryn sat up. "Mac," she asked, "have you been fucking that girl?" Mac just stared back. He hurriedly dressed. As Mac left the house, he passed Tracy's room. She was sitting up in bed, watching *Sunday Morning.*

As Mac walked up the driveway toward Laura's front door, an obviously brand-new silver Mercedes 500 SL hauling a three-wheel motorcycle screeched to a halt behind his BMW. "Hey, mister," the teenaged driver yelled, "is this the Wennerstrom house? I'm delivering this here machine to Laura Wennerstrom." He held up the Mercedes keys.

Mac peeled off a ten-dollar bill and handed it to the boy. "Thanks. I'll see that she gets it."

"Thanks, mister. It's awesome wheels. Ought to make her day."

10

*I*t is a temptation to say that Grant Radcliffe was obsessed by Mac-Donald Oliver, but that may be exaggeration. Grant Radcliffe's mind was not completely dominated by the idea of vengeance on MacDonald Oliver. Radcliffe worked long, hard hours at TOPCO and did his job superbly. He devoted himself assiduously to the needs and desires of his wife, Sarah. The existence of MacDonald Abraham Oliver, however, did haunt Radcliffe. He devoted substantial sums of money, mostly TOPCO's, and spare time to the pursuit of knowledge of MacDonald Oliver. Oliver's dossier grew fat and worn while the subject himself remained lean and healthy. Just like the picture of Dorian Gray, thought Radcliffe.

MacDonald Oliver became a sort of perversely pleasant hobby for Radcliffe. Radcliffe enjoyed adding each new morsel to the dossier and fantasizing his vengeance. Oliver would be humiliated and hurt badly:

Oliver strapped to an operating table while Radcliffe fondled the surgical tools; Oliver gagged and chained to the bedroom wall while Radcliffe raped Mary Kathryn and then Tracy. What pleasant, satisfying distraction. Something would show up, Radcliffe was sure. He was young. So was Oliver. There was time. Revenge is a dish best tasted cold.

Despite Radcliffe's fears, TOPCO had not been devastated by the disclosure of the TOPCO-Rutherford tie or by the billion-dollar judgment. It had been only momentarily staggered. Indeed, upon news of the settlement TOPCO stock had flourished.

For a while Radcliffe sweated, but no lightning bolt from the boardroom struck him. Yesterday Maynard Chase passed in the corridor and only nodded imperiously, but that was normal. At today's luncheon conference with Pearson, the president, and Gilbert, the operations vice-president, Danning Pearson told Radcliffe the dirtiest joke he had ever heard and then went on to talk of nothing but the projected profits from the Wennerstrom Process. Gilbert had invited him to join a golf foursome next weekend. Sarah apparently did not consider him a loser. Radcliffe gradually relaxed but remained wary. A plague could have a long incubation period.

None of this diminished Radcliffe's dedication to vengeance. Perhaps it was just that he hated to be shown up, made into a public liar. That was contrary to his image. Besides, Oliver had beaten him twice: first, in unraveling the fraud Radcliffe had considered foolproof and, again, in rescuing Harold Rifkin from the man's clutches.

Radcliffe convinced himself that getting MacDonald Oliver would somehow restore his own credibility and status.

Radcliffe left Oliver buried in the hot desert sand with only his head exposed. He reached for the buckets of honey and ants as he reluctantly closed Mac's file and prepared for a meeting with the operations vice-president.

Mac wanted the family to spend his sabbatical cruising *Abigail* down the Pacific coast to Costa Rica, then through the Panama Canal to San Blas. Mary Kathryn and Tracy voted for England and the Continent. Mac was determined to have his way.

After his return from Europe Mac's life took on a fairy-tale-like quality. He returned to work, and events occurred, presumably of significance but not seeming to have anything to do with him. He felt insulated from reality—at least, everyone else's reality.

He found himself happy to be back at work. He had truly enjoyed the time with Tracy, but six months spent constantly with Mary Kathryn had been a strain. He hoped never to see the interior of another boutique. He felt grateful that at least he hadn't persuaded Mary Kathryn to cruise *Abigail*. Six months with her aboard the sailboat would have driven him overboard.

Time magazine did a feature article on Mac, in which he appeared as a cross between Robin Hood and the Messiah. Mac was in constant demand as a lecturer. His favorite theme was that a fair trial ought to be the minimum standard, not the final goal. Obtaining the right result ought to be at least as important as compliance with the ritual.

Mac's share of the second annual installment of the Wennerstrom fee almost doubled his net worth. Mac's accountants instituted an investment program designed to nurture Mac and his descendants for generations.

Mary Kathryn found them a new Bel Air house, larger than the old one, but still considerably smaller than Buckingham Palace.

Mac adamantly rejected the suggestion of a chauffeured Rolls-Royce. Mary Kathryn graciously compromised on a new Mercedes 380 SEC. She insisted, however, on custom pearlescent white paint.

Marla Zimmerman married an orthopedic surgeon but kept her name. Her wedding present from the firm was a promotion to junior partner.

Jonathan Clark successfully defended a class-action suit that threatened to bankrupt the state's electric utility companies.

Cornell Sepulveda Smith donated his share of the Wennerstrom fee to charity—anonymously.

Nels Sorensen was elected president of the state bar association.

Judge Johannsen decided to take early retirement and returned eight weeks later, as judge pro tem in his old department.

Laura Wennerstrom became president of the Charles Wennerstrom Foundation, which devoted its considerable resources to alternate en-

ergy research. Mac helped her set it up. Although Mac attracted her
with what she perceived to be his animallike quality, she found him
easy to resist. The man was too tough and amoral for her taste. Laura
could hold out for a warm, caring man like Charlie. Anyway, Mac
seemed complacent in his relationship with Mary Kathryn. Laura did
not relish the role of the other woman. Mac, in turn, respected the
intensity with which Laura seemed to care about everything and everybody, although that often made dealing with her difficult. He secretly
admired her strong good looks but had no intention of churning up his
well-ordered life.

Clarence McGovern unsuccessfully sued Wennerstrom's estate for
one million dollars in alleged unpaid attorney's fees. McGovern subsequently went bald and was appointed to the municipal court. He
spent the rest of his life trying traffic cases and attempting to regrow hair.

Mac thought his achievement of the year was probably when he
placed fourteenth out of 375 in a ten-kilometer race.

Life continued to pass in living color, but it was all pastels.

Since Mac's return from his sabbatical he had tried eight uninspiring
cases, won six, lost one (but lost it well), and settled one during trial.
During the same period Mac settled twenty-seven cases out of court,
including the case of *Cal Coastal Savings & Loan Association* v. *Bulles
et al.* Seymour Bulles was a former employee of the savings and loan
association, in charge of completing and renovating its foreclosed prop-
erties, dealing with a number of building contractors and laborers. The
savings and loan association had charged Seymour Bulles with receiving
kickbacks from contractors.

Bulles had pleaded nolo contendere to a charge of grand theft and
been placed on probation. After firing Bulles, Cal Coastal filed a civil
suit against him to recover the kickbacks.

Mac was pressured into taking the case by Nels Sorensen, who wanted
to please another client, who was convinced that Seymour Bulles was
simply nominated scapegoat because the Federal Home Loan Bank
examiners were getting too close to the major culprits.

Mac had been repulsed by Seymour Bulles since their first meeting
and wanted at least to slough the case off on an associate attorney. But

the valuable client insisted that Bulles needed the best, so Mac had capitulated.

Mac thought of Seymour Bulles as greasy. It wasn't his appearance so much as his manner, although Bulles's straight, black, Vitalis-enriched hair did qualify for Mac's adjective. He managed to look Mac straight in the eye only when he was lying. Seymour Bulles, of course, denied that he had received any kickbacks. But Mac's investigation persuaded him that Bulles had indeed received some money. Mac doubted that the sum even approached the $120,000 Bulles was being sued for. Bulles claimed that he had pleaded nolo contendere without realizing that it was tantamount to a guilty plea. His former attorney had assured him that he would receive probation and that would be the end of it.

Mac filed a tactical countersuit on behalf of Bulles against Cal Coastal Savings & Loan Association for $120,000 damages for unfair employment practices, hoping that it would become such a nuisance that Cal Coastal would be motivated to settle for mutual dismissals of its case and Bulles's counteraction. Mac's hopes were realized. The case was settled on precisely that basis. Nels Sorensen, the valuable client, MacDonald Oliver, and Cal Coastal were satisfied. Seymour Bulles was not. He had grudgingly signed the release only when Mac proposed that Bulles find another lawyer. Bulles had become so enamored of the allegations in the cross complaint claiming violation of his civil rights that he convinced himself it was all true. Bulles had himself believing that Cal Coastal owed him at least one hundred thousand dollars, and he went around loudly proclaiming so. Not many people listened—but one did.

She decided it would be best if she called her boyfriend first. She didn't have a pimp—only an answering service. She was even exempt from the graft because her boyfriend was Detective Sergeant James Norelli of the Las Vegas Police Department.

"James, honey, it's me. I'm at work."

"Jesus, Amy, I know it's you. Who else sounds like Betty Boop on the telephone?" Amy wasn't really her name. The six-foot-one-inch, green-eyed, possibly blond giantess had been christened Ingrid twenty-four years ago. Amazon was her nickname, from which etymologically evolved Amy. Amy had been in the Dunes chorus line until spraining her ankle eighteen months ago. A doctor told her to stay off her feet, and she had been following his advice ever since.

"Honey, this john, Harold—Harold, that's his real name—he just quit on me."

"What do you mean, quit on me? He lost his hard-on?"

"No, honey. I mean, he's dead. He just stopped breathing. Sudden-like. What do I do?"

"Are you sure? . . . Oh, shit. I guess you are as expert as they come on whether a body is alive. Call the assistant manager. Tell him what happened. Tell him your name. He owes me one. He'll report an anonymous call and say that he found the body. You get the hell out of there."

Amy slipped out of her pink baby-doll shortie, which covered her to below her waist if she hunched her shoulders, and affectionately folded it into her purse. The nightie was the cherished memento of a heavenly six weeks with a Frederick's salesman. From the purse Amy extracted panties, a red minisheath, and sandals. She gave her hair a cursory brush, called the assistant manager, extracted all the cash except one hundred dollars from the john's wallet, gave the late Harold Rifkin a kiss on the forehead, and closed the hotel room door behind her.

After having the hotel doctor confirm that Harold Rifkin was indeed deceased, the assistant manager reported the death to the Las Vegas Police Department. "Yeah. Harold Rifkin on his registration card and in his wallet. Fifty bucks cash on him. Santa Monica address. Our doc says his heart just stopped. Harmless little old guy. Been here for months. Only weird thing about him was every month he would change to a more expensive suite. He's in twelve-twenty. Yeah, Presidential Suite number four—the one with the round bed, with the mirror in the canopy."

Mac got the call from the Las Vegas assistant medical examiner.

"Yes, sir. I found your business card in his wallet. I didn't find any names of relatives. Just credit cards, no cash. I thought you might be his lawyer."

"Yes, I guess I am." Just like the good old days, thought Mac. Bring

in the casualties. Body count, two. Charlie, now Harold. All I'm missing are body bags. Mac gave directions for returning the body and asked
about the details of Harold's death.

The assistant ME was a literal and mundane man. He answered
explicitly. "I autopsied him myself. Old Harold had a tumor in the
occipital lobe about the size of a stunted grapefruit. Probably malignant. Don't have the biopsy yet. I know he had just ejaculated, then
apparently just switched off. Sudden-death syndrome. Not unusual.
Interesting thing. You know he had the biggest shit-eating grin on his
face you've ever seen? . . . Sure, you're welcome."

Mac called Marla Zimmerman into his office. "Harold Rifkin died
yesterday in Las Vegas," he announced.

"How?" asked Marla.

Mac looked Marla Zimmerman over. He decided she was mature
enough. Mac sighed. "Marla, apparently Harold died suddenly upon
climaxing, while humping a Las Vegas pro. He is reported to have
passed on with a very large grin on his face."

"Way to go, Harold," said Marla.

11

*M*acDonald Oliver was just completing his first year of law school when Grant Radcliffe wed Sarah.

Radcliffe's motives for courting Sarah Channing Chase were not in the least obscure. He simply wanted money, power, and social position. He had assigned no order of importance to these objectives. Radcliffe was convinced that the route to his goal was via the right marriage, but he had learned well from previous failed attempts, including his literally abortive collegiate effort with the Du Pont girl. He knew that the marriage per se would not accomplish what he needed. He was hundreds of years too late for the benefits of dowry. The money from which flowed power and position would continue to be controlled by his wife. Long-term nurturing of her trust and confidence would be required before his hands would be permitted even to touch those reins. Radcliffe considered himself a good actor, but he did not believe he could sustain a lifetime of being onstage. He knew it was essential that his attention to his bride be genuine.

The only serendipitous thing about Grant Radcliffe's meeting Sarah was the manner of their initial contact. Grant Radcliffe was saved the effort of contriving a meeting when Sarah was chosen to present the TOPCO Annual Young Executive Achievement Award to Radcliffe for his structuring of a complex real estate exchange leaseback, which grossed the company a ten-million-dollar profit, financed entirely by Small Business Administration loans to TOPCO subsidiaries. Radcliffe had never seen Sarah Channing Chase before that evening, although she was on his prospects list. The physical attraction was immediate and mutual. Sarah Channing Chase was pretty in a delicate, quiet way, although cruel objectivity might have labeled her "mousy." She was small and frail, and her fine hair was blonder than Radcliffe's. Like Radcliffe's, her eyes were blue; his were pale, but Sarah's were a startling electric shade. Her eyes might have belied her timid, childlike appearance except that they were usually hidden behind large silver-framed glasses. Sarah, unfortunately, had difficulty tolerating her contact lenses.

Sarah thought Grant Radcliffe was Adonis. Never before had she met a heterosexual male as beautiful. After dinner they strolled along the terrace of the Bel Air Hotel and discovered other attractions. Radcliffe's candid disclosure of his aspirations charmed Sarah. "You've practically admitted that you're after my money," teased Sarah.

"Yes, but I'll triple your capital within three years," said Grant.

Sarah Channing Chase's little-girl looks were misleading. More than one astute old friend of the family had observed that the brains had skipped a generation, descending directly from her grandfather to Sarah. Sarah fully understood the significance of being the only heir of the only heir of the man who controlled Titan Overland Petroleum Company. She even knew that Grant Radcliffe was a species of predator. Sarah was taken with, but not taken in by, Grant. Sarah had already concluded that her enormous potential wealth would color her every relationship. Grant Radcliffe's obvious ambitions were at least balanced by a willingness to work, a competent mind, a certain charm, and fantastic good looks. She knew that Grant's affection for her was real. She supposed that it could even be said that within his limited capacity, Grant loved her, just as he said he did. Her parents would approve of Radcliffe's ancestors and alma mater. Her grandfather would be pleased that Radcliffe had already made substantial progress within the company entirely on his own merit. Besides, the baby would be beautiful. Sarah Channing Chase allowed herself to fall in love.

The engagement was brief. The wedding was magnificent. Governor Reagan, both senators and twelve hundred other beautiful guests jammed Trinity Episcopal Church. The *Los Angeles Times*, only after careful investigation of the facts, reported that the value of the jewelry worn was incalculable. The only Rolls-Royce to Rolls-Royce collision ever recorded in the history of Los Angeles County occurred in the parking lot.

The engagement reminded Maynard Chase that the only other person that he gave a damn about was his granddaughter; Chase had long ago accepted that his son's greatest accomplishment would be to avoid being an embarrassment. Maynard Chase immediately ordered a discreet investigation of his future grandson-in-law. Previously Grant Radcliffe's existence had received only cursory acknowledgment by the chairman. At the TOPCO Towers Chase and Radcliffe were separated by four floors and six intervening levels of command. The report led the chairman to the same conclusions about Radcliffe that Sarah had already reached. Maynard Chase gave the union a conditional blessing, as reflected in the manner of his wedding gift: a small Tudor house on two ridiculously expensive Beverly Hills acres. The deed recited that the property was conveyed to "Sarah Channing Chase, a married woman, as her sole and separate property."

Sarah's parents gave the couple a honeymoon trip to Europe and one hundred thousand dollars with which to redecorate and furnish the modest home. The swimming pool was less than Olympic size.

In 1970, one year after the wedding, their daughter was born. Everyone who had known Sarah as a child confirmed that the infant looked exactly like her mother. Sarah wanted to name the girl after her grandfather. The best she could manage was May Anne. Although

Grant couldn't decide whether it sounded more like a mantra or an extinct Indian tribe, he acceded gracefully. Grant would have agreed to anything that tended to please the chairman.

During the last few months of Sarah's pregnancy unseasonably warm weather increased her discomfort. Sarah took to spending cooling half weeks at her parents' Lake Arrowhead house, six thousand feet up in the San Bernardino Mountains. During Sarah's absences an almost forgotten restlessness returned to prod Grant Radcliffe. Radcliffe acknowledged its presence as he looked up the neglected telephone number.

"Ah, Mr. Radcliffe, so nice to hear from you." It was a rich, earthy female voice. "We had almost given you up. It's been over a year."

"I've been . . . otherwise occupied."

"So I've read. Congratulations on your marriage. May we be of service, Mr. Radcliffe?"

"Yes—but younger," said Radcliffe.

"Yes. We have a lovely, fresh twelve. Will that do?"

"Nicely. Is one hour convenient?"

After saying good-bye, the lady of the rich, earthy voice turned to her brood. "Trix?" she asked. "How old are you?"

"You know, Mrs. M. I'm almost sixteen."

"Well, start dressing down. In one hour you will be a virginal twelve-year-old again."

"But, ma'am, I wasn't then either."

An hour later the statuesque Mrs. M's high heels clicked loudly on polished Spanish tiles as she hurried forward to greet Radcliffe.

"Welcome back to Casa Folatre, Mr. Radcliffe. You're looking splendid. Would you care for something to drink?"

"Perhaps afterward. I—"

"Of course. Virginia is expecting you in number two."

Grant took the oversize brass key as it was offered and started up the stairway.

"Oh, Mr. Radcliffe," Mrs. M called, "please be patient with the child. She is quite inexperienced."

Grant Radcliffe knocked and entered room number two. Trix, alias Virginia, was seated cross-legged on the floor at the foot of the white-

and-pink-covered canopy bed. On the floor before her was a large volume open to a color photograph of a pony standing in a field of wildflowers. The small pale girl wore a white cotton blouse with a Peter Pan collar under her tartan jumper. The pink of her dimpled knees peeked through the space between her skirt and her immaculate white knee socks. Radcliffe could see his reflection in her black patent-leather T-strapped shoes. Her blue eyes twinkled, her blond beribboned pony-tail bounced as she looked up and smiled shyly.

"Oh, Daddy, I've missed you so," she said.

The worst that could be said of Sarah Channing Chase Radcliffe's parents was that they were shallow, parasitic alcoholics. The best that could be said was that they were otherwise harmless.

Maynard Chase's son, William, had earned the nickname Wild at Princeton in honor of his eluding two black-and-white patrol cars after a twelve-mile pursuit. William had done nothing quite as successfully since. By the time William was forty, Maynard Chase had surrendered all his expectations for William and turned his aspirations toward his granddaughter.

Sarah's mother, Arlene, had her own money from an inherited fortune built upon the manufacture of countless cardboard boxes. Arlene's interests centered on vodka and waterskiing, an unlikely combination, which she managed brilliantly.

Having a generous ration of leisure, William and Arlene spent substantial quantities of it at the Radcliffe residence, admiring their granddaughter and draining the liquor stock. William and Arlene were consistently dull but usually not obnoxious. Grant didn't mind too much, although they reminded him more than he liked of his own parents. Occasionally William would annoy Grant with an unwitty, acid remark disparaging Radcliffe's determined climb up the corporate ladder. Sarah was always there to smooth it over.

Actually Grant Radcliffe's climb was proceeding at a pace that most men would have found acceptable. A year after May Anne's birth, Grant had been promoted to assistant vice-president, real estate and development division. But Grant was not content. Although Chase and

Radcliffe remained corporate light-years apart, Grant's marriage brought him into frequent social contact with the chairman. Chase was as pleasant to Radcliffe as he was to anyone, except his adored Sarah. Radcliffe realized that so long as he kept his nose clean and produced, he would never have to worry about paying the swimming pool maintenance bills. But the aura of power surrounding the old man intoxicated Radcliffe and fed his impatience to own it for himself.

Maynard Chase was a vital man, but he was by then already seventy-three. Radcliffe worried about the possibility of Wild Chase's surviving the old man. If William inherited first, by the time the stock became Sarah's, Grant Radcliffe's chance at control would have long since been grabbed by others. Grant Radcliffe would then become a well-kept perpetual second-level executive. And what about Arlene? If William inherited the chairman's stock, he would probably leave it to Sarah's mother. That could postpone Sarah's acquisition for additional years. If William Chase inherited the chairman's TOPCO stock, Radcliffe could himself be an old man before it ever passed to Sarah. No—*if* it passed on to Sarah. William Chase was fully capable of wasting the entire fortune.

If only Sarah were directly in line to succeed to Maynard Chase's fortune, Radcliffe would have a chance at the brass ring. Within a few more years Radcliffe could hope to be promoted to a viable position from which he might make a successful play for control, upon the chairman's demise—if Sarah inherited the stock.

If only those two old rummies would drink themselves to death, thought Radcliffe. If only they were dead.

Grant Radcliffe toyed with the idea for a year: William and Arlene clutching their throats, convulsing after he had poisoned their ice cubes. William and Arlene on their way back from Lake Arrowhead, their Bentley careening out of control down the mountain road, flying over a cliff after Radcliffe had cut the brake line.

Arrowhead was the key. It took awhile to see it. It was so damned simple.

The Alps-like mountain village of Lake Arrowhead is only seventy miles from the center of subtropical Los Angeles. Winter snows and cool summer breezes make the lake an attractive haven for Angelenos who can afford it. Elegant homes with private docks line the lakeshore.

Arlene Chase had modeled their north shore house after her conception of a Swiss chalet. The place bore a strong resemblance to nineteenth-century illustrations depicting the witch's house in "Hansel and Gretel." The pink-and-blue sign hanging from the front lamppost read "Chalet Chase." A classic ChrisCraft runabout was tied up at the private dock. The old speedboat, decked in mahogany, teak, and holly, glistened under twelve coats of rubbed spar varnish. During the summer the craft was in constant use as Arlene's ski boat or as a commuter to friends' docks or the village market.

During the summer of May Anne's fourth year Grant, Sarah, and the girl spent frequent weekends at Chalet Chase. The child possessed a morose nature. At home she seldom talked unless spoken to, but she was somehow happier in the mountains. On the ski boat she could sometimes be induced even to smile. Sarah had taken May Anne to several Beverly Hills physicians and an eminent child psychologist. All had assured Sarah that the child was healthy and normal in every respect and could be expected to outgrow the phase.

At the chalet William and Arlene drank vodka, water-skied, and went to parties. Sarah looked after May Anne. Grant was not much attracted to the water. He spent his time on the deck overlooking the lake, going through reports or dictating notes.

Grant continued his fantasies concerning disposal of William and Arlene. It was nothing personal. They were simply in his way. The chairman was getting dangerously older; he was now seventy-five. It wasn't so much revulsion at committing murder that restrained Radcliffe. William and Arlene were merely obstacles. Radcliffe hesitated only because of the risk. Life imprisonment was even more distasteful than perpetual middle executiveship.

One afternoon Grant Radcliffe waved as he watched the rumbling ChrisCraft approach the dock. Carefully maintaining his priorities, William first lifted the case of vodka out of the boat, then assisted Arlene, Sarah, and May Anne. Grant thought the resemblance between Sarah and May Anne was becoming striking.

"Hey, Grant," William yelled from the dock, "still sucking up to my old man? I'll fix you something to take the taste out of your mouth as soon as I get in."

You drunken son of a bitch, Grant Radcliffe thought. I can get rid of you anytime I choose.

A few minutes later William Chase walked onto the deck, bearing tall vodka and tonics. "Here," William said. "This is sweeter than my father's ass." Grant Radcliffe accepted the drink and said nothing. "We are all invited to the Hamiltons' for dinner," said William. "The man's got chilled Russian vodka. Want to come?"

Before Grant could think of an excuse, Sarah came out. "I can't go," she said. "There's no one to sit with May Anne."

"I'll stay home with you two," said Grant gratefully.

An hour later William looked quite distinguished and almost steady as he came down to the living room wearing a powder blue dinner jacket and another drink. Arlene was already at the bar, fixing two more.

"Shall we cruise over to the Hamiltons', my dear?" asked William.

"Daddy, do you think you're able?" asked Sarah, throwing a glance at Grant.

"I'll be happy to drive you both over if you're not embarrassed to arrive by automobile," said Grant.

"Nonsense. Must go down to the shee in sips. Continue your labors, m'boy. Someday you may be chief ass kisser."

Asshole, thought Grant Radcliffe, as he mentally added another ounce to William's drink. Your funeral. He said, "Don't forget to switch on the blower before you start the engine on that bomb."

"For those of you who are already unaware, I've run that boat for sixteen years—"

"Daddy, Grant's right," said Sarah. "You always forget when you've had too much. Someday—"

"Kaboom," said Arlene, as though blowing up would be great fun.

Grant watched from the dock as William and Arlene climbed, with remarkable steadiness, into the cockpit of the ChrisCraft. A few seconds later the big V8 roared to life and the boat catapulted from the dock.

"They're indestructible," said Sarah.

"Mmmmmm," said Grant as he mixed himself another.

After dinner and after May Anne had been put to bed, Grant excused himself. "Sarah, I've got to run over to Bill Murphy's for a few minutes. I promised I'd give him a copy of my Signal Hill field report tonight."

Radcliffe drove his new 1975 black Cadillac Seville around the north shore of the lake to the Hamiltons' mansion, one of the oldest and largest houses on the lake. He pulled into their parking compound, between two other Cadillacs. I'm glad I bought a black one, he thought· it practically guarantees anonymity. He walked around to the dock. He could see it clearly in the moonlight. There was no one there. The ChrisCraft was tied up alongside several other powerboats. Grant slipped into the ChrisCraft and opened the engine cover. He turned the thumb-screw on the fuel filter and drained about a half gallon of gasoline into the bilge. He pulled one spark plug lead loose from the engine and let it dangle. He closed the engine cover, walked back to his car certain that no one had seen him, and drove back to Chalet Chase.

"Hi," said Sarah. "How are Bill and Ann?"

"Fine, I just caught them. Bill's on his way to San Francisco for the TOPCO-Exxon meeting." Perhaps, he thought, I should have actually stopped by the Murphys'.

The explosion awakened Grant and Sarah about 1:00 A.M. May Anne came flying into Sarah's arms, terrified. They could see the flames from the bedroom window.

"It's a boat," said Grant, "somewhere near the Hamilton dock."

"Oh, God," said Sarah.

The telephone call came twenty minutes later. Sarah took it, which saved Grant the effort of attempting an Oscar-winning performance. He did his best to console Sarah. She was nearly hysterical. He felt genuinely bad. It really hurt him to see Sarah made to suffer so. Damn William and Arlene. Why did they always have to be such a nuisance?

The San Bernardino County deputy sheriff did not come until eight-fifteen. By then Sarah was puffy and red-eyed but under control. Sergeant Lefkowitz offered his condolences. "I'm terribly sorry, ma'am. Apparently it was just a stupid boat accident. We get about one a season. If people would only learn . . ."

"My husband warned them to use the blower. Daddy always forgot when he drank."

"Exactly," said the sergeant.

"My husband even offered to drive them. If only they had listened," said Sarah.

"Yes, ma'am," said Sergeant Lefkowitz.

"Were they—did they—"

"Ma'am, your father was killed instantly. A piece of linkage rod through the chest. Your mother was thrown clear but drowned. We know she was a good swimmer, so I am sure she must have been rendered unconscious and never felt no pain. . . ." Sergeant Lefkowitz refrained from mentioning that Arlene's blood sample had revealed a blood alcohol level of such magnitude that no one in the medical examiner's office could figure how she'd made it out to the boat. "The boat, of course, was destroyed."

Sarah broke out sobbing again. May Anne soon joined in. Grant felt so sorry for them both. He was able to persuade the village pharmacist to sell him a strong sedative without a prescription. He got Sarah and May Anne to bed just before the next telephone call came.

"Mr. Radcliffe, this is Dave. I work over at the Hamiltons'. I'll be on the road in front of the chalet in ten minutes. I want to talk to you."

Radcliffe remembered seeing the clean-cut young man around the Hamilton place. There was something in his tone that made Radcliffe agree without hesitation. "I'll be there."

The boy was waiting in the Hamiltons' jeep. "Mr. Radcliffe, the cops came around to see me this morning. They asked a lot of questions. I told them I didn't see anyone on the dock last night. . . ." The boy hesitated.

"And?"

"And I'm going back to Montana next week to finish school. . . ."

Radcliffe's pale blue eyes stared. "And?"

"And it's pretty expensive." The boy took a deep breath. "And I was thinking about a scholarship. You know, kind of in memory of your in-laws."

Radcliffe blinked once. "I see. Would a five-hundred-dollar donation help?"

The boy tried not to swallow. "Actually, sir, I was thinking more of ten thousand dollars."

They settled on five thousand dollars, payable in cash the next morning. Grant didn't have five thousand. Every penny of his substantial salary went for substantial living expenses.

When Sarah awakened, Grant asked for the money. "Sarah, honey, this is a hell of a time to bring it up, but last night was so horrible I just forgot, and it won't wait. Last night Bill Murphy asked if he could borrow five thousand dollars. He wrote some bad checks up here yesterday to pay off his poker losings. I told him I would make a deposit to his bank account today, but I just realized I don't have it. Could you—"

"Of course, dear. I'll make a check out to Bill immediately."

There was no time for subtlety. Grant forged Murphy's endorsement and deposited the check to his own account at the village bank. Sarah never glanced at her canceled checks. Simultaneously Grant withdrew five thousand dollars cash.

He met Dave Smith as agreed the next morning. "There are several things to make clear before I hand over the money. I don't know what you think you saw, but it's important to me not to be involved in scandal. You have given the police false evidence and obstructed an official investigation. Both are felonies. When I hand over this envelope, you will also have committed extortion." Grant wasn't sure he had it precisely right, but it was close enough to be effective. "The last and most important thing is that you agree that this is a one-time payment—once only."

"Yes, of course," said the boy, suppressing a grin as he reached for the money.

"Not quite yet. I want you to know that if you ever approach me or my family again, I will kill you without a second thought." Radcliffe's eyes were ice cold. "Do you believe that?"

As Dave looked at those eyes, he believed it. Radcliffe had already proved he was capable.

12

*A*lmost immediately after what Grant had come to refer to as the "unfortunate accident," Grant Radcliffe's fortunes improved. Could it be, Grant Radcliffe wondered, that God helps those who help themselves?

Sarah, of course, inherited both her parents' property: the Beverly Hills mansion, the Lake Arrowhead chalet, an important block of TOPCO stock, an impressive portfolio of other securities, furniture, art, jewelry, automobiles, cash. Even after taxes, Sarah Channing Chase Radcliffe became an extremely wealthy person. Not only was Sarah now an important TOPCO shareholder, but she was also heir apparent to her grandfather's stock and fortune.

Grant never knew whether his promotion was influenced by Sarah's new position or his own merit. Either way his advancement to vice-president for real estate and development was satisfying progress. Grant grew even more caring and supportive of Sarah. It was not just that she held the key to his objective. He liked her style and was pleased with her retaining a childlike appearance. When Sarah was out of town, there were still occasional visits to Casa Folatre, but Grant's ardor for his wife was not diminished. He could talk to her, too, about his work. He was proud that the chairman often consulted Sarah on TOPCO policy. Although Sarah held no official company position, Maynard Chase respected her judgment and placed unconditional trust in her loyalty. Maynard Chase kept an eye on Grant Radcliffe. Grant kept watch on the chairman.

Sarah never mistook Grant's feelings for anything deeper or more complex than they actually were. She respected Grant's devotion to his work. She still adored making love to him, and she grew ever more comfortable with him.

The only ripple in the Radcliffe pool of tranquillity was May Anne. The child did well in her studies and was in no way troublesome. It was just that she remained so remarkably quiet and aloof, as if enveloped by some great sadness. The closest Sarah ever came to nagging was her frequent urging that Grant spend more time with the child. May Anne had never responded to Sarah's advances. Sarah hoped that perhaps Grant could talk to her, teach her, somehow reach her. But Grant usually begged off. He did not have the time. He was not a child psychologist. The child would grow up to be fine. She had everything, didn't she?

When Grant Radcliffe acquired the Wennerstrom Process, Maynard Chase was mightily, although privately, impressed. The old man instantly recognized the enormous profit-making potential of shale oil production.

It was during the *Wennerstrom v. TOPCO* trial that calamity descended upon the Radcliffes. Sarah had been in Edmonton, Alberta, on a goodwill mission. Grant called to say that May Anne was ill and hospitalized. Her life was not in danger; everything was being done. That was all he would tell her. She would have to see for herself. Upon receiving Grant's call, Sarah commandeered the TOPCO Gulfstream III jet and returned immediately.

Santa Monica Airport was the closest, but it had a 10:00 P.M. noise curfew. The Gulfstream captain wangled a special dispensation on the grounds of medical emergency. The state-of-the-art jet had made the fourteen-hundred-mile flight in two hours and twenty minutes.

Grant was waiting on the apron with the new red Mercedes 380 SEL. Sarah jumped in, and Grant wheeled the sedan through the gate.

"Grant, tell me, please—"

"Well, she's all right—I don't mean she's all right—I mean, she's not in danger. . . . They don't know—I mean, they haven't diagnosed her—" Grant was fumbling. "You'll just have to see for yourself. We're almost there."

Grant swung the Mercedes west on Montana Boulevard and cut north to Sunset Boulevard. Sarah was confused by the change in direction. "Isn't she at St. John's? I assumed she was when you said to come into Santa Monica Airport."

"No, dear. Here we are." Grant turned into the spacious driveway. The stone columns supporting the ornamental wrought-iron gates each bore identical brass plaques: BRENTWOOD PSYCHIATRIC HOSPITAL.

"Oh." Sarah slumped deeper into her leather bucket seat.

Sarah was stunned again when she was led into the sleeping girl's room. May Anne looked like a perfectly normal, sound asleep twelve-year-old. For Sarah it was like being outside her own body, as if she were looking at herself.

"We've sedated her," the resident psychiatrist said. "When your husband brought her in, she was virtually catatonic—in a trance. They just sit and stare, or if they are helped to their feet, they stand and stare. No speech, no emotion, no reaction. I expect that state to resume when she awakens."

Grant held Sarah tight. She was trembling. "Will she be all right? When—" Sarah didn't even know what to ask.

"Mrs. Radcliffe, there is no diagnosis yet. That may take some time. The causes can be myriad. I understand there's been a history of anti-social—"

"Antisocial? She's always been quiet and withdrawn—" Sarah started to cry. Grant held her tighter.

"Come back tomorrow afternoon, Mrs. Radcliffe. We may know more by then. We may have to ask you to move her. Capistrano-by-the-Sea in Dana Point is an excellent long-term facility for acute disorders."

Grant thought that for a psychiatrist he didn't use a lot of psychology. Grant hugged Sarah as he guided her back to the car.

"Grant, what happened?"

"Sarah, darling, I came home directly from the courtroom. It was a hard day in trial. I went to May Anne's room just to let her know I was home, and there she was."

"Was—what?"

"Just sitting there, in the corner, staring. It was as if I weren't there. I called Dr. Sorkin—"

"Did you ask Mrs. Riley? Had anything unusual happened?"

"Yes, dear. Mrs. Riley assured me that May Anne had gone directly to her room after school. Mrs. Riley was quite distraught. You know she's quite fond of the child."

"Oh, the poor thing," cried Sarah.

"As a matter of fact, dear, Mrs. Riley asked to leave. The poor woman felt somehow responsible. She said she didn't think she could bear staying in the house. I gave her a letter of recommendation and a check for an extra month's pay."

"Yes, I suppose that was the kind thing to do," sobbed Sarah.

"I thought so, dear. I'll call Jonathan Clark and tell him I can't make it to the trial in the morning. You shouldn't be alone." Grant squeezed her hand. She needed his support badly right now.

The man never reported to the chairman at his office. As usual, Maynard Chase had asked the man to come to his home. Maynard Chase's home could not be adequately described as a mansion. It was the chairman's castle, and he was proud of it. If William Randolph Hearst had only had taste, San Simeon might have looked like this.

The man was led into the study. One hundred feet away the paneled glass wall overlooked the mountains and Pacific Ocean. Both side walls were lined with two-story bookshelves, the upper tiers of which were reached by spiral staircases, leading to catwalks with carved mahogany railings. One wall of shelves was broken by a Santa Maria stone fireplace. It would have required a double garage door to cover the opening.

The eighty-four-year-old chairman sat in a dark blue leather chair before the fireplace, stocking feet propped on a matching hassock, reading reports. When the man removed his hat, his cannonball head reflected the flickering firelight.

The chairman looked up. "Grant Radcliffe," he said.

"Yes, sir. Since the Wennerstrom trial, he has developed what I would consider to be an unusual appetite for vengeance."

"Against?"

"Oliver, sir, the lead attorney for Wennerstrom. Radcliffe feels that Oliver went out of his way in the trial to embarrass and humiliate him."

"Did he?"

"I wasn't there, sir. It's hard to tell from reading a transcript. Possibly. I have no doubt that Radcliffe was humiliated—and apprehensive about the effect on his career. Whether Oliver went to unusual lengths to accomplish that, I cannot determine."

"Preparation thorough?"

"Extremely, sir. He has built a dossier on Oliver that would do credit to the CIA, but he continues to wait for an opportunity."

"Mmmmmm. Methodical and patient. Good. Maintaining fidelity?"

"If we exempt the Casa Folatre from the definition, sir—completely. His devotion to your granddaughter seems genuine."

"Do you think Radcliffe can handle top-level management?"

"I don't feel qualified to make that judgment, sir. I can only say that he is absolutely devoted to his work. I know that he is promptly aware of his division's problems and handles them effectively. I'm sure you already know that."

"Stable personality?"

"An even more difficult question. It's not difficult for a person who always gets his way. Up until now, or at least until the Wennerstrom

trial, Radcliffe has never been crossed. His daughter's institutionalization, of course. Sad, but not really pressure. The only way I know to
find how a personality handles pressure is to watch him exert it."

"Yes." The old man stared into the fire as he spoke. "Vengeance may
merely be a higher form of accounting." Chase looked up and almost
smiled. "Every business needs good accountants. Let him have his
lead."

The man knew he had been dismissed. He turned to leave, then
hesitated. "Sir, do you trust him?"

"Of course. So long as I know what he wants."

The chairman had no illusions about the life expectancy of a healthy
eighty-four-year-old. Maynard Chase had no illusions left at all. It was
long past time to consider a potential successor. TOPCO's president,
Danning Pearson, was almost as old as Maynard Chase and in worse
health. Fortney Gilbert, the operations vice-president, was practically
de facto chief executive officer already and was undoubtedly Pearson's
protégé.

Virtually single-handedly the chairman had built TOPCO into a
monumental international organization. He was proud of his achievement. He knew that monuments cannot last forever. He would be
content with a year or two less than that.

The chairman regretted not having commenced Sarah's education
sooner. For too long he had continued to hope for his son William's
maturity. Sarah had the brains, the judgment, and the requisite force of
personality, although she did not know it yet. She only lacked experience. *Sarah needs Grant Radcliffe,* the chairman thought. *Grant
Radcliffe will be her sword.* But there was something about Grant
Radcliffe that bothered him. There always had been something he
could not quite define. Not Radcliffe's obsession with vengeance. Not
his ruthless driving ambition. Those were acceptable, almost inevitable
characteristics of any candidate for the position. Not the little infidel-
ities either. TOPCO did not require a saint. Radcliffe's judgment seemed
sound enough. Oh, he'd probably screwed up on that Wennerstrom
thing, but the result couldn't be faulted. The Wennerstrom Process was

worth twenty times what it had cost. Maynard Chase didn't believe in second-guessing success.

In one whirlwind board of directors' session the chairman rammed through the creation of a new position, executive vice-president, and forced Grant Radcliffe's election to it. Fortney Gilbert had been steamrollered in the process, but the man played too much golf for the chairman's taste anyway.

Grant Radcliffe's appointment as executive vice-president at age forty-five was a triumph. He was the youngest man ever to hold the third-highest position in the company—below only the chairman and the president. *Forbes* gave him five thousand words and incorrectly labeled him a "young tycoon." The *Los Angeles Times* was more on target with the "Crown Prince."

Grant himself was ecstatic. He had done it. He was one mere step away from nearly absolute power, the presidency. That last step was virtually assured upon the chairman's death and Sarah's inheritance of his stock. All Grant had to do was retain Sarah's loyalty and devotion. He hurled MacDonald Oliver off the cliff one last time before putting the dossier away and made a note to buy Sarah some jewelry.

"I have something interesting for you," the man said as he sat before Radcliffe's new rosewood desk.

The man explained how he had discovered Seymour Bulles under some rock in southeast Los Angeles. Bulles had been in every cheap saloon in town, whining that MacDonald Oliver owed him one hundred thousand dollars. Bulles really believed that Oliver should have collected damages from Bulles's former savings and loan employer.

"Are you thinking of getting Bulles to file a malpractice suit against Oliver?" Radcliffe looked bored. "That would be an embarrassment, I suppose."

"An embarrassment is all it would be. No, I think that Seymour Bulles will charge MacDonald Oliver with embezzlement of one hundred thousand dollars."

Radcliffe's beautiful face lost its bored look. The very thought thrilled and delighted him. The man explained that Seymour Bulles was a made-to-order combination: sleazy, greedy, broke, and crazy.

"The creep really believes that MacDonald Oliver has done him out of one hundred thousand. It will be easy for him to rationalize that the end justifies any means of getting back at Oliver." The man grinned. "You understand that?"

Did Radcliffe ever understand that. He asked, "How would you persuade him to file the charges?"

"I figure a simple combination of coercion, brainwashing, and bribery will do it."

"What will Bulles have for corroboration? His word as an admitted felon is not going to carry much weight with the authorities."

"Will this help?" The man removed a single sheet of paper from his briefcase and handed it to Radcliffe. It was a typewritten receipt on the letterhead of Sorensen, Oliver, Bradford, and Smith: "Received in trust from Seymour Bulles, the sum of one hundred thousand dollars cash to be returned or disbursed upon his order." The document was dated, and initialed in ink, "M. O."

"Forgery?" asked Radcliffe.

"Of course. Although it's just a preliminary sample. The one that's actually produced will be refined."

"Where did you get the letterhead? It looks authentic."

"It is." The awful grin came on again. "The printer's clerk gave a potential customer samples of several letterhead styles for consideration."

"Won't the forgery be detected? What about handwriting experts?"

"In these days of ballpoint and felt pens, a single exemplar of handwriting is almost beyond positive authentication. The corollary also stands. One decent forgery is beyond positive identification. It is especially true when only initials rather than a complete signature are used—"

"As in Clifford Irving's hoax, the fake Howard Hughes autobiography. Will it work?"

"I can't guarantee a conviction, but Mr. Oliver cannot escape untarnished. Would you like to meet paranoid Seymour?"

"No, thank you. He might expect me to shake hands. You handle it. I'll call Oliver."

The man frowned. He made a point of never saying "Huh?" but he was tempted.

Radcliffe smiled at the confusion he'd caused. "To apologize," he explained.

Mac did not want to accept Grant Radcliffe's call. Only after Radcliffe had repeatedly assured Elizabeth Greene that he would behave, and that the conversation would not involve Mac in any ethical indiscretion, did Mac relent. Even then Mac insisted on recording the call and having Elizabeth listen on an extension.

"Mr. Radcliffe, I want you to know that this telephone conversation is being recorded," said Mac.

"I don't blame you for being cautious after my despicable behavior. I owe you an apology. It's been bothering me ever since the settlement. That's why I called. I was drunk, but that is a feeble excuse. I was highly upset—"

Mac knew courtesy required he say something forgiving, but he could not bring himself to do it. Mac managed to thank him for calling.

"Wasn't that nice?" asked Elizabeth.

"More like weird," said Mac.

Mac made no connection between Radcliffe's call and the letter he received the next day from the state bar association, informing him that Seymour Bulles had charged him with wrongfully retaining one hundred thousand dollars in trust funds. The letter requested Mac's written response, after which the state bar would determine whether further investigation or referral for criminal prosecution was justified.

Mac stalked into Nels's office with the letter. "I knew Bulles was bad news."

"You are obviously right, although we did please another valuable client. This will pass. Haven't you ever received one of these before?"

"Yes, the first year I came with you. A former client complained that

I had charged one hundred dollars for writing a letter that produced ten thousand dollars she had been unable to collect."

"Write your response and go back to work. Just because you had a good year, you can't expect to get by solely on your reputation."

Mac laughed and did both. Within a week he had forgotten the incident completely.

13

*T*he slim brunette girl stood patiently in line at the teller's window, swaying only slightly with silent rhythms emanating from the Sony Walkman plugged into her ear. She looked like thousands of other subteenagers, except for her more-expensive-than-usual clothes. Her jeans were by Gloria Vanderbilt, her running shoes were Nikes, and her sweater was obviously one hundred percent cashmere. When her turn came, the girl switched off her private concert and extracted a thick manila envelope from her backpack.

"Hi. My father asked me to deposit this," the girl said as she passed the package through the window slot.

The teller flashed her automatic Welcome-to-Wells-Fargo-Bank smile and dumped the contents onto her counter: two thick packets of currency and a deposit slip. The teller read the name printed on the preencoded deposit ticket. "MacDonald A. Oliver. Oh, you must be

Tracy. He's mentioned you. I thought you were younger. I'm Maxine."

"Hi. I'm to be sure to get a receipt."

"Sure," said the continuously smiling teller, and glanced at the deposit slip again. One hundred thousand dollars cash. One eyebrow arched slightly, but who was she to question the idiosyncratic transactions of wealthy customers?

"Just a minute, hon, while I count this." There were one thousand bills, all hundreds. "Another minute, please, hon. I've got to have this checked." Another teller was called over to confirm the currency count. She nodded her head, and Maxine punched out a deposit receipt. "Thank you, Tracy. Nice to meet you. Say hello to your father."

The girl stood at the curb for only a few seconds before the dark gray Buick drove up, pausing just long enough for her to hop in. "Any problem?" the man with the cannonball head asked as he pulled away from the curb.

"No, sir. Here's the receipt," the girl said as she removed the wig. He gave her the creeps, but Big Eddy had insisted she do the job. A smart girl never argued with her pimp.

"Here's the five hundred dollars. I'll drop you off at Hollywood and Vermont. You can keep the clothes, Roxanne."

After placing Roxanne back in circulation, the man telephoned Radcliffe. "All finished. No problem."

"Excellent," said Radcliffe. "One hundred thousand dollars well spent."

The district attorney's offices were more lavishly decorated than those of most other Los Angeles County civil servants. Ardent supporters had purchased the oak paneling and ornate velour furniture. Full-color posters of baseball scenes and autographed photographs of players hung on each wall. The overall effect was of questionable aesthetic judgment, but it left no doubt that the district attorney was a fervent Dodger fan.

The district attorney snubbed out his twenty-fourth cigarette of the day and mopped his sweating brow. The office was air-conditioned, but it was an election year. "Why don't we just toss it to the grand jury?" the district attorney asked.

Detective Lieutenant Hollingsworth, LAPD No. 5601, cleaned his fingernails. The complaint deputy chewed the taxpayers' pencil. The chief trial deputy wondered if he could defeat the bastard if he ran against him in four years.

"Boss," replied the complaint deputy, "we haven't bothered the grand jury with a felony for the past three years. Ever since the ruling came down that even after indictment the accused was still entitled to a preliminary hearing. Why don't we just file a complaint as usual? It's a lot faster, easier, and cheaper—"

"Because, dumbo," said the chief trial deputy, "the case is a hot potato. MacDonald Oliver is a big deal in this town—"

"And Sorensen, Oliver, Bradford, and Smith kick in very generously to the party," said the detective lieutenant.

The district attorney lit another cigarette. "The felony conviction of a prominent lawyer would be invaluable publicity. On the other hand, if we issue a felony complaint against Oliver and he walks, I—I mean, this office will be made to look like shit. On the other hand, if the grand jury makes the decision to indict in a doubtful case—"

"Impartial law enforcement dictates that we take a defendant to trial," said the smiling chief trial deputy.

"I don't understand," said the complaint deputy. "If we're concerned about the risk of putting Oliver through a trial unless a conviction is probable, why don't we just issue a citation first? Oliver gets the opportunity to present himself informally and give us his side of the story. If he convinces us that a complaint should not be filed, we are saved the embarrassment of having to dismiss later, and Oliver isn't put through the trauma unnecessarily."

The chief trial deputy shook his head in wonderment. Such naiveté and in his own department. "Because," he said, "citation letters don't get publicity. Indictments get publicity."

"And an incorruptible district attorney will fearlessly present a case to the grand jury, even though the accused is a prominent and powerful lawyer," said the lieutenant, straight-faced.

"Very funny," said the district attorney. "The case isn't all that weak. We've got Bulles's testimony that he gave Oliver the money in trust."

Detective Hollingsworth snorted, but the district attorney continued. "We have the signed receipt on Sorensen, Oliver, Bradford, and Smith's letterhead."

"You mean, initialed with a ballpoint pen," corrected the lieutenant. The district attorney continued undaunted. "And one hundred thousand dollars cash recently deposited into Oliver's personal account."

"To which we are conveniently tipped by an anonymous telephone call," said the grinning lieutenant.

Fucking cops, thought the district attorney. They're all frustrated lawyers. "So what do you think, asshole?" he asked.

"The case against Oliver stinks. But who are we to judge?" The lieutenant shrugged and put away his nail file. "Toss him to the grand jury."

The California Penal Code provides that grand jury investigations are secret, pending arrest of the indicted defendant. That was no reason for Nels Sorensen to be surprised by the call.

"Nels, I owe you one; as a matter of fact, I probably owe you several. The grand jury is investigating a felony accusation against MacDonald Oliver. I am sure you people know what it's all about."

"Thank you, Manny. I deeply appreciate your letting me know. Mac is important to me."

Nels called Mac in and told him. Mac sat stunned, rubbing his right eye. "It has to be the Bulles thing. I can't accept it. It's so incredibly stupid."

Nels could not bear to watch. He left his desk and stood behind Mac, his hands on Mac's shoulders. "My boy, I fear I have caused a calamity to bear on you. If my insistence on your taking that miserable case causes you grief, I will never forgive myself. I pray that it is not so. However, I urge you not to place yourself solely in God's hands. This is a time for action. Find out what you can. Do what you can. Quickly."

Mac broke out of his paralysis, nodded gratefully, and left Nels's office. Nels returned to his telephone, determined to follow his own advice.

Mac went directly to Timothy George Bradford, the resident criminal lawyer. In spite of his secret jealousy of Mac, Bradford's instincts responded professionally. "The grand jury? Highly irregular. The district attorney's policy has been to proceed by information for some time." Timothy Bradford was reminded of his own usual mean thoughts concerning Mac. "Does the district attorney have anything personal against you? Did you publicly oppose his election?"

Mac shook his head. "We've met. I hardly know him. Never have had anything to do with him." Mac managed a small smile. "I think I even made a modest contribution to his last campaign."

"The district attorney would not have dared to go that far solely on the word of an admitted felon. Obviously the district attorney has some other evidence to present to the grand jury." Timothy Bradford reached for his telephone. "Go back to work. Let me try to find out what's going on."

Dammit, everyone's always telling me to go back to work, thought Mac as he returned to his office. Some disgruntled nut and a politician are fucking you around, Mac, so relax and go back to work. Mac pulled the *Cal Coastal Savings & Loan Association* v. *Seymour Bulles/Bulles* v. *Cal Coastal Savings & Loan Association* file and waded through the stale documents, looking for a clue. There was nothing.

"I give up. I'm worthless," Mac told Elizabeth. She knew what had happened. "Tell Nels or Timothy to call me at home tonight if they get anything. I'm going sailing."

Mac got away with driving to Marina del Ray at much higher than legally sanctioned speed. Just looking at *Abigail* made him feel better. Aboard, he traded his suit for jeans, sweatshirt, deck shoes, and a can of beer. With the eingine idling in, Mac pushed the sloop out of the slip by hand. *Abigail* did not willingly back up. He jumped aboard as the bow cleared the dock. He powered out of the marina and raised the sails outside, adjusting the jib and mainsheet so the sloop balanced. *Abigail* sailed herself as Mac stretched out on the foredeck with a second beer.

Driving home three hours later, Mac was back in control. The charge was patently ridiculous. With the help of Nels and Timothy he would fight it vigorously. The whole mess would be a bad memory within a few days.

*   *   *

Nels Sorensen and Timothy Bradford were sitting in Mac's living room, toying with undrunk drinks, while Mary Kathryn stood clinging to herself as though suppressing a chill.

Nels stood. "It is serious," he said.

"They have a receipt," said Timothy, "for one hundred thousand dollars—signed—purportedly by you."

Mac stood, looking at Nels, to Timothy and back again. Mary Kathryn had come to his side.

"And there's more. They're holding back, I know. I'll keep trying to get it," said Timothy.

"Mac?" said Nels, but he could not bring himself to ask. He turned pleadingly to Timothy.

"We have to know," said Timothy, "in order to help. Is there—you know . . . anything?"

Mac knew. God, the countless times he had asked clients the same question. Tell me. Tell me everything. I can't help you unless I know the worst along with the good. Mac shrugged and spread his hands.

"Mac," pressed Timothy, "we have to know—"

The pressure of the day mounted beyond tolerance. Mac exploded. "You son of a bitch. There is nothing—I have nothing to confess!"

Three jaws hung open. None of them had ever before experienced the enraged MacDonald Oliver. Almost instantly Mac calmed back down to simple, quiet anger. "I apologize, Timothy. Everyone. I know you're trying to help. I haven't been having fun today."

"I have an appointment to see the DA in the morning," said Timothy. "Perhaps I can learn more. Good night."

Because the district attorney rated Timothy Bradford a politically influential "seven," Bradford was kept waiting only twenty minutes. "Sorry, Timothy. The responsibilities—"

"Yes, I know," said Timothy Bradford, struggling to maintain composure. He was used to being the one who kept people waiting. "You know I'm representing MacDonald Oliver. I am hoping that you will give me what information you have. It would be irresponsible to tarnish the reputation of a person of Oliver's stature without first—"

"Timothy, you're accusing me of irresponsibility?"

"No, I don't mean that. I mean we both have a responsibility to see that justice is done."

"Sure," said the DA, looking at his watch: nine twenty-five. Time for his first cigarette. "Justice is good. Timothy, I'm going to tell you everything we have. I am even going to do you a personal favor, but"— the DA took his time tamping out a cigarette and fumbling for his lighter—"in return I'll expect your cooperation."

Timothy Bradford was confused. "Fine."

"No, not fine." The DA blew smoke in Bradford's face. "I want Oliver's ass. I've got the evidence to get it, too. But we both know that, even with a strong case, trial is a risk. What's more, Oliver has the money to buy an all-out defense. That means motions, writs, appeals delay. We would be over a year getting his case to trial. I want results now."

Timothy Bradford was beginning to understand. He had forgotten it was an election year.

The district attorney continued. "You are going to help—I mean, see that justice is done. I'm going to tell you up front what we've got. You are going to use that information to persuade MacDonald Oliver to plead. In return for that cooperation, I will recommend he gets straight probation—no hard time at all—and we will make it as easy as possible on you personally."

"Me personally," repeated Timothy Bradford as he waited for the other shoe to fall.

The district attorney reached for a file. "Giuseppe Brancussi—you, right?"

Timothy George Bradford had not heard himself called that since before law school. He said nothing and waited for the rest of it.

"You and your two dago friends—"

Bradford colored and started to rise, but the district attorney waved him back. "Hey, no offense. I got a dago wife. Let me finish. You and two prominent Las Vegas and Chicago family members are the general partners of that eminent speculative enterprise entitled—just a minute—the Monte Carlo Hotel and Casino Development Fund."

"Now just a minute. My partners and I have invested ten million dollars each in that venture. That's thirty million of our own money. Just because there have been temporary setbacks—"

"Giuseppe, please let me finish. If you don't know this already, I've got bad news for you. Your Vegas and Chicago friends did not invest any ten million bucks each. As a matter of fact, they invested no bucks each." The district attorney illustrated by forming a zero with his fat fingers.

Bradford had not known. The DA waited for the news to sink in before continuing. "Now we realize that—ostensibly—you put in ten million bucks. It looks like that on paper. But in view of the fact that three hundred orthodontists and gynecologists have been induced to drop a measly one hundred grand each in this questionable venture, this office is obligated to investigate the bona fides of your purported investment—"

Timothy Bradford started to relax.

The district attorney lit another cigarette.

"—and to at least consider charging you as a coconspirator and accessory to a real estate development fraud."

Timothy Bradford stopped relaxing.

The district attorney exhaled and continued. "Now that you have a better grasp of the relevant background, counselor, perhaps we can get back to your client. We have already leaked to you that we have the signed receipt for the hundred grand. Here—" The district attorney shoved a photocopy of the alleged receipt across the desk.

Bradford picked it up. It looked authentic to him. "Can I?" Bradford started to ask.

"No, you can't." The district attorney grabbed the paper and shoved it back into his file. He pulled out another sheet, which he waved. "Just lean back and listen, will you? This office also has the bank records which show that your client, MacDonald Oliver, deposited the one hundred thousand cash into his personal bank account. Now, counselor, you can look."

The Wells Fargo Bank statement showed the one-hundred-thousand-dollar cash deposit to the account of MacDonald Oliver. The district attorney returned the document to his file. "Any questions?" he asked.

"It would help to persuade Oliver if I could show him copies."

"It is the policy of this office not to hand over copies of documentary evidence without a formal discovery order. Anything else?"

"If an indictment is returned—" Bradford began.

The district attorney laughed.

"—if an indictment is returned, will you allow me to arrange his surrender? At least he should be spared the ignominy of an arrest."

"Ignominy. That's good. I should remember that. Counselor, I'll explain this carefully so as not to offend your sensibilities. You deliver your partner, and I'll get off your ass."

The district attorney stood up. "Call me," he said as he fumbled through his pockets.

Bradford stopped at the office door when the district attorney spoke again.

"Bradford, got a cigarette?"

As he taxied back to the office, Timothy Bradford's anxiety over his own problems mounted. The district attorney must have been bluffing when he so confidently stated that Bradford's general partners in the Las Vegas project had not put up any money at all. Bradford could not believe that those two would expose themselves to the public disgrace of signing the partnership agreement, obligating themselves to put up ten million each, and then reneging. In their business a man who did not keep his word did not receive respect.

Back in his office, Bradford ordered his calls held. He dug out his duplicate original of the agreement. Bradford had signed last, after watching the other two. Bradford needed the reassurance of seeing those other two signed and notarized signature pages once again, the last three pages. There was his signature on the bottom sheet, bold and black above the neat prim signature of the notary public, the rubber stamp and the embossed seal. Bradford turned to the next to last page, then quickly to the second from the last page. Blank spaces! Both unsigned and unnotarized. The bastards had substituted the unsigned pages. Before his eyes. The bastards. The district attorney had not been bluffing. Those two had not put up their share. They had swindled Timothy Bradford—Timothy Bradford and three hundred smaller investors—out of forty million: ten million dollars from Bradford and another thirty million dollars from the limited partners.

Bradford had been concerned, even before his visit with the district attorney. There had been a work stoppage on the Las Vegas construction. Bradford's recent calls to Vegas and Chicago had not been returned. Bradford had anticipated that he was going to be hit up for an additional capital contribution—but not this.

Thank the Blessed Virgin Mary that after paying his income taxes and debts he still had his eighteen million dollars in gold bullion safely stored in the impregnable Utah mountain vaults of the Bullion Reserve of North America.

Comforted a little by the thought of his appreciating gold bars, Bradford returned to his problem with the district attorney. That bastard was unscrupulous. It would not be difficult to insinuate that Timothy Bradford had had an active part in the Vegas scam. Bradford could hear the prosecuting attorney summing up in the case of *People* v. *Giuseppe Brancussi, alias Timothy George Bradford:*

"Ladies and gentlemen of the jury. Of course, Timothy Bradford, as he now calls himself, put up ten million of his own money, just as he testified he did. But after Bradford and his two Mafia partners collected thirty million dollars from three hundred innocent small investors, the three partners met in some garlic-smelling back room. There they divvied up the thirty million. Bradford's ten million front money was returned to him. Bradford and his two family friends divided the remaining twenty million three ways. Not bad. Bradford made a cool six-point-six-million profit for the temporary posting of ten million dollars. Where is it, though? Bradford has testified that he was fleeced like the others. Bradford has shown you his bank accounts. Bradford has sworn that his ten million is gone. Sure it is. Has it gone to a numbered account in Switzerland? Or has it gone to a secret account in the Bahamas? We may never—"

Bradford shook off the nightmare and poured a drink. It was all too credible. And that bastard in Chicago. He would not be above pinning the whole thing on Timothy Bradford just to buy himself immunity.

Timothy Bradford pragmatically concluded that the district attorney had earned his cooperation. After all, there was substantial evidence against MacDonald Oliver. Bradford would be doing Oliver a service if he could successfully bargain for a suspended sentence and probation in exchange for a plea of guilty.

Bradford took another drink before walking down the hall. Mac would be expecting a report. Bradford told Mac what the district attorney had: Bulles's testimony; a signed receipt; records of the deposit into Mac's bank account.

"I don't believe it. It's impossible." Mac's right hand worried away at his false eye. "Let me see the copies."

"I don't have them, Mac. They won't release them until a discovery motion is made. We can't do that until the indictment is returned."

"You're saying I have no way of defending myself until after I am indicted for a felony? Do you realize what this will do to me . . . the news coverage . . . my wife, my child."

"It's the law—"

"The law. Do you recommend that I do anything?"

"Yes. You won't like this, but I insist that you consider it. I accept your word that Bulles is framing you—"

"Thank you."

"Nevertheless, the district attorney has a prima facie case. You are going to be stuck with the stigma of an indictment. It is already virtually an accomplished fact. Even with your presumption of innocence—"

"Presumption?"

"Even with that, there is the risk of conviction upon trial. I believe we can avoid the risk and much of the trauma. I think I can successfully negotiate a deal for your probation—"

"Wait," said Mac. He stood up. "You're saying that you want me to plead guilty—"

"Mac, it won't be that bad. Much better than—"

"—to a crime I did not commit?"

"Mac . . ."

"Do you understand, you soft-bellied son of a bitch, that I have not committed any offense? I have not stolen any money."

"I'm only trying—"

Mac held the door open. "Timothy, you're fired. Get out!"

"But—"

Mac lowered his voice. "Get out. And try not to come too close to me in the future."

It's every man for himself, thought Timothy Bradford as he made another appointment with the district attorney.

"Well?" asked the district attorney as he bungled an attempted smoke ring.

"He would not buy it. He lost his temper. He fired me." Bradford shrugged.

"Too bad. I'm sorry—for both of you. So why are you here?"

"I still want to make a deal in exchange for my immunity on the Las Vegas matter."

"You don't even represent Oliver now." The district attorney's little eyes grew interested. "What have you got to sell?"

"I'll testify—to MacDonald Oliver's confession."

"Mac, calm down. You're wearing out my carpet. I don't agree with Timothy at all, but he was only trying to help," said Nels Sorensen.

"I would prefer him as an enemy," said Mac.

"We're wasting time," said Cornell Sepulveda Smith. "You need another attorney promptly. A first-class criminal law specialist. Edward Bennet Williams? F. Lee Bailey?"

"No," said Mac. "If I hire that kind of high-powered talent, everyone will assume I'm guilty. How about L. Donald Dillon down in Long Beach?"

"I will forgive your fallacious reasoning. You're distraught, but your instincts are sound. Dillon is an excellent choice. Do you know him?" asked Cornell Sepulveda Smith.

"Never met the man. I only know his reputation."

"I've seen him in court several times. He's impressive."

"I'll telephone him," said Nels.

"We're in luck," said Nels a few minutes later. "Dillon is already downtown and will be here at four-thirty."

Donald Dillon had a rawboned farm boy look. He folded his lanky frame into one of Mac's chairs as he accepted Elizabeth's coffee. "That's it?" he asked.

"That's all I know," said Mac.

"Election years." Dillon sniffed. "The case against you sucks. It is obviously a frame. Multimillionaire attorney steals one hundred thousand dollars from client, after handing him a receipt, and sticks it in his personal bank account. It's laughable."

"It would be if it didn't hurt so much."

"It has to be Seymour Bulles. I can understand Bulles's motive, but it still doesn't make sense. Why would he put out one hundred thousand dollars to get back at you for costing one hundred thousand dollars?"

"Where would he get one hundred thousand dollars?" asked Mac.

"You could have been wrong about the extent of his participation in the kickback scheme. But we're missing something important. It doesn't even hang together as a frame-up. Time is so goddamned short. The DA's office has already closed. I'll try to reach him at home tonight. Perhaps I can persuade him to hold off until we have the opportunity to talk."

Late that evening Dillon phoned Mac at home. "I haven't been able to reach the district attorney. His wife claims not to know where he is. He may be ducking us. Take these telephone numbers. If anything terrible happens in the morning, I'll be at one of them."

Something terrible did happen in the morning. Elizabeth Greene came into Mac's office at nine-oh-five. "Mac, there are two men in the reception room asking for you. They say they are police officers."

Mac glanced ruefully at his window. "Thirty-six stories. I'll never make it. Call Don Dillon at one of these numbers. Tell him what's happened. Have someone else tell the gentlemen I'm on the phone and will be with them in a few minutes. Stall them until you've reached Dillon."

Ten minutes later Elizabeth nodded to Mac as she let the men into his office.

"MacDonald Abraham Oliver?" asked the smaller one. He was six feet two and not less than 230 pounds.

"Yes."

"Police officers. You're under arrest. Please turn around, sir, and place your hands behind your back."

Mac closed his eyes as he felt and heard the cuffs click into place.

"You have the right to remain silent. You . . ." The officer had *Miranda* down pat.

"You will have to come downtown with us, Mr. Oliver."

But we are downtown already. Mac knew he was losing his mind. "My attorney is on his way over. Can't we wait for him?"

"I'm sorry, sir. The bench warrant requires—"

Donald Dillon stuck his sandy-haired head through the door. Mac was sure he heard cavalry bugles sound. "Morning, Harvey, Fred. The district attorney would like you to call him before you take Mr. Oliver in. I've just talked to him."

"May we use your telephone, Mr. Oliver?" asked Harvey.

Mac did not trust his voice. He tried to point with his head. Dear Abby: What is the proper demeanor to be observed while standing handcuffed in one's own office?

"Yes, sir." Harvey was saying that a lot. "Yes, sir. Good-bye." He unlocked the cuffs before turning to Dillon. "You're to surrender him before eleven o'clock."

After the officers left, Mac stripped off his suit jacket. "I'm going to change my shirt. My back is drenched."

"Change it if you like, but you won't be wearing it long. Sit down while I prepare you for an extremely unpleasant three or four hours."

Donald Dillon surrendered Mac to Central Division. "Your release on OR is being arranged now. I'll be waiting outside."

Mac was turned over to the booking officer, who mumbled something into a communications box, causing an electronically controlled door to open. Mac was led through. The door closed with a solid metallic thud. He shuddered at the memories that sound evoked. The building was not old, but it had the aura of an ancient fortress. In spite of the strong odor of antiseptics, it was dirty. Hospital-green paint peeled from the walls. Halfhearted attempts had been made to scrub off various graffiti. There were no windows, but the room was bright with cold fluorescent light. The whirring of hidden ventilating fans only made Mac more claustrophobic.

Mac's freshly pressed suit and shirt were bundled into a sack, then tamped down with the rest of his clothes. He was issued denim pants designed in a universal size, a gray T-shirt, white socks, and plastic sandals. His Baume & Mercier watch, pen, keys, an orange marble, and pocket change were stuffed into an envelope. Dillon had insisted on taking his wallet. Dillon wanted his watch, too, but it had seemed important to Mac that he know the time. It hadn't occurred to him that his watch would be taken.

"Property sheet. Sign here," said the clerk. Mac signed. Handcuffs were produced. "Hold out your hands—no, in front."

Apparently they trust me to pick my nose, thought Mac. He was taken through barred doors into the booking cell. The clang of the steel door behind him made him flinch and sent his back muscles into spasm. It will be only three or four hours. A few hours only, Mac. Mac felt wire-taut. He forced himself to take a deep breath and look around. Mac Oliver was not alone. Ten or twelve other prisoners were in the large cell. Everyone was cuffed. Some were curled up on the floor, sleeping or perhaps passed out. One was vomiting in the corner. Some ignored him, and some stared. No one looked friendly, and no one said anything. The cell stank: vomit and urine; excrement and sweat. The room was completely bare of amenities. No toilet, no lavatory, not even a bunk. Bare walls, concrete floor, bodies, and stink.

Mac found a dry space against the wall where no one had thrown up lately and sat. He found himself counting. At the count of 101 he was up again, pacing wall to wall. His fists and his teeth were clenched. He wanted to strike out at his cellmates, break a few bones. He knew how stupid it would be, but he wanted to.

Mac remembered cell number one, Hoa Lo Prison, in the center of the city of Hanoi. He had been issued blue-and-white vertically striped pajamas and taken his possessions, including the Omega watch he'd been given for high school graduation. *C'est la guerre.* It wasn't a calendar watch anyway.

"Oliver. Over here."

Over here was a camera and flood lamps. Mac was made to stand against a chest-high barricade. A fresh number was inserted into a slot at chest level.

"Face the camera. Stand still." Click.

"Turn left. Head up. Stand still." Click.

"Turn right. More. Still." Click.

"Oliver, wait over there." Mac picked a new spot against another wall. Jailers with prisoners in tow walked by. Jailers alone walked by. Uniformed officers. Plainclothesmen with plastic badges. A white-coated person of indeterminate sex. The whole world and an hour went by. Mac's feet hurt. He wanted to yell. If I can't hit someone, can't I at least scream? But Dillon had warned him. Absolutely no aberrant behavior. It would delay his release by at least hours.

"Anyone seen Oliver?"

"Here. Oliver," said Mac, grateful to be discovered.

"Wadin't ya sa so? Over here."

Fingerprinting. "Right hand. First the thumb. Gimme the finger." Mac's fingers were expertly guided. Ink pad to card, ink pad to card.

"Okay. Other hand. First the thumb. Okay . . . wipe 'em off."

Mac was taken back to the booking cell. Back with the drunks, the derelicts, and the stink. Someone shuffled up behind him. "Hey, buddy."

Mac turned and snarled. The man started, backed up, and turned away. Mac had startled himself. He hadn't meant to do that. Hold on, Mac. Don't do something stupid. Think of something pleasant. Mac dutifully backed *Abigail* out of her slip and ran her out the entrance channel.

Mac was taken out of the cell. There was a lot of paper. Meaningless paperwork. Mac didn't care anymore. He was sailing *Abigail* toward

Catalina Island. He could see Mary Kathryn's back as she sat on the forward deck facing the bow. Or was it Mary Kathryn?

"Oliver, over here." Mac's cuffs were removed.

"Here's your clothes. Here's your property. Sign the property receipt. Here."

Mac dumped the contents of the envelope on the counter. He grabbed the orange aggie before it rolled off the edge. "My wristwatch?"

The clerk grabbed the paper and squinted. "There's no watch listed. Sign here. Your attorney's waiting."

Mac sighed and signed. This one had a calendar, too.

14

L. Donald Dillon had been an excellent choice. He obtained maximum pretrial discovery of the prosecution's case with minimum fuss. His attempt to have the indictment set aside and his motion for dismissal at the preliminary hearing had not been successful—that would have been almost too much to expect. Dillon would have preferred to stall the trial of the case until after the elections. He could have easily managed that, but Mac had to have the whole black incident behind him.

Dillon's maneuvering for the choice of trial judge was brilliant. The Honorable "Bleeding" Hart was scrupulously fair, a vocal socialist and a constantly criticized light sentencer. The best that could be hoped for.

Dillon selected the jury with consummate skill. Mac knew he could not have done better himself. The jurors were predominantly young, liberal, Protestant, and female. Mac thought it was almost a classic defense jury.

Even the assignment of the prosecutor seemed to be a break for the defense. The inexperienced deputy district attorney mumbled and stumbled through his examination of the jury panel. As he read his opening statement, line for line from a yellow pad, he never once looked up at the jury. His direct examination was almost painfully inept. He'd even written out his questions. If the answer failed quite to fit, his fumbling was desperate as he struggled to make up an appropriate question on the spot.

The trial moved quickly. It was all over in three days. Bulles was the first prosecution witness. His testimony on direct examination had been entirely predictable. Bulles testified that he had given Mac one hundred thousand dollars cash, in trust. He had done so because he feared that Cal Coastal Savings & Loan Association might obtain a judgment for damages against him. Mr. Oliver had assured him that the money would be safely hidden from Cal Coastal's clutches. No, he had not seen the receipt typed, but he had watched MacDonald Oliver sign it. After the Cal Coastal case against him was settled, he asked Mr. Oliver for his money back, but Mr. Oliver refused.

On cross-examination of Seymour Bulles, Dillon first established Bulles's prior criminal record. Bulles's plea of nolo contendere to the grand theft charge filed by Cal Coastal was tantamount to a guilty plea. Bulles had a record of committing the same offense of which he charged MacDonald Oliver. And Bulles had a record preceding that. Grand theft auto. Drunk driving. Drunk in auto. Public drunkenness. Petty theft, twice. Not a highly credible person.

It did not require a lawyer of Dillon's caliber to take Bulles's direct testimony apart on cross-examination. Seymour Bulles was a slow-witted, unimaginative liar.

Bulles admitted that he had been dissatisfied with MacDonald Oliver's handling of his case. Yes, he was disgruntled with the settlement Oliver had arranged. Sure, he might have said in some bar that he was going to get even with MacDonald Oliver. He did not remember. He drank a lot.

Dillon cross-examined Bulles about Oliver's refusal to return his one hundred thousand dollars. Bulles swore he had met with Mac in his office about 10:00 A.M. Dillon put the public records in evidence, which proved that MacDonald Oliver had been in department ninety-eight, Superior Court, from 9:00 A.M. until noon that day. Bulles then supposed it must have been the next day. Bulles confessed that he was no good with dates.

"How about numbers?" asked Dillon.

"Huh?"

"Did you ask Mr. Oliver why he would not return your money?"

Bulles leaned back, arms behind his head. "Nah."

"Didn't you ask him why he was refusing to give you back your one hundred thousand dollars?"

"Well—yeah. He just wouldn't say."

"Didn't Oliver say you owed it to him?"

"Yeah, I guess."

"Didn't he say he had earned the one hundred thousand dollars for attorney's fees?"

"Yeah, for attorney's fees, he said—right."

"All this happened within a day or two after the settlement?"

"Right."

Dillon waved a paid bill before Bulles. "So how come, Mr. Bulles, that a month later, when you got a bill from Sorensen, Oliver, Bradford, and Smith for eight hundred dollars' attorney's fees, you paid it?"

"I guess he figured I owed him another eight hundred—I don't know—I didn't want him coming after me."

Dillon had the paid bill marked in evidence and displayed to the jury before proceeding.

"Where did you get the one hundred thousand dollars you say you gave Mr. Oliver?"

Dillon did not think he would get away with that question without objection. A good argument could be made that Bulles's source of funds was irrelevant and immaterial. Judge Hart glanced at the prosecuting attorney, but no objection was made.

"Uh, I saved it. It was my life's savings."

Dillon had been ambivalent about asking the question at all. Bulles could have safely "confessed" that he had embezzled the money from

Cal Coastal Savings, which might have had some credibility. Bulles was immune from criminal or civil prosecution. He had already been sentenced for the criminal offense, and Cal Coastal's civil case against him had been settled. The association could not sue him again on the same claim. But "life savings"? Dillon was delighted with the answer.

Dillon quickly established that Seymour Bulles had been employed only eight of the past twelve years. His lifetime gross earnings could not have exceeded ninety-six thousand dollars. Several jurors twittered.

"Where did you keep your savings before you turned it over to Mr. Oliver?"

"Bank. In a bank."

"What are the name and address of the bank in which you had one hundred thousand dollars on deposit?"

"Uh, I mean a bank at home." Bulles smirked. "Uh, like, you know, a piggy bank."

"You kept one hundred thousand dollars in a piggy bank?"

"Well, when it got to be too much, I shoved it under the mattress."

The jury roared. It was the funniest thing they had ever heard. Bulles laughed, too, delighted at his success.

The forged receipt was less vulnerable, but Dillon punched large holes in it. The LAPD expert on questioned documents testified for the prosecution that in his opinion, the initials M. O. had in all probability been written by MacDonald Oliver. On cross-examination, Dillon managed to get the man to concede a ten percent possibility of error. Mac agreed that the concession gave Dillon a fine opportunity to argue that even the prosecution's own witness had not claimed authenticity of the document beyond a reasonable doubt.

The defense handwriting expert was a white-haired gentleman with forty years of impressive credentials. He swore flatly he was absolutely certain that MacDonald Oliver had not initialed the receipt. He explained the basis for his opinion with blackboard demonstrations and slides. He testified that while it was feasible to prove that a single set of initials had not been made by a specific person, it was impossible to prove conclusively that one set of initials had definitely been signed by a particular person.

"It's like blood typing," the old gentleman explained. "A blood test can only prove conclusively that I could not be the father or that I could be the father. The test can never prove that I am the father."

The Sorensen, Oliver, Bradford, and Smith letterhead on which the receipt had been typed was a sticky point. Marla had learned the printer occasionally gave out letterhead samples to potential customers, but the printer had no recollection of ever meeting Seymour Bulles and kept no records of the recipients. Dillon argued that Seymour Bulles had the opportunity to pilfer samples during his visits to Mac's office and that it would have been a simple matter to have the letterhead duplicated by another printer.

Dillon did better on the typewriter. The prosecution proved that the receipt had been typed on a Sorenson, Oliver, Bradford, and Smith IBM Selectric. However, Marla Zimmerman's investigation had uncovered that the offending typewriter had been out for repairs on the date shown on the receipt. Dillon was able to argue persuasively that the receipt must have been typed outside the Sorensen, Oliver, Bradford, and Smith offices.

At the preliminary hearing Dillon had unsuccessfully moved to suppress evidence of the one-hundred-thousand-dollar bank deposit. Two LAPD officers had tricked the Wells Fargo assistant manager into giving them copies of Mac's deposit records without a search warrant. The officers had bluffed the bank employee by asserting that the search warrant was still in the Hollenbeck Division office. If the assistant manager did not wish to take their word for its issuance, they would bundle him over there in the back of a patrol car so that he could see for himself.

Dillon renewed the motion to suppress the evidence of the deposit at trial. The one-hundred-thousand-dollar deposit was the core of the state's case. If that evidence could be kept out, the prosecution's case collapsed. Unfortunately Judge Hart concluded since the records were the bank's property and not the accused's, the defendant's rights had not been violated. He denied the motion.

Mac and Dillon had their only serious argument over the issue of the deposit. When Marla Zimmerman had shown the bank teller photographs of Tracy Oliver, Maxine had not been all that certain the photographs were of the girl who had come to her counter. The girl in the photos seemed younger. Donald Dillon insisted on putting Tracy on the witness stand. Not only would Tracy's denial that she had made the deposit be valuable, but the teller would be subpoenaed into court and have the opportunity to observe Tracy in person. Marla was optimistic that Maxine would not positively identify Tracy as the depositor. There was even a good chance that Maxine would realize that Tracy was not the same girl at all, and would so testify. Mac absolutely refused. He would not subject his ten-year-old daughter to the embarrassment of cross-examination. The prosecution would try to make it appear that Tracy was lying to protect her father. There was even the risk that the bank teller would mistakenly identify Tracy as the girl who made the deposit. Mac would not allow it.

What Mac could not say, and barely admitted to himself, was that he could not bear the thought of Tracy seeing him as the accused. Tracy and Mary Kathryn knew all about the charge, of course. There would have been no way to keep it from them. All the local newspapers and television newscasts carried the item of Mac's indictment. But Mac would permit neither Tracy nor Mary Kathryn in the courtroom. They were never to see him in this sorry condition. Mac was adamant.

Dillon was forced to resort to tricks that would never have gotten by an experienced prosecutor. As Dillon cross-examined Maxine, he showed the teller half a dozen pictures of young girls, all labeled "Tracy." Dillon asked the witness to identify the three photos of the genuine Tracy. After Maxine had done so, Dillon paraded three different girls to the witness stand, each of whom testified that Maxine had picked a photograph of her.

After the prosecution rested, Mac took the stand. He'd been called as a witness twice before in his life, once as an expert witness in a legal malpractice case, once by the people of the State of California in the prosecution of an embezzling Sorensen, Oliver, Bradford, and Smith bookkeeper. It was not the same. The indignity pricked. He wanted to announce to all the people in the courtroom that he did not recognize their right to subject an innocent man to this humiliation. Then he could stand up, stalk out, and go home.

The voice did not even sound like his as he heard it testify. No, Bulles did not give me one hundred thousand dollars. No, Bulles did not give me any money at all, other than to pay our eight-hundred-dollar bill. It took him two months to do that. No, I did not sign the receipt. Those initials were not made by me. I did not type the receipt. I did not cause the receipt to be typed. I never saw the receipt until after I was charged. No, I did not meet Bulles on the day after the settlement. I never saw Seymour Bulles again after the settlement until he testified at this trial. I did not ask my daughter to deposit the one hundred thousand dollars in my account. I have never asked my daughter to deposit anything in my account. I did not have anyone else take the one-hundred-thousand-dollar deposit. That deposit was made without my knowledge and without my consent. That's my name and account number printed on the deposit slip. No, I can't explain how someone else could have obtained it. No, I don't keep records of my used or unused deposit slips.

The only surprise in the trial came when the prosecution called Timothy George Bradford as its rebuttal witness. Dillon was on the edge of his chair, poised to make an objection. How could Oliver's own partner, who had even acted as Oliver's attorney on this very offense, testify against him? Mac was contemptuous but curious. He could not imagine what Timothy Bradford could possibly have to say.

Timothy Bradford had exaggerated when he told the district attorney that he would testify to Mac's confession. To be legally precise, Bradford was going to testify to MacDonald Oliver's admissions. Timothy Bradford had been aware of the distinction when he talked to the district attorney but felt dramatic license had been justified in the cause of saving his own skin.

There was nothing in Bradford's testimony for Donald Dillon to object to. No privileged communications between attorney and client were involved. Timothy Bradford simply related a conversation he overheard between MacDonald Oliver and Elizabeth Greene in a public elevator, while leaving the office at day's end. It had been two days before the indictment was returned.

"And what did you hear Mr. Oliver say?" the deputy district attorney asked.

"Mr. Oliver said, 'I owe him one hundred thousand dollars,' " answered Timothy Bradford.

"Mr. Oliver said, 'I owe him one hundred thousand dollars'?" astutely asked the prosecuting attorney.

"Yes. 'I owe him one hundred thousand dollars.' "

"Did Mrs. Greene respond to Oliver's statement?"

"Yes. She said, 'And what have you done with it?' "

"What, if anything, did the defendant reply?"

"MacDonald Oliver said, 'It's in my attaché case. I'm taking it home to change.' "

"Was Mr. Oliver carrying an attaché case with him?"

"Yes. It was the same one he has on the floor next to his chair right now."

"No questions of this witness, Your Honor," said Dillon.

Timothy Bradford hurried from the courtroom. Mac glared trying to catch his eye, but Bradford was not interested in further confrontation.

Donald Dillon had Elizabeth Greene testify to her version of the elevator conversation. Liz smiled encouragement to Mac as she took the oath. Good ol' loyal Liz, Mac thought. She was the only secretary he'd ever had.

"Yes, Mr. Oliver and I had a conversation in the elevator that day. Yes, Timothy Bradford was in the elevator, too. So were several other people I don't even know."

"Did Mr. Oliver mention one hundred thousand dollars?"

"Yes, he did. I have to back up. While Mr. Oliver and I were waiting for the elevator, Mr. Oliver had been telling me about Seymour Bulles's ridiculous claim. When we got into the elevator, Mr. Oliver said, 'According to him, I owe him one hundred thousand dollars.' "

"Whom did you understand Mr. Oliver was talking about?"

"Why, Seymour Bulles, of course. That's who he had been talking about. Mr. Oliver was simply saying that Mr. Bulles claimed he was owed one hundred thousand dollars."

"I see. Mr. Oliver did not admit that he owed the money?"

"Of course not. He didn't owe the money."

"And did you ask Mr. Oliver anything?"

"Yes. I was joking. I asked, 'And what have you done with it?' "

"What did Mr. Oliver say?"

"He said, 'It's in my attaché case. I'm taking it home for change.' "

"Did you say, 'for change'?"

"Yes. For change. You know, pocket money. I thought it was hilarious—then. We were just kidding around." Liz grew indignant and turned to the jury. "Does anyone really believe that a man would embezzle one hundred thousand dollars and then confess to it before strangers in a public elevator?"

"Objection, Your Honor," said the deputy district attorney.

"Sustained. The jury will disregard the witness's last remark. Please confine yourself to answering counsel's questions, Mrs. Greene."

Dillon recalled Mac to the stand. Mac confirmed Elizabeth Greene's recollection of the conversation and went on to explain his firing Timothy Bradford as his attorney and their subsequent falling-out.

The jury was out for only twenty minutes. Dillon was elated. "It must be an acquittal, Mac. Much too fast for conviction."

In spite of the good omen, Mac was scared. He found out why when the clerk read the verdict.

"Guilty as charged."

Mac stood at Dillon's side as the appropriate postverdict motions were made.

"Move that the defendant remain at liberty on his own recognizance pending the probation report."

"No objection from the People? Granted."

"Defendant moves for a new trial."

"Counsel, I will set a date two weeks from today to hear your motion and for sentencing. We should have the probation report by then, so that if your motion is denied, we can proceed. Is that agreeable?"

Dillon nodded.

"Mr. Oliver, you will remain free on your own recognizance at my discretion and upon the following conditions: You are not to leave—"

Mac heard hardly a word that was said. He was acutely aware of a stain on the judge's chin. He was certain it was tomato sauce.

The weeks following the guilty verdict were a kaleidoscope of horrors. Mac hurt all over. His entire body was numb. Events were fragmented and confused. Time seemed to lurch back and forth.

Donald Dillon apologizing. What for? He tried the case perfectly. Odd result, though.

Marla rushing into his arms as he came through the courtroom rail. "Hang in, Mac. We will beat it. There'll be a way."

Reporters outside the courtroom. Escape back through the judge's chambers and the side corridor.

Nels hugging him to his breast, almost in tears. Cornell Sepulveda Smith holding both Mac's hands, eyes blinking, giving assurance without saying a word. Timothy George Bradford, frozen-faced, staring. Elizabeth Greene crying.

Burt Ginter driving him home and apologizing. "I'm sorry it's so damned uncomfortable, Mac. I've been meaning to get this air-conditioner fixed for weeks."

Mary Kathryn red-eyed, waiting in the driveway, open-armed. "Darling." Tracy running into his arms. "Daddy, I love you. I know you didn't do anything—"

A large drink. Gone. No effect at all. Another. "Honey, slow down—"

Tracy with a bundle of brown fur. "Daddy, I brought you a present. He's to make you feel good. Here." The shaggy mongrel pup was thrust into Mac's arms. Brown eyes stared up at him as the tail wagged frantically. "He's yours. You can even name him."

Mary Kathryn explaining, trying to be cheerful. "Mac, Tracy says he followed her home. You don't have to allow yourself to be conned by this ten-year-old—"

Mac heard himself talking. You sound pretty normal to me, he thought. "I need all the friends I can get. He looks like a jeweler I know downtown. Bernie."

Tracy grabbed the mutt. "I'll fix Bernie a place to sleep and feed him for you, Dad."

Mr. Oliver. Safely home after another terrifically hard day in the criminal courts.

The telephone calls. Incessant. More reporters. "But don't you want your side of the story told, Mr. Oliver?"

The KLA-TV mobile unit trespassing in the driveway, set up for a long shot of the front entry as the doorbell is rung. "Don't answer it. They'll go away."

More telephone calls. Laura Wennerstrom offering, "If there's anything I can do, Mac." Great—what?

"Put the answering machine on. Are we out of scotch?"

"Daddy, you're on the six o'clock news."

"Tracy!"

"It's okay, Mary Kathryn." MacDonald Oliver, the convicted felon, spent a quiet evening with his family watching television.

The *Los Angeles Evening News*. The city's third-largest, and only evening, newspaper. Page one: TOP ATTORNEY EMBEZZLES $100M.

It was too much. His own father-in-law's newspaper. Mac stalked into the kitchen, waving the sheet before Mary Kathryn as if the article were her fault.

"Have you seen this?"

"Yes. Father called to warn me. He felt he had to print it. He can't change the news. It's a very objective article, Mac. It mentions that your attorney has moved for a new trial and that if that is denied, you have the right to appeal—"

"Somehow your father's using page one to advertise that I am a convicted criminal doesn't strike me as ideally objective. He could have at least had the sensitivity to bury it on page three."

"Mac, you know how strongly he is opposed to censorship of his news staff."

"The old hypocrite doesn't strongly oppose whatever will sell his goddamn newspaper, does he?"

"Mac, that's not fair. It's a newspaper. Don't you think it hurts him? Don't you think it hurts me? How do you think it's going to be for Tracy at school tomorrow? How, oh—" Mary Kathryn tore off her apron. "You'll just have to fix your own dinner."

Mac watched Mary Kathryn's retreating back leave the kitchen before he turned off the burners. He dumped the contents of the skillet and two pots into the sink, threw the utensils in after, and turned on the hot water. To hell with dinner. Convicted thieves don't fix dinner. They steal dinner. Bernie trotted into the kitchen on ridiculously short legs and nuzzled Mac's calf. Mac pitched him a soggy morsel from the sink. Bernie sat up and panted for more. Dog. The crook's best friend.

Everyone at the office was suddenly solicitous. It was as if an office meeting had been held in Mac's absence: "All right, folks. We're here to discuss our dearly beloved MacDonald Oliver. Mac has been badly burned. His self-respect and confidence have been damaged. Be sensitive. But no patronizing. No overt expressions of pity. Carry on as before in a cheerful manner. That's the key. But watch the jokes."

Mac tried to work. It was the only refuge left. But his concentration span was down to ten minutes. Conversations with clients and with other lawyers were painful. Everyone was walking a tightrope.

Elizabeth Greene brought in a check. "Mac, here's a payment on account. It's payable to you, but it's the firm's money. Would you endorse it, please?"

"Don't you want a witness?"

"Oh, stop it. Around here you're not a thief."

Mac recalled his lecture to Charlie Wennerstrom. The jury decides the light was red; in that courtroom the fact is that the light was red. In Judge Hart's courtroom MacDonald Abraham Oliver is a thief. But it isn't so limited, is it? MacDonald Oliver is a thief all over town. MacDonald Oliver is a thief to everyone he sees, touches, and talks to. Wherever there are newspapers, radios, and television, MacDonald Oliver is a thief.

The frequency of Mac's petty arguments with Mary Kathryn increased. When Mary Kathryn's father telephoned to justify his newspaper's policy, Mac called him a pontifical old fart. Mac regretted that. He really respected the old fart.

At the hearing on the motion for a new trial Dillon's eloquence was largely wasted on Mac. Mac kept wondering why Judge Hart hadn't been able to trim the left half of his mustache to match the right half. Mac hardly heard Dillon itemize the ways in which the evidence was insufficient to support the verdict.

"What all these discrepancies in the state's case come down to, Your Honor, is simply this: The prosecution's case is incredible.

"You would have to believe that a respected multimillionaire attorney would steal one hundred thousand dollars of his client's money;

"That this attorney, trained and experienced in logic and deduction, would hope to get away with stealing money after signing a receipt for it;

"That such an attorney, knowledgeable of investigative methods, would deposit the stolen one hundred thousand dollars cash in one lump sum in his own personal bank account—like a red flag.

"And you would have to believe that Seymour Bulles could have had one hundred thousand dollars to steal.

"The case against MacDonald Oliver surpasses belief; it falls woefully short of satisfying the People's burden of proof of guilt beyond a reasonable doubt."

Statistically new-trial motions were losing battles, but Judge "Bleeding" Hart had held the Los Angeles County record for granting new trials in felony cases for the past seven years. Dillon sat down and crossed his fingers.

Judge Hart cleared his throat. "While it is the exclusive province of the jury to find the facts, it is the duty of the trial judge to see that this function is intelligently and justly performed. In the exercise of its supervisory power over the verdict, this court should satisfy itself that the evidence as a whole is sufficient to sustain the verdict."

Dillon liked the preface. He glanced at Mac. Mac didn't seem to be paying much attention. Mac had noticed that Judge Hart's sideburns didn't line up either. Judge Hart continued. "When an attorney is charged with a crime—particularly when a prominent attorney is charged with the commission of an offense which violates the trust placed in him by his client—"

Dillon didn't understand what Hart was saying. Was Hart preaching a different standard of proof for attorneys charged with crimes?

Hart droned on. "The public's faith in the integrity of the court is essential to the administration of justice. When the accused is a member of the bar, an officer of the court, then the appearance of justice becomes a paramount consideration—"

Hart was becoming incomprehensible. He seemed to be saying that for the sake of preserving the appearance of justice, lawyers could not expect to be afforded the same rights as other defendants. An attorney was not presumed to be innocent? He had to *look* innocent?

"For these reasons, I must conclude that the evidence as a whole is sufficient. The motion for a new trial is denied."

Mac heard that part. He sighed and perversely looked forward to the sentencing. Get me out of here. Take me away. Away from compassionate gestures and understanding friends.

Judge Hart went on. "I have read the probation report. Do counsel have their copies? The defendant has an admirable history. Extraordinary. Which makes the imposition of sentence more than normally difficult. Nevertheless—will the defendant please stand?"

Mac and Donald Dillon stood together.

"MacDonald Oliver, do you have any legal cause to show why judgment should not be pronounced against you?"

"No, Your Honor." No, just lock me up in a place where I won't be a freak anymore. Just one more felon, stubbornly protesting innocence, like all the rest.

"In the case of the *People of the State of California* versus *MacDonald Abraham Oliver.* The defendant is charged with a violation of Penal Code Section Four-eight-seven, grand theft. The record will show that a verdict of guilty as charged has been returned and recorded. The probation report has been received and reviewed by this court, and copies have been furnished to both counsel.

"Does either counsel wish to make a statement or to present any evidence on the penalty issue? No? All right. MacDonald Abraham Oliver, judgment is pronounced against you as follows:

"Imposition of sentence is suspended, and the defendant is granted probation for a period of five years upon the following terms and conditions:

"Defendant shall be imprisoned in the Los Angeles County Jail for a term of three hundred sixty days;

"Defendant is fined the sum of five thousand dollars, payable within five days;

"Defendant shall make restitution to the victim, Seymour Bulles, in the sum of one hundred thousand dollars, payable within thirty days;

"Defendant shall not associate with known criminals and shall obey—"

Mac wondered if the judge knew those hairs were growing out of his nose.

"Do you understand and accept the terms and conditions of probation?"

Dillon nudged Mac sharply.

"Yes, Your Honor." You would think all those hairs would really tickle, wouldn't you?

"Very well. The clerk will prepare a copy of the order granting probation, which the defendant will sign and—"

Donald Dillon waited until the judge finished the formalities. "Your Honor, a notice of appeal will be filed this afternoon. I move that execution of judgment be stayed pending final determination of this case on appeal."

"Anything in opposition, Mr. Prosecutor?" asked the judge.

"No objection. However, it might be appropriate to require bond for the performance of the terms of probation."

"Very well. The motion to stay execution of judgment pending appeal is granted with regard to imprisonment of the defendant in the county jail, with regard to payment of the fine, and with regard to restitution to the victim, provided that within twenty-four hours the defendant has posted bond in the amount of one hundred five thousand dollars to secure the payment of the fine and of restitution.

"Is that all, gentlemen? The court is adjourned until two P.M."

Dillon placed his hand gently on Mac's shoulder. "Come on, Mac. It's all over."

No, Don, thought Mac. You're wrong about that.

15

*I*f a barometer had been mounted on the wall of the Sorensen, Oliver, Bradford, and Smith conference room, the atmosphere would have been recorded as halfway between gloomy and grim. All the senior partners and Burt Ginter, representing the junior partners, were present. Everyone knew why Nels Sorensen had called the meeting. No one, with the possible exception of Timothy Bradford, looked forward to the discussion.

"Gentlemen," said Nels, "the first and most important item on this morning's agenda is consideration of the expulsion of MacDonald Oliver from the partnership. I emphasize that my raising this question is in no way intended to imply that I favor expulsion. Nevertheless, the issue is serious. It must be faced openly and dealt with decisively.

"After full discussion we shall vote. Since we've never before had the misfortune to use the procedure, let me refresh your recollection regarding the applicable partnership agreement provisions.

"Mac, as the partner under consideration, is entitled to be present and to participate in the discussion but cannot vote. The three remaining senior partners have one vote each. The junior partners, regardless of their number, have a combined single vote. The junior partners' one vote is a reflection of the desires of the majority of the junior partners, as determined by an independent polling of them. Burt will represent the junior partners and will exercise their vote. We have, then, a total of four eligible votes. A majority vote of three in favor of expulsion is required to accomplish that result. Any questions?"

"Nels . . . everyone," Mac said, "if no one objects, I would like to be excused. It is not that I am not interested. I don't feel that I'm needed as an advocate. I believe my presence will inhibit debate, and I have to confess that I would not enjoy listening." Mac looked around. Everyone nodded assent. "I'll wait in my office. You can have me back on a moment's notice."

After Mac left, Nels resumed. "Mac's conviction is a tragedy. It is also a fact. Mac has filed an appeal, but it is not realistic to expect a decision from the Court of Appeals for at least nine months—"

"And even if they reverse, they will probably remand the case for a new trial—more months of uncertainty," said Timothy Bradford.

Nels, who did not ordinarily lightly accept interruption, merely continued. "We must accept that the status quo will be with us for some time. Let me try to summarize the negative aspects. We know we have already lost clients as a direct result of Mac's conviction. Those few with the courage to admit it are listed under Group A in the summary delivered to you earlier. The average annual gross billings for the past three years appear in the column to the right of each client's name. Listed under Group B are former clients who have terminated their association with our firm since the day following Mac's indictment. This group has either expressed no reason for leaving us or has offered some innocuous excuse. You cannot overlook that Group B is considerably larger than Group A. I had intended to include a Group C for comparison. Group C was to have listed all clients lost during the same period in each of the preceding three years. However, as it turned out, there were none. The impact on future business seems to me to be immeasurable—"

"It can only be negative. No one is going to come to us because of Mac's criminal record," said Timothy Bradford.

"Except possibly criminals," mused Cornell Sepulveda Smith. "It may be an opportunity to expand our criminal law practice."

Nels suppressed a frown. "Cornell," he said, "as an attempt at humor, that is pathetic. Let us return to business. There is also the effect on employees to consider."

"Everyone is depressed by the verdict, but there is tremendous loyalty to Mac," said Burt.

"I had in mind more tangible effects, Burt. If the exodus of clients continues, the work load will decrease. We may have to lay off employees."

"As long as we are considering negatives," said Smith, "there is the effect on our relationship with other law firms, the courts, and the administrative agencies."

"It would seem that regardless of the ultimate determination of guilt or innocence, Mac's continuing association may have an impairing material effect on this firm," said Nels.

Burt was furious. "I don't believe I'm hearing this. MacDonald Oliver made this firm one hundred thirty-three million dollars last year—with more to come. If he loses us a thousand clients, we will still be ahead—"

"Burt," said Nels, "calm down. You're too young for apoplexy. It is merely healthy to air all considerations. Mac has not yet been condemned."

"Aren't there any less drastic alternatives?" asked Burt. "How about a suspension?"

"The partnership agreement only provides for expulsion, Burt. We have no power to suspend a partner," said Smith.

"Let's get back to our responsibility to our clients and to our employees," said Timothy Bradford.

Smith and Nels only threw Bradford dirty looks, but Burt was incensed. "How about our responsibility to our partner?" he almost shouted. "Mac's still licensed to practice law pending final judgment on appeal. Even the judge who sentenced him has stayed the execution of judgment. Is MacDonald Oliver entitled to less from his own partners than he is from the bar association or the courts?"

"I believe it's time to vote," said Nels Sorensen quietly. "Burt, do you need a few minutes to poll the other junior partners?"

"No. Nothing's been said here that we haven't already considered. I have been instructed to vote against expulsion." Burt could not resist a gratuitous and belligerent addendum: "The junior partners were unanimous."

Nels smiled. "Thank you, Burt. Timothy?"

"I vote for expulsion. It is regretful, but in the firm's interest."

"Yes," said Nels. "And, Cornell, how do you vote?"

"I cast my lot with the junior partners. Against expulsion—and you, Nels?"

"I am against expulsion. Well, now that that's over, we will just have to resign ourselves to hard times."

Burt grinned. "Nels, I apologize. You continue to surprise and delight me."

"Can the rest of the business wait?" asked Timothy Bradford. "I have to get back to work."

"There is one matter I insist on taking up this afternoon," said Smith. "But we had better get MacDonald Oliver back in here first."

In a formal manner Nels stated that Mac's expulsion had been voted down. Nels did not mention Timothy Bradford's single contrary vote. Mac stood, nodding, his eyes almost closed. Mac took a deep breath and let out an almost embarrassingly audible sigh as he retook his seat.

"Cornell, you have our attention," said Nels.

Smith stood. The effect was not overwhelming. "Pursuant to the partnership agreement provision with which we are so conveniently familiar," he said, "I move that we consider the expulsion of Timothy George Bradford from this partnership." Smith sat down.

"Is that a joke?" angrily asked Timothy Bradford.

"Timothy, I am certain that Cornell Sepulveda Smith is not joking," said Nels. "Nor should we be shocked that the question is raised. I am a little surprised at the precipitant action, however. Nevertheless, the question has been moved. Let's give this nasty matter an airing, too. Cornell, since you've already started, would you care to continue?"

"Just a moment," said Mac, sighing again. "I have no more stomach for this discussion than I did the last one. In fact, everything I said seems to apply again. May I be excused?"

Timothy Bradford was silently relieved. It would take the unanimous vote of the remaining partners to expel him.

Mac stopped as he reached the door. "Oh, Nels, I've always respected your judgment. Cast my vote as you do your own." Mac closed the door behind him.

"Now just a minute," said Timothy Bradford.

"Timothy," said Smith, "it's in our agreement. Any absent partner may give his proxy to another partner, provided that the question to be voted on is known to him in advance."

That little bastard wants to lynch me, thought Bradford, but, hell, this law firm needs me now more than ever. At least Nels will be objective.

Smith stood again. "I am seldom blunt, but I will be now. I have read the transcript of Mac's criminal trial. I suspect by now everyone in the office, including the cleaning ladies, has done so. I was particularly revolted by the testimony of our partner Timothy Bradford. My revulsion was increased by the knowledge that within a few weeks before he testified for the prosecution, he had been entrusted with the representation of the defendant—"

"But I was subpoenaed. I was obligated to testify to what I had heard," said Timothy Bradford.

"Timothy," said Nels, "everyone here is experienced in the courtroom. No one here is a fool. There is no way on this earth that the district attorney would have known to subpoena you to testify to that ridiculous dialogue unless, Timothy, you yourself had already disclosed that evidence to the district attorney concerning your own client—"

"He'd already fired—" Timothy Bradford stopped. He'd said too much.

Burt Ginter was fascinated. He'd never experienced a scene like this.

"Let's vote," said Smith.

"Not yet," said Nels. "Is there anything more you would like to say, Timothy?"

"You're damn right there is. This firm needs my contribution. After the mess Oliver has gotten us into, this firm needs all the positive support it can get. I did nothing I'm ashamed of. I simply testified to what I heard. It was my duty. You don't know the pressure they put on me—"

"Burt, would you like to be excused for a few minutes to poll the other junior partners?" asked Nels.

"Be right back," said Burt. Amazing, he thought.

Nels paced the room. Cornell Sepulveda Smith stared, unblinking, at Timothy Bradford, as if observing some specimen of insect.

"Ready," said Burt, with unexpected cheerfulness, as he reentered the room.

"I don't intend to sit through this—" Bradford started to rise.

"Sit down," said Nels. "Burt, vote."

"For expulsion," said Burt. "Oh, it was unanimous again."

"For expulsion," said Smith.

"That leaves me to decide, doesn't it? I vote for expulsion," said Nels, "twice."

Timothy Bradford left the building, fuming that a man of his wealth and position should have been treated so shabbily. His eye was caught by the front-page deck, the subheadline of the *Los Angeles Evening News.* Any news relating to his gold hoard interested him. He purchased a copy from the vending machine and stood on the sidewalk reading:

BULLION RESERVE'S CHAIRMAN SUICIDE

The suicide of David Saxon, thirty-nine-year-old chairman of Bullion Reserve of America, has prompted an investigation into the company's finances. Early results suggest that sixty million dollars' worth of gold bullion sold to over thirty thousand customers never had existed . . .

Mac sat facing the other senior partners of Sorensen, Oliver, and Smith. "I am not acting impulsively. Nels, you are the closest to a father—Cornell—oh, hell. It's just not fair to you. I have to resign."

"Mac, we are your friends," said Smith. "We want to weather this with you."

"I know you do. You've already shown that. I am deeply grateful that you do, but I'm worse than useless. I am an outcast, a pariah."

"Mac," said Nels, "I cannot let you. I dragged you into this with that damned Bulles case. We'll all get through this somehow. God knows, none of us needs the money."

"It isn't just you two I have to consider. It's Burt, Marla, and the rest. I cannot ask the entire firm to share my personal disaster."

Nels Sorensen and Cornell Sepulveda Smith looked at each other. "Well?" asked Nels.

"Sorensen and Smith," said Smith, "the incredible shrinking law firm."

Mac had to get out of Los Angeles. He was just too notorious. He would move the family to someplace where he wasn't well known, like Pakistan or maybe Alpha Centauri.

They settled for Santa Barbara, a pretty coastal town about one hundred miles northwest of Los Angeles. Santa Barbara was known for its persistent adherence to red tile roofs, as well as for having the only traffic signal lights on U.S. Highway 101 between San Diego and San Francisco.

An important attraction for Mac was the small local marina in which he could dock *Abigail*. He'd had to pay only fifteen thousand dollars under the table for the forty-foot slip.

Mac leased a small office on West Anapamu Street. Marla and Burt offered to join him but were thanked and rejected. What would they all do? Find a fourth for bridge?

Mac and Mary Kathryn purchased a year-old pseudo-Spanish house, with the mandatory red tile roof, high on the Riviera, overlooking the town and the harbor. With binoculars Mac could pick out *Abigail's* mast. Mac knew Mary Kathryn would find satisfaction for months redecorating the place. Tracy would be delighted with her new freedom. She'd be able to bicycle all over town—the beach, the volleyball courts, the taco stands.

Mac hadn't figured it quite right. Mary Kathryn hated the place. She constantly and vocally mourned for her Bel Air mansion. Tracy did, however, enjoy roaming on her bicycle. She tried to run away from home twice in the first month.

It wasn't much of a law practice, but Mac didn't really feel like working anyway. It got him out of the house and gained him solitude.

Laura Wennerstrom asked Mac to help her with a legal problem. The Wennerstrom Foundation had been making substantial grants to a pair of Ph.D.'s who had so far invented nothing but excuses and were now trying to invent expenses.

Mac drove down to the city for the conference with Laura. He welcomed the excuse to get away for a day. He would have been glad to get away for a year. The meeting started at Laura's Century City office, moved to Mateo's for lunch, and, an hour and a half later, wound up in Laura's bedroom. Almost nothing had been spoken. They both wanted it to happen. It was right, they were sure. Then they were there.

God, she was strong—and warm. Her solace flowed into him, and he glowed with the comfort of holding her and of being held by her. Her generous passion softened and melted his bitterness. Her long, lean legs, her tapered fingers, and whispered words tenderly consoled his soul. Mac's pain dissolved. Everything is going to be all right, Mac, she whispered. Everything.

The decision of the Court of Appeals in *People* v. *Oliver* was rendered within a refreshingly short time. Mac wondered whether Nels or Cornell Sepulveda Smith had anything to do with that.

MacDonald Oliver's conviction was reversed, and the case remanded for a new trial. Justice Will Bronson's opinion stated:

> . . . detectives contacted the bank in which defendant maintained an account and, without a warrant or any court process, obtained photostatic copies of defendant's bank records. Defendant was charged with grand theft. His motion to suppress the evidence obtained from his bank was denied. Ultimately, defendant was convicted and filed this appeal.

In determining whether an illegal search has occurred under the provisions of our Constitution, the appropriate test is whether a person has exhibited a reasonable expectation of privacy and, if so, whether the expectation has been violated by unreasonable governmental intrusion.

Obviously, a bank customer expects that his banking transactions will remain private. Obviously, such expectation is reasonable.

We next determine whether the police unreasonably interfered with defendant's expectation of privacy. It is significant that the bank provided the records to the police in response to an informal oral request. Thus, the character, scope, and relevancy of the material obtained were determined entirely by the exercise of the unbridled discretion of the police. If this search were held reasonable, nothing could prevent any law enforcement officer from informally obtaining all of a person's bank records, even though such records might have no relevance to a crime, if any, under investigation. We rely heavily on *Burrows v. Superior Court.* . . .

Mac skipped to the end.

. . . We hold that bank records obtained without the benefit of legal process were acquired as the result of an illegal search and seizure (Cal. Const., Art. I, Section 13) and that the trial court should have granted the motion to suppress such evidence. The defendant's conviction is reversed, and the case remanded for a new trial. Upon the retrial, defendant's bank records, or any evidence from said records, shall be suppressed in accordance with the views expressed herein.

A new trial. Vindication. A fluky result like that couldn't possibly happen twice. Everything was going to be all right.

As it turned out, Mac wasn't even retried. The district attorney's office couldn't find its star witness, Seymour Bulles. The Court of Appeals decision prohibited the prosecution from using evidence of the one-hundred-thousand-dollar deposit into Mac's account. The case against Mac simply evaporated. After the authorities had failed to produce Bulles within a reasonable time, Donald Dillon easily won a dismissal.

The case of *People v. Oliver* was over. Mac could never be retried.

Legally Mac was as innocent as if he'd never been indicted, tried, or convicted.

It was funny, Mac thought. Not one word in the papers or on television. I guess, Mac, you're just not as notorious as you thought. Or is it simply that facts tending to reduce notoriety are not newsworthy?

Marla had been searching for Seymour Bulles's girlfriend, but it was the girl who found Marla. Seymour Bulles had left Juanita. She was pregnant. She'd lost her job. She was broke. And she was ready to talk.

Juanita's story was fascinating. Seymour was crazy, she said. A thief, a liar, and a drunk, too. But somehow, when he drank, he always told the truth.

A strange, mean-looking man had offered Seymour much money if he would go to the police and say MacDonald Oliver stole from him. Seymour was very happy. He would be getting even with MacDonald Oliver, and he would have much money. He would marry Juanita, and they would go away.

Seymour was told what to testify at MacDonald Oliver's trial. Before the trial he had laughed about going to his "acting lessons." Seymour said he was going to swear he had given MacDonald Oliver one hundred thousand dollars and had received MacDonald Oliver's receipt. Seymour had shown Juanita the forged receipt before taking it to the police. Juanita did not know who had forged it. She didn't think Seymour knew either.

Seymour had nothing to do with depositing the one hundred thousand dollars in MacDonald Oliver's account. When he learned of that, he was angry. He had somehow convinced himself that the money should have been his.

After MacDonald Oliver's trial, Seymour had come home drunk, with six bottles of whiskey, two TV dinners, and almost five thousand dollars. It was the down payment, he said. He would get the rest after MacDonald Oliver was sentenced.

Then Seymour left one day and never came back. Just disappeared, Juanita said, taking most of the money with him.

Marla squeezed Juanita's memory for every detail of the mysterious man who had conducted Seymour Bulles through Mac's frame-up. At Donald Dillon's suggestion an investigation was launched to discover the man's identity. Marla patiently requestioned Juanita, fishing out times and dates, overlooked details, and possible discrepancies.

Marla was convinced that Juanita was telling the truth. Mac's hunger to be cleared so clouded his objectivity that his opinion was worthless. Donald Dillon was cautious.

The girl's story hung together logically, but Dillon was bothered by Juanita's having voluntarily come forward. Dillon worried about the possibility of a devious trap. Mac suggested that Juanita be given a lie detector test. Marla thought that was a marvelous idea.

"It's no panacea," said Donald Dillon. "Suppose the polygraph results show Juanita has lied? That test will become a millstone around your neck, Mac. If it comes out, it will conclusively disgrace you. Even if the polygraph shows Juanita is being truthful, it may be of no value."

"I don't understand," said Marla.

"There is no criminal proceeding pending against Mac. His conviction has been reversed. The charges against him dismissed. His legal status is as if he had never been tried and convicted—"

"Ha!" said Mac.

"Let's not discard the idea," said Dillon. "It's still worth exploring."

Mac did not say anything. He just started rubbing his blind eye. The dispirited group sat quietly. All three were thinking about the ultimate questions—so obvious no one even bothered to mention them. Who put Seymour Bulles up to it? Who put up the one hundred thousand dollars? It had to be the same person. Why was interesting, too, but that was easy. The trio knew that when they found out who, they would learn why.

Marla proposed two polygraph examinations of Juanita be arranged. Each polygrapher would monitor the test conducted by the other. Only if the polygraphers agreed that both tests were conducted competently, and that the results were valid, would either test result be released. It was possible that Juanita would fail both tests, further dishonoring Mac. Mac didn't think further dishonor was possible. Anyway, every one of Juanita's statements they had been able to check had confirmed her truthfulness. Even cynical Donald Dillon was finally convinced that Juanita was not a plant.

The conclusions of Juanita's two polygraph examiners were identical. Each was satisfied with the other's test procedure. Juanita had answered all of their questions truthfully. Seymour Bulles had indeed confessed to Juanita that he had framed MacDonald Oliver on the grand theft charge. They would provide individual written reports to Donald Dillon, including transcripts of the questions and answers. They would testify anyplace to Juanita's veracity, if they were permitted to do so.

As the results came in, Marla kissed and hugged Dillon, Juanita, and Mac. Dillon confined himself to Juanita and Marla. Mac just stood there, grinning like an imbecile.

Donald Dillon failed summarily with the assistant city editor of the *Los Angeles Times.*

"Let me see if I've got this straight, Mr. Dillon. A gentleman has his conviction reversed on appeal, after which the case against him is dismissed for lack of evidence, so that this gentleman continues to be presumed innocent. After that this gentleman had polygraph tests given to a newly discovered witness, who confirms that he is indeed innocent, just as the criminal justice system has presumed he was. Mr. Dillon, that is not news. That is just boring."

Marla Zimmerman fared a little better with the *Los Angeles Evening News.* Mary Kathryn's father's newspaper gave the story two column inches on page eight—of Section B: LIE DETECTOR TEST RAISES QUESTIONS ABOUT ATTORNEY'S CONVICTION ON GRAND THEFT CHARGES.

Dillon thought he had scored a comeback when KLA-TV agreed to give the item twenty seconds on the six o'clock news. By 6:33 it was obvious that the *Three's Company* rerun would not include information regarding MacDonald Oliver. Dillon called the station.

"Oh, yeah, Mr. Dillon. Sorry we couldn't use that. Your guy got pushed off the agenda by that seventeen-car rear-ender on the Hollywood Freeway. Hey, maybe you can get a case out of that, huh?"

When Dillon approached the new district attorney, he was not surprised at the lack of enthusiasm. The baseball posters had been replaced by pastoral watercolors, beige nylon substituted for velour. The new district attorney did not smoke. But the facts of life had not changed. Dillon was determined to crack the man's intransigence. The new district attorney listened patiently while Dillon argued eloquently. Not only was it a prosecutor's sworn duty to assist in the vindication of an innocent man, but it would be politically valuable for the district attorney's office to come out publicly in support of new evidence, which proved that an innocent man had been charged and tried.

The new district attorney had the files pertaining to Mac's case on his desk. "Mr. Dillon," he said, "I have reviewed these files. True, your man was tried and initially convicted, but the sentence was stayed pending appeal. The Court of Appeals reversed. You moved for dismissal of the case for lack of evidence. We even joined in the motion. The case was, in fact, ordered dismissed. Your client is home free. His legal position is as if he had never been tried at all. Frankly I don't understand what it is you want."

The new district attorney waved at the stacks of police investigation reports, grand jury transcripts, booking records, pretrial discovery motions, trial transcripts, appellate briefs, reporters' and clerk's transcripts on appeal, and the Court of Appeals' opinion. "Why, it's perfectly obvious your client doesn't even have a record."

16

The corridor of the new intensive care wing glistened antiseptic white, but what was it about hospital passageways, Grant Radcliffe wondered, that always smelled so— Of course . . . of death.

"Your grandfather has had a massive stroke preceded by two heart attacks a week apart," said the young neurologist. "The second attack caused an embolism which reached his brain and destroyed tissue."

"Doctor, couldn't that have been anticipated and prevented?" asked Sarah. She looked as if she'd been up all night. She had.

"Yes and no," replied Dr. Ralston.

Typical physician's response, thought Grant Radcliffe, but he restrained himself from saying anything. Sarah was already stretched to the limit.

"I am not being evasive," continued the doctor. "Yes, we anticipate strokes caused by embolism. Yes, we have the means to prevent them.

We used to routinely prescribe anticoagulants for heart attack victims to prevent embolisms. Then we learned that while embolisms were causing strokes in less than five percent of our patients, the anticoagulants were producing adverse side effects in ninety-five percent of them. So, no, we had no way of foreseeing that your grandfather would be within the five percent."

"Can I see him now?"

"Not yet, Mrs. Radcliffe. He's still critical. I've got to stabilize him first. It's doubtful he would even recognize you yet. Perhaps this evening or in the morning."

"Doctor, it's imperative that my grandfather have every possible opportunity to recover. I know you are recognized as one of the best neurologists in the country—"

Dr. Ralston raised an eyebrow.

"Yes, I've already checked up on you, Doctor. I know you feel secure enough in your professional reputation not to be offended by my request. I want you to retain a consultant, the best you can find. You choose the man—someone you respect and can work with—from anywhere. The expense is not to be considered. My grandfather must have every possible advantage. Even if a procedure offers only slight benefit in proportion to the expense or effort, it must be done. Maynard Chase is important."

"I appreciate his importance to you, Mrs. Radcliffe."

Sarah shook her weary head. "No, Doctor, not just to me. Maynard Chase is important."

Sarah and Grant met with Dr. Ralston again that evening. How young Ralston looked. Grant Radcliffe was reminded of when he had played the doctor in the senior class play.

"How is he?" asked Sarah.

"The prognosis is extremely guarded. He is stabilized but quite weak. After all, your grandfather is eighty-five. Another attack now would kill him."

That was interesting, thought Grant.

"Let me be candid, Mrs. Radcliffe. The stroke was massive. If your grandfather survives, his entire right side will be permanently paralyzed.

Oh, he may regain use of facial muscles, but he won't use his right limbs again. He's extremely aphasic—do you understand?"

"It means his speech is impaired, doesn't it?"

"Yes, but much worse than that. He has lost the ability to express ideas in words. He won't be able to read or write."

"Is his mind—"

"That's probably the worst, Mrs. Radcliffe. His compehension will be complete, or nearly so. It's difficult to measure. He will understand fully but will be unable to communicate normally. If he gets by the next few days, he may improve substantially in the coming months, but—Mrs. Radcliffe, I don't mean to be insensitive, but I think you have to know—he will never be able to act as chairman of the board of TOPCO. His productive days are over."

"Thank you for your candor, Doctor. Yes, I have to know." Sarah sighed and stood taller. "May we see him now?"

The room looked more like a laboratory than intensive care. Maynard Chase was hooked up to an IV solution. He was wired so that his vital signs could be monitored at the nurses' station. The room was armed with advanced life support equipment and drugs. Sarah had insisted on a private nurse, although she had been assured that it was unnecessary. The nurse sat half watching the EKG machine and thumbing a magazine.

Maynard Chase looked like hell. His complexion was pale gray, the right side of his face flaccid, distorted with paralysis.

"Just a few minutes, please," said the nurse. "He's very weak."

Sarah leaned over to kiss the old man's cheek. Maynard Chase's mouth worked, but no sounds were coming out.

"Patience, Grandfather, I'm listening." Sarah bent her ear to his cheek.

The sounds barely came. "Goddamn, goddamn. No, no, no."

"Don't be surprised at his language," the nurse said. "It's the aphasia."

"You should have heard him before," said Sarah. She whispered for a long time into his ear.

Was something like a smile on the old man's lips?

*   *   *

Grant Radcliffe was impressed with the efficiency of Sarah's actions. It had not even been necessary for him to make suggestions. By late that evening she had wrested a promise from a senior O'Malley & Byers partner that the petition for appointment of Sarah Channing Chase Radcliffe as conservator of the person and estate of Maynard Chase would be ready for signature and filing by 9:00 A.M.

Grant was in the study mulling over possible moves when Sarah came in.

"Darling," she asked, "can you access names and addresses of all TOPCO shareholders on your office terminal?"

Grant was delighted. Sarah really understood. They would have to move decisively.

"Darling," Sarah continued, "we have three months until the annual shareholders' meeting. Three months to solicit the proxies we need for control of the company. We have a head start. As soon as I am appointed conservator, we will control grandfather's seven percent and my three percent. You concentrate on the institutional shareholders. I'll start with the old-line families."

"That sounds effective. Let's start with the largest holdings and work down. I'll have proxy cards printed in the morning. Our slate will consist of the five directors presently controlled by Maynard Chase plus—"

"Me for chairman," said Sarah. "And you for president in place of Danning Pearson. Oh, I have an appointment with Danning at nine-thirty."

"Danning won't help us, love. He'll want the chairmanship for himself and his own protégé to take over as president."

"I know about Fortney, darling. Shoots in the low eighties. Fix me a drink, will you?"

As the newly appointed conservator of Maynard Chase, Sarah acquired complete control of Maynard Chase's affairs and property. The power to manage Maynard Chase's affairs, however, did not give Sarah any right to act in his place as chairman of TOPCO. If Sarah Channing Chase Radcliffe wanted to control TOPCO, she would have to secure the support of a majority of its shareholders. In her meeting with Danning Pearson, Sarah had shamed the TOPCO president into giving her a fair chance to win shareholders' support. After all, Maynard Chase had hoisted Danning Pearson from the oil fields to his present position. Pearson figured the chairman's granddaughter was little more than a girl. Hell, giving her a fair chance would just make him look good to the shareholders.

Sarah wheedled the use of the fastest executive company jet. She also wangled an office, two full-time secretaries, and a computer terminal tied into the company's mainframe.

The red, gold, and blue Gulfstream III crisscrossed the Western Hemisphere at near-sonic speeds, carrying Sarah Channing Chase Radcliffe and her blue proxy cards imprinted with red and gold lettering into the homes and offices of old family friends. Sarah flew from Boston to Dallas, Houston to San Francisco, New York to London, Paris to Florence, Montreal to Chicago—wherever there were major TOPCO shareholders who had been friends of her grandfather or her parents. Sarah adroitly sold herself and her husband as the natural successors to carry on her grandfather's policies. Often Sarah had to return once, occasionally twice, but Sarah got proxy cards signed.

Sarah had a computer terminal installed in the Gulfstream so that via satellite connection, she could constantly monitor the percentage of shareholders committed to her slate and to the opposition. This enabled her to plan the most efficient route to the next largest group of uncommitted shares.

Grant Radcliffe concentrated on the institutional stockholders: trust companies, foundations, banks, and mutual funds. Grant did well, but the institutions did not succumb to quite the degree of sentimental affection that the old families had for the chairman's granddaughter.

Danning Pearson and Fortney Gilbert, meanwhile, were not idle. They were quietly and effectively gathering up green proxies of their own.

Sarah did not neglect Maynard Chase. Sarah was extravagant in her effort. A full-time physician was retained to monitor Maynard Chase's condition and to direct his therapy program. Every rehabilitating procedure available was considered. The old man drove himself merci-lessly. Within a few weeks Maynard Chase could drag himself on and off his motorized wheelchair. In a month, with the aid of a steel leg brace and cane, he could take a few steps. His ruddy color returned, and his facial muscles regained control. Sarah and Grant had him moved into their own home.

The old man's aphasia remained severe, however. Speech therapists spent hours with him daily. Computerized speech synthesizers accel-erated his progress, but Maynard Chase was not exactly conversational. Sarah and Grant could talk to him, mostly by playing an intuitive form of twenty questions. After two months Maynard Chase could sign his name with his left hand. His right was permanently paralyzed. His intellect was intact. Neither Sarah nor Grant could beat him in a game of chess. Maynard Chase understood precisely what was happening in the proxy fight and waited eagerly for the daily standings. But in the final weeks before the shareholders' meeting it was obvious that Maynard Chase was not going to take an active role in the selection of his successor.

Grant and Sarah both were tiring. Sarah had been maintaining an exhausting schedule in her worldwide quest for proxies, while also conducting the chairman's considerable business interests and even managing to continue her weekly visit to May Anne in Capistrano-by-the-Sea. Grant had been spreading himself between soliciting institutional shareholders and doing his job at TOPCO. The chairman's absence had greatly increased Grant's work load. Neither Danning Pearson nor Fortney Gilbert seemed to be of much assistance.

"The computer shows us with thirty-two percent of the votes, the Pearson forces with thirty-five percent, leaving thirty-three percent uncommitted," said Grant.

"And only a week to go," sighed Sarah. "We need an exceptionally good idea."

"Idea," said Maynard Chase. Lately he had taken to parroting the key words in Sarah's and Grant's sentences. "No, no, no, no, goddamn. Yes."

Sarah paid attention. Maynard Chase wanted the floor.

"Grandfather, do you have an idea?"

"Yes, yes."

"To get us more proxies signed up?"

"Yes."

"Is your idea for institutional or privately owned shares?"

"No, no, goddamn."

"Will it work for institutional and privately owned shares?"

"Yes, yes, shares, shares."

"Shares," said Grant. "That's it. You want us to buy up shares? If we mortgaged everything and bought on margin, we could make a healthy dent in the uncommitted percentage."

"No, no, no."

"You don't want us to buy shares?" said Sarah.

"No. No shares."

"Surely you don't want us to dump shares?" asked Grant.

"Yes, yes, dump."

Sarah couldn't believe it. "You want us to sell our stock? Just give up the fight, and the company, and walk away?"

"No, no, no." Maynard Chase looked angry. "Goddamn, damn, shares, dump." Maynard Chase lifted his cane and waved it in Grant's face. "You."

"Wait," said Grant Radcliffe. "Maybe I've got it. You want us to threaten?"

"Yes, yes, yes. Threaten."

"We should bluff," said Sarah. "We threaten to sell my stock and your stock unless the shareholders commit to us—"

"And I threaten to resign as executive vice-president unless they sign up with us," yelled Grant.

"Yes, yes." The old man thumped his cane on the floor.

"The combination of the chairman's stock and the chairman's granddaughter's stock being dumped on the market, together with my quitting simultaneously, would cause a panic in the market—"

"Yes."

"—and would depress the value of everyone else's stock. We threaten to hammer down the price of TOPCO stock unless the holdouts come along with us," said Grant.

"Threat, yes," said the old man as he leaned back in his wheelchair to rest. Sarah gave him a kiss on his forehead and went for the telephone.

The ploy was effective but not conclusive. On the morning of the shareholders' meeting the computer gave the Radcliffe slate forty-three percent of the vote, the opposition thirty-seven percent, with twenty percent uncommitted.

The TOPCO annual shareholders' meeting was held in the grand ballroom of the Century Plaza Hotel. The irony of the site of Grant Radcliffe's potential triumph being the same as that of Charlie Wennerstrom's last supper did not escape Radcliffe.

As president of the corporation Danning Pearson presided at the meeting. Just before the vote Danning Pearson graciously acceded to Grant Radcliffe's request for the floor.

"What's going on?" whispered Sarah.

"Surprise," whispered Grant as he stepped onto the stage.

"I promise not to repeat a word of the campaign speeches for the opposing slates," said Grant Radcliffe. "You all know this great company of ours was essentially built by the force and the power of one man—Maynard Chase. Maynard Chase would like to tell you his choice for his successor—"

There was a hush. Everyone knew the old man couldn't talk. This pitch promised to be pathetic or bad taste, or both.

Grant Radcliffe continued. "The person that he, Maynard Chase, believes will most effectively carry out his policies and complete his program. We all know that the chairman's unfortunate illness has impaired his ability to speak. Nevertheless, Maynard Chase remains the greatest intellect in the industry today."

Scattered applause. Grant Radcliffe held up his hand. "Maynard Chase cannot speak. His paralysis prevents it, but Maynard Chase can still use his mind. Through computer technology, I have arranged for Maynard Chase to communicate to you what he thinks."

Grant Radcliffe turned and signaled to the wings. Behind him the curtain raised, revealing a full-size cinema screen. From Radcliffe's right, a computer terminal on a stand was wheeled out, trailing a heavy-duty cable. From his left the chairman himself was being wheeled to the center of the stage. Everyone stood.

Radcliffe raised his hands. "Since the chairman cannot speak with his mouth, we have arranged for him to speak with his left hand. A standard computer keyboard has been placed before his wheelchair. The chairman will type out his statement on the keyboard. The computer will print out his words on the screen behind me, so that you can all see them as he presses the keys. Be patient. The chairman can only use one finger at a time for this."

Radcliffe turned to Maynard Chase. "Mr. Chairman, are you ready?"

Everyone in the auditorium saw Maynard Chase nod yes.

"Tell us who should be your successor to the chairmanship of TOPCO."

Maynard Chase's left hand found the keyboard and laboriously typed out one letter at a time. The message flashed on the big screen behind him: I WANT SARAH.

Maynard Chase leaned back in his wheelchair. Even the opposition stood and applauded the effort.

The vote was fifty-eight percent in favor of the Radcliffe slate. Within the hour the board of directors would meet and elect Sarah Radcliffe chairman of the board and Grant Radcliffe president of the company.

As the crowd filtered noisily into an adjoining room for the traditional refreshments, Grant Radcliffe and the chairman stayed on the stage. Sarah joined them, and the three silently basked in their triumph.

"What a marvelously dramatic idea," said Sarah as she reached for the keyboard.

"Sarah, wait."

"It's all right, Grant. I just want to say . . ." Sarah typed CONGRATULATIONS.

The big screen behind them flashed: I WANT SARAH. I WANT—

"Turn it off quick before someone sees," yelled Grant, reaching for the switch.

"You fraud," said Sarah. "No matter which ten keys are pressed, it prints out I WANT SARAH."

"We practiced, but your grandfather couldn't get the sequence right. It's the aphasia. What the hell, it's still what he wanted."

Sarah stared, unsure of her feelings. She was certain only that Grant Radcliffe had dimensions previously unrecognized by her.

17

*M*acDonald Oliver's efforts to forget the past and get on with his life were not meeting with particular success.

Mac's Santa Barbara law practice had grown. The cases were smaller than he'd been used to, but that wasn't so bad. What was worse was the type of client he seemed to be attracting. Local sharpies consistently sought to use him for legal assistance in questionable transactions. Nobody said so, of course, but Mac supposed he had a reputation as a thief who'd gotten away with it. His experience should be useful in helping others accomplish the same thing.

Mac was drinking heavily. It had been two before lunch. Now he was up to three instead of lunch. Mac's pain had been substantially eased by the time he got the afternoon call from one of his least favorite clients.

"Yes, Doctor. I know that's what you want to do. I just don't think it's fair." The prick, Mac thought. He spends more time developing real estate than he does practicing medicine, and now he wants me to help him screw his partners. "No. It isn't that I don't want your business—

"Tell you what, Doc. Why don't you take two aspirin and call me in the morning?" Mac hung up. Fuck him.

Countless drinks and hours later Mac drove home. He knew he'd negotiated the curves and dips of Alameda Padre Serra with impressive dexterity. That was why he was so surprised when he rammed the BMW into the rear of Mary Kathryn's parked Mercedes—in his own driveway.

Mary Kathryn heard the crash and came running. "Oh. My beautiful Mercedes-Benz."

Mac wasn't swaying much as he surveyed the crumpled rear end. She was right. "It certainly does," he agreed.

All Mac's friends made extreme efforts to help straighten him out. They did it directly, individually, conspiratorially, and collectively. They'd pressured Mac into consulting priests, psychologists, Alcoholics Anonymous, and transcendental meditation. Nothing was working.

Mac and Laura met frequently. Mac found it easy to arrange excuses to be away overnight. "I have a two-day trial in *Blank* versus *Blank*, Mary Kathryn," was a good standard line. Mac suspected Mary Kathryn didn't care a lot anymore.

The times with Laura were Mac's only joy. Of course, it was the comfort of holding her close, coming into her. Those long, warm legs. But that was not all. Laura tried everything she knew to reinject some self-respect and strength into him, forcing him to work, to think, to use his skills. At first it seemed to help. But not enough.

Mac was becoming sloppy and indolent. The lean, hard body she used to thrill to was becoming puffy and padded.

Laura, who had always known precisely what she felt and thought, grew confused. The same man she had resisted at first because he was so hard and tough had become disgustingly weak.

The trouble, the monumental problem, was that Mac felt disgraced.

Half the time Mac showed up revoltingly drunk. It was getting so that she couldn't stand the smell of him.

When Mac was sober, he was either sullen or belligerent.

"All you want to do is argue," Laura said.

Mac yelled back at the top of his voice, "I do not."

Even Laura tired. Finally she gave up. First her husband, the rabbit, then Mac, the self-pitying drunk. It was hopeless. Betrayed again.

On behalf of Grant Radcliffe, the man kept loose tabs on Mac. They gloated at his deterioration. At Radcliffe's urging, but almost as a lark, the man persuaded a disturbed and highly suggestible young girl to accuse Mac of molestation. The girl had a history of making such groundless accusations. But she was under age, so the Santa Barbara police felt obliged at least to investigate. The girl refused to testify against Mac. He was not even charged.

Nothing came of it. Except, of course, that a few people suspected that the man who had gotten away with at least one previous criminal offense might just have eased by another. Radcliffe and the man hadn't expected anything more. It was amusing as hell.

Shortly after that episode Mac came home one night to find nothing remaining of his family but a brief note. Mary Kathryn had left him. She had taken Tracy with her, of course. They were returning to Los Angeles. He would be contacted by her lawyers. And oh, yes, he must remember to feed Bernie.

Mac was surprised to realize that he didn't feel much sense of loss. After all, he had genuinely loved her. The past tense seemed to be the key. He guessed he just didn't feel much anymore. Period.

Mac did manage to bring himself to telephone Mary Kathryn once before the divorce settlement.

"Oh, Mac," she said, "we used to be so happy. Do you think we could ever be that way again?"

"Why the hell do you want to be happy?" Mac had replied. "I hear it's not so great."

Mary Kathryn was scrupulously fair about the financial aspects. Afterward Mac still had much more money than he could imagine what to do with. What difference did it make anyway? Like everything else in his life, the wealth was pointless.

*   *   *

Mac closed his law office and bade farewell to Santa Barbara. There weren't enough clients left to fill half a file drawer anyway. And more and more people were crossing the street to avoid him.

Mac moved back down to Marina del Rey. He found an apartment overlooking the entrance channel. Bernie was acceptable upon payment of an exorbitant cleaning deposit. *Abigail* was docked just a few feet away. A good place to get lost in—Marina del Rey. Everyone was anonymous or, at least, private. You could see all of their bodies in bikinis or shorts, and something of their faces behind the dark glasses, but that was all. No one wanted to be, or to get, too close. Which was fine. Just the way Mac wanted it.

Mac picked up the cocktail waitress a few days after he'd moved in. The lounge advertised semilive entertainment. Mac never did find out what that was. The girl took him to her place. She said she maintained better control that way. She was perhaps just a little too plump, but pretty. And maybe not too bright, but nice. Mac tried. He tried hard all night. The girl was polite and understanding. It happened to everyone sometimes, she'd said. Mac kissed her good-bye. He didn't think she'd be crushed if she never saw him again. Who needs an impotent drunk anyway?

When Mac got back to his own apartment, the letter from Internal Revenue was waiting. IRS wanted income tax, penalties, and interest on the one hundred thousand dollars that had been deposited into his account and never declared.

For the first time within his memory Grant Radcliffe knew contentment. Oh, of course, he had known moments of pleasure, times of satisfaction, even brief periods free of anxiety, but never, never before had Grant Radcliffe experienced this pervasive glow of complete well-being. There had been chemically induced imitations, but they were flawed for that very reason. Even after the cocaine spread its euphoria, he still knew it was the cocaine.

Radcliffe did not record the duration of his contentment. It was, in fact, seventeen days. At first, Radcliffe did not even recognize the stirring in his gut. At age forty-five he was the chief executive officer of one of the world's largest corporations. He was married to an extremely wealthy woman to whom he continued to be attracted. Finally the opportunities would begin for him to create wealth of his own. He had sorely damaged and humiliated his enemy, MacDonald Oliver, just as he had set out to do. True, there was May Anne, but she was getting fine care and would be all right eventually. He would think about that some other time.

Even the transition of power had gone smoothly. Danning Pearson had graciously—Grant Radcliffe suspected even gratefully—resigned and retired to his ranch to raise Hereford cattle. With Sarah's approval, Grant Radcliffe had promoted Fortney Gilbert from operations vice-president to executive vice-president, thereby converting a subversive force into a loyal follower. Each of the TOPCO senior executives moved up one step. It was a grand time.

So what did this unidentified thing within him want? Radcliffe sighed, picked up a marking pen, and slashed a broad red X across the cover of MacDonald Oliver's dossier before tossing it into the bottom drawer of his new seven-foot walnut and brass desk. He strolled thirty feet to the windows of his office. The City of Angels lay forty-nine stories below him. It was all his. Only the boardroom was above him, and with Sarah's help, even that belonged to him now.

Radcliffe strode rapidly back to his desk, yanked open the bottom drawer, grabbed the MacDonald Oliver file, and threw it back on the desk. Of course. That was it. He realized then what it was he wanted.

An hour later the man sat before Grant Radcliffe's desk, admiring the company-owned Gauguin and fondling a marble and gold paperweight in his massive right hand. Radcliffe suspected the man could have crushed it in his fist.

"What do you think? Is it manageable?" asked Radcliffe.

What would the chairman think? the man wondered. He had had no contact with Maynard Chase since the stroke. Would the chairman even care? "Of course, it's manageable," the man said. "I think a better question is, Is it worth risking all this?" He looked around as he replaced the paperweight.

Radcliffe had anticipated that his request might seem irrational to the man—perhaps to anyone. But it was how he felt, damn it. Was it worth risking all this? He tried to explain.

"If he never learns who brought him down, my revenge is incomplete."

The man shrugged. "Actually, Oliver probably suspects you by now. This may be an appropriate preemptive strike."

That was enough for Radcliffe to rationalize the move. "Do you have any reservation about doing this for me personally? It would be difficult to justify on a corporate basis."

"I don't perceive the distinction." The man suspected that Maynard Chase was no longer even lucid. "As far as I'm concerned, you are TOPCO now."

Radcliffe's new office made him feel effusive. "Why do you still do it? You must be comfortably well off by now."

The man didn't take well to personal questions. There was no joy in his smile. "Same reasons as you. I'm an achiever."

"We must be confident that Oliver will not attempt any retaliation."

"Oliver won't be able to refuse your offer. No one could possibly resist."

The man waited inside Mac's car in the parking lot behind the Santa Monica Bar. He would be able to see Mac approaching from fifty yards. The man was disgusted. The interior of Mac's BMW was filthy and smelled. The exterior paint was dull, and there were several unrepaired dents. Why was a man of Oliver's wealth still driving the same old car anyway?

Just as the man had anticipated, it was closing time when Mac came around the corner of the building, weaving only a little.

Good, thought the man. No one else in sight. He was quickly at Mac's side.

"Excuse me," he said as he sapped Mac at the base of the skull. Mac was falling before he even had a chance to look up. The man didn't want Mac's BMW found in the parking lot. Mac was stuffed into the trunk of his own car, and a disposable hypodermic was shot into the closest part of Mac's anatomy. The man had to slam the trunk lid three times before it caught.

It was a long drive from Santa Monica to Mulholland and Topanga Canyon. The man drove leisurely, enjoying the smooth responsiveness of the luxurious, although neglected, vehicle. I can see why people like these, the man thought, even though the luggage space is a little cramped.

The man turned onto the narrow blacktopped driveway and continued over the rise to the electrified fence. Although it was after 4:00 A.M., a man wearing a cowboy hat and jeans sat in a pickup truck just inside the double steel gate.

The man stopped and lowered the window. "Grant Radcliffe," he said. A flashlight shone in the man's face.

"Yes, sir. Mr. Radcliffe left instructions to let you through. He said he'd meet you outside the wine cellar about eight A.M."

Fine, thought the man as he drove another half mile to the next rise, where the oak-lined concrete road began. That will give me plenty of time to do it right. As the BMW neared the fieldstone wall, the wrought-iron gate opened and the guard waved it through. The huge Spanish ranch house set in the boulder-strewn meadow was eerie in the cold moonlight. Instead of driving to the front portico as usual, the man turned off the main driveway and parked before a rear delivery entrance. The door had been left unlocked just as he had instructed. It was certainly convenient that Radcliffe had been placed in charge of Maynard Chase's estate following Chase's stroke.

The man opened the trunk and hoisted still-unconscious MacDonald Oliver to his shoulder as if he were a pack of dog food. Inside the house and down the wide tiled cellar stairs, the man paused long enough to extract a key from his pocket and unlock one of the double doors, hand-carved with a Bacchanalian scene. He found the light switch inside the entrance and stood, uncaring of his burden, admiring the six-thousand-bottle wine cellar.

The massive beams spanning the eighteen-foot-high ceiling were carved with reliefs of flowers, vines, and grapes. Three walls were lined with floor-to-ceiling wine racks behind leaded-glass doors. The fourth wall was almost entirely covered by a seventeenth-century Alsatian tapestry depicting the crushing of the grape by barefoot maidens. At the center of the large room was a thirty-two-foot-long refectory table surrounded by thirty high-backed chairs. The table, too, was seventeenth century. Heavy, rough, scarred, and pitted, it had spent its first three hundred years in an Alpine monastery.

The man pushed several chairs aside and dumped Mac on the table. He checked pulse and pupil. Mac would be out for at least another three hours. Plenty of time.

The man left the room and returned with a canvas bag. He stripped off his topcoat and suit jacket. The wine cellar was cold. The man wondered if the room was warmed up for guests. Well, not for this one anyway. The man turned the unconscious guest spread-eagled on his back and began stripping off Mac's clothes. Then, two by two, the man removed the chairs from the table, neatly lining them up along the walls. Painstakingly the man centered Mac's unconscious form on the table, occasionally stepping back to view and returning for an adjustment, as would an artist positioning his model. Finally he was satisfied. Unfortunately Mac had let himself go badly the past few months. His muscles were still well defined but covered with a new, smooth layer of fat. A roll of blubber thickened his waistline. Too bad. It really marred the picture.

From his canvas bag the man extracted a large roll of one-inch-wide nylon webbing, a pair of heavy shears, a hammer, and a cardboard box of roofing nails. The man cut an eighteen-inch length of webbing, laid it across Mac's bare left ankle, and nailed both sides onto the table. The man repeated the procedure on Mac's right ankle, using several roofing nails at each end of the webbing. Both Mac's ankles were now securely clamped to the table. Methodically the man worked his way up Mac's body, cutting a piece of webbing to an appropriate length, placing it across Mac's unconscious form and nailing it in place. When the man had finished, he stepped back to admire his work. One webbing strap clamped each ankle. Another strap crossed each thigh. There was one across Mac's waist and another across his chest. Webbing clamped each wrist and both biceps. A single piece of webbing clamped Mac's neck. One more secured his forehead. Not bad work. Now for the final and most important touch. The man bent once again over his canvas bag and removed a large, old-fashioned woodworker's vise. The vise jaws were lined with maple hardwood blocks in order not to mar the work. Carefully, almost gently, the man placed the inverted vise over Mac's forehead. Slowly the man tightened the vise jaws against Mac's temples. The man took some pains to avoid crushing Mac's ears. He stopped tightening the vise when he was satisfied that Mac's head was immovable. With more webbing and sixteen-penny spikes, the man hammered the heavy vise securely to the table.

The man stepped back once again. Now MacDonald Oliver was virtually immobile. When he regained consciousness, Mac's motion would be limited to wiggling his toes and his fingers and opening his mouth and his good and bad eyes.

The man replaced his tools. It was not so cold in the wine cellar after all. There was a knock at the locked doors. The man looked at his watch: 8:10 A.M. Time really does fly when you're having fun. The man unlocked the door and stepped into the corridor, carrying his coat and tool bag.

"Good morning," said Grant Radcliffe. He wore a black three-piece suit with a fine red pinstripe and a dark red knit tie.

"Everything's set," the man said, "except that he is still out. He'll come around in a few minutes."

"I hope you didn't hit him too hard."

The man didn't say anything, but he felt offended. He never hit anyone too hard.

"You'll wait out here?" asked Radcliffe.

"Yes," said the man. He reached again into the canvas bag. "Take this."

A large, old-fashioned ice pick.

Grant Radcliffe took the ice pick and went into the wine cellar. The man put on his suit jacket and strolled the hallway, admiring the somber old Flemish paintings lining the white-plastered wall.

Radcliffe stood behind Mac's head, waiting for a sign of returning consciousness. Mac groaned softly. Radcliffe smiled and waited until he saw Mac's eyes flutter open . . . the startled look . . . the momentary futile struggle against the straps.

"Good morning, Mr. Oliver." Radcliffe remained out of Mac's sight.

Mac heard the voice. It was familiar. Mac could see the black threaded pipe of the vise and the wooden jaws clamping his temples, but the jaws of the vise acted as blinders. Mac could see nothing else but the heavily timbered ceiling—carved flowers, vines, and grapes. He could feel the ancient wooden tabletop with his fingers. The base of his skull ached from the blow, and his forehead hurt from the booze. He felt naked. He was freezing cold. He could not move. His head ached. And he heard familiar voices. Was this the beginning of delirium tremens, or had he just gone permanently over the edge?

"Mr. Oliver, I know you can hear me now."

That damned familiar voice. It sounded like—like—Grant Radcliffe. Now wasn't that ridiculous?

"Come around to where I can see you," said Mac. Was that his own voice—hoarse and gravelly?

"Of course, Mr. Oliver." Radcliffe came around the table and leaned over Mac's face. "Is this better?"

God. It *was* Radcliffe! MacDonald Oliver was naked and immobilized on a wooden slab, staring at carved wooden grapes on a ceiling, with Grant Radcliffe's angelic face leaning over him. Booze couldn't do that—could it?

"You probably are wondering why I've asked you here," said the angelic face. Joke. No, this wasn't some alcoholic hallucination. This was real. Real and just beginning to become more than a little frightening.

"I have the need to confess to you." That beautiful face. Mac was beginning to understand. Understanding only increased his fear.

"From the instant you went out of your way to humiliate me on the witness stand—when you threatened everything I'd battled for—from that moment I vowed my vengeance. I swore that I would find a way to humiliate and disgrace you. Do you understand, Mr. Oliver?"

Mac understood. He was coming to understand things he had only suspected. Jesus, he was cold.

"It was I who caused Seymour Bulles to file false embezzlement charges against you. It was I who had the receipt forged. It was I who had the one hundred thousand dollars cash deposited to your account. I don't expect a refund. You needn't thank me."

I'd rather kill you, you son of a bitch, thought Mac. But why is he telling me this? I'm not going to like why he's telling me this.

"I am also the person responsible for the child molestation accusation against you. In short, I am the person who is responsible for your disgrace, your despicable current condition and your immediate crisis."

Mac knew it was going to be bad. Is Radcliffe going to kill me now? Is this his final revenge? Is that why he is telling me all this?

"Why am I telling you all this? To cleanse my soul, of course. So that for the rest of my long and happy life I can cherish the memory that I have destroyed you. So that I can spend hours before the fireplace, savoring the thought that you know it was I who did it all to you. So that for all my long, remaining days I can revel in the knowledge that you, the once-arrogant, righteous, heroic MacDonald Oliver, will be impotent—unable to lift even one finger against me."

Impotent? Not death then. Jesus, what? It would be worse, Mac was sure.

"You will never retaliate. You will never even consider the thought because—"

Radcliffe suddenly brought the point of the ice pick to within an inch of Mac's good left eye.

Mac screamed. God, it looked like the same pick! He was drenched in sweat. Radcliffe held the pick steady, still an inch from Mac's eyes. Mac had known the different kinds of fear, physical and otherwise. Some he had bravely overcome. Some he had succumbed to, but never, never before had he felt such whole, complete, unadulterated terror. Whatever pitiful bit of strength left within him was dissolved in that long moment. Mac became a hopeless puddle of jelly.

He tried to talk. "How—" A hoarse whisper was all Mac could manage. He was quivering.

"How did I know they used an ice pick like this?" asked amiable Grant Radcliffe. "The details are in your citation for the Silver Star, hero. It's all in your army records in the St. Louis repository." Radcliffe continued to hold the point before Mac's eye. Mac closed his eyes. He could not stop shaking. Radcliffe carefully placed the point against the lid of Mac's good left eye.

Mac screamed again. God, don't let him blind me. Please don't let him.

"I will spell it out. We don't want to have a misunderstanding, you and I." Radcliffe's voice was deliberate, spacing the words. "Any attempt by you to harm me or my family directly or indirectly, any effort to clear yourself at my expense, any attempt at retaliation or vengeance will result in prompt and total blindness. I will put out your remaining eye. Do you understand?"

Mac could not talk. He tried to nod, but the vise would not permit his head to move.

Radcliffe's voice was confidently savage. "You must swear that you will never take action against me. Say it."

Mac opened his eyes. The ice pick backed off one quarter inch. He tried to speak. "I—"

"Say 'I swear it.' "

"Swear . . . it."

"Can I believe you?" Radcliffe made an infinitesimal jab with the pick.

Mac screamed again. "Yes," he croaked.

Radcliffe kept the pick at Mac's eye for a long time before he was satisfied. "Yes, of course, I can."

Abruptly Grant Radcliffe straightened and left the room. The door opened and closed again. Footsteps on the tile, but different, not Radcliffe's. Mac knew someone was behind him. A needle jabbed his arm. Sinking consciousness, then nothing.

Mac came to in the driver's seat of his BMW. He stank from dried sweat. He was parked. Where? Mac recognized the parking lot of a supermarket in Santa Monica two blocks from the bar he'd been in last night. Was it last night? The calendar sign on the corner insurance agency office confirmed it. Mac was dressed. Someone had dressed him. His shirt was misbuttoned. One of his socks was on crooked. His necktie was stuffed in his jacket pocket. He never did that. His keys and his wallet were intact. Mac felt physically sick with self-revulsion. Could it all have been a boozy nightmare? Mac touched the base of his skull. It was tender, but he wasn't su... why. He vaguely remembered a blow. He peeled off his jacket and rolled up his sleeve to see the hypodermic needle mark. No, it was real. It had happened. Mac opened the car door, leaned out, and threw up on the pavement. He wiped his mouth with the sleeve of his suit and leaned back, drained. Lowering the windows and opening the sunroof were an exhausting effort. He just sat there gulping air. He wanted to go home, but he really wasn't sure he could drive. He had to steady his right wrist with his left hand in order to get the key into the ignition. Mac headed south on Lincoln Boulevard. Even at his cautious rate of speed it was only a short drive back to his Marina del Rey apartment.

A hornet flew in through the open sunroof. Mac screamed and protected his left eye with both hands. He barely missed hitting a parked car before bringing the BMW to a stop. The hornet went on its way voluntarily. Mac closed the sunroof, raised the windows, turned on the air-conditioning, and tried again to drive. Only his grip on the steering wheel kept his hands from shaking. His teeth were chattering.

Mac stumbled into his apartment and headed straight for the shower, ignoring Bernie's exuberant greeting. He turned on the water full force and stepped in, fully clothed. He had the presence to toss his wallet and checkbook out before they were soaked. He slowly peeled his clothing and stood under the needle spray in the soggy heap for a long time.

Mac gave himself a cursory toweling off and donned a heavy terry-cloth robe. He ignored Bernie's yapping. Mac needed a drink. He drained half a water glass full of Glen Grant without taking a breath. That was better. He must remember to take Bernie out as soon as he got dressed. The dog had been locked in the apartment since early yesterday evening. He downed another large drink before pouring the third. The shaking was reduced to a mere tremor. Why should he hate himself? He had simply adapted to a difficult situation. Nothing useful would have been accomplished by a heroic refusal to swear his submission to Radcliffe. That would have resulted only in blindness or death. Or first one, then the other. Mac drained the glass and refilled it with the rest of the bottle. Pretending to submit was what any sensible person would have done under the circumstances. Mac took another drink. He could sip now instead of gulp. He was home now, safe. He could simply pick up the telephone and call the police. Radcliffe would be picked up. Investigators would quickly locate the place where Mac had been held. There cannot be many like that. They would find the carved overhead beams and the table. There would be clues. Why don't I just telephone the police right now? I'll be safe enough. Mac finished the whiskey. Radcliffe would not dare come after me after I'd reported it to the police. I'll rest first and think about it later. There will be plenty of time. I'm free from harm now. Mac stumbled around the apartment, checking the window latches before double-bolting the door. Bernie was yapping at his heels. Mac almost made it to the bedroom before he passed out.

Bernie stood, panting, staring at his fallen master, snoring on the carpeted floor.

Bernie climbed the unconscious body and lifted his hind leg in disgust, then peed all over MacDonald Abraham Oliver.

PART
THREE

18

*M*ac found a pair of high-impact plastic sunglasses and took to wearing them constantly. He told himself that the filtered light was comfortable. It was merely coincidental, of course, that the glasses also protected his good eye.

He stopped drinking. It was nothing conscious. Just that the alcohol did nothing to lift his depression. The only point to the stuff was that it could induce oblivion. That required such vast quantities, though. After the last episode he had been sick for a day. He had to face it. He wasn't even good at alcoholism.

For the three days after his release by Radcliffe Mac went almost nowhere and did virtually nothing. He took Bernie for his requisite ten-minute walk in the morning and evening. He went down to the dock to do boat maintenance. When he got there, he could not bring himself to do anything. He just sat in the cockpit, staring at his hands, listening to the water lapping at the hull. He tried to read. He could not concentrate. Watching television helped for one day. On the second day he'd seen it all before. The telephone rang frequently, but he didn't answer. Conversation was impossible. He listened to the taped messages on his answering machine.

Nels Sorensen: "Just wondered how you were doing. Nothing important."

Elizabeth Greene: "Just wondered how you were doing. Nothing important."

Cornell Sepulveda Smith, Marla Zimmerman, Burt Ginter, all the same.

Marina Cleaners left the only message of importance: "There's a hole in your camel sweater. Do you want us to reweave it?"

Mac looked at the mirror a lot. He looked like hell. One bloodshot eye. Unshaven, uncombed, but those things were superficial. Funny, the face really hadn't changed. There was no look of fear around the eyes. The tremors had stopped. If he talked, he would probably sound the same.

It was only his image of himself that had been shattered. That was all.

On the third day Mac was able to think a little. He had choices. He could continue to show the old MacDonald Oliver to the world while concealing the coward he knew he really was. Or he could openly reveal his weak, despicable self, eliminating all pretense.

Or he could kill himself.

Suicide was so appealingly consistent with his self-revulsion. The tendency to squash a repulsive insect, he thought. Suicide seemed so honest, too. A frank and permanent revelation of his weakness, a kind of memorial. Here lies MacDonald Abraham Oliver, killed by his own hand. Purple Heart, Silver Star, dupe, victim, quivering mass of shit.

There was a Smith & Wesson Airweight .38 Special on the boat. Mac had been persuaded to buy it before his first cruise down the Baja Peninsula. You'll need protection against them thieving Mexicans, he'd been told. In the years since, he'd learned what nonsense that was. The gun had never been needed. Over the years he had traded most of the ammunition to Mexican fishermen for lobster.

Mac brought the weapon into his apartment. The black, short-barreled revolver with black rubber grips was immaculate. He had test-fired six rounds when he bought it, then cleaned and stowed it away. What a simple, honest device. It was designed for solely one function: to kill people at short range. No pretext at sport or target shooting. He broke open the cylinder and extracted one of the Silvertip hollow-point cartridges. The cartridges were + P, loaded to high pressures for greater than normal velocity. One and seven-sixteenth inches of clean, instant death, thought Mac. The hollow point did tend to leave a messy, large hole as it exited, however.

Hell, why not just take the boat out fifty miles and open the sea cocks? It would never even be found at the bottom of all that ocean. Not as honest as the gun, though. People might even think it had been a boating accident. He could leave a clarifying note. What was a good opening for a suicide note? Farewell, cruel world? Or how about, You won't have MacDonald Oliver to kick around anymore?

There was a day-old telephone message from Tracy: "Don't forget you promised to take me to the ballgame tomorrow. Pick me up at noon. That way you can buy me lunch first."

Should he call back? Sorry, kid, I'm too busy to take you to the game today. Suicide planning takes up all my time.

Mac managed to clean himself up in time to take Tracy to the ballgame. A man's plans should not be allowed to interfere with his child visitation, right? It was grim. Tracy had started the afternoon with her usual ebullience. Mac tried to be light but could not overcome the weight of his despair. He assured Tracy that it was not her fault. She had no reason to doubt him, but by the end of the afternoon Tracy was completely subdued, as close as she had ever come to depression. Her father was not much fun.

Mac managed to spend the morning of the fourth day cleaning the Smith & Wesson, although it had been pristine when he started. There was comfort in handling the pistol. The promise of peace, he supposed.

The doorbell chimed insistently. Mac tried to ignore it but succumbed to peek through the peephole. After all, it might be something he could not bear to miss, like a Girl Scout cookie sale or a young man in a white shirt offering *Watch Tower*. It was Marla Zimmerman. Of course. Everyone else would have become resigned by now to leaving telephone messages and hoping for a response. But Marla did not accept rejection lightly. Mac put the gun in a drawer, sighed, and opened the door. He knew she would ring the bell for an hour if he didn't.

"Well, I'm just fine, thank you," said Marla as she swept by the silent MacDonald Oliver. She was halfway into the kitchen before she asked, "Am I invited in?

"Thank you," Marla continued, "I will have some coffee. No, I don't mind making it."

She inspected the contents of the refrigerator or, more precisely, the lack thereof. "These things are to store food in, you know."

She stuck her freckled face as close as she could to Mac's. Even though she was wearing high heels, her nose made it only to his chest. "My God, you look disgustingly awful. What the hell has happened?"

This is my chance to be assertive, thought Mac. "Nothing."

"Of course. Nothing. You haven't answered your telephone or returned a call for four days. Your apartment smells as if you haven't had a window open for four months. Your face looks like unsuccessful surgery. You're wearing sunglasses in a darkened room, and you've been cleaning a gun. Oh, my father had guns. I know gun oil when I smell it. So tell me again how there's nothing wrong."

"There's nothing wrong. If there were, how could I hope to keep it from a supersleuth like you?"

"Listen, you. I have a lot of time and effort invested in you. You know I don't make friends easily. Don and I are making progress, but I'm getting this uneasy feeling that you are about to do something stupid to screw everything up."

"Marla—"

"Don't Marla me. You're obviously not going to tell me what's happened, but you had better hang in there, MacDonald Oliver. I want you tough and mean. Mac, we are working hard. We are going to make everything right again." Marla brushed away a tear as she went to the door. "Here's a report on our investigation to date. Call when you're not so busy."

Mac glanced through the report. They had made substantial progress in identifying the mysterious man who had put Seymour Bulles up to framing Mac. Marla had figured out that the same man had been at Mrs. Lansing's home on the night that the house of her neighbor, Harold Rifkin, had burned down. The man didn't have a name yet, but he obviously had an employer. Marla deduced that TOPCO had to be the force behind Mac's frame-up—TOPCO or someone on behalf of TOPCO, such as Grant Radcliffe. Of course, the report concluded, there was no proof yet.

Only Grant Radcliffe's confession, thought Mac, although I don't seem to be able to bring myself to tell anyone about it. Mac's self-loathing was temporarily forced aside by anger squeezing in. The sons of bitches really took me, he thought. When did I acquire the delusion that I was invincible? I've been taken out before. Okay, so I had a failure of nerve. A failure of nerve? Mac sneered to himself. You were terrified. Maybe you still are. It's been four days, and you can't even bring yourself to call the cops. Cops, hell. You couldn't even tell Marla. You were afraid she might have suggested you do something about it.

Mac reminded himself that he had been terrified before, too. In Hoa Lo Prison. No, that wasn't the same. He had been scared witless, and he had known unbearable pain; but it was not terror. Wasn't it? Wasn't I terrorized seventeen years ago, when they hauled me into the Meat Hook Room for attitude correction and stabbed my right eye out? No, not really, because I hadn't anticipated it. The instant it happened I was so mad with pain there was no room for emotion.

Much, much later, when sanity had returned—when I could think and communicate—I'd described the pain in my eye as excruciating. This pain was not limited to my right eye or, more precisely, where my eye used to be. It was not confined to my face or my head. This pain was insatiable. It devoured me. I was saved only by the opium—opium and a competent friend, a POW who wangled opium and clean pressure bandages and saline solution and penicillin and soap. He'd known the risk of infection was critical. And he'd known that my eyeball had collapsed, that the tissue would soon grow together. He had even badgered the medic into sterilizing a glass marble, which he'd popped into my eye socket before stitching my eyelids together. That was what made the later reconstructive cosmetic surgery possible.

After I was transferred out of his cell, I never saw him again. Years later I was told he was listed as missing in action. Other POWs did not know what had happened to him. The Vietnamese denied that he had ever been in Hoa Lo Prison. They had no record of him.

Mac walked into his bedroom and picked up the orange aggie from the dresser top. He stood at his apartment window, repeatedly tossing the marble, as he gazed at yachts making their way out the Marina del Ray entrance channel.

Where was I before going back into time? Oh, yes. The subject was terror. Obviously I have no immunity against it. Why should I have expected that of myself? Having the shit scared out of me may not be something to be proud of, but should I kill myself over it? Even brave men are entitled to have a failure of nerve. As a matter of fact, only brave men can have a failure of nerve. Cowards are eliminated by definition.

Mac's anger grew. After all, he hadn't done this to himself. TOPCO had done it to him. Suicide was the wrong response. My suicide would just delight those crazy TOPCO sons of bitches.

Mac just could not give them the satisfaction of that final triumph. He already realized that he could not continue to live with despising himself. It would be infinitely better to live with fear. It would be preferable—no, necessary—to take risks even if he were blinded or killed. He laughed. What risks?

I'm worse than dead now. I have nothing left to lose. There is no risk. Only satisfaction. There seemed to be something extremely important he had to do before he died. He had to hurt TOPCO. That son of a bitch Radcliffe would surely be damaged in the process.

That was the moment of Mac's infection with the virus of revenge. He had no conception of the form or method of his vengeance. He was merely certain that it was an extremely motivating idea.

He took off the sunglasses and threw them over his shoulder. He heard a lens break as he started punching Marla's telephone number. "Hey, Marla, would you like to run in the morning?"

* * *

"Has anyone heard from Mac?" Nels Sorensen asked Cornell Sepulveda Smith. "He hasn't answered any of my telephone calls."

"Marla saw him the other day. He's stopped drinking, and Marla said he's working out for hours every day."

"Working out?"

"You know, Nels, activities such as running, swimming, lifting weights—"

"Disgusting. Although in this case I suppose it's better than the alternative. Anything else?"

"Yes, one of our people saw him emerging from the public library with a stack of books on computer science."

"Do you suppose we could persuade him to come back to work?" asked Nels.

"Let him be for a while, Nels. He knows we want him back. Just be grateful that he seems to be turning around."

Mac approached the problem as if preparing for trial or a military operation. Not a lot of difference, he thought.

The physical workouts were a vital part of the process. He struggled back up to six-mile runs. Soon he was running seven-and-a-half-minute miles again. The running, stretching and weight lifting, combined with eliminating alcohol, were melting the flab away.

As his physical strength grew, his stamina returned. That made him feel tough. Feeling tough fed his mind. Mac could not explain, but he knew that somehow, chemically, electrically, or psychologically, it was effective. The hard exercise increased his neuron activity or sped his synaptic connections, or something. His self-confidence grew. The ideas came more easily. His memory sharpened. When he was able to do one thousand sit-ups without leg restraint, he felt formidable again. He had not been able to do that since he was thirty.

Mac bought enough TOPCO stock to be entitled to ask his broker for all the back financial reports. The public library contained more than he had to know about the oil industry. There were years' worth of magazine articles on Maynard Chase, filled with useful data. A recent

Business Week biographical sketch on Sarah and Grant Radcliffe provided more general information about TOPCO's structure.

Mac was deep in the stacks of the county law library when he remembered Harold Rifkin's records. His whoop of elation got him evicted, but he was too delighted to feel embarrassed. As the executor of Harold Rifkin's estate he had stored all of Rifkin's remaining records. Half had been destroyed when Harold Rifkin's house burned down, but the records in Mrs. Lansing's garage next door had been preserved. Mac had felt the obligation to search the boxes of remaining papers before destroying them but had not been able to face the task. How thankful he was now for his procrastination. Harold Rifkin's records were a complete manual of TOPCO policy and procedure: a chart of TOPCO's structure, its subsidiaries and affiliates; a detailed history of every major TOPCO action for the twenty years before Rifkin's retirement. Bless you, Harold.

When Nels Sorensen's secretary retired, Nels asked Elizabeth Greene to work for him. Elizabeth, who, since Mac's resignation had been drifting about the office almost without portfolio, was delighted. Nels and Elizabeth shared a profound affection for MacDonald Oliver. That was why Elizabeth Greene did not feel as if she were tattling to Nels.

"Nels, Mac called and asked me for certain personnel records—former secretaries and receptionists."

"Did you ask him why?"

"Of course. He said he's opening a law office. Isn't that strange?"

Nels was hurt. Why wouldn't Mac just come back into the firm where he belonged?

Elizabeth continued. "It's going to be a second-floor walk-up on Pacific Boulevard. That area resembles the East Bronx. It's almost as if he didn't want clients—"

Nels was puzzled. "Elizabeth, did Mac ask you to go to work for him?"

"No, Nels." Elizabeth blushed. "I asked him if I could. I knew you'd understand. He almost snapped my head off. He said, 'I love you, but no.' "

Of course, thought Nels. MacDonald Oliver is up to something other than the mere practice of law.

A law office was as good a front as any. From his search of the old Sorensen, Oliver, Bradford, and Smith personnel files, Mac found an elderly secretary he remembered and trusted. The lady was discreet and delighted to work part-time. Mac did not want anyone around full-time. He needed privacy.

He had seriously considered using the legal system to pursue TOPCO. Now that he knew what he was looking for and where to look, it had seemed feasible to prosecute TOPCO with devastating civil and criminal actions: malicious prosecution; abuse of process; invasion of privacy; libel; kidnapping; assault.

But Mac knew that if he tried to use the courts, the delays would eat up years before any resolution. While all the legal actions were slowly grinding their way to conclusions, TOPCO would be after Mac. TOPCO and Grant Radcliffe would be coming after Mac in a most physical and extralegal fashion. Mac could not rely on the law for protection, and he couldn't hide. Some problems were not effectively resolved by the legal system. He decided he would rather do it himself.

He toyed with the idea of soliciting the assistance of Sorensen and Smith. Nels and Cornell Sepulveda Smith, Marla and Burt Ginter, Elizabeth and others—all devoted friends who would want to help. But it wouldn't work. He couldn't ask any of them to share the risk. His half-formed ideas of the appropriate methods for attacking TOPCO were, he already knew, unconventional at the least. Lawyers could be disbarred. People might be hurt. Mac was certain that TOPCO's response would not be passive. This exercise, he decided, was not to be one in which to involve friends. Well, maybe one. He thought for a moment. Maybe two.

Levi Asher had been sitting alone in Mac's dingy second-floor office, tossing paper clips into an ashtray on the opposite side of the room with spectacular success. Laura Wennerstrom entered so quietly that the startled Asher jumped to his feet as her shadow crossed his firing range.

"Jesus, you're big." Laura laughed. "You must be Sergeant Asher."

"It's noticeable, isn't it?" the blond giant grinned. "Call me Lever."

"Hi. I'm Laura Wennerstrom."

He counted twelve zippers on her well-fitting nylon jumpsuit. Not one looked as if it would be of any assistance in getting it off her. Lever offered her his chair and his most bashful smile. His father used to say he could charm the pants off a nun. Lever had grown to accept the idea fully before it occurred to him to question how an Orthodox Jew would know.

As Laura sat, she dipped into her bag and brought forth a chilled bottle of California champagne with three plastic glasses. The rapport was immediate. Laura poured. "Here's to our friend and host, the enigma. Where is he?"

"Mac called in," said Lever. "He'll be a little late. Traffic."

"Do you have any idea what our leader is planning?" asked Laura.

"The president has probably asked us to free Cuba," suggested Lever.

"More likely Miami," said Laura.

Mac bounded up the stairs and into the room. "Hi, you two. I stopped to pick up"—Mac halted and laughed as the duo stood and raised their glasses—"a couple of bottles of champagne."

Mac took time for a long look at Laura. He had been able to talk only to her secretary, so he'd been far from sure she would even come. They hadn't spoken in months. At first he'd wanted to speak to her. Later he had wanted to, but not wanted to. Of course, at his lowest he had not wanted to talk to anyone. Mac had hesitated to involve her in the potential danger. But he badly needed her talent, so he had rationalized: The woman has so goddamned many opinions she can easily decide this one for herself. He refused to admit to himself that it might just be nice to have her around. Dammit, she was nice to look at, though.

She was smiling at him now. She seemed friendly enough. "What's it all about, Mac? Your message only said it involved TOPCO and that I'd be interested."

Mac poured a second bottle of champagne as he talked. "The introduction is that this operation may be dangerous, is probably illegal, and—"

"I think I've seen this movie," said Lever.

"I read the book. The free world is saved, but most of us get killed," said Laura.

"Control yourselves." Mac continued, "You'll need to know about each other. Lever and I were together in Nam until I got captured. We did well together. Lever's MOS was demolition, but his engineering skills are much broader than that. Lever can destroy, build, or fix anything. Mr. Asher was, until recently, employed on North Sea oil rigs. He was summarily terminated upon his supervisor's written request. It had to be in writing since the man could not speak through his wired jaw. As I understand it, Lever, you objected to his comment that some of his best friends were kikes but you were the largest he'd ever seen—"

"My objection was that he wasn't smiling when he said it."

"Lever," said Laura, "we'll get along fine. Some of my best friends have been lawyers."

Mac continued. "Besides being a laugh a minute, Laura has a master's degree and considerable experience in—"

"You're the hacker?" asked the amazed Lever Asher. "Mac never told me our hacker is a woman. I thought they were all guys."

Laura aimed her breasts at him. "Surely you're straight on that point now—and I prefer 'computer scientist.' " She was trying hard to look seriously offended, with only limited success.

"Children, could we get back to business?" asked Mac. "Lever, I'm offering you one hundred thousand dollars in advance, another hundred thousand if we go into a second year—it can't possibly take longer than that—and a bonus of one million dollars if we successfully complete the operation." Mac didn't bother to offer Laura money. She already had four times as much as he.

"It's less than I was making, but I like the company," said Lever.

"Aren't you going to tell us who you want killed?" asked Laura. Mac couldn't tell whether she was joking.

"Of course. I plan to kill TOPCO. I want Titan Overland Petroleum Company destroyed."

Silence.

Mac's two prospective helpers looked at each other, too polite to say what they were thinking: Mac was crazy.

Mac smiled. "You think I'm crazy."

"Mac," said Lever, "I don't even understand what destroying TOPCO means. Do you mean, render its stock worthless? Do you mean, breaking it up into smaller companies? Forcing it into bankruptcy?"

"Even if we had any such specific objective, how could we hope to accomplish it?" asked Laura. "TOPCO isn't just an oil company. It's a multinational conglomerate. It has billions in assets and thousands of employees scattered over the globe."

"Too many jaws to break," said Lever. "Knowing you, Mac, I can believe you might have a way to do it. But in spite of my reputation, I'm not into wanton destruction. TOPCO is a valuable, useful industry—not some half-assed military junta. I have to know why I'm being asked to break that up."

"I feel the same way, Mac. Why?" asked Laura, not quite as friendly as earlier. She softened a little. "Does this have something to do with Charlie?"

"Yes, I suppose you're entitled. An explanation might persuade you that I'm not crazy." Mac smiled and deliberately put his right hand in his pocket. "Or at least clarify the nature of my insanity. Break out the last bottle, children, and make yourselves comfortable. It's a long, sad story."

It took a long time. Mac tried to leave nothing out. There were painful pauses as he struggled to retain his composure through the most humiliating episodes. His right arm struggled to be free to worry his right eye. He finally concluded with a recital of his near suicide after Radcliffe's threat to blind him. The story was not only sad but also sobering. Three bottles of champagne had been totally wasted.

"Oh, Mac." Laura's dark eyes were huge and wet.

Lever leaned over and covered Mac's entire shoulder with a massive hand. "When do we start, Captain?"

Laura held back. "I think TOPCO may deserve our attention, but you still haven't explained our objective or how we can hope to be successful."

Mac explained. He detailed his preliminary plans for attacking on various fronts. These plans were tentative, he explained, subject to review and criticism. Their strength was a combination of surprise and unusual motive. TOPCO was prepared to defend against competition, fair or otherwise, but not against what Mac had in mind. No, it wasn't possible to define a specific objective at the outset. Too complex, too many indeterminates. TOPCO's weaknesses had to be probed. There were many ways to devastate TOPCO. The best approach would be learned as they proceeded.

"Well," Mac concluded, "that's as far as I've taken it."

"It's impressive, Mac," said Laura. "There are obvious risks, but what the hell—Charlie would have wanted us to go for it."

Mac felt a swell of successfully applied psychology. He'd done it, persuaded Laura to avenge her father against TOPCO without even directly suggesting it. Of course, Mac had it all wrong. As Laura heard Mac's sad tale, she realized that all his troubles stemmed from his taking on the case of *Wennerstrom v. TOPCO*. She owed him full support in this. Charlie Wennerstrom would have wanted her to pay the debt. That's what Charlie would have wanted.

Lever cleared his throat. "Mac, I'm not convinced. You have some extraordinary ideas, but this has dimensions you haven't even explored. The fact that your plan has any credibility at all impresses me. I'll confess that an hour ago I would have written you off as possessed by an understandable but futile obsession. Even now the best I can see is a slim chance." Lever sighed. "But what the hell, make the check out to Levi M. Asher. One hundred thousand dollars, please."

Laura waited until Lever had said good night and left.

"Mac," she said, "I'll help you in this. I really want to." Laura didn't say she felt obligated because all of Mac's grief was the result of his committed representation of Charlie. She could see there was some pride back in him. "But there is one point on which we must agree before I can start. Okay?"

"I'm listening, Laura." Bet she wants me to promise I won't try to mess around.

"Strictly business. One hundred percent. Whatever I can do, I'll do wholeheartedly," said Laura. "But no romance. I won't be burned again. All right?"

"Laura, the last thing I want is to hurt you."

"Not good enough. Look, I had a husband with the fidelity of a rodent. Then you. The mountain turned to mush. I can't handle any more. Promise me there will be no attempt at hanky-panky, or I walk now."

Mac held out his hand. Laura shook it. He couldn't help noticing how strong her grip was.

19

*L*aura Wennerstrom did not gain access to TOPCO's computers by dialing random numbers or by guessing at typical passwords. Such sophomoric techniques she left to teenage whiz kids and to popular television programs. Laura realized that a primitive approach would not be effective against TOPCO computer security. TOPCO's computer security would intercept her incoming call, require her to punch in a password on the telephone key pad, and then disconnect her. The device would then look up the authorized telephone number matching the password and call that number back. It would not help Laura merely to steal another user's password unless she also used his telephone. Laura knew enough about the TOPCO system to realize that even obtaining the password would not be easy. TOPCO's passwords were stored in its computer in code so that no random search would reveal the master list. TOPCO's password management program also limited each password's access. A password assigned to a billing clerk who worked from nine to five would not function at night. Nor would the billing clerk's password allow access to the data of other TOPCO departments.

Laura solved the problem simply and directly. She got a job in TOPCO's computer security department.

Her forged credentials seduced TOPCO personnel into hiring her on the spot as assistant to Edgar Beard, the department head. Ph.D.'s in computer science, trained by the NASA astronaut program, did not show up every day. And the elegance of it was that before the overworked personnel department got around to verifying her credentials, Laura had already electronically altered TOPCO's records to confirm them. A lady named Morgan Wells actually did exist. She just happened to be in Australia with the air force at the time.

There had been concern about the risk of Laura's being recognized. The only person they could think of who might spot her was Grant Radcliffe, but it seemed extremely unlikely that she would encounter TOPCO's president. Nevertheless, Laura took the precaution of radically altering her appearance. Through the magic of Clairol, her Cherokee black hair became chestnut brown, and then it was shortened, permed, and feathered. Her eyebrows were reshaped and dyed to match. Daily sixty-milligram doses of Canthaxanthin deepened her creamy skin tone to a bronze tan. An extravagantly padded bra changed her previously ordinary dimensions to impressive. She purchased several Oleg Cassini pantsuits that she would have preferred not to be caught dead in. Lever Asher thought she was stunning. Mac hated the way she looked and the fact that Lever liked it. They all agreed that Laura Wennerstrom was nowhere in sight.

The office of new employee Morgan Wells was directly below, and forty-four stories under, Grant Radcliffe's. On her second day Morgan was required to take the elevator up to personnel to obtain her identity badge. As the elevator door opened at an intervening floor, Morgan Wells was face-to-face with, and twenty-four inches away from, Grant Radcliffe. If she had not been wedged in by other bodies, she told herself, she would have vaulted through the trapdoor. The elevator was too crowded for Radcliffe's taste. He stared right through her as he waved it on. Not a flicker of recognition. Laura alias Morgan was certain she had suffered permanent cardiac damage.

In the first week of her employment Morgan indelibly impressed her superior, Edgar Beard, by pointing out seven serious, theretofore unnoticed flaws in TOPCO's security system. She was immediately assigned to survey the entire architecture and to recommend improvements in its design. Within three weeks Morgan had mastered the entire security system. She knew every password, encryption key, every safeguard, every piece of hardware, and every weakness. TOPCO got its money's worth out of Morgan Wells. Upon her recommendation, several changes in the system were immediately implemented. Each user was assigned an identification number and was now required to enter his identification number and password at the same time in order to gain access. The computer was reprogrammed to detect intruders by noting suspicious patterns, such as repeated efforts to enter different passwords and random searching through files.

Morgan Wells became the instant darling of the department. Her rapid advancement seemed assured. Therefore, it was particularly tragic that she resigned under such distasteful circumstances. She was fully justified in doing so, of course. Half the department had seen old Edgar Beard practically try to rape the poor girl. Morgan had been valiantly struggling to escape without making a scene when two stenographers bravely risked their own jobs by coming to her rescue.

No one had noticed how the lonely old bachelor had been seduced and inflamed by those big dark eyes through lowered lids and the moist, parted lips. No one but Edgar sniffed Morgan's perfumed hair as she pointed out a circuit card modification. Only Edgar was aware that her breast accidentally brushed his shoulder as she came around his desk with a new flowchart. Morgan had begun to think that old Edgar just couldn't be aroused. But she had finally managed to get him up and running.

During her brief stay with TOPCO Morgan had been tempted to program TOPCO's mainframe covertly with her own secret password and identity and telephone numbers. That would have made access after she resigned child's play, but it would also have increased the risk of detection. A good security consultant could uncover any planted program. The alternative was complicated but infinitely safer. Morgan explained to Lever Asher what she needed. One visit to Radio Shack provided Lever with all the raw materials.

Once back among the ranks of the unemployed, Laura demonstrated the group's new capability. A computer system complete with high-speed printer had been set up in Mac's office. A modem permitted interchange between computers over Mac's telephone line.

"Gather around, students," said Laura as she adjusted the wig that closely resembled her natural dark hair—a nuisance, but her hair would take a while to grow back. She sat down at the keyboard and switched on power. "The old professor will show you what this gadget can do."

The office lights were out. As the video monitor lit up, everyone's face glowed green.

Laura explained, "There are half a dozen identities that are optimum. They all belong to assistant vice-presidents or second assistant vice-presidents—high enough in the company to have unlimited access to all computer banks and each highly mobile. Everyone is traveling on business about one-third of the time, which leaves his telephone lines conveniently available.

"First I'll choose an identity. This time we will use the assistant vice-president for operations. I'll dial his office number first." Laura's hands flew over the keyboard. "It's ringing now. It's nighttime, so there shouldn't be an answer. If it were a weekday, I would simply ask for the gentleman. If his secretary switched me to him, I could break the connection, or make a pitch for a charitable contribution, or whatever. If his secretary stated that he was out, I would then proceed to use his identity. Okay?" Laura looked around. Mac and Lever nodded.

Laura's fingers played the keyboard again. "Now I'm inputting the name, title, identification number, and password of the assistant vice-president for operations. Watch the monitor screen."

NAME: JAMES R. MC WILLIAM
TITLE: ASSISTANT VICE-PRESIDENT FOR OPERATIONS

IDENTIFICATION NO.: 33317
PASSWORD: WOLF 09 GUARD

"It's not working," said Lever impatiently.
"Wait. Unlimited access takes a moment," said Laura. "There."

AUTHORIZATION FOR UNLIMITED ACCESS CONFIRMED, MR. MC WILLIAM.
PLEASE HANG UP YOUR TELEPHONE AND KEEP YOUR LINE CLEAR. YOU
WILL BE CALLED BACK ON YOUR AUTHORIZED LINE IMMEDIATELY.

Laura punched a button that disconnected the telephone. A moment later the telephone rang. Laura punched the connect button, and a new display appeared on the monitor.

TOPCO COMPUTER CALLING. READY WHEN YOU ARE.

"That's Edgar Beard's little joke. He programmed it. Now we're inside. What would you like to know?"
"Wait a minute," said Mac. "I'm confused. Your little electronic friend just said that he would call McWilliam back on his authorized line, right?"
"Right," said Laura.
"So how come our telephone rang, and we're getting it here?"
"Tell him, Lever," said Laura, smiling.
"Laura designed a little modification to the circuit card in McWilliam's telephone. I built it. She installed it while she worked for TOPCO. That's all." Lever shrugged.
"That's not all, you big ape," growled Mac. "What does it do?"
"Oh. Whenever the TOPCO computer rings the McWilliam telephone number, it rings twice here first—here or wherever else Laura programs it to ring. If we pick up—connect—within two rings, McWilliam's telephone never receives the call. We do instead."
"So if McWilliam actually initiates the call, we just don't connect, and he receives the call—delayed by two rings," said Mac.
"Right," said Laura. "We only respond to TOPCO computer calls that we have initiated. And we only initiate after we have confirmed that the authorized user is not in."

"Sounds foolproof," said Mac.

"Unfortunately it's not," confessed Laura. "We could be caught if the authorized user's secretary tells us he's not in, even though he may really be. You know, perhaps he just doesn't want to take calls. Then, if he tries to use the line while we're on it, he might realize we've trespassed—"

"Or he might just think it's out of order," suggested Mac.

"Yes, but then he'd probably report it, and the serviceman could catch on," said Laura. "I think our best protection is to be really obnoxiously insistent when we call and do everything possible to confirm that the authorized user really is out before we mess with his line. Of course, even then he could walk into his office in the middle of our connection and screw us up. If we stick to early mornings, evenings, and weekends, except in emergencies, we should be all right."

"And we have access like this through six different lines?" asked Mac.

"Correct. Six different lines, six different identities and passwords. There's security for us in that, too. If we are at all in doubt about the availability of any line, we have five other choices," said Laura. "But I still haven't shown you anything. Watch." Laura's fingers danced over the keyboard again. She kept up a running narrative as she called up data on the monitor.

CRUDE OIL INVENTORY AND LOCATIONS
GASOLINE INVENTORY AND LOCATIONS
OPERATIONS DEPARTMENT, YESTERDAY'S EXPENSES
MC WILLIAM'S PERSONAL EXPENSE ACCOUNT
FLEET TANKER LOCATIONS

"Anything they've put in, we can take out. Their entire data base. We are up and running. I'm tired." Laura switched off.

"Laura, isn't the modification of six TOPCO telephones risky?" asked Mac. "What if a service repairman happens to be working on that instrument and discovers the alteration?"

"The modification to the card—the printed circuit—is so miniaturized and so subtle I don't think anyone would ever notice it unless he were specifically searching for something unusual. Even then he might miss it. The only risk is that if an instrument conks out and has to be replaced, we lose one of our six interfaces. But nobody's perfect."

They both assured Laura that she was and that it was great. "You needn't grovel," she said. "Just remember me on All Saints' Day."

Lever Asher and Laura worked together wresting incriminating data from TOPCO's memory banks. It was an effective combination. Lever's North Sea oil company experience had taught him what to look for. Once Laura understood what Lever needed, she knew how to make the computer search for it. What could not be pulled from the computer could occasionally be gleaned from the contents of Harold Rifkin's papers. The work kept Lever and Laura huddled together nightly for two weeks. Mac didn't care much for their hours, but he tried not to let it show, by staying busy on other projects.

In quick succession, calamities of varying degrees rocked TOPCO.

Almost simultaneously the Antitrust Division of the U.S. Department of Justice and the Securities and Exchange Commission began investigating TOPCO for Clayton Act violations and insider securities fraud.

The investigations had been encouraged by the congressman to whose campaign TOPCO had not contributed. Certain incriminating TOPCO records had been given to the congressman by a giant blond constituent, who claimed to have obtained them from the archives of a rival oil company, which had formerly employed him in the North Sea. How the rival oil company had managed to obtain TOPCO's records in the first place was vague but of no particular relevance or interest.

When Grant Radcliffe was informed of the antitrust investigation, he was enraged. If all the price-fixing and market allocation agreements with the other major oil producers were dredged up, it could be devastating to TOPCO's profits. What fool had leaked it? he wondered. It must have come from one of the other companies. But why?

When Radcliffe learned of the SEC investigation, he was frantic. Radcliffe had already lost count of the times he had taken advantage of his insider's advance information as TOPCO president to do a little profitable stock trading.

Two days before the news media announced the pending government investigations against TOPCO, the Monte Cristo Company, a dummy corporation secretly owned by MacDonald Oliver, sold fifty thousand shares of TOPCO common stock short. Mac promised himself that Monte Cristo would never take more than enough to cover expenses of his operation. TOPCO stock fell one and a quarter points on the news, and Mac's company covered its short sale at a sixty-thousand-dollar profit. What the hell, it paid for part of the computer system.

As the trio sat around Mac's desk devouring huge slabs of Mom's pizza, washed down with Anchor Steam beer, Lever Asher stopped long enough for a question.

"Laura," he asked, before pausing and unsuccessfully trying to suppress a belch, "can we also put anything in we want to?"

Laura held up her hands until she swallowed. "Into the TOPCO computers? Of course. We have unlimited access. We can reprogram it any way we choose. I thought I'd explained all that."

"You only said we could get anything they've put in," said Lever. "I'm going for a walk so I can think."

"Don't be petulant, dear. I'll go with you," said Laura.

Mac's eyes followed as the two left the room, but he said nothing.

Twenty minutes later they returned and announced that TOPCO was about to hold its First Annual Credit Cardholders' Sale. It was Lever's idea. Laura would design the program.

The TOPCO comptroller was at best a nervous and twitchy little man, but this news threw him into a near frenzy. He hurried to the executive vice-president with it. "Look at this. Our credit card collections are off ten percent for the month. Sudden. Drastic. Nothing like this has ever happened. Look." He waved printouts as though signaling for help.

"I'm looking, I'm looking," said the executive vice-president. "I agree, it's strange. Have you figured out why?"

"Why? There isn't any why. All the credit card statements went out at the end of the month as usual. We traditionally collect seventy-two to seventy-six percent within the first thirty days, but this month we've only collected sixty-two percent. Suddenly an additional ten percent of our credit card customers have stopped paying on time. If this is a trend, it could—"

"Yeah," said the executive vice-president. "Why don't you try searching individual accounts at random? Maybe you can find a pattern. Perhaps it's regional. Have there been any big layoffs this month?"

The comptroller twitched his way back to his own office. In an hour he was back. "I tell you, you won't believe this—"

"Don't tell me. You want me to look at this. Let's see."

The comptroller handed over the printouts but could not wait for the executive vice-president to digest the data for himself. "It's stranger than we thought. We've random-checked thousands of accounts. Statistically speaking, we've had the same number of credit cardholders paying this month as usual, but almost everyone who paid this month has paid only ninety percent of his balance. A few have paid less, but that's traditional. What is absolutely weird is that no one, *no one* has paid more than ninety percent of his account payable. And this is not regional. Our sample is nationwide—"

"I'd better show this to Radcliffe," said the executive vice-president.

Grant Radcliffe strove for calmness, but the executive vice-president sensed that Radcliffe was almost screaming.

"A ten percent drop in credit card collections? Why hasn't anyone paid in full?" Radcliffe paced the office. "Don't those deadbeats realize what this does to our cash flow? We'll have to borrow this month—"

No one thought to check the credit card statements that had been mailed out. After all, that was infallibly done by computer. A vice-president suggested customers be polled and asked why they had paid only ninety percent of their bills. He was nearly lynched. TOPCO's management dared not do anything that would leak such adverse financial information. The shareholders and banks would be crawling all over them.

The next month was worse. Almost every customer who paid on his credit card account paid only eighty percent of his balance. A few, as usual, paid less. But no one paid more. It was as if every customer had taken a twenty percent discount.

This time Grant Radcliffe was openly furious and secretly frightened. This was beyond chance. No mere quirk of fate had reduced the company's collections, last month by ten percent and this month by twenty percent. Nationwide. The shrinkage of a substantial portion of the company's income would lay waste to the quarterly profits—and even worse, if the cause were not promptly identified and controlled.

"Idiots," Radcliffe yelled. "Check the entire accounting, billing, and collection process from beginning to end. This is not accidental. This is not malfunction. Someone or something is causing this to happen. You, and you, and you, find out who or what. If your positions with this company are of any value to you, you will be back here with the answers very quickly."

This time they found it. A junior accountant discovered it almost by accident. On a whim she had decided to rerun the billing program on her own charge account. Last month, in addition to gasoline, she had charged four new tires for her aged Toyota, and she remembered the cost exactly. The computer printed out a duplicate bill that was slightly less than the cost of the tires alone. She checked this statement against the account receivable balance posted for her account. The statement was for precisely twenty percent less than what she had really owed. She ran half a dozen duplicate statements on other accounts and compared these with their respective accounts receivable balances. Every statement was for twenty percent less than the true balance due. The computer had printed out and mailed statements for only eighty percent of the amounts due.

The junior accountant ran to her boss with the discovery. Her boss did the same. Twelve bosses later, the news reached Grant Radcliffe. An executive conference was held. The computer billing program was dissected and confirmed the junior accountant's finding. The computer had been programmed to discount every bill by ten percent last month and by twenty percent this month. The computer program was easily and immediately corrected. That solved the problem but not the mystery.

"Why? How?" thundered Radcliffe.

Various theories of what had gone wrong were expounded. Dust on the printed circuit card. Moisture on the core memory. Overheated semiconductor chips. Electromagnetic influence. Sunspots. Excess humidity. Inadequate humidity. None of these hypotheses satisfied Grant Radcliffe. Radcliffe wanted to believe them, but intuitively he knew that the computer had been sabotaged. He ordered an immediate investigation of any employee with access to the program. The results were entirely negative. Very few personnel had the opportunity. Apparently no one had a motive. There was no motive that made sense. Perhaps he had been wrong. Thank God, at least they had caught it before any more damage was done.

For the next month's billings, TOPCO took no chances. The TOPCO computer printed out statements alphabetically at high speed, so all of the statements to customers with names beginning with A, and half of those beginning with B, were manually checked before the computer was permitted to proceed with the rest of the month's run. The process was exhaustingly tedious and consumed a week—not to mention several hundred thousand dollars in overtime pay. But it was worth the cost and the effort. All of the checked billings were correct. Whatever had caused the malfunction had been debugged.

It wasn't until a week after the rest of the alphabet had been mailed out that all hell broke loose.

The telephone calls overwhelmed TOPCO's switchboard. The accounting department was deluged with inquiries from confused or irate customers. All the news media treated it as the Joke of the Month.

Every statement from C through Z was for fifty percent of the balance actually due. That was bad. What was worse was that no one received a statement for fifty percent of his own account balance due. Everyone received a statement for half of the balance due from the customer two names farther down the alphabet. Mr. Caanon received a bill for fifty percent of the balance due by Caba; Caba's statement was for half the balance due by Cabanas. The computer had shifted everyone's balance two to the right, then divided by two. Everyone but Harry Zyman. Zyman got a bill for half Caanon's balance.

"I suggest this concludes the First Annual TOPCO Credit Cardholders' Sale," said Laura. "They're bound to nail us if we keep this up."

"Agreed," said Mac, "and congratulations on a brilliant exercise, but I'm puzzled. How did your trick program know to start with the C's?"

"Ah, the most fiendish, technology advanced device of all," said Lever. "Tell him, Laura."

"I met one of the programmers that I worked with at TOPCO for drinks. I bought her three martinis. She told me they were only double-checking A through B."

20

*T*he London headquarters of TOPCO lost all electrical power for twenty minutes. There was nothing remotely remarkable about that, except that the backup power source failed simultaneously, thus erasing from the computer memory all records of European and Mideastern transactions for the past five years. Radcliffe seethed. Lever awarded himself a gold star. Chaos reigned at EURO-TOPCO.

When the new wholly automated TOPCO tank farm near Karachi, Pakistan, blew up, Iranians took credit for carrying off the operation without injury, but Lever Asher nursed a minor burn on his forearm. TOPCO common was off three points. The Monte Cristo Company picked up enough to pay for Lever's trips.

Mac's obsession with TOPCO's destruction festered and grew like an invisible wart. Everything he saw, heard, and touched fed his relentless preoccupation. He lapsed into ever-wilder fantasies.

The impending antitrust prosecution will divide TOPCO into two hundred and twenty-seven minor companies. No, not a good idea, thought Mac in a momentary return to lucidity. Then I'll have to destroy two hundred and twenty-seven instead of just one.

Ah, Mac imagined, for the first time in history a corporation is convicted of capital crimes, including first-degree murder and kidnapping. The Supreme Court refuses to grant a stay of execution. All four hundred and sixty-two senior TOPCO officers are lined up against a wall and shot by a voluntary firing squad, consisting solely of Eagle Scouts. Grant Radcliffe's knees keep buckling, so they finally tie him to a post.

Come on, Mac, he thought. Be realistic. Okay, why not destroy the TOPCO fleet, twenty-two tankers and supertankers disbursed around the world? Well, that might be overly time-consuming. How about just the pride of the fleet? He lovingly concentrated on the details.

Mac already knew the *Blanco Empress* was awesome in her dimensions, the length of four football fields. With a 170-foot beam and 65-foot draft, she was wider and deeper than the Panama Canal. The registry of the VLCC, very large crude carrier, was Liberian, but her twin side stacks bore the TOPCO colors, red, gold, and blue.

Mac envisioned her white hull glistening in the murky waters of the Persian Gulf, and his imagination soared: The *Blanco Empress* has been ordered to Bahrein to take on a cargo of high-grade crude for delivery to Houston. She will drop anchor precisely on schedule, only to find that the cargo is not there. The cargo has somehow been shipped in two smaller tankers a day earlier. The radio transmissions and telexes have been flying back and forth all morning. No one seems to know what has happened or what to do. Captain Bergman—a foul-tempered alcoholic but a competent captain nevertheless, according to his personnel file— will just keep adding dark rum to his black mood and waiting.

It will be easy for the group to divert the 250,000 tons of crude oil intended for the *Blanco Empress* hold. Harold Rifkin's treasure trove will provide the TOPCO policy and procedure manuals. Properly phrased telexes will be received by the TOPCO Bahrein office, instructing it to load the waiting oil aboard the *Blanco Princess* and the *Blanco*

Duchess bound for Liverpool and Edinburgh. The discrepancy will not be discovered until the arrival of the *Blanco Empress*. By then everyone in the Bahrein office will be so involved in ascertaining that his own rear end is covered that no one will even attempt to discover how the foul-up occurred.

Getting the *Blanco Empress* to do what Mac wants will be a little more complex. Like all other ships of the TOPCO fleet, she is fitted with a shortwave transceiver coupled to a Decca Satellite Navaid. With this equipment, the *Blanco Empress* can transmit to and receive from any place in the world. The Decca also permits the ship to decode messages received in TOPCO marine code. Many commercial fleets transmit in code in order to keep company business private from competitors. Since Laura has obtained the TOPCO code, she can easily transmit coded messages or decode transmissions monitored from any TOPCO ship.

For additional security, the *Blanco Empress* and some of the other newer vessels of the TOPCO fleet are also equipped with satellite telex systems. The telex signals are bounced through the stratosphere to selected TOPCO telex stations, making interception by outsiders theoretically impossible. That will make it a little harder for Laura to design the operation. She will need Lever Asher's help. Lever will first have to worm his way onto the *Blanco Empress* crew list. Let's see, Mac mused, chief engineer should do it.

While Lever is posing as the workaholic chief engineer aboard the *Blanco Empress*, he will manage to install a Laura Wennerstrom-designed circuit board in the ship's satellite telex. That minor modification will plug the group's own telex into the TOPCO fleet system. Now they can monitor all TOPCO satellite telex communication. Laura can also send in the name of any TOPCO ship. The flaw is that the impersonated ship will also pick up her transmission if its telex is set on receiving. Maybe Laura can fix that.

It is essential that the *Blanco Empress* be made to sail without cargo. The satellite telex received by the *Blanco Empress* instructs her master to proceed forthwith to the port of New Orleans, U.S.A.—empty. Simultaneously a confirming land-based telex is received by the Bahrein office. Moving the *Blanco Empress* without cargo in her hold is unheard of. The expense and waste are appalling. But by now Captain Bergman is so eager to sail that he does not even question the order. And the TOPCO Bahrein office just wants the embarrassing evidence of its screwup out of its jurisdiction.

The VLCC's draft will not squeeze through the Suez Canal. She is forced to make passage through the Arabian Sea and around the Cape of Good Hope, before heading westward across the Atlantic.

She's got to be in international waters, Mac reasons, but close enough to land for rescue to be effected. And we will need good sea conditions to assure that rescue is successful. In the Atlantic, off Cape Town, might be the ideal spot if the weather holds. The South Africans have an effective air search-rescue capability.

Even after she's in the Atlantic, all sorts of contingencies can still wreck the plan: change of orders that really come from TOPCO head-quarters, mechanical failure aboard the vessel, or just bad weather.

Let's say that the waters around the Cape of Good Hope are reason-ably quiet, and so our decision to go is made when the *Blanco Empress* is about fifty nautical miles due west of Cape Town, heading northwest across the South Atlantic.

I will instruct Laura to send the encoded shortwave transmission. That ought to raise hell. We should be monitoring frantic radio or telex transmissions within a few minutes.

Aboard the *Blanco Empress*, magically it will seem to them, the message will be heard throughout the ship's public-address system: "Abandon ship. Abandon ship. The *Blanco Empress* has been mined with explosives which are set to detonate in exactly one hour. When the explosions occur, the ship will sink rapidly. For your safety, you must be at least five miles off within one hour. In order to persuade you that this is not a hoax, the location of one explosive device is disclosed as follows: On the forward port side of the number five bulkhead, below the intercom box. More than twelve other explosive devices have been hidden at appropriate points throughout the ship. Tampering with a device will detonate it prematurely. Even if you knew the total number of hidden devices, there is not time to locate them all. Even if you could locate them, you do not have the ability to disarm them safely. Commence abandoning ship now."

The message is repeated three times, even though Captain Bergman keeps trying to switch off the intercom. The entire crew hears it.

Lever has wired a hidden cassette player into the *Blanco Empress*'s public-address system. The coded transmission from Laura has activated the shipboard tape. The taped message will even come over the speaker Laura rigs in Mac's office. Laura has also combined a transmitter with the planted tape player, so they can monitor the shipboard announcement.

Captain Bergman will be barking orders. Mac can hear him clearly. "Check the number five bulkhead for the device. If it is there, examine it, but do not touch it. Report back to me immediately. Telex TOPCO headquarters. Advise them of the threat and request instructions. Also radio all ships our present fix, heading, and speed. Advise we may be in distress and may abandon ship. Round up the entire crew. Everyone at lifeboat stations within five minutes." It is not physically possible for some of the men to get from work stations to the lifeboats in that time. Bergman will know it can't be done, but he'll want to induce speed. He will be hoping it is a joke, a hoax, but will take precautions for his crew.

TOPCO's reply to the ship is also printed out on the group's own Santa Monica telex. Mac grinned to himself as he imagined the text:

MASTER OF BLANCO EMPRESS FROM TOPCO MARINE DIVISION. 0647 GMT

YOU ARE INSTRUCTED TAKE ALL NECESSARY MEASURES PRESERVE SAFETY OF VESSEL INCLUDING IMMEDIATE LOCATING AND DISMANTLING ALL EXPLOSIVE DEVICES. YOU ARE NOT TO ABANDON SHIP EXCEPT IN EVENT DANGER HUMAN LIFE. ACKNOWLEDGE.

VICE-PRESIDENT. TOPCO MARINE DIVISION.

This is really getting good, Mac gloated. TOPCO ambivalence is almost assured. Through a subsidiary TOPCO insures its own bottoms and cargo. Self-insurance has been one of Grant Radcliffe's innovations and up to now has saved TOPCO millions. But what has been saved in insurance premiums will not begin to compensate for the loss of the *Blanco Empress.*

When Grant Radcliffe is notified of the emergency, he'll say only, "Keep me posted," or something equally cool, but he will feel a tremor of fear. Something totally out of his control is happening. The loss will be staggering, and he is impotent to do a thing about it. Isn't this great?

Aboard the *Blanco Empress* the bomb placement will be confirmed, and it will look professional as hell. All they will find is plastic explosive wired to a black box. By then Captain Bergman will not risk the few minutes left he dares remain on board to attempt to locate and disarm an unknown number of, but more than twelve, hidden explosive devices. He will be shouting more orders: "Engines full stop. Prepare to abandon ship. Send the Mayday. Be sure to include heading and speed. Get an acknowledgment from South African Air Defense. Inform them we'll stand by the *Blanco Empress* until we're sure she's gone. Close all the watertight doors you can shut in ten minutes." Bergman will be thinking that with enough watertight compartments intact, the *Blanco Empress* might survive the explosions.

Back in Santa Monica, the group will monitor the acknowledgment from South African Air Defense. Undoubtedly a couple of rescue helicopters will be dispatched. All thirty-seven *Blanco Empress* crewmen will be in lifeboats—

Mac zealously explained the plan to Laura and Lever later that evening. "And that will be when the final encoded shortwave transmission is sent, triggering the explosion," he concluded. "Boom!" Mac paused, prepared to acknowledge the praise graciously. "Well?" he asked finally.

Then Mac watched his audience dawdle silently over lukewarm Nanking chow mein in paper cartons.

"Whose voice will be on the tape they hear on board the ship?" Lever wanted to know. "Won't that nail us if they've had the presence to record it?"

"No problem," said Laura, who seemed intent on shoveling chicken pieces from one side of her carton to the other. "It can be an electronically synthesized voice."

"Girl thinks of everything," said Lever as he raked noodles with a plastic fork.

"Can you do it?" Mac asked Laura.

"I can design it."

Even awareness of the proud vessel under his command failed to lift Captain Noel Bergman's depression. Everything was going to hell. Only last week he lost the finest chief engineer he'd ever had. The man had voluntarily roamed the ship, fixing everything in sight, even compulsively working on his off hours. Never before had the ship's systems been in such operating condition. Then the chief engineer had contracted some unidentifiable, disabling bacteria and had been shipped back home to Germany for prolonged hospitalization. Damn that blond giant anyway. Downed by an unnamed bug. That hulk had looked impregnable. Bergman knew he'd never find another like him.

Lever Asher had been gone for almost three months. As he walked in, Laura flung herself around his neck. "Oh, Lever, I missed you." She hung there and kissed his cheek. "You're tanned as an Arab."

"What a rotten, insensitive thing to say." Lever grinned.

"Everything okay?" asked Mac.

Lever brought himself to attention. Laura still hung from his neck. She resembled Fay Wray clinging to the top of the Empire State Building. "Sergeant Asher reporting. Sir. All components are in place and operational. Sir."

Mac laughed. It didn't hurt so much. "Laura, will you come down from there so Lever can take a stab at a serious report?"

Laura lowered herself to the floor and obediently sat in the corner while Lever briefed them both.

"Are you sure she'll sink?" Mac asked.

"Every through-hull fitting in every compartment is mined," replied Lever. "It doesn't matter how many watertight doors they close. That mother will sink."

After Lever finished, he excused himself to get a haircut. Laura turned to Mac. Her face was sad, her mouth open, but no sounds came out.

"This is serious, isn't it?" Mac felt pretty sure he was about to hear the announcement of her betrothal.

Laura closed her eyes and sighed. "Yes. We have to talk. When we started after TOPCO, I felt that it was right, considering all that was done to you. Oh, I knew it was illegal, but it all seemed justified. It was even fun. But that was only costing TOPCO money. Now you're not only planning to destroy useful property, you're going to be risking lives as well. Someone will be forgotten in the ship's infirmary. Or someone will fall in the rush to abandon ship, knock himself out, and get left behind. Or someone who wants to be a goddamn hero will try to disarm a bomb and kill them all. I've tried to justify this to myself, but I just can't. I've designed the system and programmed the software for you, but I can't bring myself to execute it. It's cruel; it's cynical. It's just plain wrong. Mac, please, give it up. This isn't justice anymore; it's vengeance."

Mac knew his anger was out of proportion to what she'd said, but he couldn't contain it. "And what's the difference? Why don't you explain that to me in simple words you think I can handle?"

"Mac, I don't want to fight with you or anyone else. I know I owe you a debt I can never repay. Everything terrible that's happened to you is because you helped Charlie. And I've reaped the benefits. But I just can't risk killing people. It's amoral. Just because you can do James Bond doesn't mean you should do James Bond."

"Dammit, woman, I—this operation needs you. We're so close to success. This next round will really maim TOPCO. We'll have them reeling."

"Listen to yourself. You're fighting another war. But I'm no soldier."

"No, you're sure as hell not." By now Mac knew his anger grew from something else.

"Mac, please. I've wanted to help you. I still want to. Mac, Charlie really loved you. In spite of the fact that I can't face the chance of being hurt by you again, I, too . . . care for—about what happens to you. But I can't kill for you. I can't."

Mac knew what it was. Not his reaction to a declaration of principle. She was rejecting him. Again.

"Jesus, Laura, don't you realize that I really want you"—Mac hated himself; he was practically begging —"to do what you feel is right." Mac went to the door. "Lock the door when you leave. See you around."

He was gone. Laura put a few personal things in her bag and locked the door behind her.

That night Mac walked the streets for miles, letting his anger boil over and run off. Months earlier Lever Asher had assured him that it was technically feasible to cause the TOPCO Towers to implode upon themselves, without scratching the paint on buildings across the street. Now, unable to walk farther but too upset to sleep, Mac kept his mind off Laura by trying to develop a plan that would assure emptying the buildings of all humanity in advance of the demolition.

The sun was barely up when Marla walked, unannounced, into Mac's office.

"Marla, you shouldn't be here."

"I'm awfully glad to see you, too." Marla gave him a kiss on the cheek. "I came as a friend. You've got to stop attacking TOPCO, and especially you can't blow up any more TOPCO property—"

The girl was uncanny. How did she figure these things out? Mac shoved his notes into a file folder. "Marla, I don't know—"

"Don't bother, Mac. This must stop. You cannot keep this up without injuring innocent people. Everyone but TOPCO will remain apathetic so long as it's only costing TOPCO money. But as soon as you kill some workman or clerk, the public wrath will descend upon you. The U.S. Marines will be on your ass, buddy. So far you've just been lucky—"

Mac stood and placed both hands on top of his head. "I give up. Don't shoot. What are you? Some kind of a psychic nut?"

"Mac, I've deduced this from reading the papers. Actually I figured it out weeks ago. I guess I just didn't want my suspicions confirmed—"

Mac didn't say anything. Marla Zimmerman was just too damned intuitive for her own health. He did not dare involve her.

"Mac. It finally dawned on me that if I figured it out, all by myself, without even trying, then TOPCO can't be far behind, can it?" Marla gave Mac another kiss. "That's what I came to tell you. Bye."

The morning sun rose bright and clear, but not Mac. Rocked by Laura's defection and by Marla's warning, Mac rose from the night at his desk dull and confused.

At their martial arts workout that afternoon, when Mac explained about Laura, Lever was not surprised. Laura's growing disenchantment had been evident to him. Lever was surprised only that Mac had not sensed it.

Mac was certain that he and Lever could execute the *Blanco Empress* operation without Laura. Neither of them, he argued, would be as quick as Laura at the computer keyboard, true; but everything was ready, and they had learned enough to make it work.

Lever feinted, Mac blocked, and Lever threw him hard. How could anyone so smart be so dumb? "Mac, how long have we known each other now?"

"Are you hitting me up for an advance, or is this just going to be a lecture?"

Lever threw him again, just to get his attention.

Momentarily stunned, Mac sat on the padded floor. "Okay, I'm listening."

"In Nam you never ordered a village burned. I would have done it if you'd given the order, but you never did. I was—"

"So how can I blow up the *Blanco Empress* now and risk the lives of innocent people?"

"Don't you see that's an act of pure terrorism?"

"I've got to get back—" Mac rose to attack.

"In order to get back at TOPCO, you're stooping to their level. You wouldn't before. Don't now. You'll end up being what you're trying to destroy. Mac, this costs you too much." Mac lunged. Lever sidestepped.

Mac flailed air, almost tripped, and recovered. "Toss me a towel," he said. "I'm heading for the showers."

As Mac stood under the stinging spray, he realized that Lever was right, of course. The line between damaging TOPCO property and innocent people must be respected.

They had gone to a lot of trouble to mine that ship, though. Jesus, thought Mac, what if someone accidentally sets off those explosives?

Lever had to admit accidental detonation was a risk. The *Blanco Empress* should be defused. "Why don't we just call TOPCO anonymously and warn them?" he suggested.

"You've given me a better idea." Mac headed for the telephone booth.

The next morning's *Los Angeles Times* carried the item on page one:

TOPCO FOILS TERRORIST ATTACK ON SUPERTANKER

BEIRUT—A previously unknown group claimed responsibility for planting enough explosive mines on the TOPCO flagship, the supertanker *Blanco Empress*, to sink the ship, a Christian-owned radio station said Saturday. If TOPCO officials had not discovered and disarmed the bombs in time, the mines would have been detonated by remote-control radio transmission today.

The Voice of Lebanon station said an anonymous caller asserted that members of the Khalaya al-Baath, or Resurrection Cells, intended the mines as a warning to TOPCO to cease its oil operations in the Middle East, and that it vowed to continue its efforts.

The Voice of Lebanon speaks for President Amin Gemayel's right-wing Falangist party and rarely has been accurate on terrorist attacks in the Middle East.

Before publication a *Times* reporter attempted to check the accuracy of the report with TOPCO officials, who simply issued a denial that the *Blanco Empress* had been sabotaged at all.

When Grant Radcliffe read the *Times* article at breakfast, his intuition compelled him to have a call patched through to the ship's master immediately. Captain Bergman was barely coherent. It was the middle of the night in Bahrein, after a rum-filled evening.

"Yes, Captain. I realize that you don't know anything about it. I just read about it in the newspaper. Yes, the Los Angeles paper. That's why I want you to check the ship for explosives now. Yes, I'll wait on this line—"

Grant Radcliffe sat for twelve minutes, watching his croissant deflate, before Captain Bergman reported the crew had already located three bombs.

Radcliffe continued to sit at his breakfast table, head in hands, staring at a bowl of cherries. He was dazed and totally confused. That ship really had been mined. What the fuck was going on?

Two bomb squads took four days to sweep the ship and disarm seventeen explosive devices. In spite of TOPCO's effort to cover up, the attempted sabotage of the *Blanco Empress* made the front page of almost every major newspaper in the world.

The U.S. Coast Guard and a congressional subcommittee simultaneously launched investigations into the supertanker's security. A *Los Angeles Times* editorial astutely concluded that it was a blessing that the terrorist plot had been foiled, thus avoiding an oil spill of unimaginable magnitude. The Democratic presidential candidate promised that if elected, he would appoint a commission to study alternate methods of transporting oil. Captain Bergman reacted appropriately to a suggestion that he consider early retirement.

The worldwide speculation that TOPCO was the target of a mysterious terrorist organization that vowed to destroy it as the archetype of Capitalist Imperialism pushed TOPCO stock into a nosedive.

By now Grant Radcliffe was irrevocably convinced that something more than the law of supply and demand was at work. Even though he had no proof, Radcliffe felt certain that TOPCO was under siege by a malevolent force. But he was reluctant to mount an open full-scale investigation into the cause. TOPCO had been taking a battering under his administration. There were signs that Radcliffe's position was growing tenuous. He did not dare risk adding paranoia to the list of accusations against him. He turned once again to the only person whose discretion he believed he could trust.

He met the man in a parking lot. The man was in a dark gray Buick, and Radcliffe slid into the passenger seat.

"Anything you need. Unlimited access to TOPCO records and personnel. Even unlimited budget. I must find out what is behind this. All my usual sources have produced nothing. But absolute discretion is required. Just the news that your investigation is being conducted could ruin me. Do you think you can do it?"

"It's broader than my current specialty, as you know, but I have had considerable experience. Did you know that I used to be a—" The man stopped and smiled at his own near discretion. "The change will do me good."

"I'd rather it did me good," Radcliffe murmured glumly as he left the car.

Mac squinted when Lever switched on the light. He had been sitting alone in the dark. Somehow in the dark it was easier to persuade himself that pride and hurt had nothing to do with not calling Laura. It was simply that he hadn't missed her at all.

"Hi. I just came in to pick up some notes," Lever said. "You all right?"

"Just thinking."

"You don't have the look of a commander who's winning a war."

"War sucks," said Mac.

The antitrust investigation of TOPCO's subsidiary, the Overland Petroleum Tool & Equipment Corporation, had produced enough evidence for prosecution and was being readied for submission to a grand jury when the charge was rendered moot by TOPCO's announcement that the offending subsidiary was being exchanged for forty percent of the stock of a successful computer software design company. TOPCO's stock rose two and one-eighth points.

The TOPCO credit-card-billing fiasco, as conceived by Lever Asher and executed by Laura Wennerstrom, had reduced TOPCO's accounting department to tears and had devastated TOPCO's cash flow. The cost of borrowing enough to cover the shortfall had been enormous. The publicity had made TOPCO the butt of countless bad jokes. Only TOPCO's advertising department had recognized the value of the publicity. Out of the chaos the department created an ingenious advertising campaign, centering on a discount for credit cardholders. For one month each year each credit cardholder would receive a one percent cash discount for each year the card had been held. Twenty-year credit cardholders would receive twenty percent discounts. The company dubbed the scheme the TOPCO Annual Credit Cardholders' Sale. Lever wondered if he could sue for plagiarism. Mac pointed out that the cross claim might be overwhelming.

Primarily because of the lobbying efforts of the Greener Maryland League, headed by one Oliver MacDonald, the Maryland legislature passed a bill surcharging the income tax levied against all petroleum refineries in the state. The proceeds would be earmarked to combat toxic waste. It was curious that the only refinery in the state was owned by TOPCO.

One week later Lever waved a newspaper at Mac. "Have you seen this? 'The State of New Jersey has just exempted from income tax all refineries built in the state within the past eighteen months.' "

Mac nodded.

"Of course, the only refinery built in New Jersey within the past eighteen months was TOPCO's."

Mac shook his head. "Win some, lose some."

"Mac, I think it's time for a reevaluation. I may be talking myself out of a bonus, but—"

"Mmmmm," said Mac.

"—you should consider the overwhelming futility of our operation," continued Lever. "We've been at this for almost a year. We've had spectacular successes. At this rate we will easily have TOPCO on its knees in one or two hundred years."

"Yeah."

"Mac, there's a lot of analogy to Nam here. We take a step forward, they move sideways one step. They push back one step, we move sideways—"

"It's a waltz," said Mac.

"We knock them down in the South Atlantic," said Lever, "they bob up again in Princeton, and they're not even fighting back at us. They don't even know we exist—"

"Yet," said Mac.

"Mac, consider that TOPCO may not really be your villain. Something as monstrously huge and complex as TOPCO can't be good or evil. It has some good people and not-so-good people. Consider changing objectives, Mac. If you really have to, go after the individuals you feel are—"

"Give up on TOPCO?" murmured Mac.

"—responsible for the damage to you. Mac, TOPCO is part of the commercial fabric of the world. We can't take on—"

"Lever . . ." said Mac.

"Let me finish, Mac. We can't successfully take on everything and everybody. It's like a hydra-headed—"

"Lever?"

"Yes, Mac?"

"You're right."

21

"**B**esides," said Mac, "it's becoming increasingly apparent that we can't continue attacking TOPCO without hurting innocent people. People like Captain Bergman—"

"Hell," said Lever, "we knew that would happen before we started."

"True. I guess I just didn't think I'd care as much." Mac cleared his throat. "Anyway, the revised objective is to go after Grant Radcliffe directly—Radcliffe and anyone else who has been in it with him. We know there is at least one other, but we haven't connected the man to a name yet. First we—"

"Should learn everything we can about Grant Radcliffe," said Lever. "Oops, sorry, Mac."

Mac grinned. "As I was saying. First we should learn everything we can about Grant Radcliffe. I'll start by coordinating with Marla Zimmerman and Don Dillon. Their investigation of my frame-up may help us."

Various tasks were divided. Mac and Lever gracefully converted from espionage to investigation.

Mac had lunch with Marla Zimmerman at Ma Maison.

"I'm delighted to see that you're giving up corporate crime," said Marla.

"How the hell did you know—"

"It's obvious from the fact that you're now willing to talk to me. Do you think the calamari is any good?"

Marla's investigation had produced little new information. Seymour Bulles was still missing. He had last been seen in a bar near his apartment in the company of a mean-looking man who matched the description given by Bulles's girlfriend, Juanita.

"And," Marla added, "who also matches the description of the man who burned down Harold Rifkin's house, and who followed you and Harold Rifkin to the Athletic Club."

"Doesn't this menace have a name?"

"A name? Look at this." Marla pulled two typewritten sheets from her attaché case.

"Marla, there must be fifty names here."

"Sixty-two. And we have a reason to think that he's used every one of them. But we still haven't the slightest idea which is his real name. Mac, we don't even know yet where he lives."

"The future doesn't look good for Seymour Bulles, does it?" smiled Mac.

Marla smiled back. "From where I sit, it doesn't look so good for Grant Radcliffe."

"I'll get the check," said Mac. Sometimes that girl was just too damned perceptive for her own good.

Even without the aid of Laura at the computer, the dossier on Grant Radcliffe built rapidly.

"Lever, did you know that the Radcliffes have a daughter in an institution down in Capistrano-by-the-Sea? It's distasteful to consider, but do you suppose there's anything useful there?"

"Don't know," said Lever. "I've got a microfilm of the police report on the accidental deaths of Sarah Radcliffe's parents, back eleven years ago. To me, the sheriff's investigation seemed superficial, but I'm no expert. I'd like you to take a look at it."

Reading the sheriff's eleven-year-old report on the death of Sarah Radcliffe's parents excited Mac's curiosity. He had to agree with Lever Asher's assessment. The investigation had been superficial. Something else bothered him. It all seemed too neat and pat. Finding the investigating officer was easy. He was still a sergeant with the San Bernardino County Sheriff's Department. Sergeant Lefkowitz was not much help. It had seemed like an open-and-shut accident to him. The only known potential witness had been Dave Smith, the college boy who had worked for the Hamiltons summers. Smith had claimed not to have seen anything. It was right there in the report.

"You know," Sergeant Lefkowitz said, "I do remember, now talking about it, how odd that kid acted. Nothing I could put my finger on, you know, but I knew he was holding back. Irregardless, he stuck to his story."

The name Dave Smith does not lend itself well to investigative tracing techniques. Twenty-seven wrong Dave Smiths later, Mac found him sitting at the bar in a beer joint in Big Timber, Montana. Smith no longer fitted the image of the clean-cut college lad. His paunch signaled the approach of the rest of him. A few dead strands of sandy hair remained on his otherwise barren scalp. His eyes were dull.

"Why do you want to know about it?" asked Dave Smith.

Mac thought that something like the truth might be the effective approach. "I'm a lawyer. I'm investigating Grant Radcliffe for a client."

"That means you want something on Radcliffe, huh?"

"Yes, if you've got something. I'm not interested in fiction."

"Are you paying?"

"Depends on what you've got to sell."

"What about the statute of limitations?"

Mac was surprised by the question, and that Smith knew enough to ask it. "It depends. Statute of limitations on what?"

"Oh, like withholding evidence or extortion."

"Three years." Mac knew it wasn't that simple. He just didn't feel obligated to explain the nuances.

"How do I know you ain't a cop?"

Mac pulled out his wallet. "California state bar license, attorney's business card, driver's license."

"What about protection from Radcliffe?"

"That I can guarantee you." That son of a bitch isn't going to be bothering anyone, Mac thought.

"You buying the beer?" Mac ordered two more and strove to be patient. Smith drank slowly and continuously. It obviously helped him think.

"Five thousand dollars," Smith finally said. "That's what I charged Radcliffe. Don't see why it should be worth any less now. Especially with inflation." Smith grinned. A few teeth were missing. Those remaining weren't far behind.

"One thousand dollars now. Four thousand more if I accept your story and if you back it up with a signed statement."

David Smith held out his hand while Mac counted ten one-hundred-dollar bills into it.

"Let me buy you a beer," said Smith. "And we'll take them over to the booth, where it's private." Smith's memory had not been impaired. His eleven-year recall was vivid. Radcliffe had parked his black Cadillac Seville in the Hamilton compound at 9:10 P.M. Dave had looked at his watch because he wondered why any dinner guest would come that late. Radcliffe was wearing a dark sweater. Smith recognized him because Mr. and Mrs. Radcliffe had been guests of the Hamiltons many times. Smith saw Radcliffe walk out to the dock and lift the engine cover on the Chases' Chris-Craft runabout. Smith was certain that was the boat. It was distinctive, even in the dark. He described the boat precisely, Smith could not see what Radcliffe did to the boat. He saw Radcliffe close the engine cover, return to his car, and drive away. It was 9:20.

"Why didn't you tell this to the cops?"

"I saw an opportunity." Smith flashed his ugly grin again and told the rest of what happened between himself and Grant Radcliffe. He even recalled the date he received the five thousand dollars. It was the day before his birthday.

It was all true. Mac knew it was. "Let's go get your statement typed and signed. We'll stop at the bank on the way and pick up four thousand dollars."

After Dave Smith's signed statement was delivered and paid for, Mac was still curious. "Did you actually use the money to finish school?"

"Naw. I made a down payment on a used D-eight Cat. I was going to get rich grading building sites—"

"And?"

"They claimed I fucked up the grading on the first site and wouldn't pay me. On the second one, I stripped the transmission. I didn't have any money left to fix it, so they repossessed the tractor. I lost faith in my self-confidence."

"Tough," said Mac.

"Oh, I ain't got it so bad. I work here tending bar four nights a week, eight to one. The rest of the time I got to myself. I'm free to do anything I want."

"Like?" Mac asked as he stood to leave.

"You know, whatever I feel like. . . . Hey, if you need me, I'm always hanging around here in the afternoons."

The tragic institutionalization of the Radcliffes' daughter, May Anne, did not seem to Mac to offer much potential against Grant Radcliffe. But Mac was still fishing for anything. Besides, the fine weather offered the prospect of a pleasant drive down the Pacific Coast Highway to Dana Point. Mac put on a dark three-piece suit. It would require some intimidating ruse to get at the records of the Capistrano-by-the-Sea psychiatric facility.

Mac opened the windows and the sunroof of the BMW. It was good to let the breeze fly in. As he drove, Mac tried to pinpoint his objective. Would he be satisfied simply to terminate Grant Radcliffe with prejudice? No euphemisms, please, Mac, he thought. Say it: Murder him.

Could it be morally justified as preemptive self-defense? No telling how many more Radcliffe-sponsored gorillas were lurking, ready to pounce. Mac felt the back of his skull. He knew it had healed, but somehow it still felt tender. Hell, why did he need any further justification at all, considering what Radcliffe had already done to him? Perhaps a simple killing wasn't nearly enough. Wouldn't it be deliciously satisfying to destroy the maniac first? Radcliffe was one, after all, wasn't he?

Mac strode into the Capistrano-by-the-Sea reception room and brusquely demanded, more than asked, to see Dr. Carol Young, the resident physician in charge of May Anne's case.

"The Internal Revenue Service?" asked tan, lean Dr. Young while gracefully raising her right eyebrow. Aside from her tailored suit, she looked more like a tennis pro than the competent psychiatrist she was reputed to be. "Forgive me, Mr. MacFarland, but may I see your identification?"

Mac glowered his contempt for civilians as he flashed the false identity card.

"You're investigating Grant Radcliffe?" Dr. Young hesitated. "Perhaps I should telephone your superior to confirm your authority before proceeding—"

Mac unleashed his best sneer. "Ask for Harry Steel. When you're through, let me talk to him. As long as I'm here, I may as well get permission to take a look at your returns."

Dr. Young's tan paled a little. Ah, fiscal skeletons in the doctor's closet, thought Mac.

After a few microseconds' consideration of her last year's deductions for the Bermuda convention, Dr. Young capitulated. "Oh, all right. I don't have time. Let's get this over with."

Mac covered his sigh of relief by diving into his briefcase for a notepad and reading glasses. "As I've already explained, Doctor, this is a field investigation of Mr. Radcliffe's medical deductions for last year. They seem to us to be rather disproportionate. I would like to see the files on the Radcliffe's daughter." Mac pretended to glance at his pad. "May Anne Radcliffe."

"Much of that material is highly confidential, Mr. MacFarland."

Mac's face registered disgust at the doctor's failure to appreciate the requirements of the Internal Revenue Service. "Doctor, I have no interest at all in that psychiatric mumbo jumbo. Makes no sense anyway. But I do need to see the complete files to assess the reasonableness of the claimed deductions. I assure you that the IRS will keep this investigation confidential, just as we expect you to do." Mac's expression showed his patience was exhausted. "I don't have time either, Doctor. All the files, please."

Dr. Young picked up the telephone. A monster-size male orderly brought in a three-inch-thick manila file.

"May I be excused, Mr. MacFarland?" asked Dr. Young as she stood. "The orderly will stay to return the file when you've finished."

The orderly will stay to make sure I don't steal something out of the file, thought Mac. "We appreciate your cooperation, Doctor," he said. "We'll call you if we have any questions."

"I'll certainly look forward to that." Dr. Young slammed the door.

The orderly stared sullenly from the corner. Although Mac intended to wade through the file methodically, he didn't expect to mine any gold here. He would be lucky if he got through the file without a headache.

The first two sheets were routine admission records. Names, addresses, employment information, insurance, family history.

The third sheet was the summary of the Brentwood Psychiatric Hospital resident physician's physical examination of the patient on admission. Mac's scanning eye stopped, retraced, stared. Mac felt his pulse leap. This could be something incredible. Had he given himself away? He glanced up at the monster. Still immobile. The man probably wouldn't even recognize any emotion short of paroxysm. Mac sat on his excitement, demanding calm.

The fifth sheet noted Dr. Young's interview of Agnes Riley, the former Radcliffe housekeeper, on the second day after May Anne's admission to Capistrano. There was Mrs. Riley's address and telephone number. Mac copied these, as he blessed Dr. Young for methodical note keeping. Strange, though, not a word of the context of the interview. Mac hoped that he could guess why. What was not in this file was as fascinating as what it contained.

Mac read Dr. Young's notes of sessions with Sarah Radcliffe. Innocuous stuff. Mrs. Radcliffe had no idea of the cause of her daughter's catatonic state.

The notes of Dr. Young's interview with Grant Radcliffe were no more illuminating. After each Grant Radcliffe interview was the notation "TNIH." Mac considered himself fairly fluent in medical-psychiatric nomenclature, but that one mystified him. He copied it down.

Mac returned the file to the hulk and walked back to his car. He just sat for a moment. There had never been a more beautiful day.

Radcliffe was the target. And MacDonald Oliver might have just discovered the hydrogen bomb. But the farther from Capistrano-by-the-Sea Mac drove, the more his doubts grew. Maybe his bomb was just a fizzle. He had better start with Mrs. Agnes Riley.

Mrs. Riley was right where Dr. Young's notes indicated she'd be. Mac was fortunate. It was the lady's afternoon off, and she was anxious to talk. Mrs. Riley had kept her three-year-old suspicions bottled up for long enough.

"He just up and fired me, Mr. Radcliffe did," Mrs. Riley was saying. "There's no kinder word for it. The very same afternoon they took the poor girl away. Oh, he gave me some cock-'n'-bull story about how Mrs. Radcliffe had gone off the deep end and blamed me for May Anne's condition. I'd better be out of the house before Mrs. Radcliffe got back, he said, so there wouldn't be an unpleasant scene or worse, he said. I never believed any of that. Oh, he wanted me out of the way all right. But it was because he didn't want Mrs. Radcliffe to be able to ask me too many questions. Thought he was bribing me with a month's pay and a letter of recommendation. Hmmmmmph."

"I don't understand why Mr. Radcliffe would want you out of the way, Mrs. Riley."

Mrs. Riley looked as if Mac were a little too slow to be out on his own. "I just told you, young man. So I wouldn't be questioned by Mrs. Radcliffe, the poor woman."

"What do you think Mr. Radcliffe wanted to avoid your being asked about?"

Mrs. Riley shook her head in despair at Mac's dullness. "The child, of course. Do you know he was alone in her room with that child for an hour before he came out yelling?"

"Was that unusual—Mr. Radcliffe spending time alone with his daughter?"

"It was and it wasn't. Mr. Radcliffe often spent long periods with May Anne in her room. Asked me not to disturb them. He was talking to her and teaching her, he said."

"What's so unusual about that?" Mac was thinking of the times he'd done exactly that with Tracy.

Mrs. Riley looked triumphant. She'd finally gotten through. "He only did it when Mrs. Radcliffe was out of town. And I never heard that poor child say one word to him outside that room. Not that she talked much to anyone. She would talk a little to me sometimes when we were alone. But she never once could tell me one thing that her father had taught her."

"Did you ask her that?"

"Oh, yes, more than once. I'll admit I was curious about what they were doing up there. But May Anne would just stare at me or turn away."

"What do you think went on in May Anne's room, Mrs. Riley?"

"I'm not one for speculation or gossip, Mr. Oliver," said Mrs. Riley sternly, "but it you could have seen that poor girl that day, standing in the corner—staring." Mrs. Riley raised her chin. "Something unnatural, I would have to say. Something extremely unnatural was going on in that room."

"Did you tell all this to Dr. Young?"

"Indeed, I did. Asked me the same questions as you. Almost word for word, she did. Dr. Young thought my information would be very helpful in treating May Anne's case. She was very thankful, Dr. Young was."

"As am I, Mrs. Riley. Just one more question, please. Have you ever talked to Mrs. Radcliffe about this?"

"No, she's never called me, the poor thing. And I didn't feel it was my place to contact her."

Back in his Marina del Rey apartment, Mac scrambled matzo and eggs. He hadn't eaten all day. He had something good here, but how to use it? What the hell did he do next? What a nice kind of problem to have. Where had he put the maple syrup?

If only he could get Dr. Carol Young to open up to him. Impossible. There was no ruse Mac could devise that would induce that lady to divulge her confidential medical opinion. He'd been damned lucky just to sneak a look at the file.

If only Radcliffe had a boss, Mac could go to him. That would be a good start. The matzo and eggs had not diminished Mac's hunger. He got out three more eggs.

But Grant Radcliffe was the president of Titan Overland Petroleum Company. There was no higher than that—except the chairman of the board. But that was Sarah Radcliffe. Should Mac go directly to Grant Radcliffe's wife? Ridiculous. What if she were in this, too? That was ludicrous. It had been her parents. Her child.

Even if she's not already in this, what if she decides to side with Grant?

Even if she doesn't, what if she blows the whistle on me?

Even if she doesn't, what if she just questions him?

Even if she doesn't, what if she just lets something slip?

Even if she doesn't, what if she decides to go after me independently? After all, she has a lot to protect. Name, family, company.

It is obvious that once Sarah puts Grant on to me, whether intentionally or inadvertently, he will use every force at his command to destroy me. I threaten everything he has. Status, power, marriage. Everything. I already have enough to destroy him twice over, though, if I use it correctly, skillfully. Mac chopped red onion, added slices of green pepper, then sprinkled discreet dashes of Tabasco, and carefully blended the mixture.

And of course, if Sarah decides to come after me independently, I will have to be looking over both shoulders at once. Jesus, I don't even know what soldiers she commands.

If they both do come after me simultaneously, I have no insurmountable defense. My only hope would be that after they got me, they might catch each other in the crossfire.

No, it's too great a risk to go directly to Sarah. What do I know about her anyway? Rich, spoiled brat of an heiress, with mousy looks— No, that's not fair. The woman apparently has substantial accomplishments of her own. Everything I've learned about her indicates strength, maybe even character.

But wait. You can't know how much influence Grant Radcliffe has on her. Does he have her snowed? After all, she did marry him. She made him or helped make him. Is she his unwitting dupe? Naw, Sarah Radcliffe is too sharp to be anyone's dupe. Still, a person in love—

If I don't risk going to Sarah, what are my alternatives? Mac considered and rejected anchovy paste. I can go to the cops. If I do, the charges have to leak to the Radcliffes quickly. The risks are the same as going to Sarah. I can take it to the news media. The risks will be the same. I can confront Grant directly, provoke him into coming after me, and hope I can trap him before he gets me.

Hell, what it comes down to is anything I do, short of sneaking up behind Radcliffe and putting a bullet in the back of his head, risks him and Sarah coming after me. Since that's so—

Mac broke the three eggs into the omelet pan and started mixing furiously.

Sarah Channing Chase Radcliffe had never been a timid, shy little girl. She had only looked like one. But no more. The chairmanship of TOPCO had changed that. Sarah remained slight and pale, but her presence was substantial. Improved contact lenses had finally given those electric blue eyes the opportunity to debut from behind spectacles. They were startling. With those eyes the lady could rivet vice-presidents to the wall and melt them down. More and more often she was being called Madam Chairman rather than Sarah or Mrs. Radcliffe.

MacDonald Oliver was shown into the gracious living room by a maid. Sarah Channing Chase Radcliffe came in almost immediately "Good evening, Mr. Oliver. I'm Sarah Radcliffe. I thought this would be a safe place to meet. Mr. Radcliffe is out of town until Thursday. The servants are completely discreet."

Mac was surprised at the firmness of her tiny hand. "Do you know who I am Mrs. Radcliffe?"

"You're the attorney who successfully prosecuted the Wennerstrom case against TOPCO. My husband has spoken of you, though not warmly"—Sarah smiled—"with respect, however."

Sarah motioned Mac to a Queen Anne chair. "I have to suspect that my curiosity has gotten the better of my good judgment. What could you possibly have to tell me of such vital importance—what did you say when you called?—vital importance to both of us?"

"Mrs. Radcliffe, I have to exact a promise first."

"Mr. Oliver, surely you can't expect me to promise you anything before I've heard what you have to say."

"Only that you will hear me out. I know that you will be shocked. You may be incredulous. You will probably be angered. I am sorry, but you will be saddened. You may even be frightened. . . ."

Sarah's eyes were the intensity of acetylene. "I promise to listen without interruption. Begin."

Just as he had told it all to Lever and Laura, Mac tried to omit nothing—even the most humiliating episodes.

He started with Grant Radcliffe's telephone threats to him after the Wennerstrom verdict. He told of the embezzlement charges against him and of Juanita's polygraph evidence of the frame-up.

Mac watched Sarah Radcliffe carefully when he told her of the child molestation charge against him. He perceived no reaction but sadness. Mac related his kidnapping, Grant Radcliffe's confession of Mac's frame-up, and Radcliffe's threat to blind him. When Mac described the place to which he'd been taken captive, Sarah gasped. It had to have been her grandfather's place.

"Excuse me," Sarah said, "I'm breaking my promise already, but I need a drink. Will you have one?"

"No, thank you," said Mac. The Count of Monte Cristo would not accept even a grape.

Sarah sat down with her drink. "Go ahead. I'll try to behave."

Mac told Sarah of his near suicide and of his resolve to take revenge on TOPCO. Although Sarah stayed admirably silent as Mac related his group's acts of espionage, he could see her hands trembling with anger. Her eyes could have brought down a missile.

There was a discreet knock on the door.

"Yes?" Sarah called.

As the door opened, a maid inserted half her body. "Mrs. Radcliffe, will you be having dinner?"

Sarah looked at Mac. He shook his head.

"No, thank you, June. I didn't realize it was so late. That will be all for tonight." As the door closed, Sarah turned back to Mac.

"Mrs. Radcliffe, I haven't told you the hardest part yet."

"For you or for me?"

"It won't be easy for either of us."

Mac told Sarah what he had learned of her parents' death from Dave Smith. Mac showed her a copy of Smith's signed statement.

"Wait," said Sarah. She seemed dazed.

"Are you all right?"

"Yes. I just heard Grant's voice saying to my father, 'Don't forget to switch on the blower before you start the engine on that bomb.' " Sarah waved Dave Smith's statement. "May I keep this?"

"I made the copy for you."

Sarah reread the statement and looked puzzled. "I'm trying to remember something—something about the five thousand dollars . . . something about Bill Murphy. Never mind. I'll remember." Sarah Radcliffe looked drained.

Mac glanced at his new watch. They had been talking for half an hour. "Mrs. Radcliffe, there's more. Are you up to hearing more?"

"It seems to be time for another drink," said Sarah.

Mac gave the drink a moment to work. He wanted Sarah Radcliffe as calm as possible for what was coming.

Mac told Sarah of his conversation with the housekeeper, Agnes

Riley. "Something unnatural was going on up there." Sarah jumped to her feet. Mac rose to his. She was so small, but those eyes, how they blazed.

"Mr. Oliver, I promised to listen, but this—you go too far. It's nothing but gossip. How can you expect me to give this any credence?"

"Mrs. Radcliffe, please. Listen to me, please. I'm almost finished. I know how difficult this is. I have a daughter. Please. Sit down for just another few minutes."

Sarah sat and folded her hands in her lap and faced Mac squarely. She raised her chin and waited.

"I've also seen May Anne's medical records at Capistrano-by-the-Sea—"

Sarah started to object.

"Never mind how," interrupted Mac. "I'll tell you later. I know from your reaction that you haven't been told what is in those records—"

"Please . . . hurry," whispered Sarah.

Mac gulped. "The Brentwood Psychiatric Hospital examination found semen on your daughter's body and clothes when she was admitted. Not in her vagina, but there was rawness indicated—"

"Is there more?" Sarah's voice could barely be heard.

"Dr. Young talked to Mrs. Riley. Two days after your daughter was admitted to Capistrano. Mrs. Riley told Dr. Young the same thing she told me. No report was ever made to the police."

"Does that prove something?"

"No. It's suggestive—"

"Yes." Sarah nodded. "I understand what it suggests. Mr. Oliver, I apologize for my rudeness, but it's one A.M., and I am, I think, justifiably exhausted. This is Monday. Could you return tomorrow? I know I'll want to talk more."

"Of course, Mrs. Radcliffe. I should have realized. Good night." Mac stood to go.

"Mr. Oliver?"

"Yes?"

"You can substantiate all this?" Sarah's tone was plaintive, as if she'd rather he couldn't.

Mac nodded as he started to close the door.

"Mr. Oliver?"

"Yes, Mrs. Radcliffe?"

"I don't know what I'm going to do yet—"

"I know."

22

At the same time that Mac sat in Radcliffe's living room, Radcliffe met the man in a San Bernardino parking lot. The moon was obscured by clouds. A stiff breeze swirled dead leaves over their polished shoes.

The man reported substantial progress. "I would have found this earlier if the money involved had not been so little. You'll see that the Monte Cristo Company made only a modest profit in the last year, but it was almost exclusively by speculating in TOPCO stock. This chart correlates Monte Cristo's purchases and sales with the dates of TOPCO's major setbacks. You'll notice that Monte Cristo's profits have all been made by covering short sales. . . ."

Radcliffe was startled. "They've anticipated our every disaster for the past twelve months. But why have they only traded in such limited amounts? It's peanuts. Who—"

"The officers and stockholders of the Monte Cristo Company are Elizabeth Greene and Levi Asher."

Radcliffe looked blank. The man smiled his mirthless smile. "Elizabeth Greene is Nels Sorensen's private secretary. She was formerly MacDonald Oliver's secretary."

Radcliffe looked less blank.

"Rather circumstantial, though, isn't it?"

The man ignored Radcliffe's comment. "The name Monte Cristo itself is illuminating. Do you remember *The Count of Monte Cristo?*"

"The count was falsely imprisoned and returned to work revenge on his persecutors?" Grant Radcliffe began to look fairly well informed.

"There's a little more," said the man. "Recall the public-spirited citizen who brought incriminating TOPCO records to his congressman—the records that started the SEC and antitrust investigation?"

Radcliffe nodded.

"That was Levi Asher, former U.S. Army Special Forces Master Sergeant Asher. Care to guess whose outfit Sergeant Asher was with in Nam?"

Radcliffe's face suggested that he had already guessed.

"Shortly before the mines were discovered aboard the *Blanco Empress*, her chief engineer left because of illness. There is no record of him at his indicated home address in Germany. His papers were forged. His physical description fits that of Levi Asher. Oh, yes. Levi Asher's military specialty was demolition."

Grant Radcliffe's face displayed an incongruous mix. The satisfaction of discovery. Anticipation. Anger.

"MacDonald Oliver has a law office in Santa Monica. I've staked it out. A young lady had visited the office too often for a client but not regularly enough for an employee. I'm not sure I've uncovered her real identity yet, but the name she's been using and by which you would know her is Morgan Wells. Recall the name?"

Radcliffe reverted to blank.

"Morgan Wells is a former TOPCO employee. She resigned shortly before all the trouble started. Morgan Wells was assistant to the head of the computer security division—"

Radcliffe's anger was deep. "Pick up Oliver first. We'll start with that son of a bitch."

Because he was a thoughtful and intelligent man, it didn't take MacDonald Oliver long to start missing Laura. It did, however, require another three weeks for him to admit it.

It's just pure physical attraction, he tried to tell himself. Well, she is great-looking as well as great in bed, he admitted. But Christ, that's not a basis. . . . It's more than that, though. There is some inner . . . beauty? . . . strength? Or is she just a stubborn, idealistic, opinion-ated— Isn't this where I came in?

Am I as hard and unfeeling as she makes me out? Avenging? Damn right. In my case vengeance equals justice. Goddammit, I can feel as deeply as anyone. I deeply feel the need to regain my self-respect. But I really haven't tried to make her understand that. Isn't it worth a try?

Sure, it is, thought Mac. But when he telephoned her, Laura was polite but aloof. No, she didn't want dinner. No meeting for cocktails. No, thank you, no lunch, thank you.

Mac finally persuaded her to meet him on San Vicente Boulevard early Tuesday morning. They could run the grass center divider and talk. "Running is bad for the knees," she told him. "Besides, I hate it." They compromised on a 6:00 A.M. walk. That way Laura could still make her scheduled 8:00 A.M. breakfast meeting with Lever Asher.

Oh!

Oh, well, thought, Mac, maybe we can at least be friends.

Mac had not returned from his meeting with Sarah Radcliffe until 2:00 A.M., but he eagerly rose at dawn. He threw on a faded sweatshirt, sweatpants, and battered Nikes. He could run after he and Laura had talked. He'd probably need it by then to work off his steam. No, Mac told himself, I will not permit myself to become angry.

The sky was still gray, streaked with orange as Mac unlocked the newly restored BMW and slid into the driver's seat.

The blackjack hit the base of his skull before he got the key into the ignition.

Mac came to in the old TOPCO truck maintenance depot in El Segundo, although he didn't know that. The obsolete facility had been empty for months and was scheduled for demolition. A new automated warehouse was to be built on the site.

Mac's forearms and wrists were bound behind him. He could see his ankles were taped together. His feet barely touched the concrete floor. His arms were numb and his shoulders ached. Damn. They had him semisuspended from something. The base of his skull throbbed. The nausea ebbed and flowed. Damn again. He'd had enough of being hit on the back of the head. A person could get a traumatic cancer that way. And tied up. He was sick and tired of being hit on the back of his head and then tied up.

No one was in sight, but Mac had no doubt who was responsible. The light was dim, but Mac could see that to his left and right there were rows of unused chain hoists. One had a rusty engine block hanging from it. The hoists were steel chains suspended by pulleys from overhead tracks, each chain terminating in a massive forged hook.

Mac glanced up. Another track. Of course. They had him hanging by his bound-up forearms from one of the damned hoists. No wonder his arms were numb. This was not going to be pleasant. How could he have been so stupidly careless? Nailed in his own car. Dumb.

There were voices. Voices of two men and footsteps reverberating on the concrete behind him. As they came closer, they stopped talking. Mac heard one stop behind him. The other stepped before him. His old friend Grant Radcliffe. What a surprise.

Radcliffe wasted no time on amenities. "I warned you. I told you what would happen if you tried anything."

From his waistband Radcliffe drew a long, narrow-bladed knife, almost a stiletto. Mac felt his bowels loosen. He struggled for control.

Radcliffe came closer, raised the blade, and stared. Even in malevolence, his face bore a strange beauty.

Perhaps it's still not too late, Mac thought. Maybe if I promise—if I beg. Mac tensed to suppress a shudder—and stared back.

"Hold his head," said Radcliffe. He reversed his grip on the blade, as if he were going to chip ice.

Mac's head was clamped between two giant paws. Struggling didn't budge it. Sweat erupted from Mac's back.

Radcliffe leaned forward and drew back his arm to strike. The knife was raised to the level of Mac's eye. A smile barely started at the corners of Radcliffe's mouth. "Blind . . ."

Mac roared and lashed out with both feet. The vehemence that welled up from inside him was so sudden and total that Radcliffe jumped. The knife caught Mac in the forehead. Mac's feet caught Radcliffe in the chest, knocking him to the floor. The dagger clattered across the concrete floor.

Mac's bloody head was released as the man came around and picked up the knife. The pain in Mac's shoulders was excruciating, but that didn't keep him from realizing that he had never seen the man's face. Even now, as the man assisted Radcliffe to his feet, his back was toward Mac.

Radcliffe was trembling as he caught his breath and fussed with his clothes. There was disbelief and something like awe in his face as he looked at Mac.

Radcliffe spoke out loud, but he seemed to be addressing only himself. "No nerves. None. I was absolutely certain that he was under control. I was sure that no one could stand up to the threat of blindness. Life in darkness." Radcliffe shook his head. "There is no fear in him. We can never rest if we let him—"

Radcliffe turned his glance to the man facing him. "Kill him."

Mac felt something reborn inside him. He knew what it was. Thank you, Grant Radcliffe, he thought. I'm dead now, but thank you. Radcliffe didn't know it, but he had just handed back MacDonald Oliver's self-respect.

"I'm already late. I've got to get back and close the San Bernardino deal, and those bastards have called a special board meeting for one-thirty, downtown. Some of them want my ass." Radcliffe looked at his watch. "Make it look like an accident or a routine mugging. We don't want a thorough investigation. There are too many people interested in him. I have no time left. Walk me to my car. We can discuss it on the way."

"Why not a simple disappearance?" the man suggested as the pair walked away.

I suppose I'll see his face before I die, thought Mac. He saw their backs disappear through a steel door a hundred feet away on the opposite side of the building. The door clanged shut.

As soon as the steel door slammed. Mac started trying to swing. It was pulling his arms out, but he knew his only chance was to chafe through the tape binding his hands. There would not be more than a few minutes.

"Hold still, I'm trying to cut the tape with my nail file."

Laura Wennerstrom.

"Thank you for coming."

"Wouldn't have missed it. Damn. The blade broke. That's tough plastic." Mac heard her rummaging in her bag. "Here's a can opener. I'll try it."

As the tape binding his arms parted, Mac felt his weight return to his feet, but there was no feeling in his arms.

"Hold still, for Christ's sake. I've still got your wrists and ankles to go."

The steel door opened. The man stood in the shadows for a moment before he started running toward them. He ran fast.

"Laura, run," Mac ordered. He meant away.

"I hate violence," yelled Laura as she grabbed a tire iron and ran to meet the man.

"Laura!" What a hopelessly dumb move. Mac knew she couldn't gain him more than a minute.

As Laura and the man closed, Laura's back barred the man from Mac's view.

Laura swung the iron at the man's head. The man ducked, but the iron caught him on the shoulder. Mac was sure he heard the man augh. The man clinched with Laura, while Laura continued to batter ine back of his head and shoulder with the iron. The man had Laura in a bear hug. He lifted and squeezed. Laura shrieked and sagged. Deliberately, almost tenderly, the man removed the tire iron from Laura's hand, then struck her with it across the right kneecap. Laura moaned and doubled over. With a remarkable economy of movement, the man brought the iron in a backhand swing to Laura's head. Mac heard the crack. Oh, God, Laura. She went down without another sound.

The man turned toward Mac. Mac was gone. With his ankles still bound, he had hobbled to the shadows beneath a steel staircase. There he sat, trying desperately to find the edge of the tape binding his ankles; but his arms were still devoid of feeling, and his fingers weren't working well yet.

Through the open risers of the staircase, Mac saw the man run back to the steel door on the opposite side of the room. Could he be leaving? Fantastic. Across the empty room Mac heard the bolt click shut as he watched the man lock the door from the inside. The man returned the key to his pocket and walked leisurely, almost nonchalantly, back toward Mac's side of the room. He glanced with professional interest as he passed the inert body of poor Laura Wennerstrom.

Mac used the moments to find a darker space between two empty oil drums. The feeling was returning to his arms and fingers. They hurt like hell. Mac continued to grope with the tape around his ankles. The blood from his forehead oozing into his eye did not increase his efficiency. Neither did the tears.

Fortunately, when the man returned to Mac's side of the building, he turned away from Mac to search first in the opposite direction. The man was taking his time, as if enjoying the stalk. By the time the man reached the far end of the building and started to double back, Mac had freed his legs.

As the man approached, Mac tried to decide how best to make his stand. It wasn't a question of whether to. Mac was locked in the building. He might have some limited control over where and when. Mac decided the more time he could gain, the better. His arms and fingers needed more time to regain strength. As the man neared, Mac burst from his hiding place and ran up the staircase. He was sure the exercise would do him good. At the top of the stairs a narrow mezzanine ran the length of the building. The mezzanine seemed to be lined with small offices, parts bins, and shelves. Mac could hear the man bounding up the stairs. Mac tried a door. Open. Inside the small office there were doors on each side. Apparently each office interconnected. Mac tried the one on his left. Great. With four hundred feet of offices to run through, he might be able to stretch out the chase indefinitely—at least until he had developed a semblance of a plan. Mac laughed at himself. A plan. How do you concentrate on a plan while being chased through a building by a determined monster? Time had to help. Mac thought. He had been working out almost daily. He was sure at least that his stamina was as good as the man's. Maybe he could wear him down a little before the inevitable confrontation. Mac was sure it was not to his advantage to spend much time within the grasp of those mighty arms and massive hands.

For thirty minutes the chase weaved back and forth through the tiny offices and the narrow mezzanine walkway. Once the man almost caught Mac by running ahead down the walkway and hiding behind the door as Mac opened it to run to the next office. The man was quick, but so was Mac. Mac reversed field after slamming the man's fingers in the door. He knew the man was tiring. He could hear him audibly panting now. It was almost time. Mac waited in an office until, through the tiny window, he saw the man pass on the walkway. Mac burst through the door and launched a surprise karate kick squarely to the man's head. The man was stunned and off-balance against the low railing. Another quick kick to the head sent the man over the railing. Mac came to the edge and leaned over. The man was spread-eagled on his back on the concrete floor, fourteen feet below—at least out cold, perhaps killed. So easy. Mac could see, farther out in the shadows, the silhouetted body of poor Laura Wennerstrom.

Walking along the walkway to the staircase, Mac spied a large rusty pipe wrench in one of the parts bins. He must have run by it ten times. Mac grabbed the wrench and headed down the stairs. He was considering whether prudence dictated bashing the man's head in where he lay.

But when Mac reached the bottom of the stairs, the man was not on his back. Incredible. He was standing facing Mac, and he wasn't weaving. The man came toward Mac, rapidly, purposefully. No karate kick was going to be worth a damn here.

Mac put everything he had into a two-handed swing of the pipe wrench. He aimed for the man's head. He was sure that even if the man blocked the blow with a hand or an arm, he was going to have broken bones. Mac would finish him off on the next swing. The man raised his hand, grabbed the head of the wrench, turned, and twisted it out of Mac's hand. Continuing his turn, the man brought the wrench handle against Mac's right elbow. Mac felt the bone splinter. His right arm dangled.

Mac ran back into the darkness below the mezzanine. His shoulder brushed against an engine block hanging from one of the hoists. He put his shoulder onto the engine block and drove it deeper into the darkness. He turned and held the block with both hands even though he felt nothing in his right arm. It was as if he were holding a child's swing at the peak of its arc, but the engine block weighed over two hundred pounds. Mac's arms and back strained. He could haul back on the weight for only a few more seconds.

The man was sprinting into the shadow. Mac let the weight go and added all the push he could muster. The man saw the suspended engine block hurtling out of the darkness toward him too late and raised both hands. Even his exceptional strength was nothing against the hurtling mass of steel. The swinging engine block drove the man back into the light. Mac could hardly believe what he saw. For a moment he was sure that the man's hands had been welded to his face. Then the arms dropped. There were no fingers left, only bloody stumps. Momentary ridges fanned across the frontal plane of the man's head where fingers had been. The ridges quickly filled with blood. There was no face, no eyes, nose, or mouth. Only a mask of blood. The forehead had been caved in and cracked. Mac was sure he saw brain oozing through the crevice. The man was dead. It had to be dead. But somehow through some malevolent force of will, it still stood. It not only stood but thrashed. What was left of the man circled blindly, insanely, around the floor. And it screamed . continuously, fiercely. A high-pitched scream of anguish echoed through the building.

The remnant of the man flailed for something at his hip. A bright metallic object flew into view and clattered to the floor. There were no fingers left to hold it. Mac picked it up. A .357 Colt stainless steel revolver. Mac broke the cylinder open. Loaded.

Mac felt dazed. The man had had a gun all the time. There had been a dozen opportunities to blast Mac away. Easy shots. Why hadn't he used it? Chivalry? Ridiculous. Egotism? Challenge? Contempt?

Mac raised the Colt and fired one round into the man's head. The screams stopped. It was an act of mercy. Mac knew what the pain must have been.

Mac dropped the gun and sat, staring at the floor. God, he was drained. He knew he was lucky to be alive.

He realized he never had gotten a good look at the man's face. Jesus, what about Laura?

As Mac started to pull himself up, a new shadow darkened the floor before him. God, what now? Aren't you dead yet? You win, man. I quit. Mac looked up.

It was Lever Asher. From where Mac sat, it looked like a face on Mount Rushmore. Mac spoke. He was surprised at how normal he sounded. "How long have you been here?"

"About five minutes. You were handling it all right. I sort of thought you'd rather do it yourself."

Mac managed a grin, but it was hard work. "Thanks, Lever."

Lever pocketed the gun. "I'll clean up. I'm a little put out, however. I hoped to try him out once myself. Who the hell was he anyway?"

"Lever, I haven't the strength to recite the whole list." Mac tried to indicate the body in the shadows on the far side of the building. "Laura . . ."

"Is Laura here? Where?"

"She's over by the door. I think she's dead."

"Jesus, no." Lever ran over to Laura's body and knelt. "Mac, she's breathing." Lever already had Laura in his arms. "I'm getting her to a hospital. You'd better come, too."

On the way to UCLA Medical Center Lever confirmed what Mac had already deduced. Mac knew that Laura had planted a bug—a miniaturized shortwave transmitter—in his car as well as in every other vehicle used by the trio. It was insurance, she had explained. The group was in a high-risk business. Each bug had a range of fifty miles under good conditions. Lever and Laura had also equipped each of the vehicles with unobtrusive automatic direction finders. So long as the bugs transmitted and the ADFs were within range, any member of the group could trace any other. Lever had gone after Laura when she hadn't shown up for their breakfast meeting. Laura had undoubtedly traced Mac after he failed to show up for their morning walk.

"But how the hell did you get in?" asked Mac. "The only door was locked."

"Fire escape to a mezzanine window. Laura must have come in the same way. As a matter of fact, you could have gone out that way anytime you wanted."

As soon as Mac was released from emergency, he took the elevator up to intensive care. Finding Laura's room was easy. Lever was standing outside her door.

"How is she?" asked Mac.

"She's in a coma. Concussion. Skull fracture. Broken ribs. Punctured lung. Shattered kneecap."

"God. Lever, did they say she'll be—"

"I haven't been able to get anything out of the doctors . . . 'guarded prognosis, but we're optimistic.' That kind of bullshit." Lever shook his giant head. "We'll just have to sweat her out. You don't look too bad."

The gash in Mac's forehead was stitched, and his right arm was encased in a light cast.

"Just a simple fracture. Can I see her?"

"Give it a try," Lever said, shrugging.

Mac started for the door.

"There's a four-foot-tall nurse in there who just kicked me out."

Mac went in anyway. A remnant of Laura, eyes closed, lay unmoving. Mac had helped with a lot of casualties, but never before had he seen so many tubes and wires growing out of one person. A nurse was doing incomprehensible things to some of them. She straightened and turned to look at Mac. She was at least five feet two.

"I just wanted to see her for a minute," Mac whispered apologetically.

"It's okay," the nurse said, smiling. "I just evicted the giant while I changed her sheet. You don't have to whisper. We're not disturbing this poor thing."

Mac shuddered. "Can you tell me anything at all? I recognize the EKG and the EEG monitors, but I've never seen anything like the rest of this. . . ."

"Doctors don't tell me anything either, buster. I'm just the night nurse. I can give you the tour, though. . . ."

Mac nodded.

"The needle in her head is the ventricular monitor. The CVP in her neck measures venous body pressures." The nurse pointed as she lectured. "Arterial line measures heart functions. This tube is into her pleural space from the pulmonary pump. The lung was collapsed. This balances the air pressure so it can expand. Bag down here into indwelling catheter. Gastric tube into mouth for suctioning stomach. Prevents gas . . ." She pointed to a diode plastered to Laura's forehead. "Stat temp there. This tube's into her trachea. Respirator takes over if she stops breathing. IVs for feeding and drugs of choice . . ."

Mac looked confused.

"Whatever Their Highnesses prescribe, that's what we feed into her. This is just a blood pressure monitor."

"Why the restraints?" asked Mac. It seemed unnecessarily cruel.

"Sometimes they get restless, even in a coma. We can't have her pulling out tubes and wires, you know."

A doctor entered and eyed Mac. "Don't tell me I should see the other guy. You'll have to leave for a few minutes."

"Can you tell me how she's doing?"

"Sure. Wait outside. I'll give you the rundown as soon as I've finished with her."

Lever was still leaning against the wall.

"Lever, she just has to get well. I got her into this mess. I hope you'll forgive me. I know you two are—"

"I have things to tell you about that. Look, Mac. I'm not blaming you for anything. We all knew what we were getting involved in. But that's not all. If—I mean, when Laura's better—"

Here it comes, thought Mac. He wants me to be best man, or godfather.

"—I mean, Laura and I have become really close—"

So what else is new? thought Mac.

The doctor came out and turned to Mac. Businesslike approach. "I've already told Mr. Asher the extent of her injuries. And he's undoubtedly already relayed our prognosis to you: guarded but optimistic. That's not just Pablum. There's a sound clinical basis. The knee, the ribs, and the punctured lung are routine. Barring infection, they will all heal without permanent injury. Same with the fractured skull. It's not the fracture per se that's the potential problem. It's the concussion. Her brain has been grossly insulted by the trauma. That's obvious from the fact that she's comatose. The risk is possible brain damage—"

Mac flinched.

"Yes, I know, but listen," the doctor continued. "If the cerebral fluid can be kept from causing pressure on the brain and the swelling can be controlled, recovery can be complete. That's why we've cut a flap in her skull. To relieve the pressure, you see."

Mac stiffened. His right arm twitched.

"Take it easy. I've already said we are optimistic. True, the longer in coma, the greater the risk, but she's already showing positive signs. She's restless. Moving her feet. Aside from the low blood pressure, her vital signs are within normal range. We're constantly running neurological tests. Her Babinski is okay, indicating the depth of paralysis is not extreme. Pupils are equal and react. There is every suggestion of a return to full function."

Mac visibly relaxed. "When?"

The doctor shrugged. "Can't tell. Half an hour. Tomorrow. Next week."

"Doctor, I want her to have every advantage known to medical science. Whatever the cost—"

The doctor laughed. "She's already got our head internist, chief of neurosurgery, a Nobel prizewinning cardiologist, the chief of orthopedic surgery, our head ophthalmologist, a couple of residents, and a squad of nurses. Every sign monitored around the clock." He laughed again. "We know who Laura Wennerstrom is. She's already pledged so much money to this medical facility we have to cure her just to prove we deserve it. Got to go."

As the doctor hurried off on his rounds, Lever tried again. "Mac, Laura and I have had a lot of fun together. I hope it never ends—"

Mac braced himself for the formal announcement.

"—but that's all it was. I'm trying to tell you, Laura and I were never in love. It's not me she wants anyway. I think it's you." Lever had never seen Mac look lost before. "But you never seemed to make a move, so I thought I should tell you—"

Mac still wasn't making a move.

"—so you wouldn't regret any lost opportunity. You know."

Mac had never before felt so many different emotions simultaneously. It was a flood. He couldn't sort it out, just choked back tears and barely managed to squawk, "Thank you, Lever, I've got to find the john," as he turned on his heel and hurried down the corridor.

When Mac returned, he had regained a degree of control, although he still felt confused. Perhaps meeting with Sarah Radcliffe again tonight would help. But he was sure of one thing. What the bastards had done to Laura was the last straw. Mac also felt compelled to wind it up alone. He wasn't even sure why. Possibly he just didn't want to involve Lever further. He had caused too much damage to friends already. Maybe he just needed the satisfaction of finishing it by himself. More likely he just felt like being alone.

Lever refused to quit until he had removed all trace of the day's incident. "You know, body, blood, fingerprints, stuff like that," he said.

"There's Laura's nail file and can opener, too. I'd better come along and—"

"Stop worrying. Noncoms run the entire army. What use is a one-eyed, one-armed lawyer anyway?"

Even after Mac insisted that Lever had earned his full bonus, Lever wanted to stay for the finish. Mac tried to pacify him by promising to call the moment he needed help. "Besides, you'll need time to invest the money."

"You know I'm no good with money. I'll just hand this over to Minnie."

"Minnie? Who the hell is Minnie, you closed-mouthed son of a bitch?"

"My girlfriend the cop. We've been going together for two years. We're getting married as soon as she makes sergeant."

23

Sarah had devoted meticulous attention to the decorating of the bedroom. She had always loved the way it turned out: the carving of the massive museum-quality Victorian bed; the indescribably subtle reds and golds of the silk Chinese rug over polished maple floors; the view of the garden and fishpond through four enameled French doors. But now, as she sat on the bed, drained by MacDonald Oliver's revelations, the room seemed contrived and ostentatious. It repulsed her. She didn't need psychoanalysis to deduce why. Thank the Lord Grant was out of town until Thursday. Facing him this Monday night would have been torture; touching him, intolerable.

Sarah had sensed something seriously wrong for months. Grant had never been expansive, but lately he had seemed almost secretive. His mood swings had been extreme. Sarah had charged it up to fluctuations in TOPCO's business fortunes. Well, Sarah said to herself, she'd had it partly right. Grant had continued to be attentive, even aggressive in bed, but more and more Sarah had the feeling that when they made love, Grant didn't even know she was there. She felt he was playing out some fantasy, but afterward she'd always tell herself that was nonsense. She would put it down to her own psyche.

She had always known that he was ruthlessly ambitious. Since the computer fraud he'd practiced on the shareholders at the scene of their first triumph, she'd realized he could also be conniving. I WANT SARAH, indeed. But she had loved him. Sarah managed another wan smile. How readily the past tense came to mind. Was it really that easy?

Sarah couldn't think about it anymore, but it was no surprise to her that she couldn't sleep either. She went into the bathroom and fumbled through Grant's medicine cabinet. There would be something there. Grant was a chronic insomniac. Sarah looked for something recognizable.

"Pulvules Amytal Sodium (sodium amobarbital) 65 mg, one each 24 hours. For insomnia. M. Sorkin. M.D."

Sarah swallowed one of the blue capsules and went back to bed. In spite of the medication, a brief, fitful sleep was all she managed. Sarah awoke early, feeling half hung over, but forced herself into the shower. She skipped breakfast. There was a lot to do that Tuesday.

Sarah was able to meet with Agnes Riley early. The former housekeeper repeated everything she'd said to MacDonald Oliver. As Sarah was driven away, her memory tabulated and compared what she'd just heard from Mrs. Riley with Grant's statements from three years earlier.

Mrs. Riley: He fired me, said you blamed me for May Anne's condition, said I'd better be out of the house before you got back, so there wouldn't be a scene.

Grant: Dear, Mrs. Riley asked to leave. The poor woman felt responsible. She couldn't bear staying in the house.

Mrs. Riley: He was alone with May Anne for an hour before he came out yelling.

Grant: Darling, I came home directly from the courtroom. It was a hard day in trial. I went to May Anne's room just to let her know I was home, and there she was—just sitting there in the corner, staring.

Me: Had anything unusual happened?

Grant: Dear, Mrs. Riley assured me that May Anne had gone directly to her room after school.

Mrs. Riley: Mr. Radcliffe often spent long periods with May Anne in her room. Asked me not to disturb them. He was talking to her and teaching her, he said.

Me: Grant, you should try to spend some time with the child. She doesn't respond to me. Perhaps you could talk to her, teach her, somehow reach her.

Grant: Dear, I just haven't the time tonight. After all, I'm not a child psychologist. May Anne will grow up to be fine. Doesn't she have everything?

Sarah damned her acute memory and ordered her driver to take her to Capistrano-by-the-Sea. She used the car telephone to insist on an appointment with Dr. Young as soon as she arrived at Dana Point.

As the Rolls headed south on the San Diego Freeway, Sarah also telephoned the bank where Grant kept his personal checking account. His pocket money, he called it. She'd never given it a thought. The bank officer she spoke to didn't think twice about Grant Radcliffe's rights of privacy. After all, Sarah Radcliffe was on the bank's board of directors as well as a major shareholder.

Ever since it had dawned on Dr. Young that something rang false about the visit by that alleged IRS agent, she had been waiting for the other shoe to drop. When Sarah arrived, Dr. Young did everything possible to make her comfortable and relaxed. The psychiatrist had already decided that a full disclosure of her suspicions was appropriate. The doctor came around her desk to Sarah's side and sat down beside her. She laid May Anne's open file before them.

"As you can see here, the Brentwood Psychiatric Hospital resident psychiatrist examined your daughter upon her admission there. He noted traces of semen on her body and on her underclothes. A smear indicated none in her vagina, although he observed rawness. Are you all right?"

Sarah nodded a lie. She thought she might be sick.

"Mrs. Radcliffe, I interviewed your housekeeper, Mrs. Riley, who told me that your husband had been alone with the child for over an hour before the onset of May Anne's catatonic state. Then I talked to the Brentwood resident psychiatrist. We both suspected that your husband was the culprit—that he had committed incest. Based on Mrs. Riley's statements and the girl's condition, probably repeatedly over a period of time—"

"Weren't you obligated to report that to the police? It's a crime—" Oh, God, would I have wanted her to?

"Mrs. Radcliffe, we had no proof. Possibly it's all coincidental. It just could have been someone else. Brentwood's resident and I agreed that even if our suspicions were valid, Mr. Radcliffe was no longer a threat. He is certainly not a street rapist, and May Anne was safe here—"

"But—"

"I even telephoned a friend on the Beverly Hills police force, Mrs. Radcliffe. He confirmed my conclusion. There was no case against your husband."

"Why didn't you tell me? Didn't you owe me that responsibility? I'm the child's mother."

"For a similar reason, Mrs. Radcliffe. We had no proof. I must confess that we didn't want to be sued by you or by your husband. And my responsibility is to that girl in there, who is my patient—"

"But you should have done something." So should you have, Sarah. So should you.

"Mrs. Radcliffe, I have tried, and I have made some progress. If I had disclosed my suspicions to you earlier, it would have raised hell with your life and would have accomplished nothing for the patient. I'm only telling you now to confirm what you already suspect—and because I believe we're on the verge of a breakthrough.

"Let's start at the beginning. In my first interviews with Mr. Radcliffe, ostensibly for the purpose of obtaining May Anne's medical and psychiatric history, I tried everything I knew to discreetly persuade him to enter therapy. Look." Dr. Young pointed to the file entries. "Here. Here. And here."

"Yes," said Sarah, "I see the notation 'TNIH' after every interview with my husband. What—"

Dr. Young smiled and laid her hand on Sarah's. "Mrs. Radcliffe, it's my personal shorthand. 'TNIH' means the 'truth is not in him.' "

Sarah's laugh was hysterical. Dr. Young brought her some water and continued. "You'll recall that I even suggested group therapy sessions—yourself and your husband. It was a ploy to get your husband into treatment."

"Yes," said Sarah, "I recall we both expressed disdain for the idea. We joked on the way home about being too sane already."

"Mrs. Radcliffe, in my professional opinion, Mr. Radcliffe is not nearly sane enough. He needs professional help. He is not, however, my responsibility. Let's talk about my patient. May Anne is making excellent progress."

A little sunshine feels good, thought Sarah.

"We've been regressing her hypnotically. At first with the aid of drugs—Nembutal sodium. It's sodium pentobarbital—"

"Isn't that addictive?"

"It could have been. However, we have gradually withdrawn it. May Anne's regression can now be induced quite effectively without the administration of drugs at all. May Anne's progress has been impressive this week. The rate of recovery in these cases tends to accelerate once you get them moving. We've regressed May Anne to the date of the—the event that triggered her state. She won't discuss it yet, but I'm extremely optimistic now. Once she faces it and verbalizes it, she will be well on the road to recovery. She's going to break through any day now."

"That is good news." I can use all I can get, thought Sarah.

"You'll want to see her before you leave, of course. I know you'll be pleased. You'll find that she will be much more responsive than last week. Of course, not a word of this conversation on the—the—"

"I understand," said Sarah. "I'll be careful. I have to leave this afternoon on other business, but I'd like to return tomorrow and perhaps spend the rest of the week with May Anne. Would that be all right, Doctor?"

"Better than all right, Mrs. Radcliffe. In between therapy sessions May Anne will have three to four hours free every day. I believe your daily presence can hasten her progress."

"Thank you for your candor, Dr. Young," said Sarah as she started to leave. She was going to say, "Belated as it was," but restrained herself. "Before I leave, do you have any advice for me?"

Dr. Young shook her head and clasped Sarah's hand again. "No, only compassion."

Sarah ordered her driver to head for the main office of the First Commercial Bank, then settled back into the soft pigskin seat. Her head throbbed. She was surprised to realize that she was hungry. The manager of the Laguna Beach McDonald's managed several good snapshots of the maroon Rolls-Royce, with golden arches in the background, while the driver picked up coffee and Eggs McMuffin.

On the drive back to Los Angeles Sarah tried to remember the details of her conversation with Grant a few hours after her parents' horrible death.

Grant: Sarah, honey, this is a hell of a time to bring it up; but last night was so horrible I just forgot it, and it won't wait. Last night Bill Murphy asked if he could borrow five thousand dollars from me. He wrote some bad checks up here to pay off his poker losses. I told him I would make a deposit to his bank account today, but I just realized I don't have it. Could you—"

Me: Of course, dear. I'll make out a check to Bill immediately.

Sarah Radcliffe marched into the bank as if she owned it, which to the extent of six percent was true. She was promptly seated in the manager's private office and provided with the microfilm of the records she'd telephoned about earlier. After offering instruction on the microfilm viewer, the manager withdrew, muttering something about urgent business on the third floor.

Sarah had no trouble recalling the date of the check she'd written the day of her parents' death. There it was. Five thousand dollars payable to the order of Bill Murphy. The viewer also displayed the reverse side of the check. The check was endorsed "Bill Murphy," but immediately below that was the other endorsement Sarah suspected would be there. The check was also endorsed by Grant Radcliffe and stamped for deposit by the Lake Arrowhead branch of the First Commercial Bank.

Sarah inserted another microfilm cartridge into the viewer. She turned to Grant's deposit slip for the date of her parents' death. She already knew what she would see. Her five-thousand-dollar check had been deposited that day to Grant's account. He had obviously forged Bill Murphy's endorsement. Grant had simultaneously withdrawn five thousand dollars in cash. That was the day before Dave Smith claimed Grant had handed five thousand dollars cash to him.

Angrily Sarah spun the machine's knob to wipe the picture from her view. Her anger turned to shock as she stared at the new display her random spin had selected.

It was a TOPCO check for $62,000 payable to Mark Revson, d/b/a Revson Research and Development Corporation. The check was endorsed by Grant Radcliffe and deposited to his account. Sarah rapidly scanned the film.

A TOPCO check for $36,450 to Earl A. Schwartz, consulting engineer, endorsed by Grant Radcliffe for deposit to his account.

A TOPCO check for $41,200 payable to James Caruth, marked with the notation "for economic survey." The check had been endorsed and deposited to Grant's account.

Twenty minutes of sampling added a new item to Sarah's rapidly growing list of horrors. Grant Radcliffe was stealing from their own company. She did not know the total amount, of course, but it was obvious that her husband had embezzled at least hundreds of thousands of dollars from TOPCO during his term as president. Grant simply had checks drawn for fictitious TOPCO obligations. The smug, arrogant bastard hadn't even bothered to deposit the stolen funds in a secret account.

It was only a few blocks back to Sarah's office at the TOPCO Towers. She released her car. Walking should help her think. It didn't. The sky was clear. The sun was warm. People were bustling all around her, hurrying on with their lives. She was one of the richest, most influential, respected women in the country, and her whole goddamned world was falling apart. How could she think? It was just too damned much.

Back in her office, Sarah put a call through to Bill Murphy. He was the manager of the San Francisco office now. She knew it would be overkill, but she felt compelled to dredge it all out.

"Bill, this is Sarah Radcliffe, how are you? . . . I know. . . . Bill, help me out. It's nothing important, but it's been plaguing me all day trying to remember. The night of my parents' accident at Lake Arrowhead, were you and Ann at your cottage? Did Grant and I spend that evening with you?"

"No, Sarah. I was right here in San Francisco all that week, setting up this very office. I remember calling Grant the next day and my offering to fly down to Arrowhead if there was anything I could do to help."

"Thanks, Bill. I guess I dreamed it." Sarah hung up. Bill Murphy would think she was loony, but the chairman of the board was entitled ⌐to a few eccentricities, wasn't she?

Sarah buzzed her secretary. "Order my car, please. I'm leaving early. I'll be at home, but I don't want calls from anyone but you. Tell them all that you're trying but you can't find me."

Her secretary sighed with envy as Sarah swept out of the office. Wealth, power, looks, brains, even a great husband. The woman had everything. Why should she hang around the office?

When Grant Radcliffe and the man parted in the parking lot of the old truck maintenance depot on Tuesday morning, Radcliffe felt better than he had in months. Inside the building a major cause, if not the major cause, of TOPCO's recent problems was about to disappear. Too bad he hadn't the time to hang around and watch the fun. That would have been sweet. But now he could close the San Bernardino deal with a clear head and summarily face down those vultures on the board. If he disposed of them early enough, he could make it up to San Francisco that afternoon to arrange the next quarter's bank financing.

With energy born of renewed optimism, Radcliffe fulfilled a whirlwind schedule that day before coming to rest in a suite at the Cliff Hotel atop Nob Hill. It was after 8:00 P.M. before he had a chance to telephone the man for a progress report. He sipped Courvoisier on the rocks as he listened to the familiar taped message, then left his San Francisco number. Radcliffe's spirits were much too high for him to spend more than a few minutes waiting for a return call. The night was young. He hummed "Some Enchanted Evening" as he went to his attaché case for the little black book. What was her name again? Guinevere?

When Mac was led into the Radcliffe living room Tuesday night, Sarah was already waiting. When she saw his clamped swollen forehead and his encased right arm, she gasped, "What?" Mac told her.

Sarah's electric eyes bored into him for a long time before she waved him to a chair. Neither of them could decide what she thought of him. It was Mac's turn to listen. Sarah told him the extent to which she had substantiated his story.

"All in one day? You've been busy."

Sarah thought, No more than you, Mr. Oliver, but it didn't seem to be an occasion for humor. "Mr. Oliver, do you expect me to testify against Grant? Help prosecute him?"

Mac laughed, then apologized. "I don't intend to be rude. But this has already gone so far beyond law and courts it's funny to think about bringing it back to the level where it all started."

"Do you want me to help you kill him?"

Sarah's look was so serious and her tone so matter-of-fact that Mac was stunned. "That's ridiculous."

"Are you going to execute him?"

"Of course not." Not quite true, Mac.

Sarah turned up the intensity by one thousand kilowatts. "Are you?"

"I don't know." That's better, Mac. The truth will set you free. "I really don't know. It depends on what you do—"

It was Sarah's turn to look stunned.

"No," corrected Mac, "I don't mean that. I'm trying to say that I hope that what you do—no, that's not right either. I'm hoping that whatever happens now will help me decide. I just don't know what it will take to satisfy what's growing inside me."

"I see," said Sarah. "You want it taken out of your hands. Let the fates decide? God's will be done? But why should I help you? You've done nothing but bring disaster on me. You've tried to destroy my company. You've undoubtedly wrecked my marriage—"

Mac's voice was kind, but the words stung anyway. "You were already a victim. I just brought the news."

They talked some more. The man who wanted to destroy Grant Radcliffe and the woman in whose mind he'd already succeeded. Nothing was resolved that Tuesday evening.

On Wednesday morning Sarah packed a bag and announced that she would be spending the rest of the week visiting May Anne. She did not wish to be disturbed. In the event of emergency a message could be left for her at Capistrano-by-the-Sea. First Sarah had herself driven to the office. In a whirlwind two hours she caught up the accumulated week's work and completed what had been scheduled for the next week. When Sarah left, her secretary was delighted but exhausted.

On the drive down to Dana Point it occurred to Sarah that she wanted to avoid Grant as much as she wanted to be with May Anne. Could that helpless, sick child be her crutch? Sarah supposed it was cowardly, but she could not bear to face Grant yet. She knew their marriage was over, shattered. Beyond that Sarah continued to vacillate. After all, Grant had done valuable things for TOPCO. To expose what she'd learned about him would humiliate her, dishonor May Anne, and further damage TOPCO. But to let him stay on, especially to be compelled to work with him, seemed intolerable. Sarah knew that she had to resolve her feelings soon and to make some decisions. She couldn't go home until she had.

Sarah found a pleasant, small suite in a hotel near Dana Point: a sitting room, bedroom, bath, and private patio. Her rooms were on a high bluff overlooking the Pacific Ocean. She could smell the sea air and hear the surf pounding on the rocks below.

When Sarah got to the psychiatric facility, the usually professionally cool Dr. Young was ecstatic. She actually hugged Sarah. "Mrs. Radcliffe, I'm so glad to see you. We've done it. I mean, May Anne's done it. She's broken through. An hour ago she relived that entire horrible afternoon. It was great. Oh, I didn't mean that like it sounded—"

"Was it—"

"Yes, Mrs. Radcliffe. It was her father. It had been going on for months. May Anne has finally faced it."

"As I must now. May I see her?"

"Soon. The poor girl's exhausted after that session. Years of poisonous repression burst out today. Let her sleep for a while."

Sarah went out and bought a pale blue sweatshirt and jeans. She walked the beach barefooted. She threw rocks at the surf. She hadn't taken the time to do that for years.

May Anne was like balm to Sarah's tortured soul. The child actually smiled when she saw her mother. For that brief moment Sarah had no problems at all. Dr. Young assured Sarah that it was all right to take May Anne out to eat or to the hotel if she wanted to go. Dr. Young did insist that May Anne be returned that evening. She wanted May Anne to continue in a controlled environment for a while.

Sarah bought May Anne a sweatshirt and jeans to match her own. The matching outfits were not required to heighten their resemblance. The only question in anyone's mind was whether they were mother and daughter or sisters. At fourteen May Anne was already an inch taller than her mother. May Anne's hair was longer than Sarah's. She was obviously younger. Beyond that physical distinctions faded.

They walked the beach and ate hot dogs, rented bicycles, chased sea gulls, dripped ice cream on themselves, and shopped for pseudo-Indian pottery. Sarah, of course, said nothing about Grant. May Anne realized that Sarah knew. Sarah babbled about seashells, horses she had ridden, and horses she'd been unable to ride.

May Anne was still shy, but she responded to Sarah's exuberance. Sarah even got her to laugh with a story of how she'd fallen off her first high heels in front of two hundred party guests.

Dr. Young and Sarah squeezed in a brief private session that evening.

"What's next?" asked Sarah.

"I want to keep her for a few days at least. We've accomplished so much, but this is the ideal time to reinforce it."

"Is she—will she be cured?"

"In the context of May Anne's disturbance, I don't know what the word means. She is not going to forget what has happened to her. As a matter of fact, it's essential to her health that she remember. How this affects her future, how indelible the scars are are impossible to predict. I believe it depends a lot on you, Mrs. Radcliffe."

Sarah waited for the explanation.

"Given the right environment, it might be appropriate to release May

Anne in a few days. I would want to continue to work with her regularly, however. Even the friendliest environment will cause adjustment problems. She will need two or three sessions a week."

"The right environment?" asked Sarah.

"Yes. This is delicate, so I guess I'll just be blunt. Isn't that incongruous? It's obvious that the girl loves you and that you love her. The time she spends with you is much better therapy than I can provide. But she is not nearly ready to face her father. That could precipitate a relapse of disastrous proportions. And I don't believe that it's healthy for her to return to your house. More precisely, she shouldn't be required to live there—"

"But you said it's healthy for her to remember."

"There is a distinction between facing up to the ugly past and being pervaded by it. Quite a dilemma, isn't it?"

"Not necessarily," said Sarah.

By late Wednesday afternoon Grant Radcliffe had concluded his round of bank meetings. He was pleased. TOPCO now had a larger line of credit at a lower interest rate.

Back in his hotel suite he tried telephoning the man again with no success. Nothing unusual about that. Occasionally it had taken two days for the man to return his call. Radcliffe was not worried. Arranging even a simple disappearance could be time-consuming.

Radcliffe telephoned Sarah's office and learned she had left early without an announced reason. That had never happened before. When he tried to call Sarah at home, he chose the instant the housekeeper burned her finger on a teapot. Understandably surly, Mrs. Svensen decided to forget that a message could be left for Mrs. Radcliffe at Capistrano-by-the-Sea. "No, Mr. Radcliffe. She yust packed a bag this morning and left in a rush. I couldn't even get her to drink her yuice." Radcliffe didn't think that was responsible conduct for the wife of TOPCO's president. What the hell, he would forgive her this time. Where was that little black book?

Radcliffe returned to Beverly Hills on Thursday. The housekeeper, having previously committed herself to ignorance of Mrs. Radcliffe's whereabouts, thought it prudent to stick with that position. However, she did remember that Mrs. Radcliffe said she would be back Sunday night. That bone of information provided Radcliffe some solace, but not much. Where the hell was she anyway? And why?

By Friday Radcliffe's efforts to reach the man had accelerated to four calls a day. Christ, he didn't even know where the man lived. That was sure as hell going to be changed. Radcliffe did not dare assign another investigator to find him. One of the man's great advantages was that so few within the company knew even of his existence. Radcliffe was also afraid to order the truck maintenance depot checked. If something had gone wrong, the trail would lead directly back to him. He thought of driving down and looking it over himself. But what if it were a trap? The place might be staked out by police or even by some member of Oliver's group. No, he had to find out what was going on before taking action.

Frustration overcame Radcliffe's caution by late Saturday morning. He telephoned the assistant vice-president for real property management, but he was not in his office. Damn, didn't anyone work anymore? Radcliffe could not reach him at home until after the Little League game. "Smeznek, I want you to go down to the El Segundo truck maintenance depot right now. I need a full report this afternoon on the feasibility of converting the building to temporary office space. Check out the interior—"

"But, Mr. Radcliffe, we completed demolition yesterday. That site's smooth as a baby's—clean as a pool tabletop, sir." Smeznek sounded puzzled. "The order to expedite came directly from your office on Wednesday, sir. The printout's still sitting on my desk."

Radcliffe could not think of anything to say.

"Mr. Radcliffe, sir. The order mentioned a bonus if we, you know, finished within forty-eight hours and—"

Radcliffe hung up.

Sarah and her daughter continued to spend the week as they had the first day, playing together. Sarah read to May Anne. She even persuaded May Anne to read to her. The girl read amazingly well.

The kaleidoscope of Sarah's emotions slowed. Sarah began to separate the despair and anguish. The disgust and revulsion, relief, love. And the hatred. Sarah, who had always been so admirably decisive, slowly began to identify a position she could live with.

The irony of the situation did not escape Sarah. Her poor, weak, sick daughter, near schizophrenic, recently catatonic, was keeping Sarah sane. The chairman of the board of one of the world's great companies was leaning on a fourteen-year-old mental case. For those few days May Anne was Sarah's therapy, crutch, and strength.

On Sunday afternoon Sarah hugged and kissed the child. As she said good-bye, she promised to return very soon. Then the two of them would leave together.

Sarah knew what she was going to do.

Sarah would have liked to consult her grandfather. Maynard Chase would know precisely how to proceed, but Sarah feared precipitating another heart attack or stroke. Of course, she thought—Jonathan Clark.

"Jonathan," Sarah said, "thank you for seeing me on Sunday. I've come to you because my grandfather has always respected your legal ability." "Stuffy but sound" was what Maynard Chase had actually said. "I know you specialize in litigation, but I hope to avoid it. I need advice on how best to do that."

Clark offered her a chair. "I'm honored that you come to me, but depending upon the nature of your problem, there may be others in the firm better qualified—"

"You're the only one I can trust. This concerns Grant." Jonathan Clark tried not to scowl. His recollections of Grant Radcliffe were not endearing.

Sarah continued. "Grant has boasted to me that he has this entire law firm under his thumb except for you. He doesn't seem to care for you, Jonathan."

Jonathan Clark smiled.

"Grant says you're an overweight prig."

"Somehow that pleases me. How may I help you, Sarah?"

Sarah took a deep breath. "I want to dump Grant."

Clark could not be visibly fazed. "Is that personally or corporately?"

"Both. I need to know my rights and how to go about it with minimum side effects."

"You're talking about divorce and ousting Grant from the presidency of TOPCO?"

"Divorce and removing Grant Radcliffe from any association with the company in any capacity."

"Why, Sarah?"

"Don't ask why. Tell me my property rights as his wife, my rights as a mother, my rights as chairman of the board and as holder of a majority of the proxies."

"Oversimplified version," began Clark. "What you've inherited or acquired by gift is your separate property. The same is true for Grant. Everything else is community property and will be divided equally. For example, the house your grandfather gave you and the TOPCO stock you inherited are your separate property—barring complexities, of course.

"In view of May Anne's institutionalization—forgive me, Sarah, but that's common knowledge around here—I don't believe that custody will be an issue. Nor can I imagine that you will insist on child support.

"Your corporate position may be more complex. I assume that you, as chairman holding a majority of the proxies, have installed a board of directors that is loyal to you. With the board's support you can terminate Grant Radcliffe's employment as president. You probably cannot force his removal as a director until the next annual shareholders' meeting, assuming that you will still then continue to control a majority of the vote. Of course, Grant could attempt a proxy solicitation on his own. You are in a better position than I to judge his chances of success in a proxy fight."

Sarah looked grim. "If I expose him, they're nil."

"Expose him for what, Sarah?"

"Jonathan, I don't want to say."

"Sarah, unless you trust me with a full disclosure, I cannot effectively

advise you. Mind if I light this cigar? Let me tell you the story of how
the case of *Wennerstrom* versus *TOPCO* was lost."

Sarah had heard only Grant's version of the trial. It had somehow
omitted the exposure of his lies, his deception, and his fatal failure to be
candid with his trial attorney.

Sarah nodded as Clark finished. "I see what you mean, but some of
this is too ugly. Is it all right if I just tell you the part that—"

"Sarah, weren't you listening? I've represented your grandfather since
before you were born. I've watched you grow up. If you want me to, I
can respect your privacy and still continue with our friendship. Just
don't ask me to represent you regarding private matters you don't wish
to disclose. You cannot have it both ways."

"All right, Jonathan, all right." Sarah tried to smile. "Can you brace
me with some coffee?"

Sarah told it chronologically: the probable assassination of her parents; the incest; the frame-up of MacDonald Oliver; kidnapping; assault;
embezzlement; attempted murder. "I think I've covered it all, Jonathan."

Clark had let his cigar go out. "My God, Sarah, it's appalling. I knew
the man was unprincipled, but I counted the commission of fourteen
separate felonies before I lost track."

"So you can see, Jonathan, that I can't simply expose him. It would
destroy me in the process. It would ruin any chance May Anne has for
a life. There would be more serious damage to TOPCO."

Clark relit his cigar. "You can't simply leave him in power. That's
out of the question." He blew a magnificent cloud of smoke toward the
ceiling. "Sarah, have you ever been taught how to bluff?"

Grant realized Sarah was angry about something. He hadn't seen her
in a week, b ' there was no endearment in her voice when she telephoned him at the country club to make sure he would be home for
dinner.

He tried to tell himself he would handle it. He always had. It would
help, though, if he knew what was going on. Reflection had persuaded
him that the man must have arranged the demolition of the old depot
in order to cover up any evidence of Oliver's execution. Commendable,

but what the hell was he doing now? Sarah's ire could not be related to that, though. There was no way she could know about Oliver. Perhaps it was the occasional visit to the Casa Folatre, or maybe it was Guinevere. He could deal with that.

Sarah met Grant in the foyer. That was unusual.

"Welcome home, dear," said Grant as he advanced with open arms.

"The servants have been given the night off," said Sarah as she turned and marched toward the study. "Let's talk in here."

This was serious. Grant tried to warm up the atmosphere. "I'm starved, dear. Can't we have dinner while we're talking?"

"You can eat later—if you can eat."

Grant shrugged resignation and poured himself a drink before sitting down. "All right, love, what is it?"

"I want a divorce. I want your resignation from TOPCO. Those are the main points. We'll get to the details in a moment."

Radcliffe jumped to his feet. He wanted to say, You're joking, but decided it was a bad line. She so obviously wasn't. He tried to laugh but only managed to croak, "Darling, what is it that has so upset you? Tell me so that we can discuss it."

"Certainly, Grant." Sarah's eyes blazed. "What do you want to discuss first? The execution of my parents? Or perhaps you'd like to approach it with reverse chronology. Would you prefer to start with the TOPCO embezzlements?"

Grant Radcliffe choked and gagged. The thick Persian carpet absorbed most of his spilled drink. Grant groped desperately for control. He had to think. He might have been able to handle one subject at a time, but this—how could she? One at a time. That was it. "Sarah." He hoped he sounded calm. "Now let's just discuss these wild accusations one at a time. Things are not always—"

"Grant." Sarah's smile was terrible. "I haven't accused you of a thing. Or is it that you are confessing to a connection with these events?"

"Of course not," Grant sputtered. "It was just that the tone of your voice implied—"

But Sarah gave him no time to recover. "Of course, if you'd rather, we could begin with the frame-up of MacDonald Oliver—or his kidnapping to my grandfather's house—or the recent murder attempt on him might be clearer in your recollection."

Oliver? Murder *attempt*? That meant Oliver was alive. But if Oliver was alive, then— Radcliffe's mind was not ready to accept the possibility of Oliver's continued existence, let alone the consequences of that. Perhaps Sarah had misspoken, or he had misunderstood. He floundered for something to say. "Sarah, you don't understand. The man was trying to ruin us. He was destroying your company. I was protecting you—"

Sarah was merciless. "Of course, Grant. I understand that explanation. So let's go on to another subject. Let's talk about your rape of May Anne. You can explain how your incest protected me."

Radcliffe's eyes were glazed. The bitch gave him no chance to think. Where? How? Mrs. Riley? "It's that damned busybody Mrs. Riley. Are you going to accept the—"

"Grant."

"—word of a disgruntled, frustrated old biddy like—"

"Grant." Sarah's voice was as crisp as a rifle shot.

My God, Grant thought, the woman has become formidable. I can't steamroll her. I can't stonewall her.

"Grant, it was not Mrs. Riley who told me. It was May Anne." That was exaggeration, but Sarah allowed herself some license to score the point.

"May Anne?" Grant was stuttering. "S-she?"

"That's where I've been all week. Talking to May Anne."

Grant collapsed on the couch. Everything was falling apart. It was a shambles. He stared at the floor. He could not look at Sarah. "What do you want?"

"I keep the house and the furniture. It's my separate property anyway. You can stay here until you find a place. I've already moved out." Sarah didn't say so, but she planned to sell the house and furniture. She couldn't live there with May Anne, but she couldn't bear the thought of Grant Radcliffe's living there either.

Sarah continued. "I get all the TOPCO stock. Not just my separate property but also the community stock we've accumulated. The rest of the community property will be evenly divided. I will have sole custody of May Anne. Naturally you will agree to give up all visitation rights.

"You will resign from TOPCO's board of directors and as president, effective immediately. I've had this resignation and property settlement agreement prepared—"

Grant looked up, disbelieving that this could be happening to him. Why, only this morning—

"You will see that the documents also provide that you waive all stock options, insurance, and pension benefits. It's also stated that you agree never to purchase any TOPCO stock in the future. Your connection with the company is to be totally and permanently severed."

Grant fumbled for a fingerhold. "I can fight. I'll fight you for the proxies. I can convince the shareholders that the company needs me—"

Sarah stared him down. "You have my word that once you've signed these documents, I will not expose you. Oh, yes—and you can keep the money you've already stolen."

Defeat seemed complete. "Sarah, you've left me nothing. I'll kill myself."

Sarah went to the Queen Anne writing desk. From the drawer she withdrew an ornately engraved nickel-plated .32 Browning automatic with ivory grips. She tossed the pistol to Grant. "Here, catch."

Grant caught the gun and, trembling, raised it toward his head. His eyes grew wild. "No."

The pistol was lowered. The wavering barrel pointed at Sarah. "No— you instead. I'll kill you. I'll say it was a burglar—he broke in. You struggled." Grant was shaking. He tried to steady the weapon. "I'll inherit everything, even your stock, I'll control—"

"Grant, I've got it all documented. Affidavits, photographs, photostats, signed statements, the whole story. I've left word. If anything happens to me tonight, you'll be locked up within the hour." That would have been a really good idea, thought Sarah. Too bad I didn't think of it until just now.

Sarah turned her eyes up full power. "This approach lets you walk away, Grant. Throw down the stupid gun and sign these papers."

This time Grant's defeat was truly complete. He just could not face the shame and humiliation of exposure. At least this way he would gain time to think. Later he'd think of something. Or the man would.

But for now there was nothing else to do. Grant Radcliffe threw down the gun and signed the papers.

24

Grant Radcliffe's resignation as president and as a director of TOPCO created less sensation than Sarah had feared. Grant Radcliffe had not even appeared at the special board meeting convened by Sarah. No reason was given for Radcliffe's resignation. The directors supported Sarah with no fuss at all. After all, she held the proxies which were the key to their jobs. The press and television treated the news matter-of-factly. The existence of a marital dispute was obvious. Everyone simply assumed that the breakup of the Radcliffes' marriage was the basis for the resignation. It was Sarah who held the power. Sarah's assumption of the TOPCO presidency, along with the chairmanship, was generally greeted with optimism by the press. And by the market. TOPCO's common stock rose one and one-eighth points on the news. *Newsweek* even listed Sarah Radcliffe among the ten most eligible women for the Republican presidential nomination.

Sarah had leased a beach house in the Malibu Colony for herself, grandfather, and May Anne. May Anne adored being on the ocean, and the place was secure. Sarah hired a housekeeper and a yardman. The yardman's job was not much of a cover, since the yard was mostly sand, but Sarah felt more comfortable leaving May Anne with a body-guard. Besides, he was teaching May Anne surfing and Spanish. Both people had been screened and approved by Dr. Young. May Anne was still so shy it was hard to tell, but she seemed to like them. May Anne spent an hour each day reading to her great-grandfather. They both loved it.

At Sarah's last conference with Dr. Young, the psychiatrist's prog-nosis had been mostly optimistic. May Anne could adjust to the world, but the progress would be slow and painful. May Anne's future sexual relationship, or relationships, would be difficult. Nevertheless, with love, modern psychiatry, sunshine, and vitamins, a happy and satisfy-ing future for May Anne was possible.

There was still plenty of rain remaining for Sarah, but at least her nerve ends had stopped screaming. Sarah felt relieved. Grant Radcliffe was out of her life with a minimum of difficulty. Her hatred and disgust would take a long time to fade, but it would. What happened to Grant Radcliffe next? She was a little surprised to realize that she really couldn't care much. Let MacDonald Oliver have him. Sarah couldn't worry herself about that. Let MacDonald Oliver even his score with Grant in whatever way was appropriate.

Of course, there was the matter of her score with MacDonald Oliver. That still needed evening up.

Sarah picked up the telephone. "Get me Sacramento. The governor's private line."

"Sarah, how nice to hear from you." The familiar, deep, resonate voice boomed across the microwaves. With just a little more effort, he wouldn't have needed a telephone.

"Governor, do you remember MacDonald Oliver?"

"MacDonald Oliver. Oh, the young lawyer who kicked TOPCO's ass in that lawsuit. World's highest verdict, wasn't it? And then he got into some legal difficulty of his own, didn't he?"

"Yes, Governor, let me tell you about it." Sarah talked. The governor of the state of California listened. "And there's more that may be useful, but I don't think the governor of the state would want to hear it."

"Sarah, I'm really quite flexible. I can assure you the governor won't hear a word of this."

Sarah told him the rest. It took quite a while.

"Sarah, that's awfully heady stuff. Are you asking me . . ."

"Of course, that's up to you, sir. You are the chief executive officer."

"Thank you, Sarah. Send me what you have. It will be checked out immediately. I have to go. We are keeping the entire State Assembly waiting."

The governor leaned back and put his hands behind his leonine head. He permitted himself a moment to think. What a remarkably screwed-up world. "Morris," he boomed. What a waste it had been to install the intercom.

Morris poked his head into the governor's office.

"Morris, find me someone to conduct an investigation."

For almost two weeks now Mac had alternated between holding Laura Wennerstrom's inert hand, pacing the hospital corridor, or waiting for the telephone to ring with news of some change. The doctors continued to be hopeful. Blood pressure was up. Eye signs good. Yesterday she had even groaned once.

Ordinarily an envelope from the governor's office would have interested Mac, but he was too depressed to be impressed. The heavy, legal-size bond and genuine engraved return address were completely wasted on him.

The letterhead bore the embossed great seal of the state of California.

Pursuant to the recommendation of the Community Release Board, and the general authority granted the Governor by Section 8 of Article V of the Constitution of the State of California, as implemented by statute, and the amendments thereto, you are hereby notified that you have been granted a full pardon for the reason that it has been found that the crime with which you were charged (i.e.,

Penal Code, Sections 484 and 487: Grand Theft) was not, in fact, committed at all, and you are thereby innocent thereof.

The Governor will be pleased to personally present the Certificate of Full Pardon to you at a brief ceremony to be held in his Los Angeles office at . . .

The rest was worse legalese than the beginning. The letter bore the governor's signature or a reasonable stamped facsimile thereof.

Who had put the machinery into motion? There was only one person—one person to whom Mac had related the details of the frame-up and who had political access to the governor. It had to be Sarah Radcliffe.

Mac looked at the letter again. The ceremony was in two days. They didn't waste time. Mac wanted to go, but he couldn't bear to lose telephone contact. Laura could come out of it at any time. He had to know immediately. Was her mind damaged? He decided to compromise by telephoning UCLA Medical Center every thirty minutes.

To Mac, the pardon was an anomaly. Mac's grand theft conviction had been reversed on appeal, and the charge against him dismissed. Legally he was already in the same position as if he had never been indicted at all. In that sense the pardon accomplished nothing. He was being pardoned from a crime of which he had never been convicted. But the stigma of Mac's conviction by the trial court had continued to hang over him. The Court of Appeals' reversal had been on a technical ground, irrelevant to his guilt or innocence.

The pardon was an affirmative finding of his innocence. To the extent that it was possible for governmental action to erase the disgrace, the pardon did so. It would also help remove the stain if the news media paid some attention.

Mac should not have concerned himself. The governor was a master of capitalizing on opportunities for favorable publicity. Crews from three television networks, reporters from four California newspapers, two wire services, but only one national magazine were present. Mac wondered how *Time* had screwed up.

Mary Kathryn had permitted Mac to bring Tracy. Mary Kathryn seemed genuinely congratulatory but did not think she could make it.

Mac had telephoned all the friends he thought might want to come. Marla Zimmerman gave him a hug that should have exceeded her physical capacity. Cornell Sepulveda Smith pumped Mac's hand to exhaustion—Cornell Sepulveda Smith's.

"You'll come back to the firm now?" Smith urged. "Nels would die happy tomorrow if you said yes. He sends his regrets and congratulations. He's in Washington arguing with the Federal Home Loan Bank Board."

"Tell him he'll have to hang on for a while longer." Mac laughed. "I haven't had a chance to consider the next move."

Elizabeth Greene was on vacation and could not be reached. Burt Ginter and Douglas Dillon both were tied up in trials. Mac looked around for Sarah Radcliffe but did not see her.

Flashbulbs exploded and floodlights lit. Mac's case was obviously the Good News Story of the Day. The governor shook Mac's hand with such enthusiasm that Mac could not believe it was not genuine.

"Mr. Oliver, I'm delighted to meet you. I know quite a lot about you, you know. Quite a lot." Did the governor actually wink? The governor turned and beamed for the TV cameras. "I hope that this Certificate of Full Pardon will, at least in small measure, compensate for the miscarriage of justice in your case. . . ."

It should have been a grand time, thought Mac as he hung up the telephone for the fourth time in the past two hours. "Sorry, Mr. Oliver," they always said. "There's still no change."

While MacDonald Oliver was being publicly pardoned, Radcliffe brooded and drank alone in the empty Beverly Hills house. For at least a week he had known intellectually that MacDonald Oliver was alive. Nine days ago he had located Oliver's Santa Monica office and had frequently driven by striving for a glimpse of his enemy. He hadn't seen Oliver but on several occasions had spotted his BMW parked nearby. Radcliffe knew it was Oliver's car. He had the license plate number. He obtained Oliver's unlisted telephone number and heard what sounded like Oliver's voice answer before he hung up. But Radcliffe's gut refused to accept this evidence.

Out of sheer loneliness, Radcliffe switched on the television set. He saw life-size images of the governor's head smiling at Oliver's head and saying, ". . . Full Pardon will, at least in small measure, compensate for the miscarriage of justice in your case." As Radcliffe stared at the screen, his stomach reluctantly digested the data. Jesus, it must be true. Oliver must be alive. Otherwise they couldn't show him on television.

Tears formed at the corners of Radcliffe's eyes. He began to cry, at first softly, then with uncontrollable sobs.

Early the next morning Mac telephoned Sarah Radcliffe. "I want to thank you for your part in obtaining my pardon."

"You're welcome, Mr. Oliver. I felt it was my responsibility to help even things up. I trust you're through attacking TOPCO."

"Yes, ma'am, you can count on that."

"Thank God. The balance sheet can't take any more of you."

"But not—"

"Don't tell me. That's all I wanted to know. Good-bye, Mr. Oliver."

That was not very bright of me, thought Mac. Of course, Sarah Radcliffe would not want the burden of knowing what was going to happen to Grant Radcliffe. What is going to happen to Grant Radcliffe? Mac wondered. It is time to deal with that son of a bitch. The man is completely, monstrously evil, isn't he? Yes, but am I any better? Am I the instrument of goodness? Mac was drawn into a silent argument with himself.

Mac: That son of a bitch is a murderer. He knocked off Sarah Radcliffe's parents. He tried to have Harold Rifkin killed. Who knows how many others? He almost did me in.

Himself: And you're a choir boy? What about the prison guard you knifed in the back in Nam? Just a kid. What about all the Vietnamese regulars and Cong you've offed?

Mac: I was a soldier. I had a duty to my country to kill the enemy and to escape from prison. Radcliffe killed for selfish personal gain.

Himself: And you had nothing personal to gain when you went over the wall at Hoa Lo? That was just for the folks at home, huh? What a hypocrite. Okay, what about the man you just shot at the TOPCO truck depot? I suppose that was an act of patriotism, too.

Mac: He was trying to kill me. That was self-defense.

Himself: Aw, come on. It may have been self-defense when you swung that engine block, but he wasn't still a threat when you put that bullet into his head.

Mac: He was already dying. You know I just put him out of his misery. Anyhow, I don't have to stand on that point. That bastard, Radcliffe, is totally no good. He tried to frame me for child molestation. He did successfully frame me for an embezzlement charge. I was innocent. Even with the pardon, I'll never completely live that down.

Himself: Oh, you're sweet. What about the way you framed Captain Bergman? You got him canned from his job, ruined his career. Does he get to live that down? And what about what setting up old Edgar Beard as the office rapist? How do you think that looks on his record?

Mac: Those were regrettable incidents. They were admittedly innocent victims of a war. All right, what about the incest? Radcliffe raped his own daughter. Gotcha there.

Himself: Radcliffe's sexual propensities are the result of hormonal and environmental accidents, just as yours are. For that you get no credit, nor should you be quick to condemn others.

Mac: Okay, okay. Will you at least admit that I'm a nicer guy?

Himself: Mac, that may be the entire distinction.

Mac: Aw, shut up. I didn't ask for a sermon. All I want is justice.

Himself: Or is it revenge?

Mac: Now you've dug yourself into a hole, smart ass. What's the difference?

Mac knew he couldn't let it rest. He had to finish it. He tried to tell himself he was not willing to spend the rest of his life looking over his shoulder, but he knew that was not the reason. He simply could not let Radcliffe get away with the injury. Not to himself, not to Laura. Whether it was pride, self-respect, or job satisfaction was not important. There was nothing more important to live for. Although, Mac smiled, there was just possibly Laura.

Hell, Mac thought, I've just been pardoned for a crime I never committed.

Through the grace of Sarah Radcliffe, I am not being prosecuted for the crimes I have committed.

Now I am about to commit murder in the first degree. On the basis of my record to date, I should easily get away with it.

At seven thirty-two on the seventeenth morning, when the telephone rang, Mac knew with certainty this was IT. But was IT good or bad? He grabbed the instrument on the first ring. Please, let it be something good.

It was her. It was Laura.

Not the ward nurse. Not the chief of neurology. Laura W. Wennerstrom. In person. And lucid.

She sounded weak, but all it took was for her to say, "Hello, Mac," in her special way. All his apprehension faded into vapor.

"You're all right. You are all right, aren't you?"

"I'm weak and stiff. Everything's blurry, and I've got a shitty head-ache—but, yes, I think I'm going to be okay. Come and see me soon?"

"I'm on my way."

Before taking a step, Mac had already moved into paradise. He ran down to his car and headed for UCLA.

Mac was in the elevator, halfway up to Laura's floor, when he remembered that he hadn't brought her anything. He dashed back down to the gift shop and bought $645 worth of flowers—every bouquet in the place. It took a salesclerk and nurse's aide to help carry them into Laura's room.

She looked so small and frail. Less than three weeks ago she had been the strongest woman he'd ever known. At least most of the tubes and wires were gone.

"Mac, you're a blur, but it's you. Is that a cast?" she asked, holding out her hand. The restraints had been removed.

"It's nothing." Mac squeezed her hand. "Welcome back." He looked her over carefully. She was all there. She was going to be all right. Mac's sigh was explosive.

"Mac, tell me what happened."

"What do you remember?"

"Everything up until I grabbed that tire iron and ran to attack that monster. It flashed to me then that I could not be doing this out of a mere sense of obligation. That's all I remember. Then what?"

Mac told her. She thought about it for a while.

"You know," Laura said, "I was convinced we were too hopelessly alien to each other. I saw you as amoral, irreligious—"

"How about an eye for an eye?"

Laura ignored that. "I realize now I was wrong. You're a moral, ethical man but so obsessed with vengeance that you've rationalized it as justice."

Mac hesitated. "Look, Laura, I know we're very different—"

"I was always attracted to you, of course," she continued. "But I felt like the moth to the flame. I couldn't risk being damaged again."

"No risk, no gain," offered Mac.

"We would have hard times, Mac."

They sat gazing at each other, knowing that it would be so.

Laura finally spoke.

"Mac," she said, "you know I'm intuitive."

"Hmmmm."

"You've told me everything that's happened, I know. But you haven't mentioned what's going to happen."

Uh-oh, thought Mac.

"If you carry this any further, you risk at least life imprisonment. The price is too high."

The girl is uncanny, thought Mac. She's been out of a coma for two hours, and she already knows my plans.

"You've done monumental damage to each other already, not to mention what you've both done to innocents. There's no way even to measure the consequences of your acts."

Mac could hear her strength returning.

"Mac, Radcliffe is destroyed. You're already even. Can't you see that?"

Laura raised herself and turned to take Mac's hands. Sunlight sifting through the window blinds lit the edges of her long black hair. "We owe it to ourselves to try. Perhaps we can spend our lives together. At least we have wonderful times before us finding out. And opportunities that few people are granted. Mac, a law of physics is involved here. I cannot be with you if you are in jail. End it. It's enough."

Mac did not trust himself to respond seriously. "How do I know you're not after my money?" How's that for an asininely evasive remark, Mac?

Laura sighed. "All right. Promise me you won't do anything drastic until we've talked again, and that you'll seriously consider what I've said."

Laura leaned back to rest. Mac nodded and kissed her long and full. She closed her eyes and smiled. "And thank you for the flowers."

Grant Radcliffe had started drinking in the late afternoon. He'd returned to the empty house, tired and discouraged. So far his proxy solicitation had gone almost as well as Hitler's invasion of Russia. Some of those ungrateful, weak-memoried stockholders wouldn't even see him. Grant Radcliffe, the recent president of the goddamned company. Those who did were obviously condescending and noncommittal. The assholes, all of them. But Grant Radcliffe would find a way to beat them all. He would fix a drink, rest, and think.

Radcliffe looked in the mirror. Not bad at all, really. The years had added some thickening. There were some interesting lines in the face. Distinguished-looking. Perhaps he would return to acting. He was more handsome than beautiful now. Surely the industry would no longer insist on that ancient boycott against male beauty. They could not continue to hold his looks against him. But the tedious script readings, the interviews, auditions, the goddamned agents, the groveling before producers. It would mean starting at the bottom again. He could not face all that. Why should Grant Radcliffe have to start at the bottom anyway? He fixed himself another drink.

He had money, and there would be more coming in from the divorce settlement. But he did not have the kind of capital one started a competing oil company with. The days of the shoestring wildcatters were long since over. He would be busted within three weeks if he tried that route.

He could open a haberdashery on Rodeo Drive:

GRANT'S
GENTLEMEN'S GORGEOUS GARMENTS

Wouldn't that frost Maynard Chase's hoary old balls? It would humiliate Sarah, too. That was worth considering.

"This English paisley will be quite appropriate for a board meeting, sir. I should know. Why, only last month I was telling my own directors—"

God, they would laugh him out of town, the bastards, all of them. MacDonald Oliver had put Sarah up to this. He should have killed that bastard when he first had the chance. And you could bet that Maynard Chase had stuck his nose into it, too. The old fart couldn't talk much; but he sure as hell knew what was going on, and he still liked playing God. That fucking Mrs. Riley had been in on it, too. She must have blown the whistle on him. Meddling old biddy. And who knows what stories that simple little brat May Anne had been telling. I shouldn't have had children anyway. There was no need for children to screw it up. Everything could have been so beautiful, Sarah. How could Sarah do this to him? Where was the damn bottle?

Grant Radcliffe would show them. All of them. Grant Radcliffe was not the kind of person you just kicked around. Radcliffe walked purposefully into the bathroom, gave the mirror his most dashing grin, and emptied the entire contents of the Amytal sodium bottle into his palm. He swallowed every one of the blue capsules, chased with excellent cognac.

He could hardly wait until they found his body, the ungrateful wimps. It would be too late for them. Let them all suffer.

Radcliffe was shaken by a tremor, almost a convulsion. He broke out in instant sweat. Suddenly he was frightened. What the hell was he doing? He didn't want to kill himself. He wanted to live. To live and get even. Radcliffe remembered seeing the terror in Mac's eye. That had been one of his best moments. He wanted that feeling again. The man would show up soon. They would do it together.

Radcliffe took a deep breath. He felt all right. There was time. Plenty of time. He ran out to the garage. All the cars except Sarah's Rolls were still there. Radcliffe took the closest one, the green 1940 Darrin Packard roadster Sarah had given him for his birthday. It had belonged to Clark Gable. Or was it Gary Cooper? He couldn't remember. The top was down. That didn't matter. Radcliffe started the powerful old super eight and pulled out of the garage. He would drive to St. John's emergency room. Within minutes they would be pumping out his stomach. It was only a few miles. He would take Wilshire Boulevard. That was shortest. No, too many traffic signals. It wouldn't do to be delayed by traffic. That's keeping your head, Grant. Just keep thinking straight. Sunset Boulevard was a little farther, but faster. First, west on Sunset Boulevard, Grant.

A light fog was rolling in from the sea. It wasn't impairing visibility much, but it was causing those damned oncoming headlights to glare. Grant moved the big Packard into the right-hand lane. Of course. That was much better. Not far to go now. Everything would be fine.

There was a figure standing on the corner, leaning against the lamppost. A man. His arm was extended. Was he hitchhiking? Grant Radcliffe had no time for hitchhikers that evening. The man looked familiar. There was something in his hand. Something metallic. The man was pointing it at him. Radcliffe slowed the car and peered. It was a gun. MacDonald Oliver was standing there, pointing a gun at him. Radcliffe dropped the Packard into second gear and hunched over as far as he dared without losing visibility. As he turned the big car toward Oliver, he rammed the accelerator pedal to the floor. He'd nail that son of a bitch once and for all before Oliver got him. And this was self-defense. It was beautiful . . . Radcliffe actually saw Oliver's bullet strike the windshield.

Mac had spent the entire afternoon alone thinking about what he must do, before finally deciding to go to Radcliffe. After all, he had promised Laura to give the matter serious consideration. There was no need to bother her now.

Mac stopped at his apartment door as he tucked the .38 into his belt.

No need to be foolhardy, he thought. Radcliffe might not be immediately amenable.

Mac would offer to end it, an armistice. Laura was right. You don't have to prevail over an enemy to win. Mac wanted an end to the madness. He didn't need more revenge. A chance for a real life, that was more like it. Something satisfying to work at. Mac knew he would not return to practicing law. Laura had suggested that with their money and brains they could do a lot of good. Probably.

Radcliffe might readily accept the offer of peace or just might turn nasty. Mac fingered the .38. He would have to be ready. That Radcliffe was cuckoo enough to tell time by. There is only one way to find out what is going to happen, Mac thought, as he turned the BMW toward Radcliffe's house.

As he approached the corner of Beverly Glen and Sunset Boulevard, Mac saw the flashing lights and the huddle of people. Two patrol cars, an ambulance and Grant Radcliffe's green Packard roadster rammed into the lamppost. Mac recognized the car instantly from his investigations.

Mac pulled the BMW to the curb and ran over to the scene. The Packard's vintage windshield was shattered and bloody. Alongside, a covered figure lay, unmoving on the gurney. Mac arrived just in time to see a patrolman lift the sheet and place a large, round object on the stretcher. It was Grant Radcliffe's head. Decapitated. Grisly. Not beautiful at all. For an instant the pale blue eyes were turned directly toward Mac.

The attendant drew the sheet.

Mac ran back to his car, placed the gun on the floor, covered it with his jacket, and locked the door. The BMW could be picked up later. Traffic was completely jammed. He had to get out of there.

Mac started running back to the hospital. It wasn't far. He would easily be there in time to be allowed to kiss Laura good night. If he bribed the night nurse.

The medical examiner and his assistant were each working on their second margarita. It had been a busy day.

"It's a shame about that Packard," the assistant said. "That must be a three-hundred-thousand-dollar car."

"Don't worry. They'll restore it again. Some other millionaire will be showing it at Pebble Beach next fall."

"Harvey called his widow. You know, that Sarah Channing whatever—the big TOPCO wheel. Harvey couldn't believe it. When he told her the news, she either said, 'Thank you,' or 'Thank God,' and hung up."

"The rich are strange."

"What's strange is that he was driving around with all that stuff in him."

"What's stranger is that he could drive at all. There was enough barbiturate and booze in him to kill three men. Lucky no one was standing under the lamppost. There usually is. It's a bus stop."

"The hallucinatory effect should have been grand. Wonder where he was going in such a damn hurry."

"Maybe he was being chased."

"Well, if he was, he's ahead now."